STICK McLAUGHLIN:

THE PROHIBITION YEARS

Visit us at www.boldstrokesbooks.com

STICK McLAUGHLIN:

THE PROHIBITION YEARS

by

CF Frizzell

A Division of Bold Strokes Books

2014

STICK MCLAUGHLIN: THE PROHIBITION YEARS

ISBN 13: 978-1-62639-205-2

THIS TRADE PAPERBACK ORIGINAL IS PUBLISHED BY
BOLD STROKES BOOKS, INC.
P.O. BOX 249
VALLEY FALLS, NY 12185

FIRST EDITION: OCTOBER 2014

CREDITS
EDITOR: CINDY CRESAP
PRODUCTION DESIGN: STACIA SEAMAN
COVER DESIGN BY SHERI (GRAPHICARTIST2020@HOTMAIL.COM)

Acknowledgments

When a dream born in high school takes about fifty years to come true, you'd better focus on the achievement—not look back and shake your head incredulously that it happened at all. But you only publish your first novel once, and you don't do it alone. The significance of all those paths you crossed is humbling.

I'm eternally grateful for encouragement lent by English teachers, newspaper colleagues, and some very special friends. And little did I know that many years later at a reading by an author I idolized, I'd find such a precious friend in the amazing Lee Lynch. I am sincerely honored by her enthusiasm and support for *Stick*. They are gifts I will treasure always.

There aren't adequate words to thank Radclyffe for taking a chance on this rookie and welcoming me to the generous, award-winning Bold Strokes Books family. I am proud to be a member and thrilled that *Stick* now lives in Rad's house.

And I send a wave up to Mom and Dad, who would have been overjoyed to hold this book in their hands. I did it, guys.

And, finally, I thank my partner, Kathy, for her devotion and courage, through endless readings and rereadings, the hours of plot talk, and days as an "author's widow." Chances are there'd be no *Stick* without you, honey.

To Kathy, my better half in all the best ways.
For loving, listening, supporting, and believing from the start
that a dream like this could come true.
For being my rock, forever my one and only.

PART ONE

October 1918
Dorchester neighborhood
Boston, Massachusetts

CHAPTER ONE

O ld man Henderson clamped onto the back of Stick's frayed jacket collar and nearly hauled her into his store, but lots of twisting and squirming sent her darting down the alley to freedom for the second time this month.

"Goddamn kids!" He shook his gnarly fist in the air. "I'm goin' for the cops!"

Ten minutes, a trolley jump, and five blocks later, Stick scrambled under the loading dock at Cirelli's Meat Packing Plant and took a much needed breath. She couldn't help but grin as she filled a ragged carpet satchel from her bulging jacket and pants pockets. Two cans of Boston Baked Beans, two cans of brown bread, four potatoes, assorted lollipops, and a fistful of chocolate-covered malted milk balls. It was a good day's haul, and Stick figured Mama might even shed a grateful tear before reacting with a heavy-handed slap. Little sister Dottie would think it was Christmas. Ray wouldn't approve at all. Stick knew his high-and-mighty big brother superiority would make all that hard work feel shameful.

Stashed into a front pocket, the biggest cherry lollipop was set aside just for Ellie when they met for her walk home from school. With about fifteen minutes to spare, Stick gathered up the satchel, adjusted her black newsboy cap, and crawled out into the October afternoon. Ellie liked the cap and always grinned a bit shyly when she told Stick she did. And that just warmed Stick inside and out.

Ellie was the prettiest girl Stick had ever seen, and no one could be luckier than to have Ellie alongside, smiling, laughing, walking through

"We were going past Henderson's." Baggers snickered, hitching his pants up around his broad waist and reinforcing his name. "And he comes chargin' out, sayin' he's callin' the cops. We ain't even done nothin'!"

"So I say we give him something to whine about," Davey added. He jammed his fists in his pockets and rocked back on his stubby boot heels, his face glowing with mischief.

Stick glanced back toward the school, but there was no sign of Ellie yet. She shook her head and frowned. "Uh-uh. Not getting in on that. He almost nabbed me today. Ain't going back no time soon."

Baggers elbowed Davey. "Toldja she wouldn't."

"Listen," Stick said, leaning toward them, "good thing I'm tall. If I's as shrimpy as you, Dave, I'd never got loose from the ol' man."

"Aw, Stick. Come on." Davey shuffled his feet and whipped his father's Fedora off his head in frustration.

"Yeah, Stick. You're the best at this," Baggers tried. "We get him talking, and you do that sleight of hand magic you do."

Davey was just as persistent. "I even got us some Co'Colas from Johnny-O for later. Traded him my dad's *Geographic*, the one with the naked pictures."

Again, Stick shook her head. "I'm done for today. Was a close call with him and I ain't going back to his place for a while. I got some decent stuff."

"What decent stuff, Stick?"

They all turned to see Ellie gazing up at her.

"Uh...Beans," Stick blurted. "I—I got some beans and...and bread today. But me and Mr. Henderson, though, we don't get along."

Ellie rolled her eyes. "Nonsense," she said, slipping an arm through Stick's. "Let's all go. I'll talk to him. Come on, guys."

Stick pulled back quickly. "No. I—I mean not now. It's not a big deal. These guys wanted to go, not me, so they can go. I...I came to see you."

Ellie glanced at Davey and Baggers and then blushed toward the ground.

Stick jumped into the silence. "We gotta head home, guys. I'll see you tomorrow."

The boys mumbled in disappointment as they turned away, and Stick led Ellie back across the street.

"Did I embarrass you?" Stick asked.

Ellie shook her head and then grinned. "Maybe for a second, but it…it felt good to hear you say that in front of them. I was…proud." And she looked away shyly.

"I'm the proud one, Ellie. You're…um…So, you ain't embarrassed to be seen with me?"

Ellie looked up sharply. "After all these years, Stick, why would you ever think that?"

"Well, you know I'm not like you. My family…We're…I mean we don't…Ellie, I really ain't the fine example of womanhood that you are, and—"

"Stop." Ellie halted them outside Kennedy's butcher shop and then had to push Stick aside and into the alley to let a customer pass. "You stop right now, Elizabeth McLaughlin," she said.

Stick's eyebrows shot skyward. Only her family, teachers, and Ellie ever used her real name. And it usually signaled serious talk ahead.

"All that matters to me is who you are." Ellie poked between the looped wooden buttons of Stick's jacket. Bashfully pulling her eyes from Ellie's glare, Stick concentrated on the firm set of her mouth, lips so rosy and smooth, plush…kissable. Stick's gut tightened and her heart rate kicked up. *Yep, kissable.*

"You're Stick. My *very* best friend. *My* Stick." Ellie palmed Stick's jaw. "And to me, you have everything that's important in this world. You have honor and loyalty, and you're strong and brave and have warm, yummy eyes just like melted chocolate." Ellie paused and withdrew her hand. She giggled at the blush on Stick's cheeks. "And you have the biggest heart, and I'm proud to be with you because I lo—"

Ellie's fingertips flew to her mouth, too late to catch the words. Stunned by her near admission, her eyes widened, frantic with apprehension.

A corner of Stick's mouth slowly curled upward. She set her palms cautiously on Ellie's shoulders and squeezed tenderly. "I love you, too, Ellie," she whispered. Stick's heart pounded euphorically as she lowered her head and gently touched Ellie's mouth with her own. The plush velvet of Ellie's lips set Stick to shaking all over. Feeling Ellie returning the kiss, brief as it was, nearly dropped Stick to the dirt.

Nothing in her experience compared to the sweet, consuming

sensation of kissing Ellie. Stick couldn't believe she'd been so bold, but she knew she'd be forever thankful. The whole world disappeared when their lips touched. The chill of the overcast day, the worries about tomorrow's supper, nothing mattered. Her mind went blank, swirled off to someplace like heaven. She couldn't even remember feeling her feet on the ground.

They each took a modest step back, looking everywhere but at each other. Finally, Stick reached out and delicately brushed a few loose strands of hair from Ellie's cheek. "I have a little present for you."

Stick dove into her pocket for the three-inch cherry lollipop.

Ellie recognized the shy desire in Stick's gaze and it caused her to wonder if a little romantic kiss between friends had been inevitable. A slight tremor wiggled along Ellie's spine. It was only a little kiss, but it made Ellie's heart thump and her arms feel useless and weak. She was unnerved and a bit overwhelmed to realize it was a kiss she wanted to experience again, but next time she really would like to have the security of their friendship, Stick's strength and familiarity, wrapped around her. Finally, she remembered to swallow.

Stick looked different to her somehow, or maybe Ellie was seeing her differently. The keen surveillance of Stick's eyes had softened, centered on Ellie's with a comforting glow. Stick's stern, patrician nose and long jawline lent her a proud, almost defiant look. And that slipped into a broad, humble smile. It wasn't the first time the descriptive *handsome* had come to Ellie's mind, and she almost blushed at the thought.

Tall and much too thin for her height, Stick had earned her neighborhood name, as had so many others, and only the non-locals mistook her for a boy. The locals knew that the lanky teenager with the boyish figure and striking features was one of them from birth; she was smart, street savvy, and just as tough as the boys. It was all a matter of survival in tough times, and Stick was a survivor. Ellie was ever so proud of that.

At the sight of the candy in Stick's hand, she leaned forward without thinking, whispered a quick thank-you onto Stick's mouth, and set a kiss on her lips that lasted a few seconds longer than their first. She really enjoyed kissing Stick. In fact, it was exhilarating…and perfect.

❖

"I love feeling your arms around me like this, so tight and snug." Ellie kissed Stick's neck lightly, endlessly excited by the intimate turn in their friendship. Private time was a rare, precious thing, and Ellie summoned every reasonable excuse to rendezvous like this in the shadow of her house. For Stick's strong embrace, she'd risk everything.

"I can't get you close enough, El." She kissed Ellie's ear. "You're perfect, you know."

"We're perfect."

Stick brought her mouth to Ellie's and whispered. "Are you sure they can't see us from the kitchen?"

"Stop worrying. It's okay. *This* is very okay."

A figure suddenly raced around the corner of the house and crashed into them, all three of them spilling to the ground like bowling pins.

"Holy shit!" Davey Matizano scrambled to his feet.

"Cripes, Davey!" Stick exclaimed, helping Ellie up.

He peered at them oddly. "What the hell? What're you two doin' out here?"

"Mind your business," Stick snapped as she brushed off her clothes. "What's up?"

He paused in thought, breathing hard and looking from Ellie to Stick. "Were you two...Um, I mean, did I see what—"

"What's up, damn it?"

Davey couldn't organize his thoughts, so Stick socked him in the shoulder.

"Talk, stupid!"

"Um...I-I checked your place, Stick, but...At least I found you. It's Baggers. We need you bad. He's...he's stuck."

Stick straightened to her full height and crossed her arms. "He's stuck?"

"Yeah. In Henderson's storage room, Stick. He fell through the floor."

"Jesus Christ, Davey!"

"Yeah, so come on!" He pivoted to run, but Ellie grabbed his arm.

"What's he doing in Henderson's at this hour?"

Davey froze, then looked at Stick for help. Ellie followed his gaze.

"Sounds like he's up to no good," Stick offered and clasped Ellie's hands. "We have to help Baggers, Ellie. I gotta go."

"But, Stick, if you get caught it'll look—"

"Shh. We won't get caught. Trust me. Look for me here in an hour, okay?"

Ellie set her jaw and nodded. Stick squeezed her hands and Ellie watched her race away with Davey.

❖

Within ten minutes, Stick and Davey were at Bagger's side…or rather his chest, because the rest of him dangled beneath the floor into the cellar.

Stick found a coil of rope just inside the back door, and they wrapped Baggers up good and tight and began pulling.

Baggers inhaled sharply as jagged wood threatened to pierce his rib cage. He let loose with a "Yeooowwww!"

Davey slapped the back of his head. "Shut up, goddamn it!"

"You're gonna have the whole damn neighborhood in here, yelling like that," Stick said.

"I can't help it!"

"Grab onto the rope. C'mon. Use your strength."

The floor flexed awkwardly beneath Stick's feet. "Hold it." She stepped away and stared at the hole around Bagger's beefy body. "I'll go down and find something he can stand on. Watch out for this floor."

Old man Henderson kept a kerosene lamp at the top of the cellar stairs, and Stick lit it and made her way down, pausing at the bottom to set it aside. At the broken ceiling where Baggers's legs swung freely, she piled every crate and box she could find until he could get his feet under him.

Then she heard shouting from the front of the store. Lots of heavy footsteps thundered across the old wooden floorboards above her, and it only took a second for Stick to know the cops had arrived.

Panicked, she scanned the dimness for the outside cellar door. There was no chance to help her pals upstairs. Now it was every man— or woman—for herself. She darted across the cellar and tumbled over a pallet, sending several boxes crashing down on her.

Stick charged back up and shot for the door. Footsteps stormed down the cellar steps.

She grabbed the paint-chipped doorknob and flipped back the bolt lock just as a cop yelled for her to stop. He was yelling profanities when he stumbled over the kerosene lamp on the bottom step. Fire sloshed across the floor in a wave of illuminating yellow, and Stick rocketed out into the night.

❖

True to her word, Stick was standing in Ellie's backyard one hour later. Within minutes, they were huddled together behind Mr. Weston's massive rose bushes.

"Ellie, now listen, please."

"I want to know what happened, Stick. You're filthy. Is everyone okay?" She looked off at the sound of emergency sirens a few blocks away.

"No, it didn't go too good. Listen, Ellie. It was just one big circus. We almost had him free, out of the hole, when the cops barged in. I was down in the cellar and managed to get out."

"Good. That's good."

Stick shook her head. "Not really. A cop might've seen enough to identify me. He yelled for me to stop, but I didn't 'cause I was too scared and then...then...he knocked over the lantern, and I think the place might have caught fire."

Ellie's hands went to her cheeks in shock. "Oh, no, Stick!"

"Yeah. So they must have caught Davey and Baggers, and they're probably gonna be looking for me, but I didn't do anything, really, I swear."

"I know. Shh." Ellie put her palms on Stick's flushed cheeks. "It will be okay. Go and tell them what happened."

"No! Ellie, I can't." Stick paced away and paced back. "They won't believe a word I say. Henderson already hates me. I have to go hide somewhere for a while." She bent over, braced her hands on her knees, and took a few deep breaths. It was so, so hard to breathe. Why couldn't she think clearly? Why didn't her heart explode? It was pounding so hard her body shook. "They'll figure out what really happened, right?" She straightened abruptly. "I hate to say it, El, but Baggers and Davey will have to take the fall for this. I feel bad for them, but I didn't do—"

"Stick. Slow down, please." Ellie removed Stick's cap and combed her hair back with soft, gentle fingers.

The sensation made Stick pause. She thrust her arms around Ellie's waist. Eyes closed to calm herself, she clung to her desperately and nearly crumbled at the press of tender lips to her mouth.

Stick dropped her forehead onto Ellie's shoulder. "I don't want you mixed up in this, so I gotta go now."

"Where?"

Stick's hammering heart threatened to choke her, and judging by the pale expression on Ellie's face, it was obvious. She was scaring them both to death.

"Stick, no." Ellie shook her head vehemently. "You being gone will look suspicious. You have to just act like noth—"

"Don't you get it?" Stick's eyes teared up. Vivid memories of old man Henderson played across her mind like a moving picture show at the Strand. He'd even had a grip on her a couple of weeks ago. He'd finger her as the third kid just out of spite. "El, I have to, at least for a while…until the commotion settles and the truth comes out. I gotta get away from my house and you. I will be in touch with you, though. I promise, 'cause I need you, Ellie. I…I love you."

CHAPTER TWO

The night of the fire, Stick kept to the unlit backstreets and alleys and made her way across to the South Side of Boston and the rail yard. She had walked it with Ray many times when their father was alive, when they'd bring him supper or fetch him to come home. Stick knew the yard well. She allowed her mind to escape into the vivid fantasies she'd concocted as a small girl. The broken, abandoned railcars and the hobos made up the simple houses and folks of a quiet little town all its own.

So when she picked her way through the darkness, stepping over sections of railroad ties, scattered lengths of rail, chunks of coal, and shattered bottles, she wasn't intimidated. The back acres of the yard were a vast, decrepit wasteland, and street people took it in stride. It was, even with its lost and alone atmosphere, far more welcoming than the real city she now feared as a sixteen-year-old on the run.

How in the name of God had life come to this, she wondered. She couldn't go home to anything that felt like sanctuary, even if her mother did decide to treat her decently, but separating from Ellie was what really gnawed at her guts. It was turning her aching head inside out. It made her duck into alleys to vomit. It felt like her heart was forcing itself through her chest, reaching out. She wondered if she would die from it.

Stick poked her head into several boxcars until she found one with a roof without holes. She climbed in and walked the inside perimeter in the pitch black. Determined she had it to herself and there were no men or rats lounging about, she sat down heavily in a corner. She wasn't hungry. She hadn't eaten since…she couldn't remember…but she was more numb than anything else, except for the deep ache in her chest.

Leaning back against the wall, she sighed hard and closed her eyes. They burned, on the edge of tears, but there'd be no crying. The facts would be out in short order. *You can do this. Just buck up. Hang on for a bit.* But the here and now was cold. If she was going to get through this insanity, she'd have to take charge of herself. She'd need a few provisions, a little food here and there, and a plan to see Ellie. Such were the necessities of life, she decided, dropping off into an exhausted sleep.

Come morning, Stick woke with a sore ass and a stiff neck. Shivering, she crawled to the doorway and sat back on her heels surveying the yard. Images of Baggers jammed into that hole, of Henderson's cellar awash in flame, of Ellie's scared and teary eyes…They screamed across her mind. What had she done? Jesus. She scrubbed at her face with irritation. What now?

She wondered how long she could last this way with nothing but the jacket she was wearing, not a penny to her name. This was where grown men never bathed and went days without food, where they shivered in the chill night air and froze to death in the snow. This was where you stole just to stay alive, and slept with one eye open, and stayed away from the law.

Stick blinked up at the pale early sun, thankful for fair weather. It wouldn't last, and she knew she couldn't afford to sit still. She committed the lay of the land to memory. About three acres away, two men shuffled toward the empty guardhouse near the street and, thinking they probably knew where free coffee was available, Stick paid attention.

"Hey."

The gravelly male voice surprised Stick so much she almost fell out of the car. He was taller than she was and a good hundred pounds heavier, and he stood several feet away, filthy from head to toe in a ragged flannel shirt, dark pants, and shoes with no laces. Black curly hair stood up all over his head, and his very scruffy face broke into a broad smile.

"I'm Smitty. Who are you?"

Stick was struck dumb and the big man laughed.

"You got no name? Look, no offense, but..." He squinted at her. "You a boy or a girl?"

Stick's jaw flexed. "I'm a girl. My name's Stick."

"Well, then." Smitty set his big hands on his hips. "You get in last night?"

Stick weighed just how much she should say. She already regretted using her own name. *Better learn faster than that.* "Maybe. So?"

Smitty shrugged. "Just wonderin'. We ain't got nothin' here, so hope you ain't looking for a handout. Those two fellas just went off for coffee." He nodded in the direction of the guardhouse. "Salvation Army has it every morning. It's a couple blocks over on—"

"I know where it is."

Smitty squinted at her again. "So you're from here?"

Stick kicked herself mentally. If she kept up this carelessness, she'd be in jail in a heartbeat. "You?"

"Ah, hell no." Smitty waved his hand in denial. "Pennsylvania. But the other guys, they're from here, 'cept Heath. He's been here six years now, I think. Before that, no one knows, but far away would be my guess."

Stick just nodded and turned back into the car.

"How old are you, Stick?"

She stopped and looked sideways at him. "Old enough."

"How much time you lookin' at?"

Now, she faced him directly. "I ain't running from nobody."

"You kill somebody?"

"Shit, no! I said I ain't run—"

"Ahuh." Smitty left her standing in the car doorway. "Fellas'll be comin' around soon and you're welcome to sit in. Might as well get to know everyone. No one'll hurt you."

"I can take care of myself, thanks," she said toward his backside.

"Yup. I figured."

❖

Once she left the Salvation Army building, having washed up and thrown back two cups of the strongest, sorriest version of coffee she'd ever tasted, Stick spent the day scrounging around the army base in

Southie, the fish piers, and then the Leather District. She avoided the naval barracks at Commonwealth Pier and the base in Charlestown because of that horrible influenza everyone was talking about. Sailors were dropping like flies, she heard, so she kept a safe distance.

Back in her rail car after sunset, she assessed her day's work: a pair of U.S. Army green pants and matching green socks with only one hole by the right little toe, a wool blanket a fisherman tossed at her, and two leather gloves, one small and one large. She needed a shirt or two. And some underwear was a must, but she had no idea how to land those…except off someone's clothesline. She knew it probably would come to that, but she still didn't like it.

And it turned out the guys in the yard were okay. Friendly and usually pretty funny, and they treated her like one of them.

It took a good couple of weeks to adjust to that, being "one of the boys," homeless and down on your luck, but as the days went by and things became more routine, Stick didn't see their gang as homeless or all that unfortunate. Sure they could use a good meal now and then, and a bath and a decent shirt, maybe, but they had a place to call home and friends they could trust like family. That meant a whole lot.

But the Thanksgiving holiday threatened to send Stick into the dark doldrums, missing what little festive time she used to enjoy with her parents, siblings, and neighbors. She constantly reminded herself that her mother had become someone whose company few people enjoyed, so she really didn't miss her at all. Did she? Brother Ray, at nineteen, had become his own version of God's gift to women and was too irritating to hang with for any length of time, anyway. It was seven-year-old Dottie she missed, her giggles and bright-eyed smiles, and the games they used to play. And then, of course, there was Ellie.

She mailed Ellie three postcards on Thanksgiving week, staying in touch as best she could and keeping her own spirit from crashing to the yard dirt like so much shattered glass. She wrote about past Thanksgiving nights, when they'd gather around the Westons' big kitchen table and have leftover potatoes and gravy and big pieces of Mrs. Weston's pies, either apple or squash. The Westons could be counted on to have a fat, juicy chicken stuffed with cornbread and apples, which was why there never were any meat leftovers.

At her own house, Stick's mother always prepared four baked chicken legs, potatoes, and turnip, which was cheap at the A&P, and although Stick never liked that vegetable's bitterness, she ate it to fill up. There was a cup of custard for each of them as dessert. After heating water for dishes on the old coal stove and washing and putting everything away, Stick always made a beeline for the Weston house across the street.

She'd stay till bedtime, munching down cookies Ellie made with her mom. Oatmeal with peanut bits. Couldn't buy them in a store. Crumbly, especially when stashed under a pillow. Special cookies for special moments…with a special girl.

Now, sitting on a cold chunk of railroad tie and watching the fire, Stick slouched deeper into her jacket and studied the faces of the men in the flickering light. It was Thanksgiving night, and she wondered where each man's thoughts had gone. She wondered if her first foray into the streets had been like any of theirs. She supposed that growing up, eyeballing the delicious or fun things in stores hadn't helped keep her on the straight and narrow.

She sighed and watched her frosty breath dance in the firelight. Any day now, she calculated, the police would tell the newspapers how the whole fire went down, that Davey and Baggers confessed to breaking in, and that the fire was an accident and nobody was really to blame. It was the truth, after all, so it might take a little time, but things would sort themselves out soon. The reasoning gave her hope.

It was plain to see that once this mess was cleaned up, she'd need a genuine job like other adults. She was one now. That's how it felt. She would get back on her feet, and life would get better than ever. She needed to start right away. Besides, how could she expect Ellie to even see her, if she was nothing more than a hoodlum, some street tough? How could she give Ellie sweets and flowers, the pretty things she deserved? Stick vowed to climb back to respectability. Tomorrow, she'd send off another postcard and they'd meet behind the A&P again soon, so Stick could make sure Ellie knew her intentions.

❖

Anonymous postcards arrived every few weeks, and Ellie treasured them all. Stick was present when she held the cards. That shared touch of hands. She missed Stick terribly. Nothing her mother said cheered her. Meal times were subdued; after-school homework sessions grew into prolonged, sad, and secluded hours; shopping at the A&P with her parents was torturous as neighbors always stopped to chat about Henderson's. Everyone knew the situation was deadly serious. Ellie had little to say to anyone.

She continued to save all the news clippings of "the crime" which, instead of being unraveled and resolved, had exploded with complexity. A policeman suffered severe burns in the blaze that turned Henderson's into a vacant lot of charred debris. Firemen wore themselves out fighting the losing battle. Neighbors were all gathered 'round when the police pushed Davey and Baggers into the paddy wagon. Everyone heard the boys shouting explanations of what happened, yelling in protest. Everyone heard the police urgently calling out, asking if any onlookers noticed a fleeing accomplice.

Within a day of the fire, police started throwing Stick's name around. In the neighborhood, it was plenty obvious who was missing, and everyone figured the beat cops knew more than they were saying, but nobody was giving up a local girl, one of their own, because of an accident.

No one knew where Stick had disappeared to anyway. For that, Ellie was sadly grateful because the cops came calling. The third and last time the police knocked, they chose right after supper so her father would be present.

"Eleanor Marie Weston. Have you seen Stick in these weeks since the fire?"

Her father's formal tone just made Ellie sink deeper into the sofa. "No, Dad. I told you and them before." Her eyes flickered at the two officers standing in the parlor. "I haven't. And nobody I know has, either."

"Miss Weston," the mustachioed officer injected, "the charges are extremely serious. Breaking and entering with intent to commit larceny, destruction of private property—not to mention arson. You could be considered an accessory if you don't reveal—"

"Arson?" Ellie's expression was incredulous. "Nobody would've set fire to the place!" She heard the resentment and indignation in her voice.

Both officers were nodding. "'Fraid so, miss. Lit it in the cellar. It's in the official report."

Ellie felt her blood pressure rise. All that stuff in the newspapers about corruption was true. It was city-wide. Someone must have something to gain by calling it arson.

Her mother stepped into her distant line of vision and cocked her head curiously. "Honey? Are you sure you haven't heard anything, any talk about the fire?"

"No, Mom. The only time I'm out is with you or Dad, so you've heard everything I've heard. And at school, all anyone ever mentions is how Davey and Baggers will probably get years in jail when they go to trial."

Her father's baritone made Ellie jump. "And no one mentions Stick? She's run around this neighborhood her entire life and no one mentions her?" Ellie shook her head. He sighed. "I find that hard to believe."

Ellie refused to look at the police officers. She was afraid her façade would crack. But when her father pulled a stack of postcards from his suit jacket pocket and handed them to the officers, she thought she would faint.

"Take these," he said to them, handing over Stick's communiqués. "None of them says anything but foolish dribble, but they're from her. At least you know she's still in town."

He turned and stared into Ellie's eyes.

"We'll turn these over to the detectives," the other officer said. He shot his partner a glance and they nodded. They settled their hats on their heads. "If you have anything else, miss, anything at all, please let us know."

Mr. Weston opened the door for them. "Thank you, Officers. We certainly will. You boys do good work and we'll do our best to help."

He shut the door after them, exhaled heavily, and stuffed his hands into his pockets. "They work practically seven days a week, you know, and for a pittance. They're even talking about a strike, for God's sake. They need our help, and we need to do our part as honorable citizens. And that includes you, young lady."

Ellie blinked back tears at having lost Stick's cards. "You didn't have to give them away, Dad. You know they didn't say anything." She hated the invasion of her privacy at the deepest level. And she hated sharing Stick in that way. It was a violation of their love.

"We will continue to read any more that arrive, Ellie, and hand them right over."

"But they're mine, Daddy! They don't hurt anyone!" Now tears rolled.

He waved his finger. "There are people in this city, very important people, mind you, who believe I'm a family man fit for public office, and I'm not going to allow questions about my family's integrity jeopardize the chance for that raise in pay. Your mother and I taught you right from wrong when you were a little girl. You're a young lady now. You know better and will behave accordingly."

He left for his study, pulling a thick cigar from inside his suit jacket.

CHAPTER THREE

Christmas was the hardest to take. As days counted down to single digits, Stick was sending postcards daily. Now she adorned them with little sketches of Christmas trees, wreaths, and snowmen, all around the words she wrote. Two days before Christmas, she mailed the last one Ellie would get before the holiday. So many things were left unsaid once Stick dropped the card into the mailbox on the corner of Washington and Franklin.

She saved every cent possible, especially lucky ones she found in the gutter. And she had three books now, old schoolbooks left on trains by students: arithmetic, mechanics, and history. She read them religiously in hopes it would make up for missing school. And everywhere she went, she asked about work, convinced there was a paying job out there for someone like her, strong and hardworking with brains. And then she'd get that experience she'd need to help keep a real roof over their heads. It was their dream. Stick knew she'd die before giving it up. And she knew Ellie certainly would be by her side.

And then there were the moments when the whole world turned into a blue, empty, bone-chilling gut-wrenching place with no horizon, no Ellie. Stick agonized through those times, focusing on the brilliant smile that lit up Ellie's face, her carefree laughter, the squeezing of their warm hands. And their always heartfelt, soul-baring kisses.

Hands in her jacket pockets, she walked with head down into the bitter wind, away from the holiday gaiety along the streets, and settled on a bench on the Common. Tears slowly blurred her vision just as snowflakes started to fall. There was only one thing she wanted for Christmas, and she would see Ellie, kiss Ellie, if it was the last thing she did.

She'd only been working at Maggie's Market in Southie for two weeks and had only twenty-five cents to her name, so she couldn't buy Ellie much of a present. Stick kept most of her pay in a different pocket and vowed to sneak back home as soon as she had fifty cents to give Mama. Meanwhile, she battled the guilt of not providing more. She'd *find* a few items at the A&P for her family's Christmas dinner and leave them at the back door, but she was too poor to buy presents for anyone. And all the while, she longed to offer Ellie something special. She wiped away tears with her mismatched gloves and sat up straighter to think.

By the time she reached the rail yard a half hour later, she was walking on an inch of snow and sporting a headache that would kill a horse. Ahead was the now-familiar little fire the guys had going for warmth. Stick wondered if they had any food. She had a foot-long roll of salami under her jacket, a little something she *borrowed* from Foster's Grocery over in Scollay Square two hours before. She'd share it with the guys.

That thought finally brought a smile to her face as she approached the fire ring. She still hadn't come up with the ideal present for Ellie, and it weighed heavily on her mind, but she had to admit, this sight was heartwarming. A gap in their circle drew her eye to the Christmas tree they'd erected a few feet away. It was a scrawny-looking pine, probably a reject from the lot down on D Street where they were selling trees. But a few things sparkled on its droopy branches, illuminated by the firelight.

Stepping closer, Stick saw the shards of glass, wrapped in string and connected to many others, encircling the tree several times.

"Wow," she said in a reverent whisper. "You guys did a great job!" She looked at all the faces, but none would look back. The men mumbled their thanks and pretended not to be touched by Stick's praise. She smiled fondly at their pride. They might not have much in this world, but they had that.

❖

It was almost dawn on Christmas Eve, and the fire was nearly out by the time Stick finished scraping and polishing the piece of green glass that filled the palm of her hand. Their humble little Christmas tree had inspired her, and she'd spent nearly two hours searching for the right piece, kicking up the snow far across the yard where someone had dumped bottles over the fence. It was the thick bottom of a wine bottle, and she'd sat down with it and scraped the jagged glass edges with a chunk of cement all night until they were ground smooth.

The long night disappeared with Stick hard at work, her mind drifting far from her shivering hands. *Too bad I can't ground down my own rough edges. All shiny and polished is how Ellie should see me, not as some hoodlum who steals salami from the market...some hobo who needs a good scrubbing and wears stolen underwear.*

Stick could see Ellie's small, gentle hand absorbing the warmth and desire of Stick's hand every time she touched this simple piece of glass. Ellie's slim fingers, delicate and white, would glide along these edges so tenderly, with as much adoration as her touch to Stick's cheek. Stick would make sure of it.

She held the glass up to the firelight every so often and marveled at how the circular piece went from a black-green to brilliant emerald in her hand. Then she began scraping a nick into the edge of the glass, running it over a pointed piece of cement, again and again. Eventually, the nick widened, deepening toward the center of the glass, and the more it widened, the more Stick smoothed and rounded back its edges. The guys went wide-eyed when Stick held the glass up again, this time in the shape of a heart.

Everyone had gone for free pancakes at St. Mary's by the time Stick closed her eyes to sleep. She tucked Ellie's present into her jacket pocket, wrapped herself in her blankets, and nodded off to get enough rest so she could see Ellie later in the day. A trip to the A&P for last-minute Christmas dinner necessities was the plan she had outlined in code on the last postcard, and she hoped with all her heart Ellie could sell the excuse to her mother and be there.

❖

Five hours later, with her spirit as bright as the winter sun, Stick spotted her. She tugged her cap down harder on her head and cleared her throat. Stay composed, she told herself; no falling apart, no blubbering and wasting time being lovesick. *Concentrate.*

Through the crumbling walls of the old horse barn behind the market, Stick watched Ellie shift her parcel to her opposite arm and hold the hem of her long crimson coat out of the snow with the other. Even walking tentatively, she was graceful. *And she's coming to see if I'm here.*

The breeze teased some of Ellie's hair from beneath her thick collar, and the sight of such golden silk against the deep blue sky made Stick swallow hard. Ellie was the most beautiful creature Stick had ever seen, and she loved her with every beat of her heart. She blinked away joyful tears.

Ellie disappeared around the corner of the dilapidated building and reappeared in the open doorway. She beamed at Stick, her parcel cast aside, instantly forgotten.

That happy, knowing smile nearly knocked Stick to the ground. They stepped into each other's arms and sobbed their hellos. Composure be dammed.

Stick finally drew back and cupped the chilled, rosy cheeks in her palms. Ellie reached up between Stick's hands and softly stroked away a tear. Her smile widened when Stick leaned into her touch.

"Oh, Ellie…I…I don't have the words to tell you how much you mean to me. You're everything I need in this world." She kissed the tip of her nose. "I dream of y—"

Ellie's gloved fingertips stilled Stick's lips. "I love you." She rose up on her toes to press her kiss to Stick's trembling mouth. "I hate what's happened, but don't you forget that you're all I need, too."

They kissed with intense passion, Stick wrapping her arms around the bulky coat and drawing Ellie down onto the blanket she brought. Both their hats fell away as Stick leaned along Ellie, their kisses unending. Ellie locked her arms around Stick's shoulders, wiggled her fingers from her gloves, and drove them up into Stick's hair. She sighed in Stick's ear as kisses traveled across her mouth to her cheek and neck and returned to her lips with urgent need.

"My God, I have missed you," Stick breathed, lifting her head and gazing in wonder at Ellie's face. "There will never be anyone for me but you."

Now Ellie's eyes filled. She pulled Stick's head down and sealed her lips to Stick's. She moaned into Stick's mouth, squeezing her closer with shaking hands.

Stick caressed Ellie's clenched eyes, kissed away the tears, kissed her forehead ever so slowly. "Somehow, we have to stop crying, my beautiful girl," she whispered against the bridge of Ellie's nose. "You can't go home with red eyes even if it is the color of Christmas."

She drew back, kissed the sad smile slowly, and sat them up. Ellie rose to her knees and then her feet.

"Where are you going?"

Ellie just grinned down at Stick and moved to a pile of discarded boards in the corner of the ramshackle structure. As Stick watched with great curiosity, Ellie moved the wood aside and lifted a bundled blanket from a depression in the floor. She returned to Stick and set it onto her lap.

"I've been collecting things," Ellie said. "Each time I've had to run to the market, I've added to the package." Stick just stared at it, baffled. "Go on. Unwrap it."

Stick unfolded the blanket and gave a little gasp. She looked up with disbelief from the odd assortment of very useful items. "Is all this for me?"

Ellie nodded repeatedly. "See?" she began, and dove into the pile. "Peanut butter, Stick, and that strawberry jam we like so much." She held up one item after another, and Stick's eyes just grew more dazed. "Here's some licorice sticks and peppermints, a bag of crackers, these two apples, some deviled ham, Heinz spaghetti, and Campbell's vegetable soup. I know you like that. Oh, and also some of my heavy socks, a scarf my nana made years ago, and my favorite mittens. And of course this blanket."

"Holy mackerel, Ellie!" Stick studied the lapful of treasures. "I can't believe you did all this. I...I..."

"Oh, and these too." Ellie pulled a small bag out of one of the socks. "My cookies."

Stick's head popped up. "Your special cookies with the peanuts?"

Ellie wiped a tear from the corner of Stick's eye. "How else could I take care of you? God knows, Stick, you have to eat and stay warm, be careful not to get this influenza. It's so, so dangerous. I've been going crazy, waiting for this day." She leaned close and pressed a soft, lingering kiss onto Stick's lips. "Now, keep your eyes closed."

Her opened hand resting in Ellie's, Stick felt the feather-weight touch of chain draping across her fingers, and then the press of something the size of nickel into her palm.

"Okay, open."

Stick stared down at the gold chain and the heart it carried, and tears fell immediately. Ellie quickly captured Stick's wet face and kissed her. "Merry Christmas to my love."

Stick hung her head, sagged heavily into Ellie's arms, and cried. "Oh, h-how did you do—"

"Shh. Don't worry about that."

"I-I love this, Ellie," she managed. "So much." She sniffed hard and sat up, ogling the jewelry. Ellie's hands appeared then, and she took the necklace and lowered it over Stick's head. "Ellie, I…I'll never take it off. I swear."

"I want you to have a reminder of me, of us, wherever you go. To know I'm with you, Stick, through all of this…and more."

They cried, kissed, and just held each other for what seemed like mere seconds when it came time to part. Ellie piled all the items together and wrapped the blanket around them.

"Before your kisses get my brain any more mushy, Miss McLaughlin, I need to let you know something." She stroked Stick's hands. "Your postcards. Be careful, honey. My father takes them."

Stick was outraged. "That's not fair. It's against the law to take someone's mail!"

"Shh. Yes, I know. But I guess until I'm eighteen, he can do as he pleases with me—and my rights. I'm lucky that Mama gets the mail from the mailman every day and lets me read your cards. I don't know what I'd do if I couldn't read them! She stands right there while I do, then takes them to give to Dad. He…" Her head lowered. "He gives them all to the police, Stick."

"Oh." It was another gut punch to withstand. "But at least you get to read them. I'm not stopping. I'll be careful." She set her forehead against Ellie's. "So far so good with our code."

"Thank God," Ellie said with a sob, and thrust herself into Stick's arms, crying as she kissed her.

Stick returned her kiss with equal fervor until they had to break apart to breathe. "I know we should go soon," she murmured, her eyes filling again. "I can't get you in trouble." Ellie traced Stick's jaw with a fingertip and the wisps of Ellie's short, excited breaths tickled her face. They matched her own, and she knew Ellie's heart raced just like hers. She closed her eyes to concentrate. "This mess will probably be over soon, but until then, I don't want—"

"What do you mean, 'over soon'?"

Stick leaned in and kissed her tenderly. "I heard about the trial starting, so Davey and Baggers will finally get to say how the fire was all an accident. Once that's official, I—" Stick frowned at Ellie's frown. "What?"

"Stick, listen please."

Stick cringed at the sight of Ellie's deepening frown, and when Ellie pressed her palm to her cheek, Stick knew there was more bad news to come.

"They're after you for breaking in, yes, but they're also charging you with arson."

Stick jerked back. "No! That's not true, Ellie." She moved to get up, but Ellie grabbed her arm and held her in place on the blanket. "It was an accident. Honest." Stick's eyes were watering again, and her voice shook.

Ellie pulled her into her arms. "Honey, you don't have to explain to me. You know I've believed you from the beginning. But every damn one of them is on the take."

Stick pulled away enough to search Ellie's eyes for answers. "Why, though? What do any of them have to gain by making up stuff?" She dropped her face into her hands and groaned.

Ellie hugged her shoulders with one arm and drew Stick's head to her chest with the other. "I have a theory on that. Dad says the police are trying to start a union, so I think they want people to be on their side. And a cop was badly burned at Henderson's, you know, so they have the perfect way to get people's sympathy if it comes to voting for a strike."

Stick was glued to the tale, dumbfounded, and feeling all the more lost. She was grateful for the soothing motion of Ellie's chest at every breath. She rubbed her eyes with both hands. "Ellie, what can I do?"

"Whatever you've been doing, honey. You stay safe and be smart. The truth is bound to come out. It's only right."

Stick burrowed her face inside Ellie's collar to hide from the world. She nuzzled her neck. It was hard to resist snuggling deeply into

Ellie's warmth and the scent of her honeysuckle lotion, especially when Ellie welcomed her within such a firm embrace. Stick's insides coiled. Her breathing went ragged. She was ravenous for every inch of her. This wasn't the first time, but it was the most inconvenient.

She pretended to bite the sweet skin. She couldn't help it, and growled into the crook of Ellie's neck and shoulder. Escaping to this place was heavenly. Stick licked the spot and sucked it eagerly.

Ellie's face flushed and she shivered. She playfully pushed Stick away. "Mmmm. We need to behave, Stick."

Stick reached out and slipped her fingers to the back of Ellie's neck, then dipped beneath her collar, enjoying the satin feel of Ellie's shoulder. "We've never *mis*behaved," she whispered, her lips a breath away from Ellie's. "Every part of me wants to be connected to you."

Stick sat still and quiet. She didn't know if she'd just opened her big mouth once too many times or if Ellie was seriously considering what she'd insinuated. *Again, speaking without thinking.* But boy, she meant what she said. With any luck, Ellie would put her trust—and everything else—in her hands. And then Stick would pray she'd know what to do.

Ellie finally met Stick's eyes and gave her a sheepish smile. "You really want to, don't you?"

Stick took Ellie's fidgeting hands and stilled them in her lap. She nodded. "Only if you do."

Ellie folded her fingers between Stick's. She blew out a breath and puffed a strand of hair off her forehead. She chuckled awkwardly. "Well...I've thought about it. Us, I mean."

"Me too."

"Listen, Stick..." She hurried the rest on an exhale. "I'm not experienced. Are you?"

Stick lifted Ellie's hands and pressed little kisses to each knuckle. Finally, at the last one, she looked up with a grin. "Nope."

"I guess we...we could teach each other."

"Only each other," Stick stated, gently squeezing Ellie's hands. "We love each other and...so...we'll find our own way together."

"We can't...Well, we can't right here and now, though. You know that, right?" Ellie took a breath. "It's not that I don't want to," she amended quickly.

Stick shrugged. "I suppose we can't. Too cold, huh?"

Ellie burst into laughter and shoved Stick onto her back. "Yeah, too cold, tough guy." She rested her palm on Stick's stomach and toyed with the button of her jacket. "I have to go, you know."

Stick sat back up. *Do not cry.*

"I want to give you something first." She reached into her jacket but was stopped. Ellie's possessive grip on her arm sent such a wild rush of desire through Stick's entire body that she trembled.

"Stick, you don't have to give me anything. I have you." She cradled Stick's cheek in her palm again. "We'll find a way to be together soon, Elizabeth McLaughlin. Your love is a huge gift to me."

Stick's vision was blurring, so she knew she couldn't waste time. As she leaned forward and kissed Ellie, she slipped the heavy glass keepsake, wrapped in brown paper, into Ellie's palm.

They parted but held each other's gaze for a long moment after.

Ellie spoke without taking her eyes from Stick's. "What have you done here?" Stick simply grinned. "What is it? It's heavy."

"Open it. I know it's nothing fancy like pretty ladies should have, but..." She took a deep breath as Ellie unfolded the stiff paper. "Y'see... Well...It sparkles in the light like a jewel."

Ellie gasped as she lifted the green glass heart from the wrapping. "Oh, Stick!" She raised it into a beam of light, and the heart took on its brilliant emerald glow. Tears trickled down both cheeks. "Stick, it's just spectacular." She clutched it to her chest with both hands. "Did you make this somehow?"

Stick swallowed and searched for the just the right words. *Thinking before speaking.* "I just hope you'll feel me working the glass each time you touch it."

Ellie reached behind Stick's head and pulled her into a deep, very mature kiss.

Finally breaking for air, Stick closed her fingers over Ellie's as she held the glass heart. "Simple glass I tried to make special," Stick softly told her. "I figure, if I can make something out of that for you, then maybe someday I can make something out of *me* for you."

CHAPTER FOUR

Ellie couldn't concentrate and tossed away the book she'd been assigned to read for homework. It had been unseasonably warm for mid-April and all day her thoughts returned to those fun outings in the park with Stick, their walks around town, the precious hours spent laughing on her front porch. Only able to glimpse Stick's postcards, she rarely had a clue as to Stick's well-being, hardly a connection to that other half of her heart.

And she longed for that connection, replaying their Christmas Eve rendezvous in her mind as she did every evening until all her senses responded. She could feel Stick's shoulders, her hands, her face, smell the wood smoke in her hair, taste her kisses, and could no longer deny the arousal they stimulated. Even though she'd never experienced sexual intimacy with anyone, her heart and body told her that Stick should be the one. It would be okay to be nervous with Stick; she'd understand and probably be just as nervous.

Someday. Come hell or high water.

"Ellie?" Her mother's call interrupted yet another daydream. "You're needed in the kitchen."

Ellie sighed in resignation and headed downstairs. As she turned toward the kitchen, she could see that her parents' attention was aimed at something not yet in her line of vision.

"What is it?"

Only her mother turned to her. "Look, honey. Stick's here." She stepped aside and Ellie froze in the doorway.

Her gaze traveled all over Stick's boney frame and she ached at the sight. Unruly hair bound at the back of her neck reached to the stringy collar of her shirt. An ill-fitting cotton jacket closed by its two remaining buttons topped threadbare trousers and heavily scuffed brown shoes. Stick humbly held her trademark cap in both hands. The hollowness of her sharp facial features was more severe than Ellie had ever seen. Stick abruptly broke into a smile.

"Hey, El."

Ellie choked back a sob and threw herself at Stick in a mad rush, not caring if her parents were stunned by the physical display. Now more than ever, it wasn't smart for Stick to be seen in the neighborhood. Police heat to catch Stick had increased since Davey and Baggers's trial, ever since Christmas. Ellie's heart fluttered hard as Stick lifted her off her feet, and gooseflesh rose along her arms just knowing Stick needed to see her as much as she needed to see Stick.

"Enough. Let's sit down now," her father commanded.

They sat round the kitchen table, and Ellie's mother set a bowl of leftover stew in front of Stick without asking. For half an hour, as they caught up on news of both families and neighborhood gossip, Ellie simply preferred to gaze upon her and listen. Thankfully, neither parent pressed Stick for details about where she stayed, how she spent her days. The less everyone knew, the better.

And while it was comforting to hear that Stick had just visited her mother, Ellie couldn't help but sympathize with Stick for enduring what must have amounted to fifteen minutes of hell. Stick's desolate expression grew as she quietly spoke of her brother Ray's marriage plans, that she'd learned her mother and little sister would be moving in with the newlyweds by next Christmas. Ellie knew what that meant. They all did. Stick would have no home to return to, assuming that was in the cards. Ellie almost kissed her mother when she offered their home to Stick for a temporary stay, should the legalities of her situation end positively. Her father, however, stiffened in his chair, puffed heavily on his cigar, and made it clear that until such time, Stick was not to come around his house again.

Ellie winced inside at the painful declaration, knowing it hurt Stick even more. Her father glared at Stick, seemed to dare her to challenge him, but Stick only nodded. Ellie admired the strength and maturity it required, and marveled at Stick's self-control. But when her father flaunted Ellie's intention to attend the annual Knights of Columbus ball with a neighbor's son, Ellie watched Stick's self-control waver.

"Ellie? Really?"

"Go on." Ellie's father teased her with an elbow. "Tell Stick. Tell her how you met him."

Then her mother leaned toward Stick and added, "He's a very nice boy."

Ellie could feel Stick's questioning eyes probing her face. Finally, she raised her head but couldn't look at her. "Dad had him and his father over to do some repairs to the house a month ago." With a risky glance, she recognized the heartsick gaze across the table and turned away. "His dad suggested to my dad that Tom take me." Now with watery eyes that matched Stick's, Ellie looked directly at her father. "It was the dads' decision."

Her mother gave Ellie a reassuring hug. "Oh, sweetie. Now, you know you'll have a wonderful evening with Tom. He's a—"

"No!" Ellie abruptly stood. "I told you both that I want no part of it."

Her father tapped a finger on the tabletop. "Sit down, young lady."

"I know you both mean well, Dad, but it's not what I want to do. I'm not interested in Tom...or...any of them." Her eyes met Stick's long enough for her father to notice.

He rose dramatically. "It's time for you to leave, Stick. Remember the rule I set here tonight. All the neighbors have had the police at their doors numerous times asking about you. And I will not lie to the police about this visit. Until this mess has been righted, you stay away from my home and my family. Have I made myself clear?"

Stick got to her feet. She gripped the back of her chair firmly, and Ellie wondered how much disappointment and loss one person could withstand before crumbling. Still, to her credit, Stick met his stern gaze evenly.

"Yes, sir." She went to the door he held open and paused. "Thanks for having me in and for the food. You're still the best cook, Mrs. Weston. It was real good to see you all. I appreciate it." She looked back to the table. "Ellie? Could I talk to you outside for just a minute?"

Before her father could object, Ellie passed him in the doorway. "Relax, Dad. Please." She drew the door shut behind her and the two of them wandered out of the light cast over the back steps.

"I don't want to go to that damn dance, Stick. You believe me, don't you?" Ellie waited for the downcast face to brighten. "I might come down with something that night. Some illness. I'm going to do anything I can to get out of it."

"I believe you, El," Stick answered finally. She kicked at the dirt then met her eyes. "I just can't stand the thought of him touching you... putting...his hands on you. I don't...I don't want him kissing you." She ran the tip of her finger across Ellie's lips and her voice cracked when she spoke. "These...These lips are precious. And they're mine."

Ellie smiled beneath Stick's feathery touch. "Yes, they are, Elizabeth McLaughlin, and you better kiss them before I scream." She slid her arms around Stick's waist and surrendered to the cool, tender palms cupping her face. As Stick dipped her head to kiss her, Ellie's eyes closed and she whispered against Stick's mouth. "I miss this so much. I miss you."

Stick closed all distance between them. "Me, too, El. Me, too."

Ellie explored the firm torso pressed against her, realizing as she hungrily stroked Stick's sides and back that she had never felt so much bone, the ribs and spine so prominent. The lean, athletic body of her handsome young woman was dwindling away.

Ellie drew back. "You're not eating well. I miss your muscles." She skimmed her fingertips across Stick's cheekbone and along her long jaw line. "I worry about you, you know. I think about you constantly."

Stick kissed the tip of Ellie's nose. "Please don't worry, El. I have a small job that gets me food. It'll get better. I promise."

"Where do you sleep, Stick? Every night in bed, I..." She didn't know how to finish that statement, how to convey the depth of such yearning. Stick squeezing her closer made it all the harder.

"I ache for you, El. I want to know you're safe. I want to keep you safe. Have you in my arms every night, every morning."

Now tears were running down Ellie's cheeks. "I want that too, Stick, so badly. My God, how I miss you. I want to take care of you. We need to be together. We always have been."

"I know, El, but I can't tell you where I stay and risk putting you on the spot. But it won't always be this way. I won't let it. I promise."

"There must be something I can do." Ellie dropped her head and sobbed. Stick's hands stroking her back didn't help. "I hate being helpless with you out there...somewhere."

"Please don't cry, baby. I promise you, Ellie, someday we'll live a good life together. I'm gonna make sure of it." Stick gently lifted Ellie's chin with two fingers and kissed the tears from her face. "I love you."

"Oh, Stick," she sighed, kissing her through tears.

The tip of her tongue brushed Stick's lip, but before she could shrink away in embarrassment, she felt the tentative touch in return. It was the most arousing sensation Ellie had ever experienced and she wanted more, wanted to be swallowed whole. Forgetting to breathe, she licked Stick's tongue lightly, and a little moan escaped Stick's throat.

"God, Ellie," Stick said on a quick breath. "I really, really want you in the most serious way."

Ellie melted into Stick's chest and squeezed her as close as she could. She wanted to lose herself in their sensuous kisses. The perfect world she wanted was wrapped around her, warm and secure, and she wanted so badly to provide the same for Stick. She struggled to hold back the tears and concentrated on surrendering her mouth to Stick's gently probing tongue. Her legs trembled as Stick's hands caressed her hips, as those strong fingers flexed into the cheeks of her rear, and Ellie realized it thrilled her beyond reason. There was no denying that she wanted Stick in a very serious way, too.

Her father's booming voice sounded throughout the yard. He couldn't see them behind the bushes, but he didn't have to.

"I'm going now, Ellie, before he comes storming out here."

Ellie hugged Stick tightly. "When will I see you again? Lord, I hate that we're always saying good-bye. Please make it soon, Stick."

"Soon. Honest." Stick fingered the gold chain around her neck. "Please don't ever forget I'm out there thinking of you, Ellie. Loving you."

"And you think of me, waiting, wanting you. Always, Stick. Always."

She clutched Stick to her desperately, absorbing all she could of the sweet, velvet mouth, the taste and feel of their love, and the comfortable rightness their bodies made. And when Stick withdrew, her breath fluttering against Ellie's cheek, there was little more to say. Stick pecked Ellie's nose and walked into the depths of the backyard and jumped the fence.

❖

Stick plunked herself down on a busted crate in the alley and set about eating supper. It had been a long, tough, hot day, delivering groceries to folks in Southie. All that up and down stairs had her strong legs weary, and she was just plain exhausted. Even the scrambled egg sandwich Mrs. Halloran had given her looked beat up.

But Stick leaned back against the cool brick in the alley and forced herself to take small, slow bites. This was it for the day, and she wanted to make it last. Life was pretty hard, but she knew she had to be thankful for what she did have. Delivery girl for Maggie's Market on Broadway was a decent job, one she was so lucky to land, and the fifty cents a week went pretty far when she set her mind to it. Tomorrow was Tuesday, and she knew the few Italian customers she had always stocked up for Wednesdays, so she'd get some real goodies for her efforts.

And it wasn't too far a walk back home to the rail yard once Maggie's closed at eight o'clock. Now that it was summer, she enjoyed longer days. They made it seem as if her life wasn't flying by. Plus, she didn't have to walk in the dark. Not that she minded it. She was no stranger to dark city streets; in fact, she was emboldened by them. And they came in handy whenever she journeyed back to Dorchester and snuck into Ellie's backyard. That didn't happen as much as either of them wanted, however. It was just a long way to walk after work and then back to the city rail yard—and be at work by six the next morning. Jumping a trolley sometimes made it a quick trip over, but there were no trolleys running in the neighborhood when it was time to go home.

Stick sighed as the last bite of sandwich went down. Two more just like it sure would hit the spot, she mused, and knew full well it would be a week before the opportunity rose again. She wiped her hands on her dusty pants and her mouth with the back of her sleeve. What she wouldn't give for a bath and clean clothes. These were the cleanest of what she had, and that wasn't saying much. Briefly, she wondered if her friend Ronnie, who delivered for Mason Hardware over on C Street, would ask his mother if Stick could wash a few things.

Stick reached deeply into the secret pocket of her trousers and enjoyed the feel of the four one-dollar bills. She didn't dare take them out, but in her mind, it was a glorious sight. From memory, she read every printed word on the bills. Maybe she could pay Ronnie's mom a whole quarter to wash her clothes. By Friday, when Maggie paid her, she'd be fifty cents away from having a fat ol' fin in her hand. Saturday nights were when Stick ventured back to the old neighborhood to give Mama most of the money, but maybe she would dare to hang on to an entire half-dollar for herself this week.

Of course there was always her "Ellie Fund," as she called it, smiling at the thought. So far, she had sixty-five cents stashed away to buy something special for her. And that really fine necklace with the gold locket at the jeweler's on Tremont Street was it. Stick calculated it would take her till the end of September to have the required three dollars, but she'd make it if she had to take on a second job shoveling fish guts on the docks. On October tenth, it would be one year since their first kiss, and Stick was determined to make it special.

Stuffing the four bills farther down into her pocket, Stick hauled herself off the crate and stretched. It was already dusk, and in a half hour she'd be safe and secure in her boxcar for the night. She turned to head out of the alley when a massive figure loomed before her.

She yelled as huge hands grabbed her arms and pushed her back behind the market. She twisted violently in the man's grip, thrashing left and right, and it wasn't until he backhanded her to the ground that she briefly fell still.

Broad and easily six feet tall, the man stank of fish and wood smoke. A stray from the docks, Stick quickly thought. Then white pain flashed across her eyes, and she lost her breath as he kicked her stomach with all his might.

"Empty y'pockets, boy!"

Stick tried to tuck her knees up, but her insides ached. Then he had her by the shirt collar and backhanded her again. She landed hard on her side, dirt filling an eye and an ear. Stick felt his hands at her pockets and she kicked upward with everything she could, catching him in the throat.

As he gagged and clutched his Adam's apple with both hands, Stick lunged and drove her fist into his crotch. He grabbed himself instantly, bent over in pain, howling some obscenities Stick had never heard. She scrambled to her feet, her hand connecting with a piece of the crate that had been her chair. Without a second thought, she hefted the two-foot pine board and whacked a Babe Ruth homer against the side of his head. He dropped like a rag doll and Stick sagged against the brick wall in relief.

❖

Everyone roared with laughter when Hokey's poor excuse for wine exploded out of Stick's mouth like a busted fire hose. "What *is* this shit?" She handed the bottle back to the old man. Krebs intercepted and quickly upended the jug for a decent blast. Purplish dribbles disappeared into his beard, but he paid them no mind.

"Vino Lachino." Hokey chuckled. "Borrowed it from little Caesar's kitchen up the North End today. His own private stash."

"Damn," Stick said, still grimacing, "let it stay there next time."

Again, the others laughed. Big Boy stood and grabbed the bottle. "Gimme that. I'll go add water. Shit ain't gonna last through six of us at this rate. Back in a minute." They all watched his boxy five-foot frame cross the rail yard until it disappeared into the darkened gatehouse. Everyone knew how to get in after hours. After all, it was their lone water source.

Krebs jumped to his feet and cupped his hands around his mouth. "Don't piss in it!" And everyone laughed.

Smitty hauled him back down onto his pile of bricks. "Sit. He's drinkin' it too, you dimwit." He turned to Stick at his left while reaching into his pocket. "So you didn't recognize this asshole in the alley." Stick just shook her head. "Cripes, Stick. You know, he'll be out for you now."

Stick had given that a lot of thought in the past several hours, what it would be like leaving work tomorrow. Would he be back? Would he bring friends? A weapon? She'd probably have to change jobs again, damn it, because she couldn't call the cops without being arrested herself.

A sharp click by her thigh interrupted her pondering. Smitty held up the six-inch switchblade and turned it to glint in what little light there was. "Time you woke up, girl. You're a tough one, Stick, toughest we've seen, but you're still a girl. Take this."

Stick's eyes widened. "I could never use it on someone, Smitty. Thanks, but no—"

He leaned his shoulder against hers, and even though he stank of rubbish, grit, and booze, his warm smile reminded Stick of her grandfather. A worn face in desperate need of a shave, not many teeth, and a reassuring twinkle in his gray eyes. He closed the knife and thrust it into her hand. "Never use it, huh? You ever think you'd clock a man in the head with a hunk of wood? Shut up and take this and don't give it up for nothin'."

Stick held the switchblade in her hands, nervous and a bit in awe of its potential. She'd never considered carrying anything, her left-jab-right-cross combination had proven to be enough these past few years. She almost chuckled at the recollection of Johnny-O bribing her to try out Manny's gym in East Boston. She was fourteen then. He'd even set up Davey, got him plenty pissed off at her, wanting to see Stick take him down. And when Davey called her out, she did it in a blur. A jab to his stomach and a bash to his jaw and he dropped, game over. Even Stick had been surprised.

She didn't want to carry. It led to trouble. But she was already in trouble, in more ways than one, so what difference did it make? These guys all meant well. Even Heathcliff, or Mr. Heath as folks knew him. He just sat around mostly, not adding anything to conversation, but did produce some coffee and bread on occasion. Once, he showed up with a live chicken. He'd been around the yard the longest so he received everyone's respect.

And now he tossed a small piece of wood onto their fire, where potatoes Maggie had given Stick were baking in the coals. Mr. Heath looked across the flames at Stick, his sunken eyes eerie in the firelight. "Tomorrow mornin' I'll make sure that flatfoot Robinson knows there's a big ol' bruiser on his beat, hanging around Maggie's neighborhood. So you get rid of your cap, Stick. Probably should change your hair so's not to look so much like yourself. And keep an eye out. With luck, the cops'll grab him and scoot right by you."

Stick hadn't been this surprised by Mr. Heath since he brought out his mouth harp at Christmas and had all the folks in the yard gathered round singing drunken, sacrilegious versions of holiday songs. Tall and mostly bone, he was a soft-spoken man with a gravelly voice from too many Camels. Mr. Heath was a true hobo of unknown age, a wise, traveled man who called nowhere home. Stick wondered if the man had family, and if they thought he was dead.

"Thanks, Mr. Heath. Robinson walks by at least twice a day. Maybe at closing time, he could swing his beat by the market." Heath only nodded in acknowledgment.

Big Boy finally returned with the diluted wine, and Hokey rolled the spuds out of the ashes. Stick was glad they were finally eating. She was almost too tired to sit upright, and her ribs hurt like hell whenever she moved. It had been a long day, and the next one would begin in six hours. She stared at the star-filled sky and let the summer air caress her face. Closing her eyes, she escaped her bedraggled existence and imagined Ellie's delicate touch, how it was so like that soothing midnight breeze.

❖

The murky gray first light of the morning wasn't what woke Stick from an exhausted sleep. It was the vibration of footsteps on the wood floor of her boxcar. Slowly, she peered over the edge of her blanket and saw the thin, shadowy form crouched by her old satchel. Stick's nerves vibrated and her ribs ached. Great. She had to do something. She only had her favorite cap, some spare clothes, a toothbrush, and a hairbrush in the bag, but it was hers, and all she owned.

She gripped the edge of her blanket in both hands and slowly drew her legs up beneath her. She took a deep breath against the pain in her chest and sprung across the floor, landing on the shadow and catching it in her blanket. Then the swearing began. First Stick, as she pounded her fists into the bumps in the blanket, and then the shadow, as each punch hit home.

It was during one such outcry that Stick realized the voice was female. Quickly, she jumped up and yanked the blanket away. She glared down at the slim girl, protectively curled in the fetal position.

"What the fuck are you doing in here?" Stick snapped, still breathing hard. "You're not pinchin' nothin' from me. Now get out before I bust your face!"

The girl groaned several times as she got to her feet. She was nearly Stick's height and had dark hair in a long braid down her back. The men's dress shirt she wore had once been white, Stick figured, and her trousers were too long and gathered on her shoes. There were holes in both knees.

She straightened in front of Stick, and the weariness in her light-colored eyes leaped out, even in the dim light. She had a cute little mouth and arched eyebrows that gave her a suggestive look.

Stick stiffened when it appeared the girl was squaring off with her. But a palm went up to keep Stick at bay. "No more," she gushed. "I's just looking for food. I'm real sorry."

"Yeah, well...No food in here. Now get out."

With a groan, the girl scooped her thin jacket off the floor. Blood trickled from her nose across her pale skin to her chin and she backhanded it away. She went to the opening of the rail car under Stick's watchful eye.

Stick wondered where she was from, where she'd be off to. She was willing to bet no one in the whole yard had ever seen her before.

"Where you from?"

The girl stopped and looked back. "Tonight? Hartford, but originally Chicago."

"Hm. Long way. Listen, sorry I don't have food. Maybe the Pancake House over on the fish pier will give you something as soon as they open. Nobody here has any food, so you leave 'em alone."

Stick came closer as the girl stooped to jump from the car. But instead of jumping, she whirled on Stick, snapping open a switchblade. She slashed out and Stick leaped back.

"You're no better'n me!" the girl snarled. "Got no right talking down. Who you think you are, huh?" She slashed out again.

Stick watched the flash of metal pass her midsection. She grabbed after it, locking her palm and fingers around the thin wrist, and clenching as hard as she could. She pulled the knife hand around her own body, and punched a fist into the girl's chest.

The knife flipped up into space as Stick tackled her to the floor. Pain shot through Stick's chest as her ribs protested loudly. They struggled for position until Stick used her strength to her advantage. Straddling the girl's hips, Stick seized both wrists and slammed them to the floor over her head. Black fire burned in Stick's eyes as she glared at the seething girl beneath her.

"I just told you to leave my friends alone, you stupid bitch. That's it. Ain't nobody better than anybody else. Get the fuck over yourself!"

The girl stopped squirming and looked relieved when Stick edged away. It was only another ruse, because as soon as Stick released her hands, she was punched squarely in the eye. She recoiled, mostly in shock, being able to take a hit better than most, but then threw her weight into a right cross that broke the young woman's nose and sent her to the floor unconscious.

Stick sat down hard, shaking, and cradling her hand. It hurt just as badly as her ribs, and now her throbbing eye felt bloated. *Boy, good fucking morning to me.* Stick turned at the muffled snickering by the doorway, and Smitty and Big Boy broke into applause when she spotted them.

"Girl," Smitty sighed, "where *did* you learn that? Brother? Your pop?"

Stick smiled back and shook her head. "Brother Ray," she mumbled, inspecting her hand, squeezing bones to check for breaks. "He and my dad were big fight fans. Dad learned in the navy. He wouldn't teach me, though, just Ray."

"She come atcha with a blade, I see."

Stick looked over at the weapon impaled in the floor. "Ironic, huh?" she said. She yanked it from the floor, closed it, and stuffed it in her pocket. Now she had two.

"You comin' Stick?" Big Boy asked, starting to walk away. "We're headed for Salvation Army coffee."

"Na. Gotta be at work in bit. No time. And now I got this mess on my hands. You guys mind watching my stuff while I'm at work today?"

Smitty was chuckling as he caught up with Big Boy. "Don't worry, Sluggo. We'll make sure everyone knows not to mess with you."

Stick crawled over to the unconscious intruder and studied her face. She was actually quite a doll, except for that nose. It was decidedly off-track. A flash of memory struck her then, of a tale Ray had told about Manny's gym. A fighter had his nose busted pretty badly and couldn't breathe, so his trainer moved it back right then and there. Put it in place with his bare hands. Of course, the fighter passed out, but it was faster and cheaper than going to the hospital.

Stick ran her forefinger and thumb lightly along the girl's nose and could feel the break in the bone. She cringed and yanked her hand away. She sat back on her heels. Could she do it? The girl was still out cold, so she wouldn't feel a thing…

❖

By noon that day, Stick had decided that God hated the world because it was hotter than the day before. She had to grin, though, thinking about the girl she'd left sleeping comfortably in her rail car. By now she'd be gone because no one could stay in that thing in this heat. The car stunk like baked onions when it heated up.

Stick hefted the cardboard box onto her hip and swung open the gate to Mrs. Feinstein's flowery little front yard. She inhaled the sweet scents greedily as she walked up the steps. The memory of Mrs. Weston's flower boxes had her smiling when the short, round, elderly woman greeted her.

"Dorothy, how lovely to see you again, dear."

"Afternoon, Mrs. Feinstein," Stick replied, still learning to live by her alias. "Got your order right here."

"Well, you come right in. Mr. Feinstein is in the parlor resting so I hope you'll take time for a little lemonade with me. Cut your hair, I see?" She was squinting through bifocals at close range as Stick squeezed past and into the cool, shaded house. Stick knew the woman was studying her puffy eye. She wondered if the bruise was starting to show.

"Yes, ma'am. Too blazing hot to have long hair!" She set the box on the kitchen table.

The woman drew a chair out and pointed. "You will sit here now, Dorothy. I will put groceries in the cupboard and make lemonade now."

Stick's protests were useless. Mrs. Feinstein hadn't mentioned the eye. And the lemonade was so good. It wasn't long before Stick caught her eyeing the rather abrupt haircut.

"Your mother approves of this boy style on her beautiful daughter?"

Stick stood and shrugged. Talking about her mother made her edgy. "I don't live at home anymore, Mrs. Feinstein. I bring her some money when I can, and I think that's all that matters to her."

The woman was shaking her head as she drew a change purse from the pocket of her housecoat. "Well, here is payment to Maggie..." She counted out one dollar and twenty-nine cents into Stick's palm. "And this is for you." She pressed two quarters into Stick's other palm.

"No, Mrs. Feinst—"

"You will be quiet and—"

"I can't, ma'am. It's too—"

"Eh!" The woman's raised finger called for silence. She patted her shoulder and led them to the door. "What is this here?" She hurried ahead to the screen door, Stick close behind. "You, boy! Get out! You stop this now!"

Stick craned her neck to look around the woman and saw a teenage boy yanking out the Feinsteins' flowers by the fistful. Mr. Feinstein, seventy years old and ailing, ambled across the parlor to see as well.

Stick slipped around the woman and banged through the door and down the steps. "Hey!"

In a torn blue work shirt and shabby trousers held up by suspenders, the boy looked up at Stick coming at him. He spun through the open gate and raced down the street. Stick caught him at the end of the block.

They tumbled onto the sidewalk together. Stick's rage and adrenaline enabled her to pick the boy up by the front of his shirt and slam him against the nearest wall. Next door, two tiny Chinese men emerged from their laundry to watch.

"Don't hit me! Don't hit me!" The boy's horrified brown eyes were as big as saucers and getting more watery by the second.

"Gimme one reason why not!" Stick yelled in his face, fist cocked.

"'Cause…'cause my dad…He says they're why we all ain't got nothin'!"

"What?" Stick frowned hard and shook him. "Who? The Feinsteins?"

Looking no older than twelve, the boy trembled in Stick's grip. "Yeah. The…Them Jews. It's their fault. M-my dad said."

Surprised by the boy's answer, Stick slackened her grip, then abruptly shoved him back against the brick and let go. "Your father's an idiot!"

"Don't talk about my ol' man like that!"

Stick almost stuck her finger in his eye. "Ask him if ruining old folks' flowers is the answer to everyone's troubles. Huh? You go ask him." She shoved him against the wall again. "Then ask him why he never taught you any respect. Want me to come to your house and bust up your stuff 'cause some idiot told me not to like you?" She shoved him a third time. "Well, do ya?"

"No."

"Course not, stupid."

"I ain't got no stuff anyway," he mumbled.

Stick stopped her tirade and gave him the evil eye. "You on your own?"

He nodded and lifted his chin proudly. "A month. Lost my job, and my ol' man, he was plenty mad. He…got kinda mean."

Stick cocked an eyebrow at him. "Your dad? The guy you defend? Who got you to pick on old folks? Who suckered you in?" The boy avoided Stick's eyes, looking over her shoulder at nothing as Stick went on. "Ever think maybe you can decide for yourself? How old are you?"

"Thirteen in three months." Disheveled light brown hair flopped everywhere on his head. He fidgeted with his suspenders and stood straighter, sneaking a look up at Stick.

"Hm." Stick glanced both ways on the sidewalk, organizing her thoughts. Finally, she grabbed his shoulder and started walking them the way they'd run. "What's your name?"

"What's yours?"

Stick glared at him as they walked deliberately onward. "Don't gimme a reason to pop you one."

"Looks to me like somebody already popped you."

Stick felt her patience fading. "What the hell's your goddamn name?"

"Zim. Where we goin'?"

"Zim what? And we're going back to do some gardening."

"Stevie Szymzak. I go by Zim. And I ain't doin' no damn gardenin'!"

Stick swung him up against a lamppost. "You listen to me, you little shit. You're gonna make good what you wrecked or I'll send that Polish nose of yours out the back of your head. You got that?"

Zim nodded.

"And you know why?" Stick didn't let him answer. "Because the Feinsteins've been here since the goddamn pilgrims and ain't done a thing to you."

They were almost back at the Feinsteins' before he spoke again. "Who are you?"

"You just be thinkin' about doin' the right thing, that's all."

They stepped through the gate and looked around at the scattered primroses and pansies. Mrs. Feinstein appeared on the porch.

"This is Zim, Mrs. Feinstein." Stick stood with her hand on his shoulder. "He's here to make amends." She urged him forward and whispered, "Be a man about it. Apologize."

❖

Stick managed to get through all of Maggie's deliveries by nightfall, despite losing what she estimated to be ten pounds in sweat that she really couldn't afford. She'd lost a lot of time at the Feinsteins' today and, even though Maggie understood, stuff still had to get done. On top of the heat was the tension of vigilance, keeping an eye out for the goon who jumped her yesterday as well as Officer Robinson. It had been a draining day to say the least.

The air was still thick and moist, barely breathable when she reached the rail yard that night. During her walk, she'd finished the Coca-Cola that Maggie had given her, and munched down a carrot she'd *borrowed* from the market earlier in the day, but she was thirsty all over again now. Crossing the dark, deserted yard, aiming for the tiny fire she saw in the distance, Stick toyed with the cigar-like Tootsie Roll in her pocket. She'd *borrowed* that too—for breakfast—and it was a simple comfort knowing it was there.

The fire ahead almost looked inviting, surrounded by the silhouettes of the guys. It was private from the rest of the world, had cozy light, and people she now called friends. But all Stick could think about was sleep. To lie down, take off her shoddy boots, rest the weary bones, and dream about her girl's kisses. So she passed through the firelight, said hello to the gang, and headed to her rail car.

Smitty yelled "Sluggo" at her, and everyone laughed, but the reminder of the morning's event displaced Stick's thoughts of Ellie, and that irritated her. She wondered about the broken nose. Damn, she hoped that crazy girl had skipped town.

But she hadn't. There she was, slumped against the rusted wheel, sound asleep with a saggy straw cowboy hat over her face. And as if that wasn't enough to light Stick's fuse, the crazy girl had brought a friend.

Goddamn it, she thought, why wouldn't people just let her be? She set both palms on the edge of the car floor and boosted herself up and in. Her satchel was still where she'd left it that morning, and she knelt to check its contents.

"Didn't steal nothin'," the female voice said from outside.

Stick pivoted to look back. "I see that. Good thing. How come you're still here? And who's that? I ain't taking in strays. And that includes you." Stick tried hard to get a look at the girl's nose, but the light was too poor.

Indignant now, the girl sank back on a hip and folded her arms beneath her rather well-developed breasts. "You don't need to be a bitch, you know. For your information, I waited to say thanks for lettin' me rest here, and to get my blade back...and to let you know you broke my friggin' nose."

"Really? Well, for *your* information, I reset your *friggin' nose* while you were out. So you're *friggin'* welcome." Stick turned back to her satchel. "The blade's mine now, so get lost. And take your stray with you."

That's when the second dark form appeared at the car opening, not quite as tall as the crazy girl, but bulkier, and female. "You callin' me a stray? I met your pal here at the brewery over in Jamaica Plain. We's waiting for work. You got work? You as tough as you talk?"

Stick was so tempted to jump down and engage this one. But the law of the streets said possession is nine-tenths of the law, and she wasn't in the mood to leave her car unoccupied. And the remaining tenth of the law allowed you to protect your stuff with everything you had. She walked to the edge of the opening and looked down at both girls.

"As tough as I need to be."

"Yeah, I see that now," the short girl chuckled. "Nice shiner." She offered the crazy girl a congratulatory handshake.

"You two hung around, made your point. Your business is done. Scram."

Stick returned to her satchel and shook out the two blankets she used for bedding. Hearing both girls climb into her car made her spin around quickly.

The new girl laughed at the ferocity in Stick's eyes and

nonchalantly seated herself cross-legged in the middle of the floor. "Calm down there, killer. We got stuff to talk about still." The crazy girl finally sat beside her, watching Stick warily.

"This is my place and it's time you two left. We got nothin' to talk about."

"See," the short one began, "if you'd shut the hell up and try to be nice, we'll explain."

"Get out." Stick tried to assess this one's capabilities. She wore dusty, torn trousers and work shoes, and a man's grayish T-shirt with the sleeves ripped off. Her defined biceps were evident even in the half-light. It looked to Stick as if she'd had her head shorn, what with only a couple inches of blond hair visible, and even though her face was round, almost cherubic, she conveyed plenty of power.

The girl leaned back and pulled a crumpled pack of Chesterfields from her pocket and scratched a matchstick to life. "You know, you're pretty ballsy for a girl out here alone." She squinted up through the smoke at Stick, exhaling casually. "And against two of us, you don't stand a chance. You know that, dontcha?"

Stick stood motionless, scowling down at the two young women who looked far too comfortable in her car. There was no doubt she was out-muscled.

The crazy girl leaned forward and pointed at the floor. "Sit down, tough girl. What the hell is your name, anyway?"

Stick thought twice about all of it and decided the smartest thing to do was agree. She sat opposite them and inhaled the cigarette smoke. It certainly smelled better than the car, overpowering the hint of old onions.

"You don't need to know my name."

The short girl laughed. "On the lam, huh? Yeah, I was…am. Down in Atlantic City. Boosted a car. Was the only way to see my girl, once her family moved to Philly, but cops nabbed me near the border." She chuckled at the memory. "Ran 'em through the woods for hours, then ditched 'em on foot. And here I am!"

She exhaled out of the corner of her confident smile and extended a small but broad hand. "I'm a Jersey girl."

For some inexplicable reason, Stick reached for her hand automatically. "Jersey, huh? They call me Stick." Just the sound of her name from of her own lips sent a cautious chill through Stick. She hoped she'd made the right decision. After all, Jersey had a girl just like Stick did. She couldn't be *that* bad.

She turned to the crazy girl and raised an eyebrow. "Okay, so who the hell are you?"

"Roxie."

Jersey laughed heartily. "I asked her if she danced burlesque."

Stick chuckled at the idea. Roxie sent Jersey a deadly look. "It's Roxanne. After my mother."

Stick rubbed her face hard, hiding a grin. "How 'bout we call you Rocky? Sounds better."

Jersey nodded. "Yeah, that's good. Sounds like a fighter. And you both'll have shiners by mornin' anyway."

"Right. I don't think so. It's Roxie," she huffed, and sat up straighter and looked evenly at Stick. "Sorry I drew on you. I's pissed off at stuff."

Stick offered the handshake this time. "Sorry about your nose. Hope it heals okay." She tossed Roxie back her switchblade.

"Good," Jersey proclaimed, clapping her hands together. "So listen up, Stick. You got a job?"

"Yeah. It's just delivering for a corner market, but it's something."

"Well, you heard all the pissin' and moanin' about the new law that's comin'? It's gonna be the Volstead Law or some such." Stick shook her head. She had no idea what this had to do with anything, but Jersey was working herself into a real tizzy. "Yeah, guys back home are all steaming about it already. In January booze is gonna be illegal. Imagine? All of it! So now everybody's making plans to have their own secret supplies once the Feds start gettin' rid of it all."

"People ain't gonna vote to stop drinkin', Jersey." Roxie said it like a declaration, and Stick grinned.

But Jersey was shaking her head hard. "Honest, I even saw it on the newsstands. There'll even be a department of guys hired just to shut everybody down. And they're gonna have guns."

Stick's eyebrows rose sharply. "Wow. They'll probably need them, too."

Silence fell among them as the concept hit home.

Roxie shifted anxiously. "Pretty damn scary thought, if you ask me."

"Sounds like lots of folks will end up with guns," Stick said. "But seriously. If all the barrooms stand to close, they'll find some way to get it. On the sly, like. Too much money on the line."

Now Jersey sat back smiling. "Exactly. Everyone's got ideas about how to keep the juice flowin' in and outa Jersey, New York, Boston. So I figured if we get work at the breweries now, we'd have a good shot at stayin' with the inside guys, once everything goes underground."

"There's lots of packing and loading to be done right now," Roxie told Stick. "We heard about it today at one of the warehouses near the old brewery."

Jersey leaned toward Stick. "Or we make the rounds where the trucks go, maybe get hired on to help unload, you know? The clubs and bars would give us something for unloading. Could pay pretty good."

Stick had plenty of doubts. Making illegal hooch and trucking it around didn't sound smart, not if the Feds were going to be chasing you. She had a hefty price on her head right now, so she certainly didn't need to get nabbed for some stupid federal crime.

And everything going underground with guns sure sounded like the Mob to her. There already was plenty of that nasty business around, with people fencing family valuables, and loan sharks beating the destitute to a pulp in alleys, and girls all dolled up and selling their special services at hotels. Some people—probably a very select few— already were making a fortune off everybody's pain. By the sound of things, life was going to get a lot worse before it got better.

"That's real heavy work, you know. Barrels are a bitch."

"We'll manage. There'd be three of us."

"Three girls," Stick said, struggling to be the voice of reason. "You think anyone wants girls unloading that gold?"

"So we'll show 'em," Roxie stated.

Jersey tossed her cigarette butt out into the yard. "You from around here?" she asked Stick.

"All sixteen years."

Jersey was nodding thoughtfully. "So you know folks, the stores and bars. The cops. Right?"

Stick nodded back. "But I'm not doing nothing illegal, if that's what you're thinking. I'm already in trouble, and I'm no street thug. I got family here and…and I got a girl, too." This time the tingling that sizzled down Stick's spine felt good. She was proud to state she had a special someone and that it was girl.

"Yeah?" Jersey's eyebrows shot up. "Good for you, Stick!" She rocked forward and slapped Stick on the shoulder.

"Well, whatever we do," Roxie said, "it better be for decent money. I ain't gonna bust myself up over piddly change."

Stick leaned back on her outstretched arms and thought the whole thing over. Would be hard work, but she wouldn't have to make a career out of it. Maybe after a few months she could be back on her feet. And the money probably would be good, lots more than Maggie could pay. Maggie. She'd have to get a replacement for herself. She wouldn't leave Maggie stranded. And could she trust these girls? Who was to say either of them wouldn't jump her for her pay? Did they expect to live in her car?

"I gotta get some sleep," Stick finally sighed. "Lots to think about and we can talk more tomorrow." She climbed to her feet and went to her satchel.

"You mind if we sleep inside?" Roxie asked. "Like, over there at the other end? We won't bother you."

"Na, not me," Jersey said. "Stinks in here. I'm outside." With that, she jumped to the ground.

Stick gave Roxie a long, hard stare, hoping some of her superior strength and fighting skill would come to the crazy girl's mind and she'd behave. At last, Stick nodded. "Okay, I guess."

CHAPTER FIVE

S tick was up and finished with her cold-water wash in the gatehouse before anyone in the yard stirred. She gratefully accepted coffee at the Salvation Army building, where she found a pencil to write a postcard to Ellie. She kept a few blank ones in her satchel, and this morning, she'd decided a note was overdue.

Dearest Ellie,
How are you? I am doing okay and may have a new job soon and good money. May have to move because of it but not sure. Not an easy job, but I think I can pull it off. Please take care of yourself! I hope you are well and school is still good. I miss school almost as much as I miss you. By the way, the church bell here just chimed twice.
XOXOX

Stick read it five times in a row, smiling more each time. The church bell chime was their code for Saturdays till she would visit. Time couldn't pass fast enough. They'd fall into each other's arms behind the rose bushes and kiss till their lips hurt.

Stick tucked the card into her pocket and headed off to Maggie's with a bounce in her step. She would mail it the first chance she got. A Boston postmark was pretty vague so she never worried about being tracked. And even though Ellie wasn't allowed to keep them, what mattered was that she knew Stick was still alive and well and missing her.

The postcards were all they had, and it hurt to know Ellie fought so much with her father about them. He had grabbed one away from her three weeks ago, and they hadn't spoken since. At their last rendezvous, Ellie had cried just telling Stick about it. He kept them locked in his desk until he could swing by the police station, and although she tried many times, she couldn't pick the lock. And with her mother now siding with him, Ellie said the days had just grown harder. The "interest" Stick had in Ellie, according to her father, was "unhealthy, morally wrong, even criminal," Ellie recounted, adding that she usually ended those discussions by screaming and crying and slamming the door to her room.

It all reinforced Stick's determination to save enough money and someday take them far away, like maybe even Chicago, and get a place together, work a couple of jobs, have enough money to live happily. She didn't really know if girls could aspire to such things, but figured she'd talk with Jersey about it. Even if they would be the first to try, she wanted to give it her very best shot. And for some weird reason, today she felt like their time was just a bit closer.

Stick turned the corner, and the only movement in the sleeping neighborhood caught her eye immediately. It was Zim, up against a house, scooting along beneath the windows. Curious, she stopped and waited as he disappeared behind the house and quickly reappeared with a quart bottle of milk. He crept beneath the windows and finally reached the sidewalk, where Stick stepped out from behind a tree and blocked his escape.

Zim jerked to a halt. He looked up and rolled his eyes. "What now? You followin' me or somethin'?"

"How many kids in your family?"

"What?"

"How many?"

"Just me."

"They got seven in that house."

"I know. So? They won't miss this."

"Jesus Christ, you're thickheaded. Go put it back."

"Na-uh. I gotta have somethin'."

"Go put it back and come on. I'll get you something."

"Why?" Standing his ground, he looked at Stick with suspicious eyes hooded by a frown much too deep for his age.

"'Cause I'm your friggin' guardian angel, that's why. Go!"

His expression even more suspicious, Zim kept an eye on Stick the whole time he retraced his steps. He looked almost surprised to see she was still there on his way back, and he was none too pleased.

Three blocks later, he started complaining. Stick pulled the big Tootsie Roll from her pocket and bent it back and forth until it broke in two. She handed Zim a half without looking at him.

Stick bit off a bite of her own. "You need a job."

"I'm just thirteen. Got fired, remember?"

"You're twelve. And just so's you know, you can have more than one job in life. You gotta pay for stuff, you know."

"I do okay. Don't have to pay for nothin'. Lots of kids don't."

"That's okay? Just taking from anybody?" Stick shot him a glance that said he should know better. "You'd be plenty pissed off if some kids just took whatever they wanted of yours. Just like Maggie and her little store or the Feinsteins and their flowers or the Smiths, whose milk you were swipin'."

He was quiet for several minutes, and Stick actually thought she was making progress. Zim stuffed the rest of his Tootsie Roll into his mouth and flipped the wrapper onto the sidewalk.

"So you a goddamn angel or something? Never lifted nothing?"

Stick laughed lightly. "You're one dumb Polack, if you think I could be an angel. Of course I've—"

Zim uttered a haughty snicker. "Probably why you're on the street, huh? Hiding."

"Not because I stole stuff. Look, whenever I lifted something it was never from folks scrapin' to get by." She shook her head. "Not from the little guy, you know?"

He nodded, looking up the street as they walked. "Big stores are easy."

"Don't be cocky. You get cocky, you get caught. And no, big places won't miss a can here or there, not like it would hurt the small places and the families...places like Maggie's. They get by on their own kind of miracles, just like us. Get it?"

Zim gave a quiet "yeah" and seemed to be thinking hard.

Stick elbowed him gently and he turned to her. "What if I called you a dirty rotten liar? What'd you do?"

"I'd give you a bruisin'."

Stick withheld her grin. "And why?"

"'Cause I ain't." His dimpled chin jutted forward defiantly. "Well…couple times when my neck was on the line…"

"'Cause you gotta be honorable. Not a slimeball. Now I think you have honor, and deep down, you know what's right. And I want to respect you for that, for what's inside." She tapped his chest over his heart. "Honorable person who has earned respect knows better than to hurt someone down on his luck."

"How come you're telling me all this stuff? I don't even know your name."

Grinning, Stick steered him down the alley to the back of Maggie's. "Dorothy's my name. Just telling you because you're too short to protect yourself when they come to steal back what you stole. You wanna learn to fight, come find me. I'll be around. Meantime, think about honor and respect and getting a job, making your own money."

Zim looked up the back steps of the market. "I tried corner stores like this and they all said I's too young."

"To work inside, maybe. But delivering groceries?" Stick turned to face him before leading him up the stairs. "You can walk. You know your way around the neighborhoods, and you got a fairly civil tongue in your head. Can you count?"

"Of course I can count!"

"All right. Here's the deal: Delivering for Maggie is my job, but I'm hoping to get a better one. Maggie's really good people. She helped me when I needed it, so returning the favor is the right thing to do. The honorable thing. I won't leave her with no help. I's thinking you take my job, and the sooner you start for Maggie, the sooner I start my new job. You help me, I help you, we help Maggie. Understand?"

He continued to look at her as if he'd just awaked from a long sleep. "Yeah, but I don't—"

"The pay is fifty cents a week. *Fifty*. And you get lots of tips—in money and food. Maggie is a fine lady, and I'm real sure she'd be proud to have a strong, helpful, *honorable* young man around."

Zim's hard scrutiny of Stick's face softened, and he looked thoughtfully up at the back door. "You think?" Stick only nodded. "Even though I'm short for my age, I *am* pretty strong, you know."

"No doubt. But remember about stealing: Maggie's one of us little guys. And you think someone's lifting her stuff, you find me and we'll bruise 'em up together. Deal?"

Zim slipped his hands into his pockets and studied his shoes, dejected, as if his only pastime had been taken away. Stick wondered how much of her lecture he had taken to heart.

She gave it one more shot before bringing him in to meet Maggie. "I come 'round here a lot, Zim, and if I hear you've been cheating Maggie, I'll be paying you a visit you won't ever forget."

"Yeah. I'm hearing you." He chuckled. "But you'd never catch me."

Stick backed him up against the stair railing and flicked open her switchblade right against his ear. The sharp snap of metal made Zim flinch. Stick grinned into his wide eyes, then dipped her head to whisper, "Wanna bet?"

❖

Jersey and Roxie were lounging on the stoop of somebody's triple-decker when Stick came by on her way home that evening. It had been another scorcher of a day, and Stick longed to lie on her blankets and enjoy a long, cold drink of water, not hang out on a stranger's front steps and gab.

As she approached, the girls waved and she returned the gesture, then spat the pit of the peach she'd just finished into the gutter. Both girls rose to walk with her.

"We got peaches today, too," Roxie boasted, "over at Haymarket. Jersey's still got a couple."

"Maggie gave me mine," Stick replied, knowing they'd lifted the fruit in the busy open marketplace. "What's new on the job thing? You go to JP today?"

Jersey nodded enthusiastically. "The truckers don't want nobody stepping on their toes, but a boss said he could use some help with the inventory on Thursday, Friday, and Saturday nights."

"Just three nights." Stick frowned at the curb as they stepped off to cross another deserted street. "And you think it's safe for three girls down there?"

"I put it to him up front," Roxie said. "He laughed and said his guys are so afraid of their wives and girlfriends, they can't wait to get out of work and bring home the money."

Jersey kicked a can out of her path and it bounced loudly off a store's brick façade. "I wonder if his guys have more to worry about than their gals."

Stick stiffened. "I'm not getting in with the Mob. No, sir."

"Nah, not to worry," Jersey said. "Sounds like we'd just be counting and keeping things neat and organized."

Roxie glanced at Stick, then Jersey, then studied Stick as they headed into the rail yard. "One of the guys—he even showed us a picture of him with his wife and baby—he tells us a few extra goodies sometimes get tossed their way, like cash, beer…"

"This Narragansett beer you got up here in Massachusetts…It any good?" Jersey asked, grinning.

"Yeah, it's good. So what do they have to do to get 'extras'?"

Roxie shrugged. "Dunno."

"We's thinkin' maybe sometimes a barrel or a few cases get 'lost' now and then. You catch my drift?"

Stick stopped abruptly and stared at Jersey. "And if we're the ones keeping count, who goes down when the bosses find out?"

Jersey sighed. "They don't, dumbass."

Stick rolled her eyes and walked on.

"He was a real nice guy," Roxie added. "He even gave us 'Gansetts for later, one for each of us." She pulled one from her baggy pants pocket by its neck. "Got one in each and Jersey's got hers."

"We'd start tomorrow night," Jersey said. "Show up around seven o'clock. The trucks get loaded, and we work till they're back in, around one."

Roxie sighed. "You know…I'd like to drive one of them trucks." Jersey and Stick looked at her in surprise until Roxie feigned a huge pout. "Who says I can't? I can learn."

"Sure you can," Jersey said. "I've been drivin' all kinds of things since I was about twelve. You drive, Stick?"

"Nope. Pop taught my brother a few years ago, the mechanic's truck he drove at work, but said I was too young. My feet reached the pedals and everything, but he wouldn't. Doesn't seem too hard, though."

The gang around the fire turned to check out the people walking beside Stick and she went through the formal introductions, emphasizing that Roxie wasn't a stripper. The guys laughed, and everyone scootched over on their makeshift seats to make room for them.

Conversation stretched into the night until Stick finally had to give in. Jersey and Roxie followed Stick to the rail car.

It still bothered Stick that she'd apparently lost exclusive rights to her home, but these two seemed to be good people, gullible, maybe, but decent. Once inside, Roxie produced the beers and they sat drinking and sharing stories for a while longer. Settling down, however, with Stick on her side of the doorway, Jersey and Roxie on the other in opposing corners, brought a quiet, ponderous peace to the darkness. Stick's thoughts went to the warehouse job, and she figured she might end up having to be tougher than she'd ever been. She wondered what Ellie would think of her.

❖

Classmates Rita, Connie, and Marie pleaded and whined, but Ellie insisted she had orders to go directly home after the show, so they left her at the trolley stop and headed off for ice creams at Brigham's several blocks away. Ellie, meanwhile, went straight to her backyard and sat behind the rose bushes to wait, hoping this would be the night Stick appeared. In the past, Stick usually arrived by nine thirty or ten o'clock, so Ellie knew she might only have to wait a short while—if Stick was coming at all.

She gathered her cardigan around her shoulders as the evening dew set in, and replayed favorite scenes from the dreamy *The Blue Bird* in her mind. Ironic, she thought, that the moving picture's young characters searched so hard for a happiness that really was close at hand.

The usual Saturday night turnout filled the Fields Corner Theater, and it seemed as if everyone enjoyed the picture, but Ellie had been a bit preoccupied. More than a month had passed since she'd seen Stick or received a card. If she hadn't glimpsed the message on that last card before it was torn from her hands, Ellie would have thought Stick was gone for good.

A stiffening breeze woke Ellie from a sound sleep on the ground. The bright yellow moon that had escorted her home from the show was now halfway across the sky, and Ellie shivered. She had no idea what time it was, but knew it was late and her heart began to pound.

Stiffly, she rose, brushed at her long skirt, and headed into the darkened house. Her breathing became shallow and her chest tightened. She shut the kitchen door softly and prayed that luck would have the waiting parent asleep with a book in the parlor.

Turning into the room and the gentle, amber light of her father's reading lamp, Ellie met his direct gaze. Her body chilled.

"At midnight, I was going to the police," he said evenly. "Your mother is worn out from worry."

With a glance toward the sofa, Ellie saw that her mother had lost the battle against sleep. "W-we went for ice creams, Dad, and then just gabbed too much."

"And that's why you're coming in the back door at ten minutes to twelve?"

"I didn't want to disturb anyone." Ellie worked to keep from fidgeting.

"You *know* we wouldn't go to bed until you were home safe." His tone was hardening. He leaned forward in his chair and cocked his head. "So did you get those leaves in your hair at Brigham's?"

Ellie's face and mind went blank.

"You were waiting outside, weren't you?" He stood and tossed his book aside. "Did Stick sneak into the yard? Was tonight the night she was coming to see you?" He closed to within an arm's length of her and shouted, "Was it?"

Ellie gulped down a breath. Her mother sat up, looking from Ellie to her father, and understood the situation. Ellie looked at her, afraid to see as much anger as she saw in her father's eyes, but her mother's held sadness, maybe shame.

"How would I know if she was coming, Dad? Something in the postcards *you* have?"

"Don't you talk back to me, young lady! I have those cards for a good reason. Whatever's sickened Stick's mind from the nice girl she used to be is nothing I want near my daughter. It's not normal. Do you understand me?" His eyes an icy blue, he stared hard at Ellie. "That girl is no good anymore, and I won't have you become the talk of the town like she is."

Ellie blurted words out, struggling to remain steady. "She's always been my best friend and she needs me! We need each other! Why are you hurting us like this?"

"What I'm doing is for your own good, Ellie. You obviously refuse to see it, no matter what you're told." He paced around the coffee table and back. "I *will* put a stop to this nonsense. Mark my words."

❖

Bright sunshine stung Ellie's swollen eyes. As she descended her front porch and started up the hill, she doubted her shaky legs would hold her. Not today. Maybe not ever. The image of police handcuffing Stick in the moonlight would never fade. Her father had been so proud, informing the officers that yes, he had made the telephone call, performed his civic duty when he spotted the fugitive. She would forever see Stick being dragged away, the frightened eyes reaching up to her at the bedroom window.

She was bone-tired from the tear-filled sleepless night, and the vast emptiness curdling inside made her physically sick, but buying the morning newspaper was her assignment, and her father wanted it promptly. City councilmen were due to visit soon, and he had to be up on all the latest events to be viewed a viable candidate for office. Authority and money, they were his priorities, not Ellie's shattered heart.

Halfway up the hill, a pair of scruffy girls crossed to her side of the street and Ellie agonized over having to hide her exhausted, pained appearance. She lowered her eyes as they approached and hoped they could all pass without a glance.

"Excuse me, miss?" One of the girls smiled and held up her hand as if hailing a taxi.

Ellie stopped but wondered if she should. She wasn't the least impressed by the tattered shirts and trousers. They were street people, her own age, but panhandlers just the same.

Ellie moved to resume her walk and the other girl stepped into her path.

The first girl shifted closer, and Ellie didn't like it. This one looked tough and strong. She had a nice smile, but Ellie was still a bundle of nerves.

"Sorry to bother you, miss," the tough girl began, "but do you know Stick?"

Ellie's face paled. Her eyes began to cloud up and her bottom lip trembled. "Y-you know Stick?"

The second girl came to the first one's side, nodding. "We sure do. But we don't know where she is."

Ellie broke down and cried into her hands. She turned her back to them, embarrassed.

"Look," the tough girl said, setting a hand on Ellie's shoulder, "we've heard some stuff but don't know the real score, y'know?"

"Yeah, like where she is, what the hell happened," the other girl added. "Do you know?"

Ellie sniffed several times and found a lace-trimmed handkerchief in her small purse. Wiping her eyes, then her nose, she turned to face both girls. "Yes," she said on a sob, "I know."

"Can you talk to us now?"

Ellie shook her head and glanced back down the hill toward her house. "I have to buy a newspaper at the trolley stop and get right back. My father's waiting."

"We both work in JP at the old brewery," the tough girl explained. "nights, seven till about one. Stick works with us, too, or...used to." Ellie's lip began to tremble again. "Come on," she said, leading them up the hill. "We'll walk with you to get the paper."

"Do you know where she is now?" the other girl asked.

They turned the corner and walked along Washington Street to the trolley stop. Ellie shook her head as she paid the newsboy and accepted the *Boston Post*. "I don't know. You don't know anything?"

"The police have her, don't they?"

Ellie nodded and squeezed her eyes shut. "For the...the Henderson store fire. They lied on their report and called it arson."

"Jesus," tough girl breathed.

The other one boldly took Ellie's *Post* and began thumbing through it quickly. "Something might be in here, y'think?"

All three of them scanned pages two and three, then they turned to page four. A picture of a policeman holding a handcuffed Stick by the arm was in the top left corner. Ellie gasped.

"'The district attorney anticipates a quick trial and incarceration at the Massachusetts Reformatory for Women in Sherborn,'" the tough girl read aloud. She looked at her friend, then Ellie, who'd started crying again. "Is...um...We ain't from here, so...is that far?"

Ellie nodded as she sobbed.

"Hey, please don't cry," the tough girl said. "I'm sure Stick will beat this rap. Stop now, please."

The other girl patted Ellie's shoulder. "I think we should know each other's names, don't you? I'm Roxie. I'm from Chicago."

"And I'm Jersey."

Ellie sniffed and exhaled hard. "I'm Ellie Weston." The offer of a handshake surprised her as much as the firm grip that followed. Jersey looked down at her shoes and then cleared her throat. Ellie wondered what would come next.

"Please don't take me wrong for asking this," Jersey said, "but... um...well...You're Stick's girl, aren't you?"

Ellie's eyes grew wide and she wanted to run. They'd probably catch her anyway. She didn't know if Stick considered them reliable or even acquaintances. She didn't know what to do.

But then Jersey grinned and grasped her by both shoulders. "I hope you are, Ellie Weston, because I'd hate to think our friend Stick let a gorgeous doll like you get away."

Ellie blushed to her toes. She looked down and actually laughed. She couldn't remember the last time she'd laughed. This felt good. She smiled at both girls and suffered a pang of shame for having thought so little of them at first sight.

"Yes, I am," she stated, taking a steadying breath. She quickly realized she was standing taller...proudly. "She...She means the world to me."

They flanked her as they walked silently back down her street. Ellie liked having them on her side—in more ways than one. "I don't know what to do. I...Well, you understand, I guess, huh?" She flashed a look at Jersey, seeing for the first time someone who *knew* and accepted. She was more than a little overwhelmed. "I...Oh God, we love each other so much." Tears started again and she pressed her handkerchief against her eyes. "It's killing me that I can't help her, go to her. My father and mother watch me like a hawk and it's hard for me to even go outside. I'm amazed that I met you both when I did."

Roxie chuckled. "Sure wasn't easy. First we heard about someone named Stick being arrested in Dorchester and then lucked out when this old fella we found knew her family, her dad. Sent us right to your street."

Jersey stopped walking several houses shy of the Weston home. "Look, Ellie. Bein' honest, I don't know if there's anything we can do to help Stick now. But if we have news or…or you have news, we should have a way to talk, right?"

Ellie nodded. "I…I can't have anyone throwing pebbles up to my bedroom window." Her eyes dimmed and she looked away.

"That's how Stick got caught, ain't it?" Roxie asked.

Ellie nodded toward her feet.

"Hey, you go anyplace regular like?" Jersey asked. "Like, do you go to the market every Saturday morning?"

"Usually, yes, but with my mother." She was deep in thought, then suddenly brightened. "I have to start going to the library regularly. My parents know I have lots of summer reading for my final school year, so I can plan to be there." The hope of maintaining any contact with Stick, even through intermediaries like these girls lifted Ellie's spirits. She was willing to try anything.

"That would be good," Roxie said, Jersey now nodding beside her.

"Today's Friday, so if I pick…Mondays and, say, Thursdays, I could start next week. Would ten o'clock be all right?"

Both girls nodded. "We may not always be able to come," Jersey admitted with a shrug, "and there probably won't be much news, but we'll try to stay in touch even a little, for Stick's sake."

"Oh, yes, please. I'd like that." Ellie's eyes filled again. "Do you know where the library is?"

Roxie chuckled. "Oh, we'll find it. We found you, didn't we?"

❖

Monday morning, eager for any word, Ellie huddled with Jersey and Roxie at one of the library's long reading tables. She appreciated the effort both girls made with their attire because the feisty elderly librarian would never have let them in wearing the bedraggled outfits from Friday. Ellie couldn't help but notice that both of them smelled like wood smoke. And it reminded her of Stick's hair, cool, thick, soft, and tainted with that scent of the outdoors. She was already sad enough; this didn't help.

"We went to the jail on Charles Street and they let us in to visit her," Roxie blurted.

"Oh my God!" Ellie grabbed Roxie's hands and started speaking in a flurry of hushed breaths. "Please tell me she's okay? So she knows we've met? And will continue to meet? That we're thinking of her?"

Jersey and Roxie nodded at each question.

"Did she look okay? They haven't hurt her, have they? Did she look like she'd been crying?" Ellie hid her face again. "Did you tell her I love her?"

Roxie held up a finger to make her pause. "She's okay. Of course, she's sad—"

"But mostly mad," Jersey injected.

"Yeah," Roxie amended quickly, "really mad. And no one's hurt her. She's real happy we found you and told us she'd beat the shit out of us if we lost touch."

Ellie chuckled as she wiped her eyes. "Sounds like my Stick."

"And we told her what you said, that you're missing her bad."

Jersey set a hand on her shoulder. "She said to tell you she loves you too, more than anything on earth, and can't wait to see you. Says you two are gonna start a new life together far away from here."

Ellie's head bobbed vigorously as she cried. "We sure are. We'll have jobs and a house of our own."

"Ellie, they let visitors in for a half hour on Saturdays and Sundays. We missed the time on Saturday so went back yesterday."

Roxie took Ellie's hand. "Stick said the public defender told her the state wants her tried in a hurry. He...um...doesn't give her good odds. I'm sorry."

Jersey leaned closer. "If you have the money, I think...well, you should probably go see her next weekend."

Ellie lost the battle. She cried into her arms on the table. "Even if I had the money, I could never leave the house."

"Well, I don't think it's fair of your parents," Roxie stated. "Why are they punishing *you*?"

"Yeah," Jersey said. "The big bad danger is gone. Aren't they happy?"

Ellie lifted her head and stared at the wet blotches on her sleeves. "Oh, they're happy, all right. They ruined Stick's life. They're getting even, I think, for Stick dragging me 'down the wrong path,' as they put it. And I'm being punished because I helped her all along, because I disobeyed them and *chose* to love her." She sniffed, then looked at Jersey. "I never *chose* anything."

Jersey shook her head, agreeing with her.

"I couldn't help what happened between us," Ellie went on, turning to look at Roxie. "You can't *choose* who you fall in love with."

This time Roxie shook her head to agree.

"You know?" Ellie asked rhetorically, and then looked away, to the top shelf of books in the farthest corner. "If I had a choice? It would be her. No doubt." She let out a long sigh. "So many things we never got to do." She put her head down onto her arms again. "And now who knows if we ever will."

Roxie laid an arm across Ellie's shoulders and squeezed. She whispered in Ellie's ear, "I hope you two at least got to do it."

Jersey backhanded Roxie's shoulder so hard, Roxie fell back in her chair. Jersey leaned into her face. "S'matter with you, asking that? Shit."

Ellie didn't even flinch. The question didn't shock her. She'd been thinking about *the act* a lot, and it made her sadder. It was her fault, always unable to escape her parents, and she and Stick never had enough time together. More than a year of that insanity. That was their story: never enough time together.

She spoke against her arms. "No, but…but we were going to." She sat up and cleared her throat, forcibly composed. "I will wait for her, you know. I…I don't care how long it takes till Stick's free again, till we're both free. I'm going to wait. We've always known we were meant to be together, and someday, it will happen."

PART TWO

October 1924
Town of Gardner
Central Massachusetts

CHAPTER SIX

Stick's stomach growled, and she gathered her light cotton jacket around her in an effort to smother the sound. She couldn't be a bother to anyone. Those were the rules. And if she broke them, she'd have to return and start all over.

It seemed like ages since breakfast at sunrise, and tea and an egg on toast weren't very sustaining when your nerves were eating you up from the inside. Almost noon, that's what the autumn sun told her as this fancy wagon sputtered brightly along the winding, pastoral dirt road to Gardner.

Four years had passed while she'd been confined to the reformatory. Leaving the superintendent's office, getting through the front gate, and out to the waiting truck seemed to take even longer. She fought the urge to break into a sprint. The man who came to claim her favored his left leg and was a slow walker. He'd never catch her.

She'd been a model prisoner in this odd place, the only one for women in Massachusetts, and although it nearly killed her to comply with the ridiculous rules, she achieved the goal she'd set for herself: not only earning a reduction of her eight-year sentence, but also this vaunted "pre-release" year. It loomed as her last, very critical year to serve.

Her driver's name was Carter. He was a good twenty years her senior, and for all his gruff manner, he was polite and had a pleasant smile. He also was a six-foot-tall string bean with a voice that came from his shoes and rattled Stick's nerves. Nevertheless, he had gently taken her satchel of meager belongings and set it carefully in the back of the truck.

Before climbing into his vehicle, Stick had let out a long breath and taken a last look around, recollecting with stark clarity her arrival at the ominous place. She'd never forget the entire afternoon spent bumping along deserted dirt roads, her anxiety and despair mounting until she had to get out and throw up. A matron and a policeman with a rifle stood nearby while she did.

Now, things just felt different. And from what little there was to see, they were.

This wagon, for one. Carter told her it was Ford's new Model T Runabout pickup truck, and it was quite the novelty with its low-walled open bed for cargo. In fact, there were many shiny motorized coaches on the roads now, not just delivery trucks or sedans with hired drivers. It appeared that anyone could have his own automobile...car...and go wherever he wanted. Well, almost anyone.

She worked earnestly to keep her mind from wandering. There just weren't many more sights to see besides open farmland, and beautiful, sprawling meadows with the occasional farmhouse and outbuildings. It was a refreshing site for sure, but her spirit insisted on seeing its desolation. She spent the rest of the way reminding herself of how far she'd come, of her accomplishments, that if she could just buck up for one more year, she'd make a brand new start. She'd be twenty-three when the chains came off.

And she'd start all over, all right. She promised herself as much from Day One behind the bars of the Charles Street Jail. When this was over and she got her life back, by God, she'd make sure she never fell into that position where men with power played with her life as if she was a pawn in their chess game. She would never have to pick change out of the gutter or steal off someone's clothesline ever again. She'd get her share of what life had to offer and hold her head high.

In total, that one night in Henderson's store and some crooked justice cost her more than just these years, and Stick fought off the melancholy of loss. The anger and loneliness had been crippling for months. Nearly a year passed before she initiated casual conversations with other prisoners. She never had visitors; no one she knew had the means to travel so far or the money to pay for it.

And she had refused to allow her keepers the rights to her mail. Inspection of all letters was required, and prisoners were expected to consent. Denying the reformatory permission to read her mail meant all outgoing letters were forbidden and all incoming correspondence was withheld until the prisoner was ultimately released. Even though desolate weeks and months became numbing years, she still had control of this much. Her life was being manipulated and violated enough.

Throughout her term, Stick often wondered if there would be a bundle of mail waiting…letters from the one person who would always own a piece of her heart. It had been so long. She passed the early years fantasizing about their love, discovering everything about each other as they grew to adulthood, making love, making a future. She passed the latter years, right up to the present, with a more realistic outlook, conceding that time and people change. Beyond everything else, she needed to see pride and self-respect in her daily reflection.

Stick absently fondled the tiny gold heart at her throat. It had been returned to her when she signed the probation agreement. She decided that, when she finished this year and any mail was handed over, if there was none from Ellie, she'd stash the necklace away for good. Maybe.

Carter turned onto a narrow, tree-lined drive and within a minute, they arrived at a massive, immaculately landscaped Colonial home. He promptly hobbled around the vehicle and opened her door, just as a finely dressed woman addressed her from the porch.

"Miss Elizabeth McLaughlin, I presume?"

Stick stood straight, poised in her broad-brimmed hat and ankle-length blue dress, her purse in both hands in front of her. It was easy now, practically a reflex, and she could play the role to perfection after years of classes and practice. How to keep still, how to be a lady and know your place, how to provide the finest in domestic service, such were the goals of the reformatory. Being released to a qualifying family, serving well and properly for no less than one year, was the final phase of her sentence. And looking up now at this woman with the harsh glare, Stick knew it would be a hard one. The resentment and anger she harbored had not abated.

"Yes, ma'am." Stick nodded crisply in greeting.

"You'll address me as Mrs. Waters. And you'll curtsy. There'll be none of that nodding business."

"Yes, Mrs. Waters." Stick curtsied. And ground her teeth. *Thinks she's the damn Queen of England.*

"Carter, show our new maid to her quarters. Use the rear door. Oh—and, Elizabeth, I'll see you in the kitchen momentarily."

The woman turned on a heel and reentered the house. Stick looked at Carter in amazement. Without meeting her eyes, he silently retrieved her satchel and walked past.

"Follow me, please."

The path to the back of the house was lined with a multitude of ornamental bushes and neatly trimmed pine trees. Stick couldn't fathom Carter managing such landscaping alone. And when they turned into the backyard, Stick exhaled in surprise.

"Carter, this is gorgeous." The property at the rear of the home was vast, acres of meadow and trails extended in all directions. Even the horse and car barns obviously received meticulous care.

"Thank you, Eliz—I mean, Miss Eliz—eh…Miss McLaugh—"

Stick smiled. "Please call me Mac, Carter. My friends back in Sherborn shortened my name to Mac to tease the administration. We used it so much that it's what I go by now." A grin brightened his scruffy face. "But while at work," she added, "and since the lady of the house will be using it, let's go with Elizabeth."

"Thank you, Mac. Um…Anytime you're allowed, I'll show you around."

He opened the back door and held it as they entered.

"I'd love that, Carter. Thanks."

"And here is your room. The kitchen is straight ahead at the end of this little hallway."

The tiny yet sunny room barely accommodated a twin bed, dresser, night table with oil lamp, and ladder-backed chair, which was where Carter placed her satchel.

"There is a closet here," he said, unlatching the handle and swinging open the narrow door.

Mac wondered if it had once been used to hide a stand of Revolutionary War rifles. That's all it seemed sized to hold. She certainly couldn't step into it. But she would make do. It was only for one year.

She sighed as she slowly looked around. "It will be fine, Carter. I appreciate you showing me." She automatically offered a handshake and smiled with relief when he quickly accepted.

Stick was tempted to question Carter about his boss but decided to wait till she knew him a bit better. She looked forward to it.

He stepped to the doorway. "Don't forget to curtsy, *Elizabeth*."

They shared a grin before he left.

Mac hung her hat on the bedpost. She had a mean urge to fluff up her neatly bobbed hair. Old habits die hard, she mused, and headed for the kitchen. It wouldn't do to be late.

The yeasty scent of baked bread drew her into the warm room. A heavyset woman wearing a full apron as white as her hair turned to acknowledge her, and a broad smile overtook the full cheeks.

"Welcome, dear lassie. I'm Mrs. Finnegan, the official cook of the Waters estate. You must be...Elizabeth?"

Mac curtsied, thinking she'd best get in the habit. "Elizabeth McLaughlin," she answered, eagerly shaking the chubby hand. "I'm pleased to meet you."

"Dearie, I'm in no need of your curtsyin'. I'm just the cook, I am." She leaned closer, and a strong hint of cinnamon tickled Mac's nose. "You best be saving the curtsyin' for the family."

"How big a family is it?" Mac wondered if she'd end up crippled from all this stupid curtsying.

"Oh, just Mrs. Waters and her daughter, Olivia. We lost Mr. Waters to a heart attack just a year or so ago. Such a darlin' man. And Miss Olivia's fiancé is off to Europe now. Reginald is spending most of the year studying architecture, he is. So she's pining away for him. Poor girl, half the time doesn't know what to do with herself."

"Gossiping again, Mrs. Finnegan?" Agnes Waters marched into the kitchen, the draped silks of her royal blue dress flowing around her. She cast a wry grin at the cook. "I'll admit my daughter could use a hobby. We'll see what she brings home with her this time." She turned steely, blue-gray eyes on Mac, ran them down and back up her frame. "Olivia will be home for lunch shortly, and I will introduce you. In the meantime, come with me."

Mac moved quickly and stayed two appropriate steps behind while Mrs. Waters took her on a narrated tour of the home. In short order, Mac realized that housecleaning now was her full-time occupation. The downstairs featured a large parlor, reception room off the foyer, dining room, and library, as well as the kitchen, pantry, laundry, water closet, and the tiny rooms for the maid and cook. After a stately ascension of the grand, central staircase, Mac learned that the second floor offered three guest rooms, a study, and the master bedroom and Olivia's, which shared an elaborate bath for those primary residents.

Mac was exhausted just thinking about keeping a shine on every surface. *At least it'll keep my mind occupied and keep me in good shape.* She hoped she could do a satisfactory job. She *had* to.

Back downstairs, Mrs. Waters led Mac to the laundry room off the pantry. She pulled down several bundles of black fabric and some of white from the linen cabinet and set them on Mac's quickly extended arms. "Your uniforms. Starched white blouses and black full-length skirts. They could very well be an appropriate size. If not, I trust you're capable of making the necessary adjustments. We have a decent Singer there in the corner."

Mac pivoted to see the sewing machine.

Mrs. Waters continued. "The Waters estate has no electricity this far from the city, so I'm sure it's not what you were used to at…well, before joining us."

"Steam," Mac told her. "We had over one hundred sewing machines running on steam."

Mrs. Waters's disinterested gaze focused on Mac. "'Running on steam'…what?"

Mac was puzzled.

Mrs. Waters's shoulders straightened; her nostrils flared. Mac realized her mistake too late.

Mrs. Waters raised her chin haughtily. "How do you address the lady of this house?" Her tone was venomous.

Mac lowered her head and curtsied immediately, her eyes remaining on the floor. "My most sincere apologies, Mrs. Waters. It won't happen again."

"In that, you are quite correct. See that it doesn't. I suggest you return and organize your quarters now. You will be serving lunch in approximately one hour."

Mac curtsied at the dismissal. "Yes, Mrs. Waters."

Mac watched her flounce out of the pantry and through the kitchen. It took several moments before she thought to move her feet.

A year of this, Mac told herself as she hurried to her room and unpacked. No choice, but boy, she'd love to knock Her Majesty flat on her ass. Mac quickly dressed and discovered the blouse fit her well, even if a bit scratchy at the neck and short in the cuffs. The skirt rose almost to mid-calf and she debated its acceptability. She'd consult Mrs. Finnegan.

Stepping into the kitchen, Mac spotted the cook beyond the cloud of steam from the kettle. She was stirring a sizeable pot of soup atop the huge coal stove.

"Excuse me, Mrs. Finnegan? Could I ask your opinion on this uniform, please?"

"Of course, dearie." She shuffled closer. "My, you surely be a tall one, aren't you?" She grinned as she examined Mac's appearance. "The skirt should be lower, I fear. The missus will be checking, you know."

"Yes, ma'am," Mac said, turning quickly and issuing a thank-you over her shoulder.

At the sewing station, Mac located scissors and swiftly took down the skirt's hem. She stepped into the skirt of her second uniform, grabbed the first, and returned to the kitchen.

"I'll never have time to heat an iron, Mrs. Finnegan, and this hem is so wrinkled." Mac took a short breath and asked, "Could I hold this in your steam here? To relax the fabric, that is?"

The cook's thick silver eyebrows rose with delight. "Clever lass," she said with a wink, and pulled her soup pot off the stove to make room. "I'll help you hold it over the kettle."

Together, they managed to erase practically all wrinkles from the newly lengthened skirt and Mac was thrilled. She pecked Mrs. Finnegan on the cheek and rushed back to her room to change.

Grinning fondly, Mrs. Finnegan called after her. "Time to set the table, dearie. Ten minutes."

Mac arranged the luncheon of hearty chicken soup, freshly baked bread, and rich vanilla custard at the far end of the long dining table, linens and silver all in proper positions. She assumed her own proper position at the kitchen doorway upon hearing two sets of footsteps descend the staircase. Mrs. Waters's clipped voice preceded her into the dining room.

"I'm reminding you, Olivia, that finally we again have a maid for such things."

"Mother, I was merely excited to be home. Besides, there's no logical reason why I cannot—"

"In the future, she will greet you, and you will leave her to the task of carrying your parcels or luggage."

The younger woman sighed as the two entered the room.

"Ah," Mrs. Waters began, nodding toward Mac. "This is Miss

Elizabeth McLaughlin, our domestic for the coming year. Elizabeth, my daughter, Miss Olivia Waters."

Mac promptly lowered her eyes and curtsied. "Pleased to meet you, Miss Waters." She steadied her breathing. Olivia Waters was one striking redhead, one whose luminous green eyes locked on to her with undeniable curiosity.

As her mother took her seat at the head of the table, Olivia moved thoughtfully to her place at her mother's left. "Welcome to the estate, Miss McLaughlin. Have you been here long?" She sat carefully, placing the napkin across the lap of her dress, and looked back to Mac for her reply.

"Just within the past hours, Miss Waters." Mac wasn't sure if response in mid-conversation required a curtsy, so she did to be safe.

"I presume she was still unsettled when you arrived," Mrs. Waters said, "which is why she failed to attend the door for you."

Mac spotted Olivia's irritated glance at her mother just prior to offering another curtsy. "My apologies, Miss Waters. It won't happen again."

Olivia raised a delicate, bejeweled hand, bangles clinking on her wrist. "There was no prob—"

"Elizabeth, that's the second apology you've issued since you arrived," Mrs. Waters injected. "I do not wish to hear another."

Mac curtsied. "No, Mrs. Waters."

"Very well. We'll have tea now."

Mac and Mrs. Finnegan ate their lunch in the kitchen while the Waterses dined and chatted. Mrs. Finnegan shared tales of Ireland, of her family's sailing adventure, and their optimism, and Mac was mesmerized. She, in contrast, shared the sad tale of her life—avoiding mention of the *scandalous* relationship she had enjoyed with Ellie. Mrs. Finnegan was equally spellbound, and Mac was thankful for the warmth of their exchange.

Overall, Mac's afternoon and evening sped by in an exhausting blur. She cleaned the dining room, swept out every room in the house, filled every lamp and all the heaters with kerosene, scrubbed the toilet, sink, and mammoth claw-foot tub in the upstairs bath, dusted both the master bedroom and Olivia's, even polished their vanity mirrors, and then served dinner.

She was sharing a cup of tea with Mrs. Finnegan when she was summoned.

"Elizabeth?" It was Olivia, from the parlor. "Bring us two whiskeys, would you, please?"

Mac rose immediately and straightened her skirt. Mrs. Finnegan touched her forearm.

"The left side bookcase, lassie. Lowest shelf, behind the books. You have to look close, but you'll see the books aren't real."

Mac found tiny crystal glasses in a kitchen cupboard and put them on a tray. Once in the parlor, under the watchful eye of both Waters women, she located the prohibited alcohol and served the drinks with curtsies.

"Honestly, Olivia. This is how you spent your time in Boston these past few weeks? You bring this home?"

Intrigued by Olivia's vibrant, refreshing persona, Mac awaited her response and sensed the keen eyes upon her as she took up a silent position by the door.

"Thank you, Elizabeth," Olivia offered, delaying an answer to her mother.

Eyes lowered appropriately, Mac curtsied again. "You're welcome, Miss Waters."

"That'll be all for now, Elizabeth," Mrs. Waters stated.

With a slight nod of acknowledgment, Mac curtsied and left the room. She dallied in the hallway, however, curious about their mother-daughter interaction, and rearranged the flower vases close enough to the parlor to overhear their conversation. Olivia had given her a prolonged once-over, even seemed a bit distracted by her, and Mac grinned as she eavesdropped.

"Now, Olivia, as to your pastimes, I don't feel—"

"She's rather striking, don't you think, Mother?" Olivia ignored her mother's blank stare and finally shifted her gaze from the doorway. "And quite tall. She appears more than capable." *Quite the handsome woman. Enchanting eyes. Yet she seems unsettled in her own skin.*

"Eh…capable…Well, we shall see," her mother said, frowning.

She raised her glass toward Olivia. "Now, this. You know I have precious little illegal substance in this house for a reason. Your father would—"

"Now, Mother, let's not misrepresent Father's occupation. He had many friends in shipping, in the *interstate commerce*. How else would he have accumulated his fortune if not for investments with the right men for the right products?" She grinned knowingly at her mother and sipped the straight rye whiskey. It made her blink.

Her mother shuddered after her sip. "This is boorish stuff, Olivia. At least before the Volstead, your father made certain we had refined Irish whiskey."

"Times are quite different today, Mother. In the city, money and liquor flow like water, regardless of the law. All sorts of liquor. And as we well know, it comes by land and sea," she added with a giggle. "The men in charge have fabulous private clubs for drinking, dining, dancing, for entertainment. And the women! Oh, Mother! You should see the glamour."

"You and the Stowe girl visited these places?" Her mother shook her head.

"Indeed we all did, Mother. With Charlotte's fiancé and two of his friends escorting us. In fact, we danced the night away many an evening."

"Olivia!" Her mother's eyes flamed as she leaned forward. "You are engaged to be married! Are you not aware of the impropriety of such behavior?"

Olivia waved a dismissive hand and sipped the last of her whiskey. "Shush, Mother. I'm twenty-two. I do believe that ladies and gentlemen can associate in public without disgracing anyone's family honor."

Her mother sat back in a huff. "Well, I have doubts that your fiancé would accept this calmly."

"Times are changing, Mother. Women are more determined than ever to carve their own place in the world, have their voices heard. Earning the right to vote was just a first step. Nowadays, particularly in the cities, more and more are attending college, pursuing higher paying—"

"A lady knows her place, Olivia."

"Mother. Look at you. A well-respected, highly intelligent woman who does what? Drinks tea and talks about art exhibits? Attends mah-jongg parties? Works crossword puzzles?" Now Olivia frowned at her mother. "You have so much to offer...in public speaking, tending accounts...You could run for public office."

"That's enough." Her mother stood and stared down at her. "Stop with this and come to your senses. I have no such desires. If you recall, your father considered public office and found it quite unappealing."

"Only because his associates convinced him he was best suited for commerce. Father could have been a United States senator. Who knows what you could achieve? I certainly intend to experience as much of what life has to offer as I can."

"This conversation is over, Olivia. I'll have you respect the status that generations of Waterses have attained, and not subject it to disgrace. You are a Waters and shall represent that name with dignity."

❖

Mac trotted out of the house with a hot, freshly buttered corn muffin wrapped in a napkin. The damn skirt billowed around her legs like a loose sail, and she cursed the thing.

"Hey, Carter." She caught up with him as he tied the reins of a muscular palomino to the hitching post outside the barn.

"Morning, Mac. For me?"

She handed him the muffin, pleased to see his eyes light up. "Haven't seen much of you these past few days. Do you eat out here or sneak into the kitchen?"

He actually laughed, a deep, resonating sound Mac felt beneath her feet. "Most times out here in the barn," he finally answered, tossing his head toward the side door. "I have living quarters there. Mrs. Finnegan keeps me supplied."

"Ahh. I think you should be eating in the kitchen with us. Doesn't seem right to me."

"Propriety, girl." He set a heavy, understanding hand on her shoulder. "You'll learn the propriety of things in no time."

"Oh, I get it," she responded sharply. "Those with money believe it's their right to keep you in your place. Yeah, I know all about it."

Carter gripped Mac's upper arm and tugged her into the barn. He lowered his head before speaking. "Mac. You gotta keep your opinions to yourself. Otherwise, they'll get you back where you came from."

Mac shook her head at the unfairness of it all. "That apply to you too, Carter?"

He straightened and stretched his back. "Well, now. Let's just say I go back a ways with Mr. Waters, and he gave me a job when I couldn't get nothing after the war. I know which side of my bread's buttered. Can't complain."

Can't? Won't, most likely.

"Well, I still don't think it's right, you working so hard around here and not associating with anyone, missing out on things inside. I'll be bringing you goodies whenever I can, Carter, and don't protest."

He shook his head, grinning.

"So who is that?" Mac asked, pointing to the golden horse.

"That's Sunny. Miss Olivia's pride and joy. She's quite the rider, you know. Did circuit competition when she was younger." He led them back to the hitching post and proudly stroked the horse's mane. "These days, though, she's always off on some junket and seldom has time to ride. I keep Sunny exercised well enough so she's ready whenever Miss Olivia gets the urge. Like this morning."

"Oh. She'll be out soon, I suppose? I'd better get back to work." Mac glanced toward the house nervously. "Wouldn't do to have them think I was slackin'." She backed away from Carter. "See you later. I'll bring down another surprise when I can." She headed off to start her laundry chores.

Olivia exited the back door just as Mac gave a wet cotton sheet a vigorous shake. "Good morning, Elizabeth," she said brightly.

Surprised, Mac turned and tossed the sheet back into the laundry basket to curtsy. "G-good morning, Miss Waters. I didn't see you approach."

Olivia's eyes glittered in the sun, her smile sparkling and radiant. No denying she was stunning, so poised in her riding outfit, her hair so fiery against the black jacket, and she knew it. Mac could sense it but couldn't help the lump that formed in her throat. It seemed to cut her breath short. And she got the feeling Olivia knew that, too.

"Such a lovely day, don't you think?" Olivia gazed about at the azure sky and colorful foliage of trees lining the meadows.

"Yes, Miss Waters." Mac stood in place, forgoing the laundry, forgoing the curtsy.

"Do you ride, Elizabeth?"

"Oh no, Miss Waters. Never been on a horse." She remembered to lower her eyes respectfully.

"It's exhilarating. Many people from this area have ridden since childhood. Where are you from?"

"Dorchester, Miss Waters."

"Ah, I see. A city girl."

"Yes, Miss Waters."

"My mother tells me this is your first position as a domestic. If you don't think me rude for being frank, you're no child, so what was your profession prior to this?"

Mac's eyes lowered again. She had no clue what to say. But she still had her pride.

"I...I worked for a market in South Boston, Miss Waters."

"Is that something you aspire to? Or is domestic service your calling?"

"I...Well...I would hope to have my own business someday, Miss Waters."

Olivia sank back on her hip, crossing her arms thoughtfully. She tapped her riding crop against her shoulder, obviously pondering the response.

"What line of business?"

By now, Mac wanted to get back to hanging sheets. This interrogation made her nervous. So did Olivia herself; her gaze was too direct. *Not fair that it's improper to look her in the eye. The way she looks at me...*

"I...I haven't settled on any one concept yet. My priority is service to your family, Miss Waters."

"Well." Olivia stepped closer and tapped Mac's bicep with the crop. "You are a hard and diligent worker. I predict success for you."

Mac curtsied. "That's much appreciated. Thank you, Miss Waters."

Olivia nodded and started for the barn. "I'll be taking Sunny out now for a few hours," she announced over her shoulder. "Please prepare my bath for later?"

Mac was taken aback by the directive posed as a request…and that Olivia actually used the word "please" again. "Yes, Miss Waters," she called to the attractive backside. *Flaunting or flirting?*

❖

One of the lessons Mac learned at Sherborn was to keep your hands to yourself. Not that she'd ever made advances toward another prisoner, even though the thought crossed her mind numerous times, but she'd seen what happened to others. Solitary was a decidedly miserable place to be stuck. Maryellen Rolston and Bea Henrich became shadows of themselves, withering away on bread and water for a month in their isolated rooms. And the superintendent locked Susan Mulcahey away just on a rumor a matron reported.

So that afternoon outside the closed bathroom door, Mac forced those sad memories to mind as a measure of self discipline and pretended not to watch Olivia arrive in only a floor-length cotton robe.

"All steamy in there, Elizabeth?"

Mac curtsied. "It is. Take care not to scald yourself, Miss Waters."

Olivia looked so deeply into her eyes that Mac fought back a shudder. She looked down, respectfully.

"And the towels are inside?"

"Yes, Miss Waters."

"Elizabeth," she said, her voice unusually soft, "look at me."

Given permission, Mac met her gaze directly. Olivia's eyes were impossibly enticing, and probed so deeply into Mac's reserve that she shifted uneasily on her feet.

"Come," Olivia said, her hand on the doorknob. "Talk to me. Keep me company." She stepped into the stifling bathroom and dropped her robe.

Mac had hardly recovered from the invitation when Olivia's naked form presented itself. She swallowed and turned her back to shut the door. She stayed that way until she could tell Olivia was settled beneath the water.

"Elizabeth. Now don't be bashful. There's nothing to see that you haven't seen of yourself. Sit. Tell me about yourself. How did Mother come to hire you?"

Mac didn't think her legs would hold her, but she edged her feet toward the dressing chair across the room and sat, relieved. Dots of perspiration rose across her forehead and the back of her neck. There was no way she'd look at the beautiful—nude—Olivia reclining in the tub.

"Um..." Mac began and heard her former instructor screaming about proper speech. "I...I was among those who completed training and were eligible for hire, Miss Waters." She knew that statement would only lead to more questions but couldn't think of a better response quickly enough. Her mind was spinning too fast. The heat in the room was merciless.

"Training where?"

Mac hardly heard the question. She struggled to keep her eyes properly averted as Olivia sponged the hot soapy water up her arm and across her chest.

"You can look, you know. I won't bite."

Mac's gaze rose and took in the full, creamy breasts with pert nipples at the waterline, the stroke of Olivia's hand as she soaped them luxuriously. Nerves knotted Mac's stomach, and arousal competed with hot steam to drench her from head to toe. She lifted her eyes to Olivia's and took a deep breath. *Concentrate on the questions.*

"I was trained at the Massachusetts Reformatory for Woman at Sherborn, Miss Waters."

Olivia stopped the sponge at her opposite shoulder, her eyebrows raised. "The prison? You're joking."

"No, Miss Waters."

Olivia let her arm and the sponge plop into the water with a splash. She sighed with resignation. "You know, I think that since you are sitting here and I'm quite naked, indeed bathing before you, we could forgo the protocol. Don't you think? My name's Olivia. This 'Miss Waters' business keeps Mother happy, but drives me nuts, quite honestly. I'm sure it must you, as well."

Mac's jaw almost dropped. No instructor at Sherborn ever prepared them for a boss who wanted to be a friend.

"Oh. Well...As you wish...Olivia."

"See? Much better." Olivia was smiling again, and washing. "Now, Elizabeth." She raised her right leg, bent at the knee, and lavished it with the sponge. Mac swallowed hard. This *very* special treat was torture.

The room, excruciatingly hot. "You said the prison? Truly? What on earth did you do to be put there?" She abruptly lowered her leg and drew herself up into a full sitting position. Her breasts bobbing free of the water, she grinned devilishly at Mac. "Are you a murderer?"

"I am no—" She caught her defensive reaction in time, softening her voice. "I was sent away because of a false report."

Olivia's eyes never left Mac's face. "What did the report say?"

"That I committed arson."

Olivia's head snapped back a little. "Did you proclaim innocence? How many years were you there?"

Mac straightened in her chair and rubbed her wet palms on her thighs. Her shoulders flexed and her mouth hardened. Her entire bearing became defiant. "This is my fifth and final year. And I *am* innocent."

"Dear Lord. Five years?" Olivia reclined again and slipped beneath the water, soaking her hair. She popped up and reached for the shampoo. "I believe you."

Mac cleared her throat. "You do?"

"Don't ask me why, but yes. I do." Olivia dunked her soapy head. When she surfaced, it was a while before she spoke. "I think it's in your eyes."

Mac leaned forward on her knees and stared at the floor. Frustrated, she ran a hand back through her hair and scruffed up her neat bob before she knew what she was doing. *Now she's reading your eyes... What the hell's next?* Then she remembered her place.

Mac sat up straight and fussed with her hair. *Don't you dare forget yourself.* She adjusted the stifling collar at her throat and smoothed out her skirt. God, she hated this costume.

Apparently, it showed. Olivia sent her another grin. "You're not used to those clothes, are you?"

More heat blazed into Mac's cheeks. "I should be by now."

Olivia stood then, water streaming down every delectable curve of her shoulders, breasts, stomach, hips, the thatch of auburn hair between her thighs. "And I would think you'd be used to this," she said, gesturing at her nude body.

Mac was off her chair in a flash, towel unfurled and offered to block her view. She kept her head down, blushing profusely.

Olivia laughed. "Please tell me you've seen naked women in your day, Elizabeth." She took the towel and wrapped it securely around her torso. Mac exhaled with relief, but then Olivia leaned toward her confidentially. "And you've probably seen your share of naked men."

Mac met her eyes as they stood inches apart. The scent of Olivia's lavender soap flooded her senses, fogged her mind. The urge to touch the rosy skin, taste the sweetness of it, warm her cheek against it, was startlingly hard to withstand. She hadn't been this close to succumbing since…

"Do you have a boyfriend, Elizabeth? I mean, did you before they sent you away?" Mac blanched at the topic and Olivia set a hand on her shoulder. "I'm sorry," she added quickly. "I didn't mean to—"

"I try not to think about those days."

Olivia squeezed her shoulder before letting go.

"You need to think about your future," she offered, exchanging the towel for her robe and grinning when Mac politely averted her eyes. She pressed her palm to Mac's bicep. "You will be through here before you know it, so be thinking of what lies ahead."

Mac relaxed and just smiled. She couldn't remember the last time anyone genuinely wished her a happy future.

Responding with a warm smile of her own, Olivia shuddered to think Elizabeth hadn't the slightest clue about the world that awaited her. A single woman could easily be overwhelmed by the whirlwind of life these days and with no support, no close family or friends, Elizabeth appeared primed for existence as a lost soul. Hearing that Olivia believed her innocent obviously had shocked her, and that tugged at Olivia's sense of justice. She doubted that anyone had ever believed Elizabeth, and felt oddly drawn to offer a reassuring hug.

She stepped into the hallway and looked back at Elizabeth, whose next chore was to clean up after her. Olivia suddenly wished there was a professional maid to tend to the chores, not a vibrant woman in her prime who was being forced to work as punishment for something she didn't do. She couldn't imagine the pent-up anger, the weariness, what it took to tamp it all down under someone's thumb. She couldn't conceive of how that would change a woman.

Nor could Olivia decipher the look in Elizabeth's eyes, but at least now she knew why it was there. She couldn't tell the sadness from the frustration from the resignation. But she felt something in the connection their eyes shared. Maybe it was as simple as kindness.

Elizabeth still stood by the tub, discarded towel in hand. "Thank you, Olivia."

Olivia put a steadying hand on the door frame and tried to see beyond the questions in Elizabeth's eyes. "Next time we talk, I want to hear about your plans." She flashed a smile and left for her room.

CHAPTER SEVEN

Mac had the house spotless. She'd busted her butt to do so, roared through all the dusting, sweeping, scrubbing, and polishing so she could sit back and put her feet up for the next three glorious days. It was Thanksgiving, and the Waters women and Mrs. Finnegan were spending the holiday with relatives. Carter drove the big Studebaker to take all three to the Framingham train station, from whence they'd reach Boston and part on separate trains. And then Carter was driving halfway to Cape Cod to visit his old friends and expected to return with a giant gift sack of fresh-picked cranberries.

That left the Waters estate solely in Mac's hands for the entire day. And she put it to good use, squaring away all the tedious chores so as not to have any worries during her holiday. Yes, she struggled to keep her spirits up, but the little calendar she hung next to her bedroom lamp said she'd soon be crossing off another month of her sentence. She was restricted to the estate but determined to make the most of her time.

She drew a bath upstairs and treated herself to a long, hot soak, even used a dab of Olivia's lavender shampoo and soap. She sipped a cup of tea while she soaked, tea she spiked with a dash of that rye whiskey. It was a holiday, after all.

And she let the sensual memory of that conversation with a magnificently naked Olivia come to mind. Such a delicious-looking figure, Mac thought, smiling as she sipped her tea. She wondered what the proper Miss Waters would have done if Mac had kissed her, right here beside this very tub. Olivia had seemed so uninhibited, stepping so close to her. Mac looked at the floor where they had stood, and knew that Miss Waters wasn't really as proper as she led everyone to believe.

Well, hell. Neither am I.

Mac dried off, restored the bathroom to perfect order—while naked—and ran down the stairs to her room. The house was cold, but running through it stark naked and laughing like a child was a liberating treat unto itself. *Just my luck, I'll catch some influenza.*

Almost so excited her hands shook, she opened the box of things she'd had Carter pick up at the store from her three dollars a week salary. Mac pulled on a new pair of dark brown canvas breeches and nearly shouted with joy. With new black stockings and her spare, scuffed Oxfords, all topped by a man's crisp white shirt and red suspenders, she went parading through various rooms, beaming like a fool. It was a great Thanksgiving.

There were two things she'd been able to keep since her arrest: her old black newsboy cap and Ellie's necklace. The latter was always on, close to her heart beneath every blouse. But the cap hadn't been worn in more than five years. It was a reliable old friend, something she'd swiped at Baggers with many times, a rain and snow shelter when the weather turned bad on the streets, the perfect hiding place for candy bars or a bottle of vanilla…the element of her attire that Ellie called "naughty."

Mac stood before the little mirror on the back of her bedroom door and set the cap on her head just right. She gave the brim a roguish, slightly downward tilt over her forehead, the way she used to wear it, and with her bobbed hair, her sharp facial features, and the shirt and suspenders, she looked unmistakably male. And, she dared to admit, quite dashing.

She threw her head back and laughed roundly. "Bah!" she sighed, and went to the kitchen to make more tea.

"Hey! Who are you?" Carter yelled at the stranger in breeches and cap at the stove. His burlap bag of berries hit the floor and thousands upon thousands of them bounced madly everywhere.

Mac spun around, her eyes wide. "Carter!" She took one look at the flood of red on the floor and broke into a fit of laughter. "Oh, shit, Carter!"

He just stared at her. "Mac?"

It took two hours with them both on hands and knees, but they finally rounded up all the renegade berries.

Carter sat at the table with a weary exhale, staring at Mac's eyes beneath the brim of her cap. "You better know how to make juice and sauce and muffins and every other damn thing, now that we have all these berries."

"Mrs. Finnegan left me recipes," she said, grinning mostly at his effort to make conversation. "You'll see." Mac set a cup of coffee in front of him. She'd found the percolator under the sink and coffee that was God knows how old on a shelf in the pantry. Enough tea. She wanted coffee. She hoped to express that desire to Mrs. Finnegan when things returned to normal. Her shoulders sagged at the thought.

"So you ran the streets, huh?" He obviously was intrigued by the conversation they'd shared on the floor.

Mac joined him at the table with her own cup and warmed both hands around it. She'd have to get a really good fire going in the stove soon.

"For almost three years. Lived on them for one."

"Dressed like that? You could pass for a man, you know. Swear to God." He held up his open palm.

Mac chuckled. "Hey, this is me. It's how I live, who I am, Carter. Dressing any other way feels odd…like the maid's costume." Carter laughed. "Seriously," she went on. "Of course it always helped that boys got to go places, do more things than girls. They don't get hassled or…Well, it's safer not looking like a girl on the streets, you know? It's big to me, being my…natural self after such a very long time."

"Hm." Carter grunted into his cup. "I guess I do see your point."

"I did what I could to help my brother put food on our table."

"Didn't you ever…you know…" His hand flailed through the air, as if he'd snag the words he needed. "Well, didn't you ever get all gussied up for dates with fellas? Go dancing or bowling? Or to the show? You know, what girls do?"

"I was just a kid. Then when I was sixteen, I had to go off and hide. There's no way to get 'gussied up' when you're living in a boxcar, Carter."

He let out a slow whistle.

"But…see…I already had someone special. *She* was my reason

for living, for shooting for that light at the end of the tunnel." Mac saw his eyebrows rise and was surprised when no exclamation was made. "It was her father turned me in. I never saw her again."

"Whoa, shit, Mac," he whispered. "That's some tale. I'm real sorry."

Mac patted his arm. "You're one sweet guy, Carter. Thanks for understanding."

"Ain't never known a woman who was...well, *that way*, but I don't see how it matters to the kind of person you are. From where I sit, Elizabeth McLaughlin's just an honorable woman who stepped into a bad mess and dresses any ol' way she feels like." He put his hand atop hers. "Your family know any of this about you?"

Mac shook her head. "I only dare tell people I trust."

Carter's eyes softened and he nodded. "I appreciate that, Mac. That's nice of you to say. Thanks. Guess you couldn't trust your parents. Weren't they around to come visit you all those years?"

Mac sat back in the chair. "Well, my dad's passed on, but my mother, no. And honestly? I don't know where she and my sister are now. Or my brother, Ray. Somebody back in the Square once told me they were going to Charlestown, I think." She sipped and her thoughts began to drift. "The reformatory was too far for anyone to go. And they probably were ashamed of me."

"They could've stuck up for you. Didn't they care that you were innocent?"

Mac looked at him evenly. "I suppose they didn't believe it."

Carter took a long drink of his coffee and shook his head. "Wow. Must be so hard to have it come to this, you being somebody's servant, and all. I mean, you started roaming the streets at what? Fourteen?"

Mac nodded as she spoke, slowly turning her cup in circles. "Oh, it's an eye-opener, Carter, that's for sure, being in the reformatory for so long, trying to keep true to who you are while they poke you and shape you into what they think you should be...like you're their own hunk of clay. After a while, you just let 'em because it's too damn exhausting to fight back, but you hang on to what's in your head." She tapped her temple. "And you don't *ever* forget that somebody used you."

She flexed her long fingers around her coffee cup, feeling bitterness and resentment rising to the surface, hearing it in her own voice. She sighed before taking another sip, and considered Carter's reaction to all that she'd revealed.

❖

The Waters women were arguing in the parlor about how and why to decorate for Christmas, seeing as how neither of them expected to be home for the holiday. Then they started arguing about that, where Olivia intended to go, and what, God forbid, she planned to do. In the kitchen, Mac rolled her eyes at Mrs. Finnegan.

"You'll have some more free time, lassie," Mrs. Finnegan whispered as she worked. "I'll be off as well. The missus has her Christmas with her sister as usual, but it does sound like Miss Waters will try skiing again up to the Adirondacks camp with her Beacon Hill chums."

Mac just smiled and shook her head. She'd get her hopes up when the time actually arrived. Meanwhile, she returned to reading the old copy of the *Post* she'd saved since Thanksgiving weekend. She always found something new in it that fascinated her. Olivia had brought it home, but thrown it away.

"Have you ever been to a show at the Bowdoin Square Theatre, Mrs. Finnegan?" Watching the smiling customers come and go from the Bowdoin had been a frequent—free—pastime, back when she had Sundays off from Maggie's deliveries.

"Once, just a year ago. You get stage acts *and* moving pictures there." She poured vanilla batter into a floured pan. "The picture shows have such wonderful actors, nowadays. There's a Rudolph Valentino who's most handsome. For his picture, *The Sheik*, the papers named him the 'Latin Lover.' The ladies near to swoon for Valentino, didja know?"

"You don't say." Mac lowered the paper and stared. "Does it cost a lot to get in?"

"It's up to ten cents now. Time was, a nickel would do."

Mac nodded as she went back to reading. "I remember that," she muttered, recalling all too well that she could never afford to waste five whole cents to watch a bunch of pictures flicker by. Nickels went for important things like bread or a Joe & Nemo's frankfurter or a trolley ride if it was raining…or postcards.

"Says here that the big mercantile in New York, the Macy's store, treated the whole city to a parade on Thanksgiving. Must have been a real doozy—but I bet it cost so much they never do it again."

Suddenly, Mac sat forward, eyes glued to the paper. "Wow. I could buy my own Ford!" Mac's memory brought forth her eagerness to drive and her father's refusal. She was so tired of being thwarted at every turn.

"Indeed, lass. With enough savings, yes. There are many to choose from now."

Mac turned the page. "And here, there's an Oldsmobile coach that's a real beauty." She whistled. "Three times the Ford's price, though. Guess I'll stick to them."

Five minutes later, she was reconsidering. "Look," and she stepped to Mrs. Finnegan and folded the paper in half to point to the advertisement. "This one's called 'Champion.' The company says 'Convenient personal car for women.'" Mac fell silent. "Oh." She resented the insinuation and she mumbled under her breath, "Women don't need *special* cars." From over her shoulder, Mrs. Finnegan giggled. "Look at this. It says 'The seats make into a full-size bed in car for camping.' What's camping?"

By the time Mrs. Finnegan finished explaining about sleeping outside, cooking over an open fire, and drinking out of canteens, Mac thought twice about her "Champion." Camping wasn't a sport. Camping was her past. She'd start saving toward four hundred dollars for one of those Ford Model Ts.

Mac tossed the paper on the table and sat down, eyeing the various now-familiar front-page stories. The Volstead Act must have been some huge deal, she figured, and there must've been something good in it for somebody or some people, if it took all the alcohol away from the whole damn country. Were all the brewers and drivers, warehouse shippers… all the bars and liquor stores gone? *Shit, that's a lot of folks.*

As far as Mac could tell, the little guy—as usual—got the short end of this Prohibition thing. If you owned a restaurant or a dance hall, you probably could have a great thing going on the sly and make a killing. Advertisements for those places were everywhere in the paper, and Prohibition didn't appear to be hurting those folks. No question in her mind that there was plenty of alcohol to be had, if you knew who to ask. Sure looked it.

And right there in the *Post*, it showed this mighty spiffy-looking guy with the weird initial first name, J. Edgar. This Hoover guy was in charge of some new government bureau that investigated crimes. *The country needs police now, too?* Not that there wasn't really bad stuff going on all over the country; the newspaper confirmed that there was. There were gangs of hoodlums everywhere, it appeared, and carrying guns, shooting people, stealing hooch, and robbing banks like outlaws in the old *Buffalo Bill Weekly* that Ray used to buy for a nickel.

Even Boston had some outlaw types. There were Irish gangs, and Jewish gangs, Italian gangs, and Mac knew there was no way in hell they were all pals. Just like she knew for a fact that city officials— including the cops—stopped at nothing to get what they wanted. Most likely hooked up with the gangs, she thought. They might as well all be in it together; they all had the same mentality anyway. You did things their way or else. And she knew what that was like, too.

Seemed everyone had a price or a price on his head. Mac knew it in her gut and she nodded absently at the newspaper. *Yep, they're raking in the dough.*

❖

Every time Carter or Olivia went to town these days, they brought home the *Post* for Mac, and it wasn't long before she knew all the goings-on, all the key players in Boston politics and crime. She always perused the entertainment pages, curious about the clubs, the top-name performers giving shows, and the moving pictures and songs of the day.

More than any other part of the *Post*, lodging held her attention for hours. Houses for sale, cold-water flats, and rooms for rent, they were everywhere. Everywhere Mac wanted to be. She knew she might never have the eight thousand dollars for some of the homes listed, but she should be able to afford something like eighteen dollars to rent a flat for a month. Then again, did she really need to spend so much on a whole flat?

It made her wonder what a domestic *really* earned. She had no idea. As a prisoner of the Commonwealth, she earned three dollars a week, but on the outside? For a wealthy family like the Waterses? Maybe five times that, she guessed, but then there was the impossible price: you literally submitted to servitude and surrendered your freedom. *I'll sleep in a boxcar first.*

She began searching the paper anew with every issue, hoping a profession she could learn, master, and enjoy would strike her. Olivia had put the thought in her head, that lovely day in the bath, and Mac had focused on her future ever since.

The job, whatever it ended up being—and Mac was firm in her position—would not cost her her dignity or self-respect. People would show respect and common courtesy for who she was, because if there was one thing that mattered most, it was that Mac could and would be herself. The search was never-ending, but not discouraging.

Mac now saw the upcoming ten months as opportunity to plan, hopefully to learn, and definitely to save. If freedom meant a single room with no heat, and handouts from the church and Salvation Army, she'd jump at it. She could get by on saltines and water, or Fig Newtons, or Vanilla Snaps maybe if they were cheap, or even Cheese-Tid-Bits. Mac chuckled at herself. What she would have given for any of them just six years ago.

❖

With Christmas the following Thursday, Mrs. Waters declared the household would celebrate the holiday on the Friday evening prior. The Waters women and Mrs. Finnegan again would be traveling in the Studebaker to the station, this time on Tuesday, and returning after celebrating the New Year. As far as Mac was concerned, they could take double that; she couldn't wait. It would be the same as Thanksgiving, except the break for her would be much longer.

Carter hooked the sleigh up to Teddy, Sunny's Morgan buddy, and came back with a fine spruce for the parlor. Mac was directed to serve brandy cordials to everyone, herself included, while they assessed and Carter wrestled with the positioning of the tree. She, Mrs. Finnegan, and Olivia combined forces to string popcorn and small red velvet bows all over its eight-foot height. Mrs. Waters bestowed upon them elaborate stories of her childhood while hanging ornaments from the special crate

Carter had retrieved from the attic. The intricate, hand-painted glass figurines had been made and shipped from England nearly fifty years ago, she said, and Mac had to admit, she'd never seen anything more delicate—or expensive.

Having left the women to their devices for some time, Carter finally reappeared blanketed in frigid air, dusted with new-fallen snow, and lugging a sizeable wooden crate. He set it carefully in the middle of the rug and stepped back. When Mac refreshed his drink and hovered nearby, hoping he'd give her a clue, he simply winked.

Olivia went to his side and brushed the snow from his shoulders. She turned to the others and gaily announced, "Merry Christmas to everyone from me!"

Mac and Mrs. Finnegan grinned at each other.

Mrs. Waters's look of consternation was no surprise. "What is it, dear? Carter, if you would do the honors?"

The box inside the crate was labeled "Victor," and Mac recognized it from the advertisements she'd seen in the *Post*. Olivia cleared a side table, and Carter freed the phonograph from its trappings and set it in place. As he hurried back outside, everyone huddled around to marvel at the remarkable technology and the attractive walnut craftsmanship.

"This too," Carter proclaimed, returning with another large box. He popped open the crate and its inner box and removed a mammoth, gracefully curved horn. "The sound comes out through this," he said, attaching it to the phonograph. He located the brass crank and screwed it into the side of the machine, then looked mischievously around the room.

From the back of the foyer closet, Olivia retrieved a flat box several inches thick, and she opened it for all to see as she reentered the room. "Music records!" she announced. "It's about time we entered the twentieth century, don't you think?"

Mrs. Finnegan giggled, Carter laughed, Mac hooted, and Mrs. Waters just shook her head in amazement. They all clapped and exclaimed their thanks, watching Olivia set one of the black records on the platter and crank the machine to make the platter spin. Then she lifted an arm-like rod that swung on a pivot and set its ball end on the edge of the disc. She stepped away, holding her breath.

Tinny crackling noises drifted out of the large horn, followed by quick, staccato notes from violins and horns that swung right into "Toot, Toot, Tootsie!" and Al Jolson's voice, just as if he were standing in the room with them.

"Oh, my gracious!" Mrs. Finnegan shouted. She grabbed Olivia's hand. "Miss Olivia! This is wonderful! Thank you!"

"Olivia, dear!" Mrs. Waters said loudly to be heard over the music. "Mrs. Finnegan is quite right. This is wondrous."

Bouncing to the beat, Olivia made her way over to her mother's chair and leaned down to be kissed on the cheek.

"I'm glad you like it, Mother. We are rather behind on the newest gadgets! I couldn't wait to give it to everyone." She turned at Carter's tap on her shoulder. "What do you think, Carter?"

"Amazing, miss. Read about them, but couldn't imagine the real thing."

"Well, we'll be getting you in here a lot more often to enjoy it."

Olivia found Elizabeth, grinning from ear to ear, her foot tapping out the beat. "Fun, isn't it?" she asked, guiding her by the elbow closer to the machine for another look.

"It's like magic," Elizabeth said on a sigh. "Thank you for thinking of us, Miss Waters. That's very, very generous. I-I could listen to it all night." She lowered her eyes and curtsied.

Touched by Elizabeth's genuine appreciation, Olivia thought she spotted tears pooling in the soft, warm eyes and was disappointed that she couldn't see them. And Olivia definitely wanted to stop that damn curtsying, but it wasn't her place to say anything. Seeing Elizabeth subjugate herself just for speaking or for being spoken to nagged at Olivia. Knowing what she knew about her and having shared some very personal time, Olivia couldn't help but interpret each curtsy as Elizabeth's acceptance of a punishing blow. At some point, probably sooner than later, Olivia knew she'd speak to her mother about this foolish antiquated protocol.

The record ended, and Olivia realized she'd been staring at the floor between them. "Oh! Let me play another."

"What other records to you have there, my dear conniving daughter?"

Olivia placed the entire box in her mother's lap. "Choose something, Mother. Something we can dance to."

"Oh, poo." Her mother waved away Olivia's dancing idea. She

selected "It Had to Be You," and Olivia read the label as she returned to the machine.

"A foxtrot, Mother. Are you up for it?" She set the needle on the spinning disc and reached for her mother. "Come on. Up with you!" The music started, and the bopping beat filled the room.

Holding Olivia's hand, her mother stood looking down at their feet. "It's been ages, dearest daughter. I haven't—"

"Yes, Mrs. Waters," Olivia finished for her, dancing all by herself at the end of her mother's arm. "You haven't since Saturday nights with Daddy. And that was a year ago. It's time to dust off your moves."

Olivia released her mother and danced around her. "She is a fine dancer," she told the others. "I think she needs encouraging!"

"Olivia!" her mother exclaimed, and turned pink in the cheeks.

"Show us how it's done, Mrs. Waters." Carter was the brave one to speak first.

"We could learn a few steps by watching, if you don't mind, Mrs. Waters," Elizabeth dared to say, then curtsied.

Olivia and her mother looked up at Elizabeth. "You don't know how?" Olivia realized she knew the answer and wanted to crawl under the rug for asking. "Oh...I..."

"It's fine, miss. Everyone here knows why I never learned, Miss Waters."

Olivia watched Elizabeth drop her eyes and curtsy. Olivia was starting to hate it.

"Of course you can learn the steps." She turned to her mother and took her hands. "All right, Mrs. Waters, enough of your dilly-dallying. Let's go."

And so it went for several hours, and several more rounds of brandy, slurred singing, and all twenty records in the box at least twice.

Her mother danced magnificently with Carter to "Rhapsody in Blue," after teaching him the steps and restarting the record three times. Even with his bad leg, his effort (and the cordials) put a smile on her face. And Elizabeth insisted she learn with a very bashful Mrs. Finnegan, so Olivia directed them around the room to the song "Tea for Two." Mrs. Finnegan laughed so hard at their fumbling, she grew teary eyed and short of breath.

Fanning herself with both hands, her mother took advantage of a break between records and departed rather unsteadily to freshen up in the upstairs bath. Carter then went to Mrs. Finnegan and bowed from the waist. Olivia shared a grin with Elizabeth as Carter gallantly offered Mrs. Finnegan his hand.

"If Miss Waters is merciful with her song choice, oh lovely cook, might you honor me with this next dance?"

Mrs. Finnegan's plump, flushed cheeks actually reddened further with a blush. She rose to her feet, swaying and smiling as the easygoing "All Alone" began. "She took pity on us," she told Carter.

Olivia turned to Mac. "A classic waltz, Elizabeth?"

"I'm sorry, I don't know this either, Miss Waters."

As she began the curtsy, Olivia took her arm and kept her upright. Confused, Elizabeth met her eyes, then remembered her place and lowered them.

"The waltz is as easy as one-two-three, one-two-three," Olivia said softly, drawing Elizabeth to her. She took Elizabeth's right hand in her left, and placed her other atop Elizabeth's left shoulder. She splayed her fingers, enjoying the feel of it, and steadied her breath. "Now put your other hand at my waist."

The relaxed, freewheeling tenor of the entire evening disappeared for Mac at the feel of Olivia's hand in hers. Knowing she also had to touch Olivia's waist, Mac tensed all over. Only at her trial had she been this nervous.

"Relax, Elizabeth." Olivia looked up into Mac's eyes and smiled gently. "I wish you would look at me."

"I...I shouldn't...I mean, I'm not...You...I mean—"

"Shh. There's no need to be nervous."

Mac looked directly at her and was lost. Olivia's eyes sparkled. Mac liked holding the soft, small hand. She liked the warm, sweet curve of Olivia's hip. She liked the lavender scent of her. She liked being lost in those eyes. Mac stopped breathing. She blinked and looked away. "I-I need to watch my feet. I don't want to step on—"

"Shh."

"—your feet—"

"Shh, I said."

"—Miss Waters."

Mac appreciated being moved to the rhythm of the song. She was grateful for the simple steps because dancing with Olivia was at once nerve-wracking and exhilarating. The emotional combination made her dizzy. The slight, feminine hand she cradled was velvety soft, comfortably relaxed, and grasping hers in return. Olivia was supple and warm at the waist where Mac gently pressed her other hand. So compelling was the urge to feel Olivia against her body, Mac actually shivered. She felt weak in the knees, and the knots in her stomach cinched tighter. She wondered if Olivia could feel her trembling. And when she recognized the sensations as desire surging through her system, a wave of nostalgia struck hard.

So long ago and still so real... Memories, exquisitely real, rose from the shadowed corner of Mac's heart and threatened her tenuous composure. Theirs had been a young but true, consuming love, one to which Mac knew she'd forever compare all others. Its passion ruled her soul still, and Mac stood defenseless against its resurgence.

Weakened and her eyes closing, Mac drifted back into the world of Ellie's arms as they squeezed her shoulders. Hushed, intimate words caressed her face. Firm and determined muscles shifted so fluidly, fit so perfectly against her chest, torso, and hips. Adoring eyes filled Mac with a yearning she could hardly restrain. Ellie's satin lips came to her mouth and claimed the heart Mac so willingly surrendered.

The memory nearly staggered her. She bowed her head and exhaled hard, as if to force it back into the recesses of her heart where it lived. The parlor moved around her, it seemed, more like she was the stationary spectator amidst her past. Yet somehow she was in motion, and the air around her was charged with the very real presence of a statuesque woman in her hands, with music that taunted her heart.

Raising her eyes to Olivia's, Mac did her best to concentrate on the rhythm that drove her feet. *Appreciate this moment. Thank her with a smile.*

Seeing Elizabeth's focus return to the present, Olivia wondered where she had gone. Someplace, she gathered, where only pain of the past, of loss, generated such a distant, forlorn gaze. Olivia searched her eyes as she returned Elizabeth's smile. And it was then that the words being sung penetrated Olivia's psyche. Jolson cried from the pain of his loneliness, from the heartache of missing his special someone. She could not have chosen a song that would hurt Elizabeth more. Olivia wanted to rip the record off the turntable.

But then she was distracted by a flood of arousal, as Elizabeth's fingers unconsciously flexed into Olivia's hip.

"Do you miss him, Miss Waters?"

Puzzled momentarily, Olivia needed a few seconds to get past the tender stroke of Mac's breath to her cheek. She found nothing inappropriate in her question about something so private. Rather, she was taken aback that Elizabeth concerned herself with Olivia's heart at all, particularly at a moment when her own surely ached. But Elizabeth's eyes were welcoming and sincere, and Olivia's heart opened in return.

"I've seen so little of Reggie this past year that I could be growing accustomed to life without him. That sounds callous of me, I'm afraid. I've found various pastimes on which to focus my attention, and that helps."

"You have an ideal life ahead, a loving future husband coming home to you."

The music stopped and Mrs. Finnegan and Carter giggled as they curtsied and bowed to each other. Olivia and Elizabeth just stood unmoving for an extra second before Elizabeth withdrew her hands and stepped back. She forced a smile and curtsied.

"A wonderful dance lesson, miss. You're an expert dancer. Thank you so much, Miss Waters."

Olivia responded with a similar curtsy, then leaned forward and grinned. "I hate curtsying."

Sending a discreet little cough into her handkerchief, her mother drew their attention to the staircase. "There's no dancing instruction at the reformatory, Elizabeth?"

Everyone watched her blush and look toward her shoes.

Olivia barely refrained from chastising her mother. "I would not imagine that training for domestic service included such a thing, Mother."

Elizabeth cleared her throat. "One Christmas, a band came and played at a general assembly," she said, glancing at Mrs. Finnegan and Carter. "And once, for the senior women, a recital of sorts. But there was never any dancing, Mrs. Waters." She curtsied.

Olivia released an aggravated sigh. "Well, now that we have this Victrola, there'll certainly be more of it around here. It will liven up the dead of winter ahead."

CHAPTER EIGHT

Dressed comfortably in her breeches and shirt, Mac set the dining room table for Carter and herself to sit opposite each other, and quickly returned to the kitchen.

"Here you go," he proclaimed, standing up from the oven with a pan of stuffed, roasted chicken. "She's a beauty, Mac."

They transferred it to an antique porcelain platter, and he took it into the dining room. Mac followed with bowls of boiled potatoes, carrots, squash, and cranberry sauce, then went back for the bread. Carter poured them brandies while Mac lit the seven-piece candelabra, and they both sat down, beaming across the table.

"Well!" Carter gushed. "Good Lord. Thank you, Mac. This is one of the finest spreads I have ever seen."

Mac nodded eagerly. "And you are very welcome, Carter. To think, it's all ours. Should keep us fed for a few days."

Grinning, Carter raised his cordial glass.

"To a very special friend. Merry Christmas, Mac."

Tears blurred her vision but didn't stop Mac from touching her glass to his.

"You are what friendship is all about, Carter. I'm never going to forget you or this Christmas."

They clinked glasses and drank, then dove into the food Mac had spent two days preparing from Mrs. Finnegan's directions. Even the pumpkin pie looked like pumpkin pie.

Their dinner conversation covered a world of topics, from current events to stories of their past, and Mac couldn't help but feel her fondness for Carter grow. Farm boy, soldier, lifelong friend, Carter exemplified everything she hoped to be: strong and resilient, smart and kind.

She put down her fork and sat back. "All this"—she gestured to the opulent dining room—"came from...bootlegging? You and Mr. Waters?"

Carter nodded as he speared a piece of chicken on his plate. Mac was glad when he looked her in the eye to answer.

"A topic not voiced anymore, but yup. We were in the same unit during the war and stayed in touch afterward. Jed made some pretty well-off connections working in Boston, brought me in on the action, and we moved stuff out west from here for three years. Damn, but didn't the money roll in like coal down the chute. When he passed last winter, the missus put a stop to it all."

"And so you stayed on here."

"I have no family left anyway. Besides, it was the right thing to do."

"But you could still make a fresh start, Carter. Couldn't you?"

He shrugged and resumed eating. "I'm getting old, Mac, and the need for my skills is dwindling with every day of this modern age. I have a fairly easy life with the Waterses, and they are good to me, so no. It's called not looking a gift horse in the mouth." He chuckled at that image and sipped his brandy. "You, however...Girl, you have everything to gain."

Mac frowned at him and waved her fork negatively. "Carter, what skills do I have? How to turn down a bed? Polish mahogany? How to crank that High Speed Wizard clothes washer?" She slumped back in her chair. "I need the practical stuff, you know? This dinner here is one of them. I never learned how to cook. Even if my mother *had* wanted to spend time with me, we never had much to cook anyway, so I was never home. But now, I think I can. I like it, in fact. And there are so many other things I'd like to try."

"Well, there you go. Your enthusiasm will get you far, Mac. Your choice of clothes may not, but your spirit will."

She snickered and stuck out her tongue at him. She gave her head a half shake. "Better happen fast, Carter, otherwise I'll be back on the streets with nothing, come next October."

She watched him lean forward to concentrate on his plate again. Carter had that bum leg, but he was a self-sufficient, self-made man.

Understanding and open-minded. Mac envied that and respected him greatly. Carter shoveled up the last of his squash with the last chunk of chicken, then set down his fork with finality.

"Goddamn!" He leaned back and rubbed his belly. "You showed some outstanding skill here, Elizabeth Mac McLaughlin, I do say! Can't eat another bite. And that's mighty unfortunate because I sure want to."

Mac laughed with him.

"Thanks. Did come out pretty good, if I do say so."

"What say you and me clean up here and go in that fancy parlor to talk? We can get a fire going, and I might even have some surprise beverages in the barn we can share."

They were on their feet quickly, piling dishes and collecting silverware.

"If you want to, Mac, I think there are some skills I could share with you while you're here."

Mac stopped halfway to the kitchen. "Yeah? Such as?"

"Well, for instance, you been rattling on and on about that Model T you're saving for. Once you get it, what are you going to do with it? You even know how to drive? What if something breaks? You don't know anything about cars, but I do." Mac's eyebrows rose. "And you know how to use a hammer and saw?" She shook her head, speechless as opportunities assailed her. "Well, I might need help fixing the stall that Teddy kicked down. Big damn dumb horse."

Mac bit her lower lip as her excitement mounted.

Carter was still talking as he walked ahead into the kitchen, his arms full of bowls. "And I know you lived a harder life than most and had to be...tough, but...you ever shot a gun? You must know how to fight, right? Protect yourself?"

Fight? Oh, yes. It was one skill in which she took great pride. But guns?

Mac hurried after him. The water in the stockpot she'd left to simmer was ready, and she filled the sink with it and began scrubbing, her mind a million miles away. It was a lot to absorb, Carter's generous offer and all it represented, and she was ready to take him up on all of it.

They spent the rest of Christmas night in front of the fireplace, a roaring blaze warming them in the upholstered wingback chairs drawn up close. Carter sent her memory reeling when he set six unlabeled brown bottles of beer on the table. They took their first long drinks and she soon had him laughing at tales of her old friends at the rail yard diluting stolen wine.

"Hard to find friends like that nowadays," he said on a sigh. "I gotta say, Jed Waters was a good friend. It really is why I ended up here, caring for his place. The family's been almost as close as the one I used to have." He took another swig of his beer. "I remember when Miss Olivia was just sixteen. The mister and missus had one helluva time with her. Was always crazy around the house. Wild child, she was." He laughed at the memory. "Think it's why the missus's hair is all gray today."

Mac shared his laugh, trying to visualize a rambunctious Olivia Waters. All that propriety and style powered by brains and an irrepressible spirit. "She and her mother fight a lot?"

"Ha. Oh, yes. As determined to do things her way as Jed. Only time there was peace around here was when he was home. A few days each week. She was either on that damn new telephone for hours or missing. The missus hated that Jed bought Sunny for the girl one Christmas. You could never find her once she learned how to ride. Just so independent."

Hours later, in bed and fuzzy of mind, Mac pondered the life a young girl might enjoy on this estate, the grand Christmas festivities, the galas, extravagant gifts. She wondered about Olivia Waters's version of fun and friends. Had it been her, Mac firmly believed, she'd have ridden miles every day to spend time with a special someone. Mac considered herself lucky, despite everything, to have grown up with Ellie just across the street.

❖

How Carter's new truck ended belly-up in the snow *inside* the corral, Olivia couldn't imagine. Peering out the kitchen window and into a slanting, late afternoon sun, she could see that the gate had been splintered nearly in half, but it made no sense that he'd drive in two feet of snow in the first place, let alone crash through the gate.

Large chunks of snow flew into the air intermittently from somewhere on the other side of the truck. Carter was trying to shovel himself out, obviously. She wondered if Teddy or Teddy with Sunny could pull the truck free.

Olivia left her purse on the kitchen table and re-buttoned the coat she had yet to take off. She wrapped her scarf around her neck and settled her hat firmly on her head, wishing she had her long hair again just to keep her neck and shoulders warm. The drastic bob she sported now had been a present to herself and quite the center of her friends' attention.

When her best friend Molly broke her leg on their third day, Olivia chose to accompany her home on the train, abbreviating their much-anticipated skiing vacation. Being a congressman's daughter, Molly called for a driver to pick them up and deliver Olivia all the way out to her front door. He then hauled Olivia's luggage into the foyer, and Olivia thanked him profusely, a bit surprised that Elizabeth hadn't helped.

As she had when she arrived, she tried calling out, but the house remained silent. Thinking back to the previous night at the New York lodge, Olivia remembered that no one had answered the telephone at the estate when she'd called to announce her change of plans.

Confounded and more than a little upset, she crunched along the snow-packed path toward the corral. Carter called out to her from the horse barn, and Olivia went to join him, looking back at the truck and the flying snow.

"Carter," she said on a heavy, frosty exhale.

"Miss Waters, you're home early."

"My God. What happened?" She turned back toward the truck again. "What poor friend of yours did you weasel into shoveling for you? And where in God's name is Elizabeth?"

"It's a long story, miss." He tossed his chin at the outside. "Just a little accident, actually. Don't you worry, though. We'll have the corral back in shape tomorrow morning."

"We?"

Carter grinned as he nodded. "Won't take long to fix that gate with Mac's help. Of course, we gotta get the truck out first."

Olivia watched him lead Teddy from his stall. Still surprised and a bit irked, she was mostly confused.

"So how did this happen? And, again, where is Elizabeth? No. Wait." She pointed outside. "His name is Mac? A friend of yours?"

Carter stopped working on Teddy's harness to respond but his eyes suddenly grew wide.

The nervous expression set Olivia on edge. "What's wrong?"

"Er…well…That's…that's Elizabeth."

Olivia's eyebrows shot up as her jaw dropped. "Elizabeth…*Mac*?" Admittedly, the nickname he had for her was rather cute. She looked at the truck and back to Carter. "*That's* where she is? She's shoveling for you?" She stormed out to the truck.

Through the broken corral gate, Olivia went directly to the far side of the truck, impressed to find it almost entirely cleared, right down to dirt. But the vision of Elizabeth—completely unexpected and totally foreign—jerked her feet to a halt. Stooped and shoveling with abandon, this slim figure before her huffed hard breaths into the air like a locomotive, and dressed in breeches, boots, jacket, and cap, certainly didn't resemble anyone Olivia had ever met before.

Who was she, really? Should they re-introduce themselves? Olivia didn't know how to react. In a steady but anxious voice, she tried out the name Carter used. "Mac?"

The shovel chucked into the snow bank and froze in place. Olivia watched acutely as Elizabeth slowly straightened, exhaled a visible breath, and turned.

"Miss Waters."

Olivia didn't mean to stare but couldn't pull her eyes from the wary expression. She tried to gauge the mindset behind the steady gaze. No defiance or insolence. Nervousness, however, was evident. *She knows I've caught her in the role of this alter ego, or whatever this is.*

Olivia approached slowly, hands in her coat pockets, her head slightly cocked in curiosity. Her eyes never left Elizabeth's and, from several feet away, she searched for the proper opening question. "I… Honestly, I…Oh my. I don't know where to begin."

"I'm responsible for this disaster, Miss Waters. A driving lesson that went very badly. So I'm doing my best to help. Starting with the truck. Miss Waters."

Olivia gave the truck a distracted glance. She returned her eyes with slow deliberation.

"*Mac*?" she queried, bewildered.

"Yes, Miss Waters?" Suddenly, Elizabeth appeared to understand the question. Her puzzled expression dissipated as her face slackened and frown lines eased. "Oh. I mean, yes, Miss Waters."

Standing perfectly still, Olivia inspected every inch of her. She could practically see Elizabeth sweat. Moist cheeks, jaw, and neck shimmered in the winter sunset, and when Elizabeth swiped away a droplet at her eye, Olivia fleetingly thought of offering her handkerchief.

But this was no casual encounter. Nor was it a simple employer-employee interaction. There was more to this than Olivia could pinpoint. An intimacy that made her rather unsteady.

She flicked her eyes up to Mac's cap, which sat jauntily askew over part of her forehead. Caked with snow, it hinted at the daring, adventuresome personality that Olivia suspected lay restrained beneath the feminine façade she'd come to know.

The short jacket hardly qualified for winter apparel, and it dawned on Olivia then, where she'd seen it before. It was Carter's. Elizabeth had to be freezing under the thick canvas material.

And the breeches and tall boots...Well, obviously, they weren't Carter's. Elizabeth somehow must have purchased them for herself. They looked to be a perfect fit, and lent Elizabeth such a remarkable air of strength and stability that Olivia could only shake her head. She envisioned her half dozen friends on the ski slope ogling such an independent woman...envious...charmed...

Elizabeth shuffled her feet and adjusted her jacket collar. The antsy movements drew Olivia from her musing.

"I'm sorry to keep you," she said hurriedly. "I'm sure you're getting cold."

"Well..." Elizabeth shrugged. "It's just..." She gestured toward the setting sun. "The daylight."

Olivia nodded, holding Elizabeth's gaze for an extra second. "Yes, of course." She had so many questions, she didn't know where to start. "We'll continue this inside when you're done."

Rather than look and sound like a bumbling fool, Olivia wrapped her arms around herself and followed the path back to the house.

Carter appeared at the rear of the truck with Teddy in tow.

Mac still stood staring distantly at the kitchen door, and exhaled hard when she noticed him.

"I'm sorry, Mac," he said, and the big, black Morgan bobbed his head and issued a frosty double-barreled snort as if in agreement. "Mac...jeez. I don't know why she's home early. Maybe she telephoned while we were out here. We *have* been spending days and nights in the barn."

Mac nodded. "We'll find out soon enough."

❖

Mac stomped off the excess snow on the back step and hurried inside. She seriously doubted that Olivia carried her own luggage upstairs, so she draped her wet mittens over the drying rod behind the stove and rushed to the foyer.

Sitting in the parlor next to the fire, Olivia intercepted her. "In here, please."

Mac stepped to the doorway and inhaled the nostalgic scent of the wood smoke and Christmas tree. She wanted so badly to just linger and gaze at the view; Olivia, so vibrant, enchanting in such a setting, the firelight warming her skin, making her jeweled eyes dance.

She took a breath and shook off the dangerous mental image. She was unsure of her next move or words. *You should have changed, stupid. Does one curtsy in breeches? Apologize now for your actions, your dereliction of duty, your appearance. Do I insult the Waters family honor just by being Mac? Does she now think I'm a sneak and second-guesses everything I've said and done?*

Olivia waved her into the room, her eyes steady and unreadable.

"Come stand by the fire. And take that jacket off or you'll never warm up."

With cautious strides, Mac reached the hearth without breathing. She made a conscious decision to look only at the flames. *I hate it when my head spins this way.* She unbuttoned the jacket and slipped it off, gathering it all in one hand at her side, feeling as if she'd bared her soul.

Knowing inquisitive eyes were upon her, she dared try for a distraction. "That's a terrific hairstyle. Very courageous of you, Miss Waters."

"I appreciate you saying so."

Mac continued to stare at the fire and wondered if the compliment had even registered. She figured Olivia shook her head at the sight of her men's white shirt and red suspenders. Her back and shoulders tingled from the inspection she knew was under way. Even her ass, her legs felt warm from it. She was unnerved, disconcerted, and close to resenting such unabashed gawking. She removed her cap and slicked back her wet hair.

Olivia cleared her throat. "Do you prefer the nickname to your real name?"

"I do," Mac said quietly. "It's how I came to be known at the reformatory, Miss Waters."

She kept her eyes on the fire. It was better than looking at her feet and appearing ashamed. Because she wasn't. This was who she was. The only problem was that it would cost her her freedom.

"And is this your preferred style of dress?"

"It is. Since I was young. It's more practical, Miss Waters."

"Practical." Olivia paused as if considering the word. "Then, after five years in a prison dress, you must feel liberated."

"Yes, Miss Waters."

"Please," Olivia said, standing quickly. "I'd prefer it if you'd call me Olivia."

Mac turned her back to the fire and fussed with her jacket. "I've violated too many rules already, Miss Waters. It's against proper—"

"I'll be the judge of that."

Olivia went to the bookcase and poured each of them whiskeys. Mac enjoyed the view, the sway of her hips and the expensive fabric around them. The hunter green dress was rather short, hemmed with fringe at her knees. Quite a bit on the risqué side. But such alluring legs were practically irresistible and Mac found it hard to turn away before they started back in her direction.

The coy smile on Olivia's heavily painted ruby lips said she knew where Mac's eyes had been.

"This will warm you up." Olivia held the glass just out of reach until Mac's eyes found hers. "Now, what's my name?"

Mac couldn't help but grin. And Olivia apparently appreciated it and smiled back.

"Olivia," Mac softly conceded, taking the offered glass.

"And what's yours?"

"Mac."

Olivia set her glass to Mac's. "There. We've gotten *that* far, at least."

Their fingers pressed together and they quickly looked up from their glasses. The engaging sensation that rippled up Mac's arm gave her pause. *Did she feel that too?* They both promptly downed their whiskey.

Mac frowned at her empty glass. "I'm not sup—I can't be... friends with my employer."

Olivia took her glass and crossed the room to refill it. "Well," she said at last, and sounded somewhat annoyed as she returned. "I don't see the harm." She handed the drink to Mac. "Actually, in some cases, isn't that impossible to avoid? Wouldn't you agree? In our case, you've even seen me naked...*Mac*."

Mac's wind-burned cheeks warmed and out of the corner of her eye, she saw Olivia smile fondly. Mac released a slow, calming breath and did her best to avoid eye contact. "It's a regulation that, in providing our service, we don't become too...familiar."

Olivia sipped her whiskey and took a half step closer. She arched a brow and slipped her index finger beneath one of Mac's suspenders, gripped it between forefinger and thumb. Slowly, she slid her hand up several inches to Mac's shoulder and back down to just above her breast. The back of her hand warmed Mac's chest, caused her breath to catch.

"*This* is being 'too familiar,'" Olivia whispered, and withdrew her hand at last. She smiled softly, her eyes momentarily falling to Mac's lips, and then turned and sat down, gesturing Mac toward the opposite chair. "I would very much like to be simply Olivia and Mac—to each other."

Mac nodded, almost begrudgingly. This was dangerous. It would be hard to do, and she doubted she could avoid slipping in front of Mrs. Waters. She smiled faintly.

"Mac, I think we both know that Mother will never approve of any of this, you addressing me casually, using a man's nickname, and goodness, wearing those clothes!" Olivia slapped her palm to her cheek in mock horror. That brought a wry smile to Mac's face.

With a seductively arched brow, Olivia leaned forward. "I, on the other hand, have no problem with them at all. In fact"—she sat back regally—"I'll go so far as to confess that I find you to be the most handsome woman I've ever seen."

Mac's eyes grew wide and Olivia smiled, nodding in confirmation.

"Oh, absolutely. I'll tell you, Mac, that my friends and I associate with quite the happy-go-lucky crowd. All types of men and women from all walks of life. We travel through affluent circles with lavish parties, and we visit the speakeasies with their wild shindigs. All have outrageous goings-on, the drinking, narcotics, the back room rendezvous. And I don't say this to shock you, but yes, my friends and I have partaken on more than a few occasions. There are women as brave as you, dressing as they wish, being true to themselves, and we are as intrigued by them as we are envious. I dare say, quite charmed."

Mac had barely caught her breath, hardly made it past "most handsome woman," and Olivia had added "brave," "envious," and "charmed." Mac leaned forward on her knees, running a hand through her hair again in frustration.

"Frankly, I don't know if any decision of mine is worthy of envy, Mis—I mean, Olivia."

"Oh, *so* untrue, Mac." Olivia rose and hurried across the rug to her.

For some reason she could not sit idly by while Mac minimized her self-worth. Boldly, she knelt, took Mac's hands, and sat back on her heels. "Here we are," she began earnestly, "on the eve of nineteen hundred twenty-five, well into the twentieth century, and we are women still bound by outdated traditional and foolish *man*-made rules just as surely as by ball and chain. Don't you see? The time has come for women to step out, be proud of who we are. We will make the world a far better place."

Mac absorbed every word, felt Olivia's vehemence down into her fingertips, and agreed with this new-age mind set, but she frowned at the tempting woman kneeling before her.

"Your enthusiasm is infectious, Olivia, but it just isn't that easy. I am serving a *prison sentence* here. I have to be the woman they've created 'for the public welfare,' or some such…shit." Olivia grinned at

Mac's cursing. "But I do agree with your point. Once my sentence is done, I will be myself, no matter what. And no tradition, no etiquette book, no protocol, and no fucking law will stop me."

Olivia's grin broadened into a smile as the passion poured out. Mac's eyes blackened with fervor, her large, placid hands escaped Olivia's grasp and flexed into vehement fists. Her crooning voice dropped an octave and nearly growled. Olivia was enthralled by the emergence of Mac's heart onto her sleeve.

How friends, family, lovers must thrive around such vitality, Olivia pondered. Someone with so much heart and drive…Someone obviously impossible to dismiss. Olivia welcomed the lively dance of Mac's eyes across her face, almost tangible in their touch, and suddenly she wanted nothing more than just that. A touch.

"God," Mac groaned abruptly, dropping her face into her hands. "I apologize for letting loose like that…forgetting my place. You're being unbelievably kind, and I truly appreciate that. It means so much to me. But I seriously don't think society will be ready for changes like me for a long, long time."

Olivia would not let this moment pass. She couldn't. She straightened up on her knees, reached out, and lifted Mac's face with both hands. Mac's eyes closed at the contact and Olivia willed herself to continue. She slipped her palms along Mac's firm jaws and combed her fingers through her hair, sweeping back the unruly strands. Her hair was cool and still damp with sweat and snow, and Olivia fought a powerful urge to cup Mac's head to her chest and just hold her.

But cold fingers tenderly encircled Olivia's wrists and drew her hands away. Their faces just inches apart, Mac lowered her voice to a whisper, and her breath caressed Olivia's lips.

"You are an amazing woman, Olivia, and, God, so beautiful. But you know this should not happen."

Olivia bit her lower lip anxiously. Her hushed words shook. "Mac, I…I want to be kissed by you."

Mac clenched her eyes shut. When she opened them, they fell upon Olivia's plush lips and she looked up quickly.

Olivia didn't want her to speak, to voice the uncertainty in her eyes. She wanted more of that undaunted vitality, that courageous attitude—and action. But Mac disappointed her.

"Olivia. So help me, I want to kiss you, but we can't. I can't."

"Tell me why."

"Because I don't kiss my…"

"You don't kiss your who? Your boss?"

"Or girlfriends. They're friends. Kissing is…It's for…that someone special, when you're in love."

Olivia sat back on her heels but clung to Mac's hands. "That same someone special you said you try not to think about? He must have been very special to have you holding on, despite yourself."

Mac knew it wouldn't be worth ruining this moment with an inquisition, the curious stare, maybe even the dismay incurred by telling Olivia about Ellie. She stared at their entwined fingers. "I'll get past it."

"Well, if there comes a time you want to talk about him, I'd be honored to listen." She squeezed Mac's hands. "And, by the way, I think it's an impossibly difficult challenge, but you are incredibly sweet and noble to save your kisses for love."

Mac shrugged and swiped at the pesky strands of hair crossing her vision. "Sorta childish, I guess, considering this day and age. No Puritans around anymore, are there?"

Olivia smiled back and shook her head. "No, Mac. No Puritans." She used her fingers again, and combed Mac's hair back. "Today's modern woman wouldn't stand for Puritans. Feelings are nothing to fear."

Mac turned to face her, to disagree, but found Olivia's lips just a breath away. *This should not happen. Don't start what you can't finish.* Olivia closed the distance between them, leaned into Mac between her knees, and a consuming wave of heat rolled through Mac's body. The tenderness of Olivia's kiss, the delicate draw on her lips was exquisite, and the tiny moan that rose from Olivia's throat nearly melted Mac where she sat. She deepened their kiss and Olivia responded in kind, leaning closer for more.

All the air left Mac's lungs and her heart beat drowned out the fire's crackling, their shortened breaths, and most of her conscience. Olivia's similar desire was evident in her kiss and the temptation to take her into her arms vibrated in Mac's hands. She withdrew carefully.

This would be all they could share and Mac hoped Olivia

understood. Words failed her when she recognized the sympathy in Olivia's hazy eyes and wondered if her own cautious reluctance was as readable.

Olivia tightened her grip on Mac's fingers. "There's a fire inside you, Mac," she whispered, "and for someone who's battling for the right to live her own life, I know it'll take something far greater than a kiss to ignite it." She ran a fingertip across Mac's lips. "But I will remember that one for a lifetime."

With a twinge of loss, Mac watched her rise gracefully and straighten her dress. Truly stunning, she thought, the seductive figure, the perfect complexion, enticing smile. But as she looked up into Olivia's hauntingly remarkable eyes, deepened by the shadowy remnants of makeup, she saw much more. It was one thing to imagine Olivia, bewitching and titillating in full makeup, dolled up for a night on the town... How all the men must drool. But no imagination was required for Mac to appreciate Olivia's heart and soul.

"I guess..." Olivia chuckled as she turned away. "I guess we got distracted, didn't we?" She settled into the wingback, her eyes distant. "Actually, I think *I* took us off course, Mac. I apologize."

Mac offered a resigned smile. "It was a special kiss, Olivia. *You* are very special."

Olivia's smile was toward the fire, remote and reflective. "So..." she began on a deep breath, "please tell me about this driving lesson. Obviously, you need more. And I just may want some as well."

Resolutely, Mac dropped back into the recesses of her chair. Her body was thrumming, warm and energized, nowhere near ready to turn off the staggering emotion Olivia evoked in her. She grinned at Olivia and could only shake her head.

Ten more months could take forever.

CHAPTER NINE

Lounging in April's late-afternoon sunshine, Mac lay on her bed reading the tattered three-day-old *Post* that she'd nearly memorized since Carter brought it home from town. The idle hour before supper preparations gave her time to think, clear her head. She often needed to nap by this time of day but seldom slept; her busy brain usually refused to relax. There was always so much to think about.

Grabbing ten or fifteen minutes throughout the day had been all she looked forward to through the dreary winter. But once the good weather arrived, the Waters women's social calendars filled up, and by April, both were frequently away, significantly lessening demands on Mac's time. Just the opposite was true for poor Carter, however. He was dragged all over the countryside, frequently as far as Boston, taxiing one or both of them on errands, visits, or to civic functions. Olivia had put the man through four driving lessons thus far and still couldn't be trusted not to crash or strip the gears.

Mac, on the other hand, chomped at the bit to race on the road. Her driving skills made Carter beam proudly, but she had grown bored with puttering across meadows. She kept a close eye on the prices of Model Ts in the *Post*. She tacked a clipping of the car to the wall by her calendar for inspiration. She didn't have even a quarter of the price saved yet with only six months to go. However, she did have thirty dollars set aside for renting a room and for food and clothes until she found some work. But she'd give nearly anything to buy that car.

Which just made finding work that much more of an imperative. She set the paper aside and stared at the smooth plaster-and-beam ceiling. Funny how some people were just born into certain worlds, she thought, like she was to a poor Boston family, scraping by—stealing to put food on the table…Like Olivia, born into the high life, never knowing what it was like to worry about a meal or an income. Mac couldn't help but be amused by Olivia's worries about her hair and fashion accessories, all that makeup or showing off those glamorous legs…

Mac smiled. And glamorous they certainly were. As enticing as her sparkling eyes, the soft touch of her hands, and the surrender in her kiss. She replayed *that* moment in her mind for the thousandth time. Olivia hadn't made any further advances or even called her "Mac" privately in the past months, and Mac had to admit it was a bit disappointing. But there were several occasions when she'd caught Olivia's prolonged gaze and wondered if Olivia revisited their encounter as vividly as she still did.

Mac strained her ears for activity elsewhere in the house but heard none. The tranquility was heavenly. Mrs. Waters was attending her Daughters of the American Revolution convention in Saratoga and wouldn't be returning for a week. Olivia was upstairs dozing before Carter transported her to the Framingham train for yet another weekend romp with friends. Mac gave serious consideration to changing into her "normal clothes," despite upsetting Mrs. Finnegan, just to poke around the estate, the gardens, and the barns.

But Carter's raised voice caught her attention. He never yelled. She gathered up her skirt and raced out to the horse barn but found it empty. Behind the car barn next door, however, three delivery trucks were lined up, two from a Boston hardware store and the other from a Charlestown bakery. Carter's voice was drowned out as another man shouted him down.

Mac peeked around the back door until they came into view. Carter was up against a towering pile of crates and surrounded by six men, one of whom had a pistol pointed at Carter's chest.

"Ten thousand, just like it's always been," the gunman yelled into Carter's face.

"And I told you those days are long gone," Carter snapped back. "We ain't been on your route for a year now, not since Jed died, so don't expect to just appear and get money."

The gunman stepped close enough to jam the barrel tip under

Carter's chin. Mac ran a hand back through her hair nervously, wishing there was something she could do.

"The boss says Waters takes it from here. Says we get paid for the drop, you got that?" He shoved harder and slammed Carter's shoulders against the wall of crates. The clinking of glass was loud in the barn, and Mac realized what the boxes contained. "So you get your gimpy ass into that fancy mansion and get us our fuckin' money."

"Nobody home knows where the safe is, let alone a combination."

The gunman slashed the pistol across Carter's face and he dropped to his knees. Mac nearly lurched out into the open to help him. *Fucking sons of bitches. If I had a gun...*

Mac brought herself up short.

There *was* a gun. In the horse barn, the old US Army Colt .45 revolver that Carter taught her to use last month. Everyone had been away then, too, and Mrs. Finnegan had fumed royally at the impropriety of it all, but Carter had given her daily lessons for a week. She knew enough. Mac retrieved it from the dusty little box beneath a bench in the tack room and shakily dropped as many bullets as she loaded. The gun held only six, so she stuffed a handful into her skirt pocket. *Goddamn uniform. Breeches would've had more pockets. Yeah, like you're even going to shoot the thing.*

By the time she returned to the car barn doorway, the men had bloodied both sides of Carter's face. Two men held him upright, while another punched Carter's stomach and face alternately. Blood splattered from his cheeks, nose, and mouth with each blow.

"Enough," the gunman ordered, and the men let Carter fall to the floor. The gunman used the toe of his boot to turn Carter's face toward him. Then he pointed the gun at Carter's forehead. "Either you get in there and get our money or we go tear the fuckin' place apart and get it ourselves. Your choice. Of course, you make us do all that work and I'm gonna blow your fuckin' brains out."

The others laughed at the proposition, and the gunman barked without taking his eyes off Carter. "Jack, go see what you can see in the windows up there. Don't need no wife and kids or fuckin' servants callin' the cops once they hear the shot."

Mac didn't think her heart could pound so hard and not burst. She couldn't breathe.

Move! Now!

She ducked back around the corner of the building and gripped the Colt by its barrel, then raised it over her head and waited.

Within seconds, she heard the rapid scuffling of shoes in the gravel, and when the one called Jack hustled past her position, she stepped up and smashed the pistol butt onto his head. The severe impact knocked him unconscious and the gun from her hand, but she caught the Colt in a crouch before it hit the ground—just as another figure rounded the barn.

Before either of them had an instant to think, Mac lunged up out of her crouch and whipped the Colt barrel across his face. She even heard the bone crack as the bridge of his nose broke and he collapsed to the ground.

Mac raced to the house and nearly ripped the door off its hinges. "Mrs. Finnegan!"

Mac bolted across the kitchen and flung open the door to the cook's private quarters. Mrs. Finnegan had been knitting, and needles and yarn flew out of her hands at Mac's entrance.

"Telephone..." Mac said on half a breath. "Police! Hurry! Guys hurting Carter! Call!"

Mac was gone, racing back to the barn. With her skirt bunched in one hand, Colt in the other, she listened to her feet pound like heartbeats, and wondered just what the hell to do next.

From her hiding spot at the car barn's back door, she watched the gunman pace. He looked down at Carter occasionally, maybe to see if he was still breathing. Which he was, she noted.

"We give 'em fifteen more minutes," the gunman declared. "They're probably taking care of whoever's up there. Then we go in. We'll take him, too."

Mac found it incredibly ironic she was praying for the swift arrival of the police.

The man stood over Carter and extended his gun arm, taking serious aim at Carter's face. He chuckled and Mac shivered.

"Could take out one eye at a time," he boasted to his men, still squinting down the barrel at Carter. "Ever tell you guys how I took out that Kraut prisoner in France?"

"Ahuh."

"Yep."

"Twice."

The gunman angled his head, apparently trying out different firing positions. "You bet. Kept mouthin' off at us. So I took off his right ear. Son of a bitch still wouldn't answer our questions. That's when I put the next shot dead center in his left eye." He lifted the pistol and turned to grin at his accomplices.

They grinned back, obediently, and began wandering around the barn. One of them offered to try his hand at safecracking once they found the Waterses' treasure. Another offered to make Carter "disappear." The third was enthralled by Carter's Runabout pickup and thought it should be part of their payment.

The gunman sighed impatiently. "We find the safe, we rip it out of the fuckin' wall. If we don't find it, we'll take enough stuff from the house to keep the boss happy and get us our cut. And yeah, that truck should be worth some serious dough."

Then Mac nearly fainted when she saw Olivia brazenly walk through the barn's front doors.

She had fire in her eyes and an antique Revolutionary War rifle aimed at the men.

"Just what do you think you're doing?"

How could I forget she was in the house? Mac blinked in hopes the vision would be different. *That thing hangs over the fireplace. She can't think they'll fall for it.*

"Well, sweet Jesus. What have we here?" the gunman said.

"You heard me, mister. You better put that gun down or I'll shoot."

All the men laughed roundly.

"First of all," the gunman said, slowly closing on her. "I'm the one with the real gun here."

"This is a very real—"

"Second of all, that thing doesn't even shoot bullets, Miss Davey Crocket."

"It most certainly—"

"And third of all, even if it did shoot something—assuming you knew how to load it and it didn't blow the fuck up in your pretty face—it would only be once." He glanced over his shoulder at the three men, grinning. He turned back in a flash and yanked the rifle from Olivia's hands by the barrel. "Now. That's much better. Bet you're Jed's daughter?"

Olivia jammed her fists onto her hips, her face nearly as red as her hair. "I certainly am, and I don't know what's going on here, but I can clearly see you've hurt Carter—"

"Eh, so he's not so cute anymore. A good tape job on those ribs and he'll be the same gimp he's always been." He hurled the long rifle into the far corner of the barn.

Olivia steamed. "The police are on their way and they're going to take you all in!"

The man sitting on the Runabout's bumper quickly jumped to his feet. "We can't hang around here, Vito, money or no money."

"Yeah," agreed another. "Boss'd rather lose the load than hand us over to the cops…I think."

Vito fingered the fine silk of Olivia's sleeve and then ran his fingertips through her hair. Olivia slapped him so hard he took a sideways stutter step.

With his men snorting in amusement, he backhanded Olivia across the face. No sooner had she landed hard on her ass, he reached down, grabbed her upper arm, and gruffly hauled her to her feet. "Then we take what we can of value and leave."

"Get your hands off. Let me go, damn it!"

He dragged her along as he stormed toward the back door.

"You're taking her with us, Vito?"

"Why not? Don't you think she's worth a pretty penny?" He pulled her to his side and snickered. "I bet Miss Waters just can't wait to go for a ride with us boys. Ain't that right, sweetheart?"

As Olivia cursed like a sailor and twisted against his grip, they made their way to the doorway where Mac waited.

Where are the damn cops?

Mac unhooked the upright oak crossbar used to keep the barn doors closed and prepared to let it swing down onto selected heads as they emerged. She cocked the hammer back on the heavy Colt and aimed it at the doorway.

At the first sign of their hats, Mac let the twelve-foot plank go. As it crashed directly atop one man's head and across another's shoulders,

Mac rushed at the group from the side and shoved the tip of the Colt's barrel directly into Vito's ear.

"Drop it!" she shouted at his face.

In severe pain, he tried to lean away, but Mac grabbed his jacket and pulled him closer, pressing the gun barrel inward.

"Don't even *think* about moving an inch!" she yelled, tossing her head for Olivia to separate herself from the stunned man. "Drop that gun or, so help me God, I will put a bullet in your fucking head."

Vito held his breath. She could tell he was debating whether to believe a crazed maid.

The man behind him froze in place. "Two of us can take her, Vito."

Mac screwed the barrel farther into his ear with all the strength she had. He winced and squeezed his eyes shut.

"Go ahead, Vito," she said, jerking him by his jacket with each word, which only drove the gun barrel farther into his ear. "Tell him, Vito. Tell him to just bump me," she insisted, jerking him again. "Go on. Let's all see what happens when my finger twitches on this trigger."

Vito let out a slow breath. "Rudy, shut up."

"Okay, Rudy," Mac said quietly, "you come out here and join your moaning pals. Out here. Slowly. So we can see you."

They heard the sirens approaching as Rudy stepped gingerly around Vito and came out of the barn.

"And you, Vito, my new friend," Mac said, "now's a good time to drop your gun."

❖

The dapper young man took hold of Olivia's hand atop the dining room table and Mac almost let a snicker slip out.

In his three-piece Brooks Brothers suit and white bow tie, Reginald J. Lowry Jr. was the epitome of high style. However, his subdued monotone deflated all emotion in everything he said and seemed to take all the flare and excitement out of the tale Olivia now told. Mac wondered if he even raised an eyebrow at anything; surely Olivia must arouse him. That was one thought too many, she told herself, and returned to the kitchen.

"Is he even breathing?" Mac whispered to Mrs. Finnegan.

"Oh, dear lass," she said with a laugh. "You'll become accustomed to his reserved manner soon enough. I dare say we all have some readjusting to do, he's been away so long."

"Oh, he's reserved all right. Maybe his bow tie is too tight." Mac shook her head. "I just don't get what she sees in him." She refilled the creamers and sugar bowls, and tea and coffee pots, and headed back to the dining room, wishing she was someplace other than Reginald's welcome-home dinner party. Anyplace but close enough to witness this ridiculous affair. What a vivacious, intelligent woman, someone as beautiful and full of life as Olivia found attractive in this tree stump, Mac couldn't imagine.

Three rings and multiple bracelets glittered in the chandelier light as Olivia positioned her forefinger and thumb like a pistol and stuck it in Reginald's ear. "Just like that," she stated, boasting a smile as genuine and brilliant as her jewelry.

"In his ear?" Disbelieving, Reginald turned in his seat slightly to look at Mac, who stood at her post in the doorway.

Olivia looked as well, her eyes ablaze, and winked when she caught Mac's eye. Mac simply grinned, absurdly moved by the secret signal, and politely averted her eyes. Reginald and the other guests looked back to Olivia. He frowned. "Goodness, my love!" Now he had her hand in both of his.

Olivia was too animated to sit still. "I tell you, Reggie, it was a scene fit for the Shubert! Elizabeth told him"—Mac cringed inside, knowing it wasn't Olivia's style to even consider censoring her words of that day—"'Drop that gun, or so help me God, I'll put a bullet in your fucking head.'"

Mac's stomach dropped.

Everyone at the table gasped at the vulgarity and all heads turned toward Mac. She didn't dare look up. *Jesus Christ, did she have to say that at the dinner table?*

Olivia, meanwhile, was completely caught up in the memory. Clapping her hands together in delight, she continued, "Oh it was perfect! Just the language that thug understood in an instant!"

Mrs. Waters glared from the far end of the table. Mac could feel it, hot and scorching like a clothes iron pressed to her face.

"The language of a thug, indeed," Mrs. Waters growled.

Reggie sent Mac another reproachful look. "My dearest Olivia. All I can say to that is...such profanity while in your presence better have achieved the necessary goal."

Mac wondered if Olivia truly took stuffed shirts like him seriously. Maybe she, and everyone else for that matter, was just used to him, or oblivious, or maybe they were just ignoring him. *Actually, they're all like him anyway...except for her.*

"Reggie, he was so afraid, I was able to escape his grasp. Elizabeth was holding them at bay with her pistol when the police arrived."

❖

That "Great Gangster Caper," as Olivia fondly named it, kept the household abuzz—and on edge—for months. Till after the Fourth of July. After hearing about the ordeal, Mrs. Waters obsessed about repercussions, about revenge, claiming she knew "that type" never gave up on "matters of honor." And the "Caper" had cost one of Boston's major bootleggers ten grand worth of honor. That was a lot to forgive and forget.

Mac spent many an hour pondering the event and the fate of those men. The police had confiscated the alcohol as evidence, except for several cases that Detectives Moore and Boranski left with Mrs. Waters and Carter on the sly. But it wasn't until summer began that Mac learned through Carter that the thugs had somehow avoided prison time and were back in Boston. *And you wondered why you never had to testify.* Some things never changed, she realized sadly. *These bootlegger gangs have friends everywhere. And apparently, booze can get you anything because everyone wants it.*

But still it intrigued Mac that the Waters name had significant connections to this illegal trade. The "interstate commerce" business Jed worked had been so much more than the family let on, and obviously was still going strong without him. *This Volstead prohibition is quite the joke.*

So it didn't surprise Mac that Mrs. Waters had grown agitated since the "Caper." She knew plenty about the business and the type of men who ran it. Mac wondered how much Olivia really knew, although such a socially active young woman most likely hadn't paid much attention to her father's affairs at the time. Chances were good that Mrs. Waters did everything in her power to distance her precious daughter from that life and its criminal influences.

That explained Mrs. Waters's managerial approach regarding Mac at the estate. *After all, the paperwork for your pre-release listed you as a low-life arsonist who lived off the streets, obviously not above stealing and violence.* Mrs. Waters piled on the chores and doubled them if she even perceived of a flaw in Mac's work. It aggravated Mac no end, but reformatory life had taught her how to reserve her bitterness for her private time. Still, it didn't help having that needy, stuffed-shirt milquetoast floating around the estate. Reggie almost pushed Mac to her breaking point with endless requests for tea and freshly laundered shirts.

The increased workload succeeded in keeping Mac housebound to the point where lesson time with Carter nearly disappeared. Having to withstand this imprisonment and its degradation was one thing, but losing the small pleasures that bolstered her pride and self-esteem and lent her hope for her future threatened to spill her spirit into a well of deep depression. *If you've already "bucked up," can you "double buck up"?*

❖

Mac began forgoing midday meals to spend time in the barns, refusing to miss an opportunity to drive the pickup around the estate or study the mechanics of the vehicle. Occasionally, she'd rush out to wherever Carter was working and grab a hammer to help. And she'd become quite enamored of the Colt .45, developing a fine eye at target practice whenever Carter managed to take Mrs. Waters out for one of her excursions.

Often, Mac took advantage of time alone in the horse barn to revitalize an old, tried-and-true skill: punching a suspended burlap sack of hay into oblivion. She had to hand it to her brother Ray for teaching her the art of boxing at such a young age. As his sparring partner of three years, she was impressive; as a skilled boxer-turned-street fighter, she was ferocious.

When the house retired at night, Mac burned her lamp past midnight, voraciously studying the Runabout's owner's manual, analyzing Carter's firearms catalogs, and dreaming about items in the latest one from Sears Roebuck.

So many fine, remarkable things fed her fantasies. You could rig a canvas on a folding frame over the Runabout's bed and sleep under cover anywhere you wanted. There were also large knobby tires you could put on the truck to master any terrain.

And Mac was intrigued by the wickedly expensive little rifle called the Thompson submachine gun, which cost half the price of her beloved Ford. The damn thing could fire more than eight hundred cartridges a minute! Mac had never even *seen* eight hundred rounds, never mind a gun that could waste them in the blink of an eye. It was nicknamed "The Bandit Gun" in an advertisement for law enforcement types, and Mac easily understood why. She didn't doubt that bandits had them, too.

And just when she thought she'd seen it all, there was good ol' Sears Roebuck selling houses by the "kit." Three or four thousand bucks got you a home you put together yourself. She just had to shake her head in awe and accept that she'd need a lot more carpentry lessons from Carter. And one hell of a good job.

Mac longed to talk about all these things, about the world that awaited her. It was late August and, thank God, she only had two months to go, but she was almost as anxious as she was excited. She longed for someone her own age to whom she could relate, someone who could clue her in to what was in store. Carter and Mrs. Finnegan were good listeners, but Mac sorely missed the Olivia she'd met during the winter.

Remembering that special afternoon in the parlor sent a little thrill down Mac's spine. The conversation had been relatively brief, but powerful. Olivia opened herself to Mac, shared things that sat deep inside, and drew Mac a bit out of herself, let her actually breathe.

Olivia's spirit just sparked everywhere she went. There was a contagious enthusiasm in her voice, her smile...and her eyes. She broadcasted an optimistic, fearless anticipation that surged toward Mac's heart like a dawning sun lightens the sky.

Olivia may have wanted a special, intimate friendship back in December, but she respected Mac's rejection. Mac appreciated that, knowing her heart couldn't be trusted and that salvaging her life was everything. Nevertheless, it had stirred Mac's battered heart to be the one sharing serious conversation...to be the object of Olivia's desire and her sensuous kiss.

It had been quite some time since a kiss had set her back so. At Sherborn, Penny McMichael sneaked a kiss in the laundry room, and the sly Abigail Willis cornered Mac in the library a time or two, but those encounters never stirred enough arousal to overcome the fear of repercussions. Olivia's kiss, however, stole Mac's breath and nearly all her rational thought. It was a kiss Mac yearned to repeat until she lost all composure and restraint, and surrendered everything to a single soul. Until she found heaven on earth again—with Ellie.

Part of "bucking up," Mac lectured herself, was overcoming obstacles by focusing on the present and doing it right.

CHAPTER TEN

Mac was elbow-deep in rich black earth, harvesting potatoes from Mrs. Finnegan's insanely large garden. She volunteered for the hard labor to spare Mrs. Finnegan all the shoveling, weeding, kneeling, and carrying. She also knew that, inevitably, it would be added to her list of chores, which now included lugging bushel baskets of green beans, cucumbers, tomatoes, summer squash, sugar beets, and whatever else came out of the garden across an acre of meadow back to the kitchen. Mac had the hardest time rationalizing a garden the size of Massachusetts for a household of five. And she thought that whoever made such decisions went one step too far when they planted it in the next county. There'd never be a chance of packing on the pounds working this estate.

To Mac, that was an indisputable fact, and she had the body to prove it. She'd always appeared too thin for her height; after all, the name "Stick" hadn't come from nowhere. But the reformatory's routine "ladylike" chores and lard-based meals had rounded her body's sharp angles somewhat and softened her look. And she deeply resented it, accusing the prison system of trying to define her gender to suit the men in power.

However, after ten months of domestic servitude, the last four of which included tending the "farm," as she called it, Mac's physique changed and she stole looks in Olivia's long dressing mirror whenever she could just to marvel at it. What she saw helped bolster her shaky self-confidence: not only would her piercing eyes be taken seriously, but she'd be physically capable of tackling any job she wanted.

The line of her jaw sank a bit deeper beneath her cheekbones and chiseled a more austere expression. Arm movements actually made her biceps bulge and tighten the sleeves of her blouses. Her thighs were as strong as steel, and the muscles across her stomach were so rock hard they stood out in relief. That she had to take in the waistband of her skirts came as no surprise.

It wasn't until a crisp day in October that Olivia approached her again as friends, interrupting Mac's apple picking chore in the orchard. Astride Sunny after a morning ride, she ducked low-slung branches and called out.

"Morning...Mac."

Mac glanced around to see if anyone heard her. Relieved, she allowed herself a smile and similarly informal greeting. "Good morning, Olivia. Have a nice ride?" She emptied her apron pockets into the large basket nearby.

"Wonderful." Olivia dismounted fluidly.

Mac picked a fat blemished King apple off the tree. "Can Sunny have this?"

"Of course." Olivia led the palomino by its bridle to the apple on Mac's open palm. "Special treat for her. And Kings are her favorite." She laughed when the horse finished chewing and nearly pushed Mac over with a nudge of its head. "That's a 'thank you,'" she said.

Scratching Sunny's velvet nose, Mac chuckled into the big watchful brown eyes. "You're welcome." To Olivia, she added, "And I've been thinking..." She cast her eyes to the ground and back, modestly. "I owe you many thank-yous for treating me so decently. Right from the start. I've only got about two weeks left."

Olivia's eyes softened and she smiled warmly. "I've never really been comfortable with it, I want you to know, your...your being our domestic." Releasing Sunny to wander, she strolled to the base of the giant King apple tree and sat down delicately. "Please come sit."

Mac gathered her skirt and sat beside her. They leaned against the wide trunk and gazed into the neighboring trees.

Olivia gave a short laugh. "Even seeing you do that." She flipped her hand toward Mac's skirt. "The 'proper lady's sit' makes me want to laugh."

Mac stared at the scuffed Oxfords she always wore outside. "Glad I can provide some humor for y—"

"Oh, silly." Olivia sat up and seized a pinch of Mac's skirt. "I didn't mean laugh in a funny way. What I find so irreverent is your act.

I know this isn't you," she said, giving the fabric a little shake. "I learn a lot chumming around Boston. You do when your name or your money gets you inside any private club you choose." She elbowed Mac and winked. "It's true. What better way to learn about the real world than to throw yourself into it?"

She brought her shoulder to Mac's and spoke confidentially. "In June, when Molly's physician declared her leg healed, we all gathered at the Stowe homestead and painted the town! I met the most attractive couple at a South Boston club, one of them so fair and fashionable, the other so dashing and alluring—and both of them women."

"You're joking."

"I swear, I couldn't help but see you as finely turned out, tie and tails, gloves, spats."

Mac felt her heart rate increase, and she needed to get up and pace. *This is how she sees me? No longer saving herself for "him"? She knows.* The back of her neck itched from her starched ruffled collar. She raised her hand to adjust it and ran it nervously through her hair instead.

Olivia sat quite close and her eyes twinkled. She set a palm on Mac's forearm.

"Mac, I know you wear your breeches because you believe they're 'practical,' as you call it, but wouldn't you just love to wear the formal outfit?"

"You mean…as in the man's tuxedo?" The newspaper was full of advertisements for pricey clothes like that. She'd seen them, liked them, and knew she'd never afford them.

"Yes," Olivia insisted.

"You mean, really wear it? Not as some…some costume, like this?" Mac tugged at her collar.

Olivia's giddiness vanished. She looked stricken, as if she thought she'd spoken offensively. Mac was afraid to be honest and allay Olivia's obvious concern. She took in and let out a deep breath. *Say it. Say yes, you'd love to wear the tux.* At last, she grinned a little and shrugged.

"I…Well, I…um…"

Olivia's smile grew until Mac blushed. She wrapped her fingers around Mac's hand.

"I thought so," she said and leaned close again. "You would turn heads, you'd be so handsome."

"Olivia, I could nev—"

"Of course you could!" She shook Mac's hand once for emphasis. "Those women I met wear whatever they wish all the time." Still clasping Mac's hand, Olivia sat back against the tree. "Maybe years from now, there will come a day when we meet and those eyes of yours won't turn way. They'll flash when they see me. And I'll be impossibly attracted to you, willing you to ask me to dance."

Mac laughed lightly, flattered. She dared to squeeze Olivia's hand. "And I thought *I* was the dreamer."

Olivia sat up again, her expression serious. "You are a realist. *I* am the dreamer."

"Oh, is that right?" Mac grinned and cocked a brow in challenge. "So what else does the lovely Miss Olivia Waters dream about?"

Olivia's gaze drifted up into the tree branches and settled on Sunny munching another apple. "Lots of things," she finally said. "Mainly my independence, I suppose."

"How will that work once you're Mrs. Reginald J. Lowry Jr.?"

Mac watched Olivia consider her question, and delicate lids shuttered the dreamy eyes.

"We grew up together," Olivia said at last, giving Mac a sideways look. "Did you know that?" Mac shook her head, truly surprised. "We did. And have always been there for each other, through thick and thin, as they say. Reggie is a very caring, thoughtful man, very respectful. We know each other so well, there's nothing we'd keep from one another, and nothing we'd do to prevent the other from enjoying life and finding happiness."

"So he wouldn't object to his wife 'painting the town' with her friends?"

Olivia's lips curled into a mischievous grin. "Oh, he probably would, but I'm equally certain he'd find me tedious company, should I tag along on all his junkets."

Mac frowned. "I guess I don't understand how you plan to live an independent life even though you'll be joined as one."

"Reggie and I have always been 'joined as one' and have always sought to make each other happy. If he feels complete by traveling for his work and enjoying the company of others, then far be it for me to stand in the way of his pleasure. Likewise, if I find contentment by spending intimate time with friends, he would never deny me such happiness."

Mac nodded to acknowledge the statement, but she was deeply unsettled by the philosophy of it all. How a lifetime commitment of marriage could be opened to include "intimate" happiness with others was beyond her. *Ellie and I were "joined as one," and we knew there'd be no one else...Once upon a time...when we were so young.* Mac absently touched her fingertips to the top button of her blouse, pressing Ellie's ever-present gold heart underneath to her skin.

She knew without question that she wanted to be Ellie's sole source of intimate joy and would happily die working toward that end. That Olivia saw commitment so differently disturbed her. It wasn't anyone's place to judge, but Mac's heart found their differences disappointing.

Olivia tripped a finger beneath Mac's chin affectionately. "Just because you and I could dance the night away in each other's arms doesn't mean I'd need to divorce him."

Mac was so unsettled by Olivia's revelation that she grew irritated. "If you weren't single, I wouldn't have you in my arms in the first place."

To Mac's surprise, Olivia grinned. "Your nobility only makes you more attractive." She sat back, appearing quite satisfied with herself.

Mac leaned forward. "May I ask you a question?" *Enough of this cat-and-mouse game.*

"Of course."

"I've yet to hear you say you love him, so why bother getting married?"

"Our futures will be secure. Actually, Reggie and I and our families have been anticipating this for as long as I can remember. We'll have a home, financial stability, and the freedom to enjoy our lives."

"So you can have your cake and eat it, too." Mac wanted to get up and pace, but flouncing around in a damn skirt would only add to her irritation.

"I don't appreciate that, Mac." Olivia turned where she sat to face her. "Why are you getting so upset? Are you mad?"

"Well...Yes, I guess I am."

"Did I do som—"

"No. Yes. Well, no, not yet." Mac could tell Olivia was holding back a smirk. It made her even madder. "Someone vows to have and to hold you till death, you shouldn't be out painting the town, being intimate with anyone else. That's…That's all."

They stared at each other for a moment until Olivia looked away. She watched Sunny meander among the trees for several minutes. Mac remained silent, wondering if she'd crossed the line.

"He's really kindhearted, you know. A true gentleman. He's handsome…in a businessman sort of way, very prim-and-proper, which is probably why Mother adores him. They're so much alike." Olivia caught Mac's eyes firmly. "But I'm not that prim-and-proper type, truly, and I won't pretend to be at the expense of my happiness. I'm…I'm not my mother, Mac, and I refuse to become her."

So she'll marry someone like her?

"Look, Olivia. I'm sorry. It's none of my business. I'm sorry I threw my opinion at you like that. Jesus, it seems I'm always spewing out stuff to you and apologizing for it. We should talk about other things." She offered Olivia a hopeful grin. "I'm very, very thankful you are who you are. I like you a lot. Please know that I treasure your kindness. I mean…You could've fired me, sent me back a few times already. I apologize for forgetting my place."

"Mac, I'm not going to fire you."

"Well, I have messed up enough and I suppose I deserve—"

Olivia laughed lightly. "I can't think of any reason to fire you, Elizabeth Mac McLaughlin, unless, for instance, you refuse a direct order."

"Have I done that?"

"No, silly. But if I told you to kiss me right now, would you?"

Mac sat back hard against the tree trunk. *Now, this isn't fair.*

"No. You're engaged to—"

"Refusal is cause for dismissal, Miss McLaughlin."

Mac shook her head. "You're playing dirty pool."

"Told you I knew my way around, and I love a good game of pool."

"Olivia."

"Oh God, Mac, relax. I'm not married yet. In fact, not till next summer."

Mac shook her head. "You're engaged. No kissing." Without a

doubt, just *thinking* about kissing Olivia was dangerous. She needed to stand her ground but didn't want to insult her. Mac crossed her arms over her chest and sent her a petulant look.

As much as she wished for Olivia's happiness, Mac simply didn't believe that legally marrying Reggie Milquetoast would accomplish it. Lord knew Mrs. Waters worshipped the ground he walked on, for being the white knight to rescue her daughter from Old Maid Sin and Damnation, but for this couple, marriage would be an adventure of their own making. At least they weren't going into it blindly.

Olivia cocked her head and met Mac's stare. "Okay, then. Tell me about this love that's left such a mark on you."

"I'd rather not get into it."

"Refusing again, Miss McLaughlin?" Mac simply stared at the ground. "I think you need to speak of it. I will sit here and wait for as long as it takes."

Mac wondered how they always wound up so entrenched in intense conversation. It was unique, this relationship of theirs, and deep down, Mac appreciated every moment of it.

Olivia blinked. "Whenever you feel comfortable."

The breath Mac seized was almost painful. "I may never be comfortable with the subject." She picked a nearby blade of grass and focused on breaking it into tiny pieces. "We were so young, so inexperienced, but we felt it. We knew the love we shared was very, very special, that we had what it took to make it last. And that's what we dreamed about."

"You were sixteen?"

Mac nodded. "Had turned seventeen. Young, I know. We grew up together, too. 'Joined as one' since we were little. Then I went to prison, and half of me was ripped away. The reformatory got to play with what was left."

Olivia reached for Mac's hands and brought them into her lap.

"Please don't be insulted, Mac, but because I'm still a little uncertain, I have to ask. And, believe me, I won't be shocked or appalled. This love of yours…it's a girl, right?"

Mac withdrew her hands and sat straighter against the tree. "Her name is Ellie."

"You still love her very much."

Mac returned a small, pained smile, and unbuttoned her collar to show Olivia her necklace. The dime-size open-frame heart glistened in her palm.

"Mac," Olivia said on a hard exhale. "It's truly lovely!" She examined it closely and lifted her eyes to Mac's. "All this time?"

"The reformatory returned it to me when I came here. Thank God."

"When's the last time you two met?"

"From her backyard to her bedroom window, almost six years ago. Her father turned me in."

Olivia gave a little gasp, fingertips flashing to her lips. "Oh, Mac. How tragic. She never visited you? Wrote letters?"

"Her father always controlled everything. And letters…well, they weren't allowed, unless I let the reformatory read everything coming and going. And I damn well wasn't going to let them touch my heart, too."

"Ahh, I remember now," Olivia said softly. "Shortly after you arrived, Mother told me about your mail, how anything sent to you is forwarded to Sherborn until your final release." Mac nodded. "So, do you think there are letters from Ellie waiting for you?"

Mac refused to let Olivia's optimism penetrate the protective barrier she had spent years erecting around her heart. "No. It's hard to imagine the reformatory actually saving five years of mail for me. I'm sure that if anything did arrive, it was tossed away. And after all that time with no word, I couldn't blame her if…she found someone else to love." Mac's eyes moistened. "I hope she did, I suppose, because most of all, I want her to be happy."

"Oh, Mac. I wish I knew what to say. I think you're one of sweetest people I've ever met and deserve the good things in life. I want *you* to be happy."

Mac detected her own heartbeat in her throat. "That's very kind to say. Thank you." She was on shaky, emotionally unfamiliar ground, having someone truly know her and still care. Until now, she'd told only Carter, and his acceptance had rocked her as well.

Mac blinked away tears and eagerly changed the subject. "And you deserve to be happy, too, Olivia. He better treat you well." She covered Olivia's fidgeting hands with one of hers and squeezed gently. "Are you in love with him?"

Olivia stared down at the back of Mac's hand as she spoke. "Reggie is very thoughtful and has always treated me with kid gloves, always so polite, respectful. I do think he's a rare man and I love him for that, but I know that's not what you asked. I just don't see it as a necessity in our case."

"Those are important things, the respect and thoughtfulness, the kindness, but I think being in love is what makes all the other stuff work, don't you? It's like the glue that holds all the puzzle pieces into a picture. Without it, the pieces barely stay together."

"But we've been together for so long, Mac. While what you're saying might apply to some people, what Reggie and I have is just... different." Her voice wobbled and she looked away.

Now Mac was certain Olivia was trying to convince herself. She scrambled for the proper words. "I'm not too wise on the subject, considering how much experience I've had with the real thing, but I have spent years thinking about it. How it should be. How I want it to be. For me."

Olivia bowed her head, nodding. "I guess I have to admit that Reggie doesn't have half of the love and compassion you share so easily." A tear fell on Mac's hand.

"Olivia, you reassure me in my struggle so unselfishly. I'm sure what you're facing isn't easy either. I think marriage is serious business." Tenderly, she lifted Olivia's quivering chin to speak into her eyes. "Things will work out, I'm sure. If your heart knows it's right, you won't be sorry."

Mac searched the watery eyes to lend all the sincerity she felt. But she couldn't help reacting to the uncertainty and angst she found. The yearning to comfort Olivia arose and, without thinking, Mac leaned closer and placed her palm to the tear-streaked cheek.

Olivia reached up and held the hand in place.

"Olivia!"

Mac jerked to her feet as Reggie ran into the orchard, his usually stoic face fraught with worry. He dramatically dropped to his knees at Olivia's side and seized her hands, then turned on Mac.

"I saw you touching her," he snarled. "Don't deny you put your hands on her!"

"Reggie," Olivia said.

"Darling, are you all right?"

"Reggie, please try to calm—"

"How can you ask such a thing, Olivia?"

Mac wanted to distance herself from this potential nightmare as fast as possible. She wished he'd listen to Olivia, but he was nearly raging.

"Darling, I know. Unspeakable! How dare she lay a hand on you!"

"Stop, Reggie. You don't understand."

"Understand? It's perfectly clear, Olivia. This woman…this lowlife…Can't you see she's one of those sick—"

"Reggie!"

Mac stiffened. She met his glare without deference. Holding herself back was a struggle. Like second nature, old street survival skills reared up in her defense. She didn't think this milquetoast had it in him, but if he advanced on her, she would not back down. Her hands balled into fists.

Reggie took Olivia's hand and helped her up. "Come with me, darling. It'll be all right." He drew her behind him and stepped toward Mac, his chest puffed with bravado. He stabbed a bony finger onto her sternum so hard she winced. "I will see you are summarily dismissed forthwith. You pulled a fast one on Mrs. Waters all this time, didn't you?"

"Reggie!" Olivia exclaimed.

Mac almost growled at him. She ground her teeth to keep from speaking. Options flashed through Mac's mind like leaves in a hurricane. One thing was clear: now she'd be returned to Sherborn, whether she defended herself or not, so it didn't matter if she dropped this piece of chicken shit to the dirt. She flexed her right fist, testing it. What used to be her rifle-shot jab was now a cannon-blast right cross. *One shot to the face and he'll drop.*

"You…You're a sin against God! You're through!"

Mac had never hesitated to throw a punch when necessary—until now.

Reggie spun around, scooped up Olivia's hand, and practically dragged her off.

Mac watched in disbelief. *Jesus, please tell me this did not happen.*

Olivia wrenched her hand free to snatch Sunny's reins. As they stomped away, their conversation was a loud combination of his rants and her declarations. Just before they disappeared around the barns, Olivia glanced back, but Reggie pulled her onward.

Reggie Milquetoast.

CHAPTER ELEVEN

They're hardly speaking to each other now. What's going on?" Mac stacked luncheon plates, cups, and saucers next to the sink and turned for Mrs. Finnegan's response.

The muscles in Mrs. Finnegan's forearms flexed as she kneaded the bread dough harder. "The help aren't privy to such things, lass."

"Stop."

Mrs. Finnegan's fingers stilled, several knuckles deep in dough.

Mac crossed her arms and frowned at her. "I know you want to tell me."

When Mrs. Finnegan resumed kneading, Mac hurriedly washed her hands and joined her, working her own ball of dough. Now shoulder to shoulder, Mac whispered, "Okay, out with it."

"It's been three days now. You have barely a week left, and Reginald is fit to be tied, keeping a civil tongue about you."

"I guess he really doesn't have the guts to do otherwise, the milquetoast."

"To the contrary, lass. He's certainly conveyed some disparaging details to the missus…How you used your charlatan ways to disguise your mental illness and endanger his future bride—"

Mac's face heated with fury. "That pathetic son of—"

"And the very Waters name itself." Scowling at Mac's choice of words, she gathered her loaf of dough onto a cutting board and left it to rise on a shelf near the stove. Mac followed suit.

"That's all bullshit and you know it."

"Elizabeth."

Mac didn't have to see the worry in Mrs. Finnegan's eyes to know what she meant. She lugged the coal hod closer to the stove. If she stayed busy, her mind wouldn't collapse and crush her. With a heavy leather glove, she swung open the stove door and shoveled in three scoops of coal. Mrs. Finnegan stood nearby, wringing her hands.

"He claims your advances have left Miss Olivia easily shaken, edgy, her common sense upturned."

Mac nearly slammed the little cast iron door shut.

"Jesus. That's insane talk. Has he made it his life's work to send me back?" She returned the hod to the cellar doorway and paced back to Mrs. Finnegan. "I just can't figure out why. Is he after Mrs. Waters's favor? As if she doesn't already think he's a prince. Is he making sure the hero gets written into the family will?"

Mrs. Finnegan glared at Mac and forcibly cleared her throat.

"You think that's it?" Mac pressed. "I've followed all the rules here with respect since Day One, and you know it. If she is going to believe the ranting of some pantywaist society boy over what she sees with her own eyes, then the missus is losing her own edge in her golden years."

Again, Mrs. Finnegan cleared her throat. Louder this time.

"Common sense should tell her," Mac persisted, crossing her arms in frustration, "I would never do such things, let alone risk being sent back to prison. If I thought she'd give me a fair listen, I'd speak up, but I don't dare. Mrs. Waters is queen of the house." Mac tipped her chin up, mocking. "She shows so little respect for her own daughter, a grown woman, that there's no telling what she'd do to a lowly domestic."

"Elizabeth!"

The sharp call from behind silenced Mac. Mrs. Finnegan shuffled into the pantry.

Chilled, Mac felt Mrs. Waters's icy stare pierce her back. She knew she had forgotten her place and gone too far, least of all spoken too loudly. Before she could turn and meet that hard look, she heard, "I will see you in the library directly," and then the rapid staccato of heels leaving the room.

Mac washed her hands by rote and straightened her uniform, Mrs. Finnegan silent as she watched from the pantry. Mac gave her a nod of farewell and headed for the library.

❖

Mrs. Waters's eyeglasses were perched on her nose, a blizzard of papers before her on the desk, and she nailed Mac with a glare the moment she appeared.

Mac curtsied and fleetingly wondered if it even mattered anymore.

"Sit there," came the directive, and the long index finger pointed toward a leather chair. Mac promptly obeyed. Mrs. Waters gathered several sheets of paper and held them up. She even shook them at Mac. "These arrived this morning. Evaluation forms pertaining to your service here. Forms I am to return within five days. Forms from which your release will be determined."

Mac stared at her freedom in Mrs. Waters's clenched hand. Gooseflesh rose along her arms, and she cast her eyes downward. This was it. Her heart hammered. More of her life to be lost. Inwardly, she cursed the woman and Reggie, the well-to-do, the system, life in general. Mrs. Waters continued to speak and Mac struggled to hear without feeling.

"There is no question in my mind as to how I shall complete them. When you return to the reformatory, the only remaining question will be for how long. The state commission will set an appropriate extension of your incarceration. You realize it could be as long as the original eight years."

Mac steadied her breathing. Too many emotions churned in her gut. Too much rationale pounded in her mind. She knew this was her only moment to defend herself, and she hoped her voice would be even and calm. She met Mrs. Waters's glare.

"My domestic service has been exemplary. I respectfully disagree with you, Mrs. Waters. I haven't given you any reason to recommend denying my release."

Mrs. Waters slammed her palm to the desktop. "How dare you!" Mac started slightly but refused to look away. "After your behavior toward my daughter?"

"Anything Reggie told you was a gross misinterpretation, Mrs. Waters. Have you asked Olivia?"

Her jaw dropped. "*Reggie* and *Olivia*?"

Mac kicked herself. She *knew* she'd slip in front of her some day.

Mrs. Waters leaned over the desk and almost snarled. "They are *Mister Lowry* and *Miss Waters* to you! Yet another demonstration of your impropriety toward them, your disrespect of them and this household."

"That is totally untrue, Mrs. Waters." Mac took a breath. "What has she told you? Have you talked with her at all about his allegations?"

"What I do or don't do are certainly none of your concern. You are well aware that my daughter's mind is preoccupied with their nuptials, the life change that becomes a bride and wife. And her judgment is not at issue here. You are under *my* employ and as such—"

Mac's self-control wavered. She dared to harden her gaze. "I beg your pardon, Mrs. Waters, but your daughter has a very clear, intelligent mind and deserves to be considered, not—" Mac caught herself. She sat back and this time looked away, toward the shelves of books, urgently reaching for inner calm. *Does it matter anymore?*

Mrs. Waters rose like a queen from her throne.

"One week from tomorrow, Carter will deliver you to the reformatory. Until that morning, you will remain in your quarters unless performing the duties of your position."

Mac stood up. She ground her teeth and focused on controlling her escalating rage. The overwhelming despair threatened to push through in a panic. It crept into her throat and swelled till she could hardly breathe. Mac forced a hard swallow to keep it at bay. Her nostrils flared as she gathered a breath with her mouth sealed shut. There would be plenty of time to acknowledge despair.

Mrs. Waters concentrated on making a neat pile of papers, obviously avoiding eye contact. "That will be all." Without another glance, she rounded her desk and left Mac where she stood.

❖

Mac stood in the pumpkin patch, stretched out a kink in her back, and took in what she knew would be one of her last gazes upon this beautiful landscape. The foreground lay in brilliant orange to the acres of golden meadow and the fully dressed red oaks and yellow maples that surrounded the property. The air was crisp and scented with a combination of garden earth and pine, and she wondered if she could ever own land that felt, smelled so invigorating. She inhaled as deeply as she could. There were only three days left.

"Hey, Mac." She turned at the gravelly voice, pleased to see

Carter for only the second time this week. He grinned and carefully maneuvered his old boots among the sprawling pumpkin vines. "How you holding up?"

"Okay, I guess. I missed you. How's the leg? Gonna make it through another winter?"

That made him chuckle. "Hell, yeah. I'm too crotchety to go without a fight." Falling silent, they both scanned the garden and meadow. "Mrs. F said she heard Miss Waters arguing with her mother the other day. She tell you?"

Mac shook her head. "We don't have time to chat. Not anymore."

"Mrs. F don't like it either. We both miss you. Miss Waters does too. Told me so."

Mac just gave a little snort and stared at the pumpkins around their feet. Things were beyond words now.

"Mrs. F said they were arguing about you...Miss Waters trying to make the missus listen to reason."

"No luck, I'm sure."

Carter shook his head. "They haven't spoken since." He jammed his hands deeper into his pockets. "Looks to me like that woman can't wait to have her daughter's wedding be the social event of the season. I think Lowry's got her scared to death that the world will shut out the highfalutin Waters women if the escapades of one Elizabeth McLaughlin get out. Whether they're in his imagination or not. Of course, he thinks *not*."

It was Mac's turn to chuckle. "So I better be back where I belong when high society comes calling."

"That's the gist of what Mrs. F heard. I guess mother and daughter battled most of the day."

"And Olivia left yesterday?"

"To Molly Stowe's in Boston, yup. Didn't speak all the way to the train."

The hollow that opened in Mac's chest when this nightmare began over a week ago, gapped just a bit wider and threatened to steal her breath. Carter's confirmation made Olivia's support feel twice as distant. Mac's gaze fell to the ground, and she labored to stand tall. Loss riled her anger.

Mac kicked a small pumpkin off its vine and absently picked it up. The size of a grapefruit, it was young and promising, smooth and peach colored. "Wonder if Olivia will ever get the chance to be her own woman." She glanced at Carter. "She firmly believes so. Did you know that? She intends to live life as she wants, married or not. Says she and Reggie have an understanding."

"Bet it ain't what the missus has planned."

"Hell no," Mac said, and reached back and hurled the pumpkin as far as she could. It splattered near the garden gate. She stared at the mess for some time, her own young life shattered on the ground.

"Mac, you know I'll come visit you." She looked up and he nodded. "Ain't gonna be like before."

She turned away when her eyes began to fill up.

"In fact, you can bet good money that me and Mrs. F will be making regular visits." He put an arm around her shoulders and she leaned against him. "I just know it won't be long, girl. And when you're out and famous, you better not forget us."

With a light laugh, Mac hugged him hard and stepped back. She sniffed. "How could I? You're one of the kindest, most generous guys I've ever met."

"And you best not forget all you learned. I didn't spend all that time for nothin', you know."

They grinned at the memories of months spent as master and apprentice.

"Someday, Carter, I'll pull up in a shiny new Ford and take you out for a spin," she said through runny eyes. "Take you and Mrs. Finnegan out to a swanky joint for a fine dinner."

Carter laughed and offered his hand. "Make it a Cadillac and you got a deal."

❖

Mac counted the knots in the beams of her bedroom ceiling one more time, trying to nod off for the night. Her mind had worked so hard these last few days, it didn't know when to stop. She was exhausted from thinking, from wondering, worrying, wishing.

This afternoon in her room, having read everything available so many times she hardly saw words anymore, she tried on her long blue cotton dress to see if it still fit. Worries about it proved justified: it hung off her slimmed-down frame like drapery and snugged too tightly in the shoulders and arms. So she spent the rest of the afternoon and evening stitching it into a comfortable, more form-fitting size. She hated it. But then, she hated lots of things that lay ahead. Come morning, she'd play the maid one last time and serve breakfast to the woman who controlled her future.

Her bag was packed, such as it was, with several changes of undergarments, a few books, hairbrush, and scuffed Oxfords, as well as her breeches, shirt, and suspenders—and her beloved newsboy cap. No doubt they would be confiscated again until she was released. And they'd take back her necklace, too.

Mac's eyes filled up at the thought. Without the necklace, she was totally alone. At least when she wore it, memories of Ellie kept her heart beating. How life could be filled with loss and then refilled with still more confounded her, even made her stomach ache. She blew out the lamp and rolled onto her side and doubled up. A tear rolled off her temple onto the pillow.

Had this year been just like the others? Twelve months of restraint? Of denial? She went back to her first day at the estate and logged events and changes in her mind. There were many. No, this hadn't been a year like the previous four, after all. She would spend the next however many the system forced upon her just remembering, practicing whatever she could, planning her future. Because she *would* have one, despite the system, despite Mrs. Waters and Reggie and whatever it was that society insisted. If she concentrated on what she gained this year, her future *would* be brighter. *It's out there waiting. Keep playing your cards right.*

She tossed and turned for hours, replaying every dramatic scene she'd lived since her arrival. Her mind would not shut down. She rolled over again and noticed the silhouette of tree branches outside her window, the night sky finally lightening behind them. She squeezed her eyes closed in an effort to empty her mind.

❖

"Visitation is on weekends from one to four." Mac took in all she could of the pastoral countryside on their way to Sherborn. Carter didn't have much to say, so she filled the quiet herself for a while.

"Visitors can bring in an item or two, as long as they're small. They get thoroughly inspected, of course."

"Better dresses than that blue thing you're wearing?"

Mac feigned indignation. "This is high fashion, now that I've sewn it up with some style. I'll be the Olivia Waters of the whole place!"

Carter laughed out loud at that, and it warmed Mac's heart. He'd left such a profound mark on her, and she knew she'd be eternally grateful. They'd always have those initially fearful moments with the Colt, the stomach-lurching sessions behind the wheel, the Thanksgiving they spent two hours on the kitchen floor gathering cranberries. And, of course, the "Caper," when she'd actually been his hero. She'd miss him terribly.

Almost as much as Olivia.

It was probably for the best that they hadn't said good-bye. Olivia no doubt planned her absence for that reason. But Mac couldn't get past the emptiness of having lost a very special moment with a very special friend.

She wanted to wish Olivia well with the wedding, their "open" marriage. She wanted to say, yes, they might meet again some day. She wanted to thank her for being a freethinking, spirited woman, for believing in who Elizabeth Mac McLaughlin really was. And yes, she wanted to hold her close, feel the full length of that vivacious body against her, and kiss the sweet, painted lips until they both swooned. Just once.

Mac snickered at her reflection in the passenger window.

Carter downshifted the Runabout and drove through the gates and up the long drive of the reformatory. The compound's welcoming sign caught them both by surprise and Carter stomped on the brake.

"Since when?" Mac asked. She cringed, reading "Massachusetts Correctional Institution—Framingham" and feared that other things had changed as well. She just stared at it, the two-story brick façade with its institutional windows, and the groomed lawns that would become her home once more. She was numb all over.

Carter proceeded slowly to the granite steps of the main doors, shut off the engine, and turned to her.

"I'm carrying your bag in."

She shook her head. Words were clogged in her throat.

"Yes," he insisted. "I'm going in with you."

Mac just sat frozen and fought back the tears.

"Listen, Mac, I'll be here next Saturday. Maybe Mrs. F will come then, too." He squeezed her hand. "You remember what I said, right? It's not gonna be like before. You're gonna have visitors now. Friends who care. You remember that, girl."

Their footsteps echoed on the dark green linoleum, the hallway quiet with work sessions and classes under way. Mac led them around the corner to the superintendent's office and looked up at Carter as she gripped the doorknob.

"Thank you is nowhere near enough to say, Carter. You're a wonderful man and I love you dearly." She hurried her arms around his neck and clutched him close. He dropped her suitcase and nearly lifted her off her feet, returning the hug.

Mac stepped back and watched him wipe his eyes.

He pointed at her and spoke in his deep, hard voice. "You damn well better not forget what I told you, Mac."

They both sniffed back runny noses, and Carter grabbed up the suitcase. Mac opened the door, and they approached the secretary's desk.

"Well, Elizabeth McLaughlin," the woman exclaimed, sitting back and removing her glasses. "Welcome back."

"Good morning, Mrs. Kelly."

"Today's the day, isn't it?"

"Yes, ma'am," Mac answered dutifully. "I'm to see Superintendent Hayes."

The secretary was already rising from her seat. "That you are. One moment, please."

Mac fidgeted, shuffling from one foot to the other. Carter placed a steadying palm on her back as the secretary returned.

"Right this way. Superintendent Hayes is ready for you now."

They started forward and Mac looked anxiously at the secretary.

"Mrs. Kelly? May my friend come with me?"

"Certainly, Elizabeth."

Carter guided Mac into the Spartan office and up to an imposing oak desk.

Superintendent Hayes was a remarkably stoic, harsh-looking woman, and the black hair fluffed around her sunken cheeks did nothing to soften her demeanor. On her desk, the framed photograph of what appeared to be her family seemed out of place.

"Good morning, Miss McLaughlin."

"Good morning, Superintendent Hayes."

"Have a seat."

"Thank you. Permit me to introduce a dear friend, Carter Langston, who's driven me here today."

Hayes continued to organize papers on her desk and spoke without looking up. "How do you do, Mr. Langston?"

"Fine, thank you, ma'am."

Hayes opened the desk's center drawer and retrieved a manila envelope. Mac knew her life was inside and suddenly felt the room grow cold and still. The ticking of the antique grandfather clock in the corner was the only sound, and it grated on Mac's last nerve. The ticking away of years, the ticking of a bomb about to destroy her life.

At last, Hayes finished reviewing the paperwork.

"You have been a model member of Sherborn's population during your term with us, Miss McLaughlin, and as such, last September you were awarded a three-year reduction of your eight-year sentence."

"Yes, ma'am."

"I have here the evaluation forms of your employer, covering the past twelve months of your pre-release year. Please summarize for me now your employment by Mrs. Agnes Waters during that time."

Mac shifted in her seat. This wouldn't be a quick interview. She knew whatever she had to say would be refuted in Mrs. Waters's paperwork, undoubtedly painting Mac as the devil incarnate.

"I served both Mrs. Waters and her daughter, Olivia, and then also her fiancé, Reginald Lowry, as a full domestic, responsible for wardrobe, dining, housekeeping, laundry, and gardening work, twenty-four hours each day whenever needed. I worked hard and diligently, always respectfully, and, in my opinion, to the standards Mrs. Waters required."

"I see." Hayes scanned the papers, apparently searching for some detail. "Mrs. Waters further states that on a date last April, there was an incident during which you became involved with certain criminal types at the estate. Some gunplay was included. Is this true? Please elaborate."

That Mrs. Waters would even bring up the incident was a shock.

Not only was she not present when it happened, but having bootleggers consider your house part of their regular route didn't seem like something Mrs. Waters would want discussed publicly. Mac glanced at Carter and saw that he was equally surprised.

"I...well, I came upon some sinister characters in our barn. They wanted money from the house and were holding Carter here at gunpoint and beating him to within an inch of his life. And then Miss Olivia Waters unwisely entered the scene and they took her hostage. I...I had...seen a gun in the horse barn, so I used it to disarm the man and hold them until police arrived."

Hayes peered at Mac. "Had you ever held a gun before, Miss McLaughlin?"

Mac shook her head vehemently. "No, ma'am," she lied.

"Hm. Quite remarkable."

Hayes shuffled to another page, and Mac flashed a curious look at Carter. He only raised an eyebrow.

"Well," Hayes finally said, "I see no further reason to delay, considering this information"—she waved the papers—"and the telephone interview I had with Mrs. Waters yesterday."

Now Carter sent Mac a stunned look. Mac felt her shoulders slouch.

Hayes then went to a cabinet across the room and unlocked its doors. She withdrew a large, bulging envelope, checked the writing on the front, and relocked the cabinet before returning to her desk. But she remained standing, holding the envelope in both hands.

"Based on the evaluation of your tenure here, your reduction in sentence, your pre-release eligibility, and your outstanding performance over the past twelve months, no further review is required by the commission. I am hereby authorized to terminate your incarceration forthwith. If you'll be so kind as to sign some forms with my secretary, Miss McLaughlin, you will be free to go."

Both Mac and Carter just stared up at the woman.

"I beg your pardon?"

"You heard correctly."

"Honestly?" Mac asked, convinced there was another shoe yet to drop.

Hayes actually smiled. "Yes, Elizabeth. And this is for you."

Mac took the envelope and needed only a second to realize what it contained. Mail. *Ellie?*

"I—I don't know what to...to say." Her voice broke, and she dropped her head, struggling to hold back a sob. Carter set a long, strong arm around her shoulders.

"C'mon there, *Miss McLaughlin*," he said quietly. "It's time for you to leave this place." He helped Mac stand and steadied her.

She could only stare at the superintendent, dazed. She did the only thing that came to mind and abruptly offered a handshake. Hayes accepted with another smile.

"We're quite proud of you, Elizabeth. When Agnes Waters asked if we had anyone like you for a replacement, it made me extremely proud." She came around to their side of the desk and set a palm on Mac's shoulder. "Now, let's go see Mrs. Kelly and sign some things, shall we?"

Ten minutes later, Mac stood with Carter at the prison gates, once again gazing at the institution. She ran a hand through her hair and let out an exhausted sigh.

"My God, Carter. I just can't believe it."

"Whatever Mrs. Waters said, whatever she wrote, she did the right thing, Mac."

"Yeah, she did." Dumbfounded, Mac could only stare at the ominous building and marvel at the mystery of her release.

Carter tossed her suitcase into the Runabout and waited patiently by the driver's door. Mac turned where she stood and smiled broadly. She broke into a dead run and threw herself at him, laughing hysterically.

"I'm free, Carter!"

He laughed with her, swinging her around in a circle. "Hey, get in the truck and I'll treat you to lunch."

Once settled inside, Mac took his hand.

"Guess it's finally time for me to go home." *Home. Where the hell is that?*

The word echoed in the truck's silent cab. Carter seemed to be wondering, too. He ran a hand over the scruff on his cheeks and the sandpaper rasp disturbed the ponderous quiet.

"Yeah, but...Well, Mac, um, where...?"

"Boston," she said, now somber. "I have some money, and looks like I need to get a room in a hurry. And of course, I have to find some work."

Carter just stared through the windshield. "Right, I suppose."

"So…The Framingham station?"

He nodded and started the Runabout.

"Find a secluded spot off the road, would you please, Carter? I'm not waiting any longer to dump this damn dress."

He teased her about her wardrobe for the ten minutes it took to find an overgrown woods road. Mac wasted no time retrieving her "practical" clothes from her suitcase and took the opportunity to stash her mail envelope inside. Holding it since leaving the prison had started to eat at her, but she wasn't about to open it until she had the privacy to go through the contents. Back in breeches, shirt, and suspenders, she emerged from the woods and hopped into the truck. "Thanks, Carter. I'm ready now." She adjusted her cap. "Let's go."

He simply grinned and shook his head. "You are one intriguing woman, Mac McLaughlin."

The first five minutes of their drive were silent until he asked, "You remember the Waterses' mailing address, right?" Mac nodded. "How about the telephone number?"

"Yes, Carter."

"Okay."

They hardly spoke the rest of the way. On top of everything racing through Mac's bewildered mind, she worried about Carter worrying about her. She almost chuckled at herself because Carter had reason to worry. *Where the hell* are *you going?*

❖

"There's a restaurant inside where we can have lunch," Carter informed her, pointing to the station house as they parked the truck. "Next inbound train isn't for an hour or so."

She hardly heard him, too preoccupied with the array of automobiles and trucks—even motorcycles and bicycles—in the lot. Spotting her beloved Ford, the exact model she'd dreamt of buying for these past months, Mac excitedly lost her breath.

Carter managed to coax her, stumbling and gawking, into the station and provided a tour. Fascinated by the ease with which she could hop a train to popular exotic locales like Florida or California, Mac gathered all sorts of information to read and bought her one-way ticket before they settled down to hot pastrami sandwiches and cole slaw.

Mac whispered across their little table. "What are those men drinking?"

"Bevo," he said with a grin. "Substitute for beer. Gotta thank ol' Anheuser Busch for coming up with the idea."

"Bevo," she repeated. "I'd like to try it."

Carter laughed and they each indulged, toasting numerous times as they awaited Mac's departure.

And when a train whistle finally sounded, Mac chugged down the last of her Bevo in a hurry.

"Train's here. Come on."

She wiped her mouth and was out of her seat before hearing Carter say it wasn't her train. She only caught a glimpse of him signaling their waitress as she burst through the doors toward the platform like an child on Christmas morning. By the time Carter made it outside, the outbound train was debarking passengers from Boston and Mac was lost in the throng.

The hustle and bustle seemed far more frenetic than Mac remembered of her days lingering around Boston's North and South stations. *How young was I?* Now, apparently everyone had somewhere to go. Folks were in just as much of a hurry way out here as they were in downtown Scollay Square. And so many dressed in finery. The shimmering dresses and slick business suits, the hats and shoes. Even babies in fancy stroller contraptions were gussied up.

As the train pulled out for western Massachusetts, Mac stood amidst the cloud of steam that drifted over the platform and watched families reunite, couples chat excitedly, and preoccupied executives hustle off. She tried to take it all in. This look, sight, and sound of the "general public" she hadn't seen in five years had changed so much, it left her awestruck and a bit lost.

She stepped aside to let a couple with an infant pass. Hardly older than Mac, the woman glanced coldly at her over the top of her baby's bonnet. Mac's appreciative smile faded quickly as the woman flicked disapproving eyes from Mac's cap to her knickers and back. Mac looked down at herself, wondering what had obviously repulsed the woman.

"Told you you'd turn heads."

Mac spun around at the familiar voice, her heart skipping. "Olivia!"

They hugged immediately, lingering. The urge to kiss Olivia stunned Mac and she held her out at arm's length, nearly breathless.

Olivia pulled her out of all the foot traffic. She tugged the open sides of Mac's light jacket closed across her chest. Then she reset Mac's cap at a tilt.

"Hello, Mac."

Mac's face tingled from the smile she couldn't stop. Her knees even trembled. "Hello. I-I can't believe you're here…that I get to see you, after all."

"Some things simply must be fate, don't you think?"

Mac just nodded. Olivia was strikingly beautiful, as always, elegant and poised in her long cashmere coat with matching, snug cloche hat. Statuesque, a refined princess among commoners in the crowd. Mac took the slight, gloved hands in hers and felt Olivia squeeze her fingers.

"You are a sight for my sore eyes, Miss Olivia Waters."

Olivia sighed. "And you breathe fresh air into my life, Elizabeth Mac McLaughlin. I'm so glad everything worked out for you." She brought fingertips to Mac's cheek. "You're heading to Boston now, aren't you?"

Mac nodded again and forced a swallow past the lump in her throat. She heard the whistle of the next train, the one inbound to the city, but neither of them moved an inch. Mac willed Olivia's fingers to remain on her face. Words wouldn't come to mind. Her eyes moistened and, to her surprise, Olivia's did, too.

"You've changed my life, Mac. It meant so much to me, talking with you, us listening to each other's thoughts…Hell, you helped me hear my *own* thoughts."

"That worked both ways, Olivia. Your spirit and energy worked wonders on mine."

Mac waited on a breath. They really had become special, intimate friends. And to Mac, their friendship highlighted an entire year of her life. It touched her deeply that Olivia, for all her high-society upbringing, shared that appreciation.

Grinning, Olivia tapped Mac's chest. "That spirit and energy take a lot of hard work, I'll have you know, but the times we spent talking helped make life that much easier and I'll cherish them always."

Mac's Boston-bound train slowed to a stop with a heavy, steamy sigh, and passengers began trickling off the cars. Carter appeared then, holding Mac's satchel and standing apart to allow them privacy.

"Mac, you mustn't think of this as good-bye. We'll always have so much to talk about."

"Really, it can't be good-bye," Mac managed, "but it may be a long time till then."

"Will you keep in touch?"

"I'll try."

Olivia abruptly began rummaging through her purse and at last, withdrew a battered business card. She tucked it into Mac's jacket pocket.

"The grandfather of a good friend," she explained. "A highly respected Boston attorney. Joseph Ginnetti. He has several properties downtown, apartment buildings, and rooming houses. Just if... Well, in your search for a place, he's someone you can trust."

Mac tenderly cupped Olivia's jaw. "I'm going to miss you."

"Oh, how I'll miss you, too, Mac. I...I think my heart is breaking just a bit."

"Mine, too."

Olivia set her palm on Mac's chest. "You're a very special woman, so caring and strong. Stronger than you think, Mac. I just know you will do very special things, but promise me you will be happy."

The conductor yelled a boarding call for inbound passengers, and Carter stepped slightly closer, catching Mac's eye. Fleetingly, she questioned the coincidence of timing between Olivia's arrival and Carter's availability with the Runabout to transport her home. *But he was just as surprised by my release as I was...wasn't he?*

Mac stroked the satin of Olivia's cheek with her fingertips.

"I don't exactly know what happened today, Olivia, but I'm a very happy woman right now. And forever grateful."

Olivia sent her a coy smile, her eyes twinkling. "Let's just say that—thankfully—there are some things Mother values far too highly for her own good. The social status that befalls a Waters wedding is one of them."

Mac shook her head, amazed. "You truly are remarkable. I am blessed to have shared your life. Thank you for being so beautiful, inside and out."

Olivia reached up and tugged Mac down into a kiss.

"Go find her, Mac," she whispered against her lips. "Go find the lucky woman who's meant for you."

PART THREE

October 1927
Dorchester neighborhood
Boston, Massachusetts

CHAPTER TWELVE

Mac focused hard on the two heavily laden trucks that crept along the distant causeway in Nahant. Their headlamps illuminated precious little of the narrow sandy road from the beach. She squinted against the buffeting concoction of October mist and saltwater spray, and settled deeper into her coat, its collar straight up until it bumped the Fedora on her head. Fifteen minutes and she'd lead her group through another successful hijacking.

She checked her watch, pleased to see the truckers kept to the schedule she'd observed twice before. On this run, however, they'd hardly reach this deserted little tourist village on the mainland. And they definitely wouldn't reach the Flaherty gang's Charlestown storehouse. This load of whiskey would go right into hers.

She glanced behind her, along the dark street where a lone Model T sat parked in front of a boarded ice cream parlor, and strolled back into the alley.

"This will top off tomorrow's shipment perfectly." She didn't have to look up at the burly driver of her own lead truck to know he appreciated her good mood. Tonight, they would come through with flying colors on the deal she'd made with rail contacts in Harrisburg. Relieving Boston gang boss Jimmy Flaherty of four hundred cases of Jameson would turn the Irishman inside out. And net her operation some serious green.

Gleeson snickered. "You'd think by now they'd have a pilot car or something. I mean, considering how easily we took Minsk's haul. And, Jesus, we lifted Ambrosino's the same way just last month. Stupid."

"Hey, Flaherty thinks he's untouchable. The luck of the Irish and all that." She readjusted her Fedora and swiped the salty mist from her cheek. "Just the same, we'll stay away from these shore runs for a while." He was right. Gleeson always stated the obvious, even when he'd been her boss at the brewery, back when she was just a kid…just Stick. But she treasured his presence more than ever now. Mac counted her blessings that he and many others she'd rounded up from the old days lent their hard-earned knowledge of the industry and Boston street life to make their operation run so smoothly.

She turned at the sound of footsteps. Jersey grinned and gestured back to the mouth of the alley with a club the size of rolling pin. Cocky as ever, she had a hard time standing still and practically bounced on her toes. Mac grinned at her enthusiasm, taken as always by the energy and focus in her eyes, and a wave of something close to gratitude rushed through her.

"They're struggling over that road," Jersey said, slapping the club into her palm. "It's a wonder those pieces of shit don't just rattle all apart. Their trucks are junk."

"More stupidness," Gleeson said, from the driver's seat, "trusting all that in jalopies."

"As long as they make it this far," Mac said. She set a hand on Jersey's shoulder, the proximity of her old friend always lending her a jolt of confidence. "We all set out there?"

"The girls are ready. Got to admit, I've never seen them look so good."

"Either one of them could stop traffic just walking down the damn street," Gleeson quipped.

"And we've got seven people on each side," Jersey continued. "We'll be on them like a bat outa hell." She gave Mac a reassuring sock in the arm and jogged toward their second truck.

Mac climbed in beside Gleeson. She took off her coat and rolled up her shirtsleeves, wondering not for the first time if *this* was the job where kickback would hurt.

"Their heads are going to be spinning, Mac," he said, wiping moisture off the inside of the windshield with his palm. "Flaherty won't hesitate to pin this on the Italians. And the Jews will laugh their asses off when those boys go at it. Pick a nationality. We've already got them at each other's throats. It's a good plan, Mac."

She looked at him sharply. *It is, but for everyone's sake, is it good enough? Why do I always worry?*

"I don't give a shit about them. What matters is our people don't get hurt." She made it sound like a commandment. *They're family, this collection of old friends and supporters, and it's my job to be smart enough. After all, they are putting everything on the line—again.*

"These big jobs are working out well. We've all got some extra dough and don't have to kill ourselves at work no more. And you guys landed that big Victorian in Dorchester." A satisfied grin wrinkled his haggard face. He elbowed her arm. "To think, it's been...what? Over a year now since we moved up to the big money?" Gleeson answered his own question with a nod. "Remember those 'short hauls' right after you appeared in the city?" He laughed roundly. "Boy, what we risked for short money."

Mac pressed her shoulders into the seat to relax and nodded at his gift of gab, his recollections.

"Got us out of those backbreaking jobs, huh? You lugging hides in the Leather District and me, those friggin' eighteen-hour days at the alleys."

Gleeson pointed at her and grinned. "Your own fault there. If you hadn't pushed that old man to add pool tables, people would've just had to settle for bowling and you could've gone home early most nights."

"Yeah, yeah. But the short hauls did the trick."

"I remember Jersey saying you and your schemes came along just in time, too, because Roxie almost joined the girls at the Ladyslipper Review."

Mac turned quickly. "The one beside the Howard Theater? I never knew that."

"Yup. Damn shame to miss out on that, now let me tell you."

Mac laughed with him, but it unnerved her to learn Roxie had come that close to turning to burlesque.

Within months of returning to Boston, Mac had managed to connect with key people from her past, offering them what had been a small-scale money-making venture. Hijacking illegal alcohol shipments hadn't been anyone's ultimate dream job at the time, but Mac watched with immense satisfaction as they all warmed to the idea of "paying back" the gangs, the cops, and the crooked politicians for the suffering and loss imposed in years past.

She checked her watch again. "Five minutes. Stay on your toes." She handed Gleeson a black cotton hood and several short lengths of rope, which he stuffed into his jacket pockets. Mac jammed the same items into her trouser pockets while Gleeson babbled on.

"And *you*," he said. "What if Jers hadn't stopped to save your drunken ass passed out in the snow? You would've had a hell of a time tracking her down after your stint playing housemaid."

"She delivered all over the city back then. I would've found her eventually." She fumbled under the seat and produced leaded police-issue nightsticks for each of them. "Hell, I found Zim waiting on tables the first time I stepped into Stoddard's. I'm just glad you guys were still around. *And I wasn't playing housemaid.*" She chuckled. "Now pay attention. They'll be passing in a minute or so."

A gust of wind blew more mist into the cab. She wiped her face with her sleeve and found a rag near her feet to clear the windshield. *Someday we'll have enclosed cabs. This old hack is no better than the one we had at the start.* She focused hard, but those early petty raids stuck in her head. *These aren't short hauls anymore. Damn, we've been lucky.* Each time out, she prayed they'd emerge unscathed.

The mouth of the alley glowed dimly as the delivery trucks began their pass through town. Over the low idle of her own truck engine, Mac heard car doors slam and women's curses rip along the deserted street, and knew Roxie and Millie had tackled each other like rival alley cats. On the street, literally.

Gleeson's oversized belly jiggled as he snorted at the raging, grunting voices. Mac nodded agreeably. It had to be a wild scene out there. The vehicles passed the alley, downshifting to a crawl, and an angry male voice bellowed for the brawling women to move aside.

Gleeson leaned sideways and jutted an ear out beyond the cab. "Idling now."

Mac pointed with her nightstick. "Go."

Without headlamps, Gleeson and the truck behind him roared out of the alley and up to the rear of the delivery vehicles. Simultaneously, an imposing Packard whirled into view up ahead and Roxie and Millie jumped aside. It skidded to a stop facing the lead truck, blocking the road and blinding its occupants.

Hooded figures swarmed the delivery trucks and fists and clubs flew. The second truck's sideman pivoted in his seat and swung a shotgun into position just as Mac appeared at the cab. He jumped at the sight of her, and Mac made the most of his hesitation. She yanked the gun away by the barrel, and the blast blew out the storefront plate glass across the street. She smashed his forehead with the nightstick and dragged him out and onto the road. She pointed to the shotgun in the cab and told a member of her crew, "Take that, and tie and dump him with the others."

She signaled Zim and he raced to her side.

Winded, he puffed hard and aimed alert eyes up at her through cut-outs in his hood. "Jesus, Mac. You hit?"

"No. We're good, but that fucking shot was probably heard for miles. Cut all the lights and speed everybody up."

He spun and ran to the front, where he hurriedly waved away the Packard, and Roxie and Millie's car. Jersey and Mac were already moving the delivery trucks. They led the procession to an abandoned marina less than a mile off the main street and transferred the hijacked liquid gold in record time.

❖

"Jesus, we need guns. They got all kinds of 'em, damn it." A rugged young man stood up in the dimly lit basement and pointed at the leadership table up front. "The Southie Micks are the biggest. How you think they got that way, huh?"

He took two steps forward, a hand raised as if to argue further, and Jersey and Zim rose so quickly on either side of Mac that their chairs fell over. He stopped.

Still seated, Mac spoke calmly. "Relax, Danny. I think the time for guns has come, too."

Gleeson reached up and tugged Danny back to his seat. Zim sat down as well.

"Most of us have them, Mac," Hank said, "but we all agreed it's too risky to get caught with 'em."

Danny shook a finger. "Yeah, but things are different now. The big boys are more prepared than ever."

Jersey stared hard at him as she addressed the room. "We've got the firepower we need for our future jobs, so calm down. Anyone who needs a piece will have it."

"Each time we've intercepted a delivery," Mac said, "it's been very clean. We've pulled them off without guns. Those guys hardly ever get off a shot. Our last few jobs have looked like Irish hits, and soon enough, Johnny, Saul, and Ricky's boys in Eastie will retaliate in their own ways. There'll be a war like this city's never imagined. Flaherty's Irish Mob will be in for the fight of its life…and we'll still be standing after the law cleans up their mess."

From the back of the room, Millie laughed. "Hey, Mac, can't you just see Beacon Hill when that happens? None of the damn politicians will want to look involved, but they'll be at war with each other."

"Nothin'll get done on the Hill for months," Nicky added.

"Nothin' gets done now," Gleeson said, and everyone chuckled.

"Word on the street," Ralph began, "says there's a dame at the DA's office who might make a good connection. Some new blood."

"Who's your source?" Mac asked.

"Son of my sister's friend is a waiter at Locke-Ober. You know how it is over there, Mac. This waiter, he hears a lot when those stuffed shirts come in for a cigar and fancy dinner. And they let anyone reserve the private dining rooms upstairs, not just the fat cats."

"And he thinks she's got potential? Why?"

Ralph shrugged. His thick gray eyebrows twitched as he frowned. "He said everyone at the table was really talking her up. She's a looker, I guess, but cold, not interested, not impressed by the big names or the headlines. He said she's probably related to some big shot to get that kinda job."

Mac sat back. "Sounds like she could be on anyone's side. Find out whose and set it up if you think she's for real."

Ralph acknowledged the order with a tap to the brim of his cap and looked across the room. Buddy, a ruddy longshoreman, and his daughter, Vonnie, both nodded back at him.

Nicky edged his chair closer to the table. "The Italians are due next, Mac. Ambrosino's man's taken a liking to me, so the wheel job is probably mine."

"You've only been hanging with his boys a month, for God's sake."

He held up two fingers.

"They do like him," Roxie injected, pressing forward at the end of the table. "I've seen him doing the town with those guys…at Bella's, at the Howard."

"Hell," Zim mumbled, "You been to the Howard? I haven't hit the Howard in ages."

Nicky chuckled at the scowl Mac sent Zim. "So I'm Nicky *Colletta*, remember. Nicky *O'Dowd* don't exist."

"Don't push Ambrosino, Nick. If he picks someone else to drive, you just make sure you're riding shotgun with their boy. After all, we wouldn't want Big Johnny to have another load hijacked, now would we?"

A mischievous grin spread across Nicky's wide face. He slicked a palm back over his black hair and nodded. "At least not till we've gone five blocks and some thugs bash in our windshield."

"And, Nick," Mac added in a near whisper, "I don't want Johnny's guy coming to and telling him you were a setup."

"Got it."

Jersey unwrapped a pack of Chesterfields as she issued instructions. "Jackson, you, Millie, Danny, Gleeson, and I will rendezvous with Nicky's truck and transfer that load. And make sure you bring along a few of your Townie boys."

"You guys better make it look like I fought like hell before you hauled me off," Nicky said, "and I left my blood all over everything. Don't forget."

"I got the blood from Dimitri's butcher shop," Millie said.

Jackson grinned at Nicky. "And I'll slice up your seat."

❖

Ellie Harrison finally sat across from her husband at their kitchen table and tried to make sense of his ranting. Allen's jittery mood had him pushing the fried fish supper she'd prepared all around his plate. His mumblings about his bank job, their financial status, and Mayor Curley's office weren't adding up. Weary from a day's work and plagued by the deepening chasm between them, she sighed heavily.

"Allen. Stop, please. Your father's a vice president at the Shawmut, so why's the mayor—?" She grew anxious as he set down his fork, his slim form shrinking farther into his chair. They had been married a year, just settled into their small apartment in Hyde Park—and a baby was on the way. "Is he letting you go?" She knew her meager salary as a clerk in the DA's office wouldn't see them through.

"No. Nothing like that. Just the opposite, actually." He leaned forward on his elbows, removed his horned-rim glasses, and rubbed his eyes. "There's a promotion in store for me, Ellie, if I succeed at this new task he's given me."

She stopped eating and held her breath. Well-known among Boston's aggressive powermongers, Gerald Harrison lived for his bank. In contrast, son Allen, having been raised to strive for the same life, had yet to advance beyond the role of bank teller and amounted to a social embarrassment for his father. Ellie couldn't imagine what Gerald had in store for her mild-mannered, hard-working husband. The fact that the mayor apparently was involved prickled the fine hair at the back of her neck. Lord knew what the conniving Mayor James Michael Curley had up his sleeve.

"Father has appointed me his liaison between Curley's office, the city council, and"—he brought his eyes to Ellie's—"and Jimmy Flaherty."

"What?" Ellie fell back in her chair. Allen nodded at her outrage. Ellie shook her head. "No, you can't mean he expects you to deal with the Mob."

"He expects an answer tomorrow right after at our usual Friday meeting."

"But...but the *Mob*? Damn it, Allen. That's unfair. It's dangerous."

"I've been thinking that I'll just liaise with the Southie councilman, Kelleher, and leave it at that."

Ellie shook her head again and leaned forward. "Oh, Allen. I've seen the charges piling up against these mobsters and how the cops all look the other way. It amazes me every day, the things that go on, and no one—especially Curley—does anything about them. He's part of it, Allen, and now your father, too? And he wants to bring you into it?"

"My father has only his investors and customers at heart, Ellie. He's not involved in any of that stuff you type up at work. If the bank can profit for its clients, then this is a simple and sound business move."

Ellie stared back at him, wondering where his common sense had gone.

"Do you know what he wants?"

"Curley's looking to expand his support base before the next election and wants to help the Southie businesses with their cash flow. So many are struggling, Ellie. In exchange for us offering them extended credit, of course on Curley's behalf, the city will send more business Shawmut's way."

"And Flaherty gets a piece of this pie, too?"

"He has interests in a lot of those businesses anyway, so, yes, I suppose he'd take some of the money, but...he would provide the protection." He spoke softly, as if the walls had ears. "Outsiders threaten the shops, his group gets to...take care of things."

"His 'group'? His gang, you mean. Allen, everybody knows how Flaherty takes care of things."

"Well, the police will be spared the bother."

"The *bother*?" Ellie shot up from the table and practically dumped her plate into the porcelain sink. Dish and silverware clattered loudly. "*Bother*? Isn't that their *job*?"

"The police brotherhood will be compensated."

Ellie's eyebrows rose. The crooked cops and the political cronyism she documented every day for the DA sprang to mind. She hurried back to him and put a hand on his thin shoulder. "Allen. Listen to yourself."

He shrugged beneath her hand. "Oh, I have, dear. And I'm counting on my pitch being a winner. Branch manager, Ellie. A fifteen percent raise." He pressed his cheek to her stomach. "The next Harrison boy will climb the ladder just like his father and grandfather."

❖

"I'm telling you, Mac, that ugly vein in his neck almost popped, he was so bullshit." Nicky O'Dowd struggled to keep his voice down. Around him in Dorchester's underground Blue Velvet speakeasy, Jersey, Zim, and Roxie smirked at him. Mac sipped her whiskey and waited for more of Nicky's inside information.

"So, we's back at the warehouse in Charlestown, all of us bleeding like stuck pigs. One guy's arm's hanging off, all busted—"

Jersey snickered. "Went like clockwork," she said. "Sorry Jackson cut your arm, Nick, but you took that bash to the head like Valentino."

He grinned at her praise. His acting job the other night made him look like the rest of Ambrosino's delivery boys, all beaten into submission.

"You sure you're okay?" Mac asked.

Nicky dismissed her concern with a wave of his hand. "So in comes Big Johnny, and he explodes. Says he wants the S.O.B. behind the 'jacking. His big goon, Tito, says they don't have a clue but got some leads and Johnny whacks him across the chops. Says he wants *the guy*, not leads. So Tito says," and Nick puffed his chest to perform the impersonation, "'No doubt it's the fuckin' Micks.'"

"Perfect," Mac said.

"Yeah, then Bennie tells Johnny about Saul having nightmares, thinking he's next 'cause Flaherty ain't hit the Jews in a while." Nicky guzzled half his beer and wiped his mouth with his sleeve. "So guess what Saul did? His boys went and lit up Flaherty's Green Harbor Lounge on Castle Island."

"Oh shit. Here we go," Roxie muttered, and reached for one of Jersey's Chesterfields.

"Yeah," Nicky said, glancing at her and back to Mac across the table.

"Saul may have thought he was next on Flaherty's list," Zim reported, "but our people say Rick in Eastie thinks he is. Squirming little wimp wants a summit with Ambrosino and Saul."

Mac finished her drink and signaled the waitress for another round. "So Saul's bullshit at Flaherty, Rickie's looking for a fight with Flaherty, and after our raid the other night, Ambrosino will be going after Flaherty." She shook her head at her associates. "Tough being in those Irish shoes."

"But wait, Mac. There's more. After last night, y'figure Flaherty's gotta be winding up for something big, right?" Nicky dug into his shirt pocket for his cigarettes. "So this is the best part!" They all grumbled impatiently while he put a match to the Camel and exhaled, grinning like a fool. "The guys said Tito was all fired up after Johnny called him in the office. Guess he told him Saul's looking to take over the city and that it ain't right for a Jew. So Tito and a couple boys go visit that puppet city councilman Flaherty has. I's glad they left me doing a motor job, 'cause they do a number on him, stuff a cod down his pants—even carved the friggin' Star of David on his forehead to send Flaherty after Saul."

Chapter Thirteen

When Mac strolled through the French doors reading the evening *Post*, the warmth of home washed over her. Entering the comfortably furnished parlor, she didn't mind that her second-in-command lounged on the embroidered sofa half-asleep, that another associate drank coffee while staring dreamily out the huge front windows, or that yet another preoccupied himself with a new pair of suspenders.

She dropped into the roomy upholstered chair next to the fireplace, tossed the newspaper onto the coffee table, and looked around the room, waiting. "We've made ourselves at home pretty quickly, huh?"

They all turned to her and smiled. They found seats and gave her their full attention.

"Best piece of luck that's come our way in a long time, Mac," Jersey said. She straightened her pale blue dress shirt and tucked the tail back into her pants. She yawned, scratched her mussed head, and looked longingly at the sofa where she sat.

"Lucky we had the means when this place went on the market," Mac added, letting her gaze wander up the walls of floral paper to the ceiling far above.

"Such a nice couple, the Maegers," Roxie said. "I can't imagine coming to a strange country and working your ass off to save up just to go back where it's so difficult."

Mac shook her head. "Don't think I'd move to Europe these days, even if I did have family to look out for, which they did."

Roxie, who seemed to survive only on caffeine, sipped at her third coffee of the afternoon. "I wish 'em well, but their loss is our gain." She lifted the lid to the big Borgia radio and tuned in WBZA's orchestral sounds.

Zim snapped his new suspenders against his chest repeatedly and grinned at Mac. He knew that old habit irritated the hell out of her. She was just about to make some wisecrack when he observed, "What about you, Mac? You like being back in Dorchester? I mean, these big-ass Victorians are far from your old neighborhood, but still..."

Mac just shrugged and picked up the *Post*. The room went quiet. They all knew better than to bring up the past. She had no desire to ever go back to that subject. Reminiscing was fun for the others, they'd come so far and achieved a relative level of success, but Mac's past was just too much loss, and thinking about it was as unwise as slicing somebody with a blade.

Zim swaggered across the worn Oriental rug and crouched before Mac, both hands on her knees. "How can you resist my apology when the only man in your life is this handsome? Come dance with me, baby."

He never did grow much past Mac's shoulder, but his light brown hair and eyes, coupled with a sly, heart-stopping smile and powerful build, drew plenty of female and male attention wherever he went. Zim wore a white T-shirt stretched taut over his beefy, muscular torso, and his biceps bulged when he folded his arms across his chest. He wore white T-shirts almost year-round.

Mac grinned down at him. She shoved his shoulders and he landed on his ass. "God, you're cocky."

"It's 'cause he went to the show this afternoon," Roxie teased him.

"Don't say it." Jersey feigned outrage, staring at him. "*The Sheik* for the fourth time?"

"No. It ain't running at Fields Corner anymore," Zim tossed back, indignant.

"Oh, I know," Roxie said, chuckling now. "The *Son of the Sheik* is over in Bowdoin Square."

Zim's playful expression hardened against their teasing. "It's his latest. So what?"

Mac laughed. "Zim, you are not Valentino."

Breaking into a humble grin, he straightened and ruffled his unkempt hair. "No, you're right, Mac, but I'm learning. Besides, I'm better lookin'."

The women groaned and Zim laughed even harder.

"Well, I say we need to get out more," he declared. "Nothin' wrong with going to the show. Or a club. We should hit Stoddard's for dinner some night, do some dancing."

They all swore they would, just to get him off his tangent, and eventually, they managed to do some work. He brought the accounting ledgers down from the attic where they were stashed inside a deceased chimney. A whiz at mathematics, Zim rattled off projections for the foreseeable future, the status of several small monthly bills, and their current overall financial condition.

They huddled over the coffee table, watching Zim point to various columns of figures and grasping the issues as he explained them with great patience. Roxie mussed his hair appreciatively, and their interaction sent Mac's memory back to the day Stick had left him as Maggie's delivery boy. She marveled at how far he'd come, how appreciative he still was for the generous Irish woman who taught him the ins and out of inventory and good business, how he never failed to thank Mac for his happy life.

"I think the next time we all get together in Roxbury," Mac said, "I'm going to urge us to slow things down a bit. We'll see."

"But aren't we running a little low?" Roxie moved to the edge of the sofa cushion and glanced at Jersey for confirmation.

Mac pointed at the ledgers and looked at Zim. "A little, but we'll manage. It's true that every cent we could spare went into this house, but we didn't cut our own throats."

Zim was shaking his head. "Nope, we did okay. We don't have the bankroll we've been enjoying, but we have enough to do what we gotta do."

"At least we can swing it, if we have to slow things down for a while." Jersey met Mac's eyes across the room. "Saw Jackson downtown yesterday, under the clock at Filene's, and he says it's all over the street now, Ricky Demarco sweating his balls off in Eastie because Ambrosino won't call a summit."

Mac sat back, her fingers steepled together over her nose.

"Well, that's sort of the news we've been waiting for, getting them all worked up at each other. So no summit?"

Jersey frowned. "Jackson's guy didn't know if it was definite. You think Ambrosino will go for it?"

"Shit, I don't know." Mac rubbed her eyes in frustration. "Now would be the perfect time for Ambrosino to think Saul's after him, wouldn't it? I mean, Saul's looking to line up with the Italians, and maybe Ambrosino is considering it 'cause Flaherty is pissing everyone off. So what if, all of a sudden, instead of making nice, Saul hits Ambrosino? So much for that alliance."

"And if Ambrosino sticks up for little Rickie and hits Flaherty," Jersey added, "then nobody's gonna be lined up with anybody." Grinning, she sat back and clapped her hands together sharply. "Damn, what a fine mess things would be."

Roxie frowned at both of them. "Yeah, but can we pull off both hits?"

Zim was scowling, struggling to keep up. "You mean we make it look like Saul picks off Johnny's trucks *and* that Johnny picks off Jimmy's trucks?"

Jersey nodded at him from across the room.

"But first," Mac said, "call on the street people and find out what these big boys have coming in. We need to sweeten our own pot as much as we can, so let's make sure they're the trucks we really want and in the spots we want them to be. Everyone is going to tighten up now, remember. As much as I'm sure Ambrosino is bullshit about losing shipments, he's not going to be pushed into anything he's not crazy about—even if it's little Ricky Demarco the Wimp."

"I'm surprised Johnny hasn't erased the Demarco gang already," Jersey observed. "I mean, why have two Italian gangs so close together? Why does he put up with such a scrawny pain in the ass?"

"Good question," Roxie added.

"Maybe he's blood," Zim said.

Mac got up and stretched. "He may not be keen on aligning himself with Ricky, but he sure won't be aligning himself with Saul if he thinks the guy hit him. And as for Flaherty, well, hell. He's just overdue. And when he goes after Ambrosino to get even, Johnny will think Saul set him up."

"I'm curious what everyone will have to say at the meeting," Roxie said through a yawn. "About this setup, keeping Demarco around—"

"And about that new sharp cookie at the DA's office," Jersey said, "that woman Ralphie's getting the scoop on."

"They say she's good lookin', huh?" Zim's eyebrows rose expectantly, which made his hairline jump and his hair flop forward.

Roxie leaned into his shoulder. "Heard she's married, Sheik."

Zim reared back, devastated. "You don't know nothin'. You're just sayin'."

Roxie couldn't hold back the laugh, and they were all teasing him as they left the parlor, Zim shutting off the last lamp. Everyone headed up the main staircase to their rooms, except for Mac, who went to the refrigerator for a 'Gansett. She grinned when she opened the heavy door. No more iceboxes, she thought.

Mac headed out to the front porch and settled on the top step, her back against a white post that held up the roof. It was a quiet night, the hint of autumn's chill curling around her shoulders and reminding her of years past. She never minded the night, walking for miles, hot and humid or bitter cold and wet. She was on her own then, her own boss, making her own way. Until, of course, *they* changed her life. And then *they* kept her on a leash like a dangerous animal to erase prime years of her life, grinding away at her dignity and self-respect.

But she had emerged more determined than ever to be her own person in a life of her own making. And now here she was, on the brink of avenging herself tenfold. A couple years out of prison and she had a decent car (the Model T wasn't new but did the job), owned a city home with electricity and appliances, and had a job that netted her more money in one month than most folks earned in a year. *Oh, what would the illustrious Mrs. Agnes Waters say now?* She shook her head at herself. Her life had come to *this*.

Mac gazed around the neighborhood with the questioning eyes of a stranger. It wasn't *Mac* who had seen this place before, had dreamed of an easier, happier life. It wasn't *Mac* who had been forced to check her self-worth, freedom, and friends outside the gates in Sherborn for so long. It wasn't *Mac*'s heart that broke a little more every day for years, until she was forced to pile the pieces into a corner and ignore them—not forget them—just to survive. That was *Stick*. It was *Stick*'s life that had been left behind the moment the cuffs clicked shut. A whole year of waiting, jail, trial, and five more of *that place*. Six years could really make a difference, a long time that right now seemed to have passed in a nauseating blur.

And *Mac* was someone new. She'd always been smart, alert, and extremely cautious, but she'd also become assertive, defensive, cynical, and frequently aggressive. All things that Stick never was or worried too much about. But Stick had watched Mac learn and mature, glean what she could from those around her, both in the Sherborn prison and the Waters prison. Eventually, *Mac* became the one watching, then the one in charge, as *Stick* faded completely into her past...just like the fun times of her youth and family, like the only love she'd known and lost.

❖

Mac returned from the water closet down the hall and shut the door to her room behind her. She'd stalled long enough. She'd had her freedom and this room for two days already and only ventured into the autumn sunlight she loved and the city she once knew on a couple of occasions for food. She lifted the bulging yellow envelope from the bureau drawer and dumped its contents on the bed.

Single-sheet-thin envelopes fluttered over the blanket like leaves. There were dozens of them, and Mac's stomach knotted, just imagining the messages within.

She began sorting by return address, most of which she didn't recognize, but a few were from home. She opened those first, only to learn what she'd assumed all along: her brother Ray's wedding had been a swell occasion, and he soon would be moving them all to Philadelphia, where he said industry would be booming by 1920. In the meantime, Ray had them all happy and well fed in a large flat in Lynn. Now more than ever in her youth, Mac wondered how his paycheck stretched so far.

And that was the last of the half dozen letters from her mother. Six years ago. Mac gathered them with a swipe of her hand and dropped them into the trash bin next to the night table. At the window, she stared down at the Model Ts, Chevys, Nashes, and other automobiles she'd only seen in pictures. Through the gritty glass, she watched them maneuver through the god-awful chaos on Boston's Tremont Street, letting vendor carts, pedestrians, bicycles, trucks, and trolleys weave their way along. Everyone with somewhere to go, to be, with some purpose. She sighed heavily and turned back to the envelopes that awaited her.

Mac stepped to the edge of the bed and gazed at them, nearly hypnotized by their presence, a tumult of simple white squares riding the lumps of a dusty blanket and battered striped mattress. So what if her own flesh and blood had moved on without her? These letters...this outpouring of emotion that she sensed awaited her from an array of mysterious locations...this really mattered. God bless Ellie.

It took some time, but Mac soon organized the envelopes according to postmark date: more than a dozen from the rest of that turbulent, traumatizing 1919, and fifty-four throughout the first devastating year of prison, and nearly three dozen during year two...

But only sixteen made the pile for 1922. Mac slowly sat back on the bed as her body chilled. The blood seemed to harden in her veins. There were no more letters. She stared at the most recent pile and watched her own hand reach for the last letter. Did she really want to read it?

"My darling Stick...As always, I write with excited hand and trembling pen, just from the sheer possibility you will indeed share this touch and read my words. My love, I do so hope this letter finds you well. That will always be my wish. Now, however, the moment has come that I never anticipated, when I must admit to myself, as well as you, that this letter is my last.

"The heaviest of hearts leads me to end this one-sided correspondence because it simply is too painful to maintain. As much as it will hurt me not to write, it will be torture if I continue. Somehow, I must focus on my studies now, here in Maryland where I am staying with Aunt Lorraine and Uncle Eric, and force my attention to becoming the legal secretary everyone is urging me to be. The college promises a position for me here in Washington, DC, several years from now when I graduate, so it is unlikely that I'll return to Boston.

"Please know that with both arms and all my heart, I held on to our love, our special connection for all these months, even as they turned to years without a word of response. It seems you have decided that we shan't follow the same path through life, so I can only offer my sincere hopes for your happiness and success. But, my love, please

*know that nothing will ever take you from deep within my heart. It is
where I will hold you close, always. I write this and shall mail it today,
forever 'our day,' and in so doing, send you my love for our lifetimes.
My darling Elizabeth, I wish you a life filled with all the happiness you
most certainly deserve, and I dream that some day we will celebrate
love. ...Forever yours, Ellie"*

*The name blurred as a tear smeared the ink. Mindlessly, Mac
pressed the paper to her shirt to blot up the liquid. She took a breath,
and air chugged raggedly into her lungs, past the knot of devastation
in her throat. Silent tears streaked her cheeks in a steady flow. She sat
frozen in place, peering and blinking hard at the letter, discerning the
October 10 date, and violent sobs escaped. Their anniversary, their
first kiss, just sixteen years old. Oh, what they knew then...*

*Mac clutched the gold heart that hung from her neck. Tears flowed
for hours, through the remainder of that pristine October day and into
the night. She wouldn't take off the necklace. She couldn't. Not yet, at
least.*

❖

Mac set her empty beer bottle on the front step beside her and
rubbed her stinging eyes. How clearly she could summon the memory
of the Sherborn admissions matron, the surprised, amused reaction
when Mac refused to surrender the rights to her mail. She'd stood
strong but, in the end, paid the ultimate price. *Such a stubborn fool.
How abandoned Ellie must have felt.* From the back of Mac's mind,
from their last Christmas together when postcards meant everything,
Ellie's words rang true: *I don't know what I'd do if I couldn't read
them.*

Mac closed her eyes. Behind them, she could summon anything,
anytime, any*one* she wanted. But she didn't dare. It was wiser, safer, to
be practical. She knew only too well how dreams hurt.

Her entire life had changed, turned around, if not upside down.
This house, for instance, and the ones like it nearby, comprised a
neighborhood she and Ellie dreamt of calling their own when they
were young. Trolley rides to the park across town often brought them to
this area, and they strolled past these mammoth architectural wonders
where the well-to-do lived, imagining what the rooms looked like, what

the people inside had for supper, if they had a tiny icebox, too…if they had servants.

"Sitting out there with all your friends?"

Jersey's voice from inside the screen door was soft and low. Mac chuckled and waved her out.

Jersey sat and handed her a fresh beer. "Figured you'd be ready for another by now."

"Thanks."

They drank in silence for several minutes, and Jersey finagled a beat-up pack of Chesterfields out of the back pocket of her trousers. In a front pocket she found matches.

"Jesus, when you gonna stop those things?" Mac whined, even though she'd smoked more than a few in her day. "They're friggin' awful."

Jersey lit one, exhaled, and handed it to Mac. "Here. Shut up."

Mac could only laugh and accept the battered cigarette as Jersey lit one for herself.

After a long pull off her beer, Jersey looked away, issued a belch that echoed down the deserted street, and looked back at Mac. "'cuse me."

"Such a lady."

They laughed and stared off into the darkness. "We been in this place a couple months now, Mac, and this is the first time I've seen you out here in the middle of the night. You wanna talk about whatever it is?"

"Eh. Stuff I have to come to terms with."

Jersey nodded, squinting against the smoke as she inhaled another drag. "Being back, right? I mean, I know Dorchester is a big hunk of the city, but you must feel like you're almost home again, huh?"

"I remember going by this very place when Ellie and I were kids." Mac dragged off her cigarette. "We used to pretend it was haunted, all overgrown and stuff, until new owners came in." She looked at Jersey's thoughtful expression in the dim light. "Guess those were the Maegers."

"Funny how things change."

Mac didn't know what to say to that. Things surely changed, all right, but she couldn't find anything funny or ironic about any of it. To Mac, it was all just sad.

They finished smoking in silence.

"Ever wonder if and when our time's gonna come, Jersey?"

"Huh?" Jersey halted the bottle rising to her lips. "You mean, like get hit?"

"Well, yeah. A hit or raided or...just...ratted out."

Now Jersey peered at Mac and set her bottle on the step next to her foot. "You been dwelling on that shit out here tonight? That what's got you all knotted up?"

"It's not impossible, you know."

"Of course it ain't, Mac, but you can't be dwelling on it either. All we can do is our best. That's what you said from the beginning, from way back when we started at the brewery, remember?" Mac nodded. "And you're right. Look where we are, Mac." She waved her arm back toward the grand house. "It's Stick and Jersey and Roxie, here in this great house with little Zim the Polack." She grinned.

Mac gave her a hard look. "But no, it isn't. We're us, yeah, but we aren't on the up-and-up like we used to be. That was a long time ago. And this place...We stole to make the cash, Jersey, pulled some pretty big jobs, busted a helluva lot of heads, sliced up a few guys, too." Mac tipped her bottle up and drained it. "So, we're no better than them."

Jersey slapped Mac's upper arm hard with the back of her hand. "Knock it off. Don't say shit like that. We *are* better than them. A whole lot better. For Christ's sake, Mac. So we sunk our wad on getting this house, but it was for us. Four of us. We didn't sink our wad into booze or gamblin'—or that heroin shit I think Johnny's into now. Where does our cash go, Mac? Huh?"

Mac looked away from Jersey and down the silent, dimly lit street...her neighborhood now. "Yeah, yeah, I know. It goes to—"

"No shit, Mac. We all take our cuts, but we also dish it out. You go take yourself back nine, ten years ago. Where was your money comin' from? Huh? Nowhere, that's where. And did you know where you'd get your next meal? Was somebody dropping greenbacks in *your* mail slot back then? Fuck no there wasn't. So don't be dishin' out that bullshit that we ain't better than them."

Mac stared at Jersey, then pulled her into a hug. Jersey's return hug was just as solid, and welcoming and warm.

Mac pulled away from the comfort, sighing. They glanced away awkwardly. When she looked back, Mac was relieved to see that the confident grin had returned.

Jersey laughed lightly. "Come on," she said, urging Mac to stand with her. "We have a lot to get through by Sunday. And even that'll be a busy day. That Double T's bed is hanging on, but going to need a lot of work. And then there's a meeting to get lined up."

Mac closed and locked the door behind them and they started up the stairs. "I appreciate what you said out there, you know. I...I don't take stuff like that lightly."

At the landing, Jersey reached up and clamped a broad, solid hand on Mac's shoulder. "You came out of the joint older, tougher, and wiser than when you went in, Mac, but I got to know Stick a bit before that all went down. And Stick made me realize I could hang around and have something to call my own. Roxie, me, even Zim, we held jobs all that time. Shit jobs. Wasn't easy, but we did. And now you're back. You're still the same Stick inside, I don't care what you say. We know it and we're with you."

Mac just smiled. She felt her eyes filling up and blinked away the tears.

Jersey sent a playful punch into Mac's upper arm. "Hey. Next time you want to worry or sulk all night, just lemme know." She winked and disappeared into her room.

Chapter Fourteen

The driver swore loudly and spun the wheel to no avail. Watching from a dark third-floor window across the street, Mac grinned when Jersey elbowed her arm. The top-heavy truck, aiming for a shortcut to Ambrosino's storehouse in the North End, went into an uncontrollable sideways skid on cobblestones slicked with twelve gallons of crank case oil. His side man grabbed the door and the dashboard to keep steady.

At nearly thirty miles per hour, the old Hack slammed its right-side wheels into the tall granite curb and tipped over, sending several geysers of ale some twenty feet into the night sky. Mac and Jersey spun from the room and hit the stairs to the street.

The men were climbing up and out of the driver's door when Mac and Jersey exited the alley, and on Mac's signal, a dozen hooded hijackers emerged from the shadows. The truckers were summarily hooded, bound, and dragged into the darkness, where someone with a club knocked them unconscious.

Mac's Double T long-bed rattled to a stop, and five more people jumped to the ground. Barrels and wooden cases of bottles swiftly passed from one truck to the other, and the entire area was vacated in less than ten minutes.

The hit-and-run scene replayed twice more that evening, as Mac executed an elaborate plan to play the key parties against each other all at once. She knew Ambrosino wouldn't waste time evening the score with Saul for that messy loss in the North End. And the hit in East Boston an hour later left Ricky Demarco believing the Irish Mob had brazenly crossed a territorial line. And 'jacking Saul's load of top-shelf stock in Somerville would push him right into Big Johnny's face.

It took several hours to finish stashing their haul on the Pennsylvania Railroad's monstrous southbound train in the Southie yard, and Mac kept careful watch as each raid's load moved. Zim stood alongside, madly scribbling inventory into the small notebook he kept in his suit jacket. This was the first time they'd amassed a shipment of such volume, requiring an extra rail car to pack away all the goods for stops outside of Harrisburg, Pennsylvania, and Munson, West Virginia.

"Final tally is a lot more than we were told to expect, Mac. By two hundred cases. Glad your connections are still so good." Zim tucked his notes away. "Your boys are a godsend, keeping that yard guard so sauced all this time."

Mac just nodded. She owed the rail yard hobos a lot. Smitty and Big Boy worked the rails for her operation now, hopping cars with a couple of armed escorts she provided to see transactions through and bring home the cash. Most of the other guys from her days—Stick's days—at the yard were long gone from this dreary, dirty place, but not from her heart.

"I'm glad the sun doesn't come up for another couple hours," she said. Seeing the lay of this land any more clearly than she already did was not high on her priority list.

She noted Jackson's fatigued stride as he approached. He wiped his hands on his pants and turned to look at the rail car as its door slid closed.

"We're all beat, but what a night." He grinned and stroked his chin with forefinger and thumb several times, a habit over his trademark goatee whenever he was in a pondering mood.

Mac slung an arm over his shoulder. "Got that right. Let's get the trucks back to Roxbury and everybody off the streets."

❖

The documentation had been erased and typed over. That much was clear, and Ellie frowned as she filed papers away. She stopped at her coworker's desk, waited for Alice to stop typing, and leaned over to whisper, "Somebody's been changing things on these reports. and I know it's not you or me."

Alice glanced back at Theresa, the DA's senior clerk, who was typing blindly from a report on her desk. "She wouldn't, would she?"

"Who else?"

"It's bad, I gather."

"Well, that incident with the Southie city councilman, Kelleher?" Alice nodded, expectant eyes glued to Ellie's face. "We all know he was found strangled in Dorchester, but now the report says 'accidental death by asphyxiation.' Says he choked. At his house."

"No!" Alice sat back hard. "I saw that police report the morning it came in." She pressed a hand atop Ellie's on her desk. "Everyone was talking about the Mob. Now it's changed?"

Ellie nodded and carefully scanned the room of busy secretaries. "Scares me to death, Al. My father's probably going to be appointed to take his place. He got a call from Councilman Deegan yesterday, saying that if Dad's interested, they'd like to swear him in as soon as possible."

Now Alice patted Ellie's arm. "But, honey, that's wonderful. Your father loves politics and he's as straight an arrow as there is. No one's going to boss him around. Southie needs someone like him."

Ellie thought about her father's ambitious nature, his need to wield the upper hand, and saw him fitting the bill eagerly. Too eagerly. She almost felt sorry for his future constituents. But then there was the Mob influence. The initial word on the street about Kelleher had fingered the Saul Minsk gang in Somerville for the murder, but there wasn't even a hint of that being mentioned anymore.

"It's lunchtime and I'm going for a walk," she said wearily. "I need some air."

A serious headache threatened from the back of her mind, back where the fond memories of her father lived, back where she'd stashed her reservations about working on the DA's organized crime unit when she was hired. Intuition told her that such past events were stepping to the forefront now—together—for a reason. There was so much she didn't know, yet she felt as if she should.

She collected her coat and purse and took a deep, cleansing breath as she left the building. She was buttoning up against the November wind when a pair of police sergeants tipped their hats to her.

"Blustery day, miss," one said.

"Surely is." She stopped abruptly and they straightened up from leaning against a paddy wagon. "I don't mean to interrupt," she said, stepping closer, "but aren't you Sergeant Browning?" He beamed proudly at being recognized. "I see your name often when DA O'Rourke submits his briefs. I'm with the secretarial pool, and we see all the names of you fellows who never get any of the credit."

His colleague knocked Browning's shoulder. "Works like a dog, this one, feeding detectives and making the higher-ups look good." He tipped his hat again. "Sergeant Valeriani, miss. North End squad."

"How'd you do?" Ellie sent them her most charming smile and moved slightly closer. "You sergeants must hate it when politics gets involved, all your hard work going for naught."

Browning and Valeriani exchanged curious looks.

"Well…We, um…" Browning stumbled and Valeriani readjusted his hat.

"We just do our jobs, miss. Can't say as politics plays a part—"

"Oh, I just meant with things like that poor councilman, Kelleher, for instance."

Both sergeants' expressions grew stoic.

"Sad incident, that one," Browning offered simply. He appeared to scan the street dutifully in each direction.

"Yes, very. No politics there," Valeriani quickly added, and turned to Browning. "Something he was eating, wasn't it?"

"Chicken bone in the soup. That's what I heard."

Ellie let enlightenment show on her face but didn't buy a single word. "Such a shame. Hundreds turned out for the wake, too, the papers said. I heard it was a closed casket. Is that true?"

"True. I had the detail," Browning said. He checked his watch and glanced at Valeriani. "It's about that time."

Valeriani touched his hat with two fingers. "Pleasure chatting, miss, but we have a meet—"

"A friend of mine used to be a neighbor of the Kellehers," Ellie persisted, "and wondered why the casket was closed. Did you ever hear why?"

Browning stepped up and set a massive hand on her shoulder. The weight of it nearly dipped her to one side.

"Lots of questions from a pretty little secretary. Now I'm sure we've taken up most of your lunchtime, so we'd all best be moving along."

Both sergeants backed away then, wishing her a good day before driving off.

Ever since she'd been a young girl, Ellie'd known about police involvement with unscrupulous characters and shady deals. One such deal had altered her life, in fact, when the deepest, truest love she'd yet known was yanked away. And now, formally trained as a legal secretary, she recognized trouble, could read between the lines quite easily, and didn't hesitate to act on her concerns. She'd had no choice as a sixteen-year-old, but she did now. And spotting that blatant do-over on the Kelleher file, with her father poised to fill that vacancy, just made her blood boil.

Unspoken but generally accepted, the ethnic mobs in Boston had their pockets full of councilmen, and Ellie wasn't keen on her father diving in to join them. She hadn't enjoyed an endearing relationship with Jonathan Weston for many years, but he *was* still her father, and Mob influence wasn't something she wished on anyone. Including her husband, who would now have to pitch his Mayor Curley scheme to his father-in-law, of all people. Allen wasn't thrilled about Jonathan taking the post either. She knew he cringed at the idea of speaking to him, even more than he cowered before his own father, and having to deal with Jonathan as city councilman would bring Jimmy Flaherty twice as close to her family.

Zim and Jersey and two of their guys spent most of Sunday cursing their 1924 Ford Model TT truck in the abandoned trolley barn. Their actual objective was to repair the long truck bed and its stacked-plank walls, but they kept up a steady barrage of hints—loud enough for Mac to hear beneath the hood—that it was time to invest in something newer. It was a miracle the old beast had held together for their last job. One too many beer barrels caused an avalanche that nearly splintered the entire bed onto the street.

"It's time to break out some dough!" Zim said, pausing his hammering to yell.

"I'm no skinflint!" Mac shouted back.

"Yes, you are!" Jersey said.

"Hey, this is a tough old truck. Great for kegs and barrels and you all know it," Mac replied. She hadn't been convincing, though, and by late afternoon, other associates checked in and joined the outcry for better wheels.

Gleeson pointed out that their 1923 bakery delivery truck, which was a tall Ford you could stand up in, was never big enough, and the '24 Dodge Brothers pickup was only good for short hauls. He strolled around Mac, pitching his idea for a '26 International flatbed; they only had to put up their own side racks, he lobbied over Mac's grumbling.

She kept her head down, her concentration on the wrench she cranked, refusing to be swayed. Ralph endorsed a beefy "gang truck" being retired by Edison Illuminating. Roxie added her two cents, scowling at Mac's backside while campaigning for a newer Double T, but was immediately advised that having doors and being "cute" didn't count.

Mac emerged from under the hood, wiping her hands and growling at everyone around her.

"If you guys only worked as much as you yap." She secured the hood and tossed the rag onto a bench. "If you *must* know, we've got a sweet '26 Graham coming this afternoon." She pointed at Roxie while everyone cheered. "And no, you can't drive it."

Ironically, the only one of Mac's gang who actually owned a car was Mac. She bought the staid black 1924 Model T Fordor sedan within six months of leaving the Waters estate because it was the spitting image of the advertisement she'd hung on her wall. Even though she'd been tempted to return for Olivia's wedding last year and cause a ruckus, she still hadn't managed to go back and show it off. The four-hundred-dollar price was manageable at the time, and now she was quite thankful she'd selected this Fordor: its front passenger seat had been customized to fold forward, and they could stuff quite a few guys inside quickly. The fact that there were plenty of Fordors rolling around Boston also made her quite inconspicuous and, of course, that was a plus.

At suppertime, Mac dragged seven of them down Dudley Street to Ciro's Tavern for some of the best franks and beans in town. For twenty cents a plateful (fifteen on Saturday nights), you couldn't beat it. Like every other such establishment, it was legally a "tavern" in name only nowadays. Just how much alcohol you could buy there was directly proportional to the amount paid the local flatfoot patrolling the neighborhood. In Ciro's case, it was in Mac's best interest to guarantee the tavern always made its payoffs on time: wiry old bartender Ciro had big ears and no mouth, meaning he was a terrific source of street news for Mac's gang only. Truckers, delivery boys, and cabbies were always coming by for lunch and sneaking in some beers and a few stiff shots. Information was plentiful, current, and usually correct.

And Ciro, at a feisty sixty-eight, had taken a particular liking to Mac, Jersey, and Roxie. He didn't give a damn who fought for the Micks or the Wops or the kikes. Ciro the Greek just loved the idea of women getting the job done. And he did everything he could to help. In return, Mac slipped him protection money and made sure he got shipments of 'Gansett for free.

"You got wheels ready to roll?" He filled a tall glass with ginger ale for Mac.

"Yup, thank God. Don't know what we'd do without that Double T."

"Break in the Graham right away," Jersey grumbled into her beer.

Ciro pointed a crooked finger at Mac. "So next time you not throw the shit up on the long bed, no? Bed broken is your fault."

Mac was nodding and forking food into her mouth at the same time. Never made any sense arguing with Ciro. He'd hang in there for hours, even after he knew he'd been bested, so the smart thing to do was to just agree from the start. "But we may not need it too soon, after all."

"No?" He stopped wiping the bar.

"Been thinking we should slow down, let things play themselves out."

"Hmm. Maybe you on right track, Mac." Smiling at his own rhyme, he removed Jersey's nearly empty beer mug. He reached down behind the bar, plunging into the ice chest nearly to his armpit, and pulled out a fresh bottle bearing a counterfeit Hires root beer label. He pried off the cap, refilled Jersey's glass, blew the suds off onto the floor, and then filled it to the brim. She grinned as he slid the beer to her along the glossy bar top. "I hear…how you say…'big doings' come soon."

Mac and Jersey gave him questioning looks, forks and drinks set down.

"You know Angie Ricci? One of Ambrosino's boys." They shook their heads, and Ciro leaned closer, lowering his voice. "Well, he ride in Thompson's cab today. Head hanging so low. Said not happy to have big war."

"Shit." Jersey sipped her beer quickly, as if Ciro wouldn't talk if she was drinking. "What's that mean?"

He slapped his towel over his shoulder and set a hip against the bar. "To me it sound like Johnny to fight Saul. Soon. Because of what Saul say to Jimmy."

Mac and Jersey shared a knowing glance.

"So Saul fingers Johnny to Flaherty? And Johnny gets back at Saul for it...while Flaherty's hitting Johnny." Mac sat back as if shoved. "Fuck. Yeah?"

Ciro sprang upright. His bushy black eyebrows twitched at her. "Do not you curse like sailor! Dirty words not for lady to say!"

"Sorry, Ciro." She elbowed Jersey for snickering.

The big boys were saving them the trouble of pissing them off at each other and Mac nodded appreciatively. Apparently, Ambrosino was going after Saul, and Flaherty after Ambrosino. They were going to trip over each other in a big way, and Mac took it as a stroke of luck when she saw the opportunity in the Mobs' chaos.

"Now, I say," Ciro whispered, leaning on his forearms to make them hang on his every word, "you...watch how they have their war. You stay away."

Nodding as they cleaned their plates, neither Mac nor Jersey looked up.

❖

Two nights later, the steady stream of "hitting the fan" began, and Mac sized up each episode as the news rolled in from her connections on the streets.

"Tito Delgado, Big Johnny's captain? Took four rounds to the upper body outside the La Traviata Restaurant in Cambridge." Nick delivered his news so fast everyone at the supper table had to stop eating to concentrate. He eagerly accepted the 'Gansett Roxie offered and took a breath. "He'd just finished dinner with Ricky and two of his boys, and was third man out the front door. Tito's second man out and one of Demarco's also bought it. All the cops got was that a Tommy fired from a black Chevy. Word is that Flaherty's done talking."

Hank brought Buddy into the parlor a week later, interrupting a morning discussion about weapons, and said they all needed to set up a scoreboard to keep track of the goings-on around the city.

"Looks like Ambrosino got even, Mac," Buddy said, and removed his knit cap and scratched his head as if it would help him think. "They're saying Jimmy Flaherty himself, and ten guys were inside. Somebody chucked a couple sticks through the window and blew the front thirty feet off the fucking restaurant. Had the best corned beef in Southie, too. Damn shame."

Mac, Jersey, Zim, and Roxie took a moment to check each other's expressions.

"Flaherty go down?" Jersey asked.

He shook his head. "Close, but nope. Four did, though, including his second, Blackie MacDonald."

"Shit," Zim muttered. "Here we go."

"Getting crazy out there, Mac," Hank said, leaning on the door frame and filling the entryway with his brawny presence.

Mac set her pencil on the coffee table and ran a hand back through her hair. "Maybe you're right and we do need a scorecard…a chess board, maybe. From where we sit, looks like Saul's yet to make his move."

Buddy predicted correctly that it wouldn't take long.

On Thanksgiving eve, Ralph, Jackson, and Millie arrived at the Victorian and disrupted the lighthearted chaos of too many so-called cooks in the kitchen. Ralph dropped a fatherly palm on Mac's shoulder and steered her to a chair.

"Sit down. Somebody hit the North End this morning. Burned the Saint Ann Orphanage to the ground. Broad daylight."

Mac stood right up. "Holy—"

"None of the orphans were hurt," Millie added quickly, "or the nuns, but they found Father Michael's body. A thirty-eight slug in the forehead."

"Gleeson's grandson sells the *Post* on that corner," Jackson said, holding his palm at chest height, "little guy, Rusty, said there were four of them. Parked on Foster and walked casual as you please right up the front steps and right back down when they's done. Said he watched all the nuns bring out the kids."

"Such a thing as going too far?" Zim muttered, as everyone sat down.

"So now the talk is that Saul's to blame," Ralph continued, "to get back at Johnny."

"And of course, it's Saul," Millie said through a snide smirk, "because only a Jew would shoot a priest."

Jersey laughed. "People actually fall for shit like that?"

"People fall for all sorts of bullshit," Ralph grumbled.

"We know that the law does," Roxie said.

"And these meatheads sure do," Jackson added.

Mac stared at the salt shaker on the table and reached absently for her pack of Luckys.

Jersey offered a light. "Your thoughts?"

Mac inhaled the cigarette to life and exhaled hard toward the overhead light. "If these assholes get off playing with each other, I say let them have at it. Let them focus on each other instead of business. A distracted bunch of idiots running wild sounds like prime pickings, if you ask me." She dragged off the Lucky again and gazed around the table. "Taking out innocents—a fucking priest, no less—makes me even more eager to take my shot."

And during the next two weeks, while all three gangs, the mayor's office, and most neighborhoods clamored for speedy justice from the DA, Mac directed her pesky little group to reel in its biggest haul ever. She leaned on good street info, timing, teamwork, and pure luck and kept her people rolling nonstop, intercepting convoys all over the city. When the dust settled and she read the inventory Zim had logged, Mac was duly impressed. They had hijacked two of Ambrosino's shipments, two of Minsk's, and one of Flaherty's, with emptied distribution trucks reportedly found scattered in Revere, Everett, Charlestown, Somerville, Allston, Watertown, Southie, and Dorchester.

Mac took in the subsequent news articles with a considerable level of satisfaction. All the papers agreed: Someone had thrown a match into the Mobs' collective gas tank. Mac hoped the ruthless bastards would burn each other out.

The more she read, the more she was convinced of that probability.

The three major gangs raged. They pointed fingers and sent each other ever-escalating messages, always striving to out-duel the other. Torched pool halls and gin joints led to car and storehouse bombings, which led to bodies floating down the Charles River, and, eventually, to flat-out ballsy daylight assassinations in public. The Boston newsmen were in perpetual motion, with extra editions printed every few days. Everywhere she went in the house, there were newspapers. Young boys hawking them on street corners till long after dark were making a fortune.

❖

Jersey banged through the front door that afternoon and tossed a copy of the *Post* to Mac. She sent another copy off to Roxie at the end of the sofa before sitting down with a bounce. Mac wondered what had her so animated.

Jersey couldn't sit still, her lips seemed to be holding back a smile, but when she caught Mac's gaze, she smiled broadly.

The warmth of sunlight seared into Mac's chest so deeply, she consciously had to take a breath. She forced herself to stand, willed the feet she couldn't really feel to carry her to the sofa.

Mac labored to concentrate on her group's issues and held up the *Post*. "Must be something big."

Jersey slid over and pushed Hank into Roxie to make room for Mac. She pulled her down to join them on the sofa and took the newspaper back, opening it to page two.

"Starts on the front page, but most of it is here," she said, splaying open the pages across her legs and Mac's, and pointing. "The U.S. attorney general—the fucking *United States attorney general*," she stressed, "is forming a task force, with our attorney general, the district attorneys, and the state police. All to bust up these dickheads. And if we can get to that woman in the DA's office, get some info to keep us clued in, the whole ball of wax could be ours."

Mac and everyone else studied the news story intensely. She could feel Jersey's eyes on her, feel the excitement radiating off her skin, the heat of the powerful thigh pressed against her own. Jersey even smelled of crisp, fresh autumn air, and Mac inhaled the scent greedily.

She couldn't concentrate. After all, it had been a very, very long time since she'd given her heart any consideration and...maybe it was time to think twice. *Who are you kidding?*

"At the meeting the other night," Roxie reminded everyone, "Ralphie said this Mrs. Harrison woman is really sharp. She lives in Hyde Park with her husband, and her folks live in Southie now, but she grew up around here, so I guess she knows how it's always been in this city. I thought it sounded good for us."

"Just last night, Nick told me Big Johnny's nosing around City Hall about her," Hank said. "Guess she's been asking questions Johnny doesn't want brought up."

"More like he thinks a woman should be seen and not heard," Jersey grumbled, "just lay around and be the toy."

Roxie flipped a hand in the air. "Yeah. 'Clean my house, make my supper,' blah blah bullshit."

"She's been asking questions?" Mac frowned at Jersey.

"Nick says Johnny's starting to get hot 'n bothered about her 'cause she's got the DA's ear. She's the curious sort, I guess."

Zim tapped the coffee table. "Ambrosino's had a contact in that office for over a year. Something's up if he's worried."

Mac leaned back on the sofa. "Let's be careful where we step here. Who knows what or who's pushing this Harrison woman, or what her agenda really is. Sounds like she's got something important invested if she's daring to rile up the powers that be. And don't forget that she could spell trouble for us just as much as for them."

Roxie sat forward suddenly. "Well, I like her already. I say we go *really* check her out. Like the ol' accidental-bump-and-buy-ya-coffee thing."

Zim finished his beer and thunked the bottle on the end table. "No time like the present to start building a solid friendship, I always say."

Mac frowned at the newspaper and folded it back up. She looked directly at Jersey beside her and swallowed hard. "We'd need to prepare on two fronts. Think about it." She glanced over at Zim and then turned to Hank and Roxie.

"Don't forget that if the Feds bring in all the boys and the gangs fall, when all the networks get busted up, we'll be left standing out like a sore thumb. Common sense says they know enough about us to want to have 'a little chat.' We'd have to lay low for a while but could use the time to start making our own connections for the future. Pretty safe to assume we wouldn't be the only game in town for long."

She rapped the newspaper into her opposite hand. "Now, this... Harrison woman. Inside details about the DA's movements? Or, hell, about this federal task force? We don't even know if she's good for it. Think about what would it cost us, what's in it for her. Why would she get involved helping us skirt the cops when she's already making a stink about the way things are?"

"I still vote for the one-on-one coffee thing," Roxie said. "Figure out a way to ask her."

"I'll admit, she's got me curious." Mac shrugged. "I would like to hear what she has to say."

Hank spoke into his worn pack of Camels, digging for the last one. "Don't you even think about meeting her, Mac. Gotta be some other way to find out what she knows." He looked up to see everyone watching. "What? You can't," he declared to Mac. "Say she's a plant for Saul or one of them, or she's a Fed, and here you are on a silver platter?" He snorted and lit the cigarette.

❖

The bicycle courier named Vonnie was relatively new, but she walked through the large office as if she owned it, weaving among the desks until she found the one that offered the bowl of peppermints. She selected just the right piece, clearly delaying her departure until Ellie Harrison noticed her and grinned at the routine.

For Ellie, the courier *was* a breath of fresh air in the stuffy district attorney's office, a sunny, momentary escape from the tedium of filing, making phone calls, and typing depositions and briefs. It was an important job and paid as well as any woman could expect, keeping food on her table and the landlord at bay, but the days were long and very busy lately. Of the eight clerks in the department, only the two new hires were her age, also married about a year, and the rest had either appointed themselves as Ellie's mothers or had declared themselves above fraternization.

"Hi, Mrs. H. It's a gorgeous day out for December. You should take your breaks outside today."

"That so, Vonnie?" She sat back and flexed her stiff shoulders. "Thanks. I just might. And I've told you before, please call me Ellie." She leaned toward Vonnie and whispered, "Calling me 'Mrs. H' makes me feel old."

Vonnie beamed at her. She was smitten. It was obvious to the entire department. Ellie knew she'd hear the side-of-the-mouth remarks from her coworkers as soon as Vonnie left.

"I'll try to remember." She popped a second mint into her mouth. "Well, time to go. See you 'round." Vonnie's cheeks pinked as she smiled and left to pick up her next assignment.

"Take care, Vonnie." Ellie watched her leave. A flashback of memory washed over Ellie, as she vividly recalled a taller, similarly cocky young woman enlivening her spirit with a smile.

Alice grinned from ear to ear, returning to the room with an armload of folders. She'd seen Vonnie leave, and they'd exchanged waves.

"Saw your young friend bounce out of here on cloud nine," Alice quipped, settling in at her desk. "Oh, and I passed your dad in the hall. He was coming in with Archie Tanner again. They must have another meeting, you know, like classes for the new councilman." She grinned at her own teasing. "Listen, maybe he'll take you to lunch this time."

Ellie raised a brow. "Right. We'll see." Her father's appearance with Deputy Mayor Tanner was his third this week, and she happened to know that the assistant DA sometimes attended as well. She wondered why the entire city council wasn't involved, why her father was always being singled out. Then she considered the Curley, city council, Flaherty scheme her husband had yet to propose. For a moment, she considered snooping through her colleague Theresa's in-box for hints. Theresa was the DA's senior clerk, but she had the inside scoop on everything.

She shook her head at herself, acknowledging the power her father still had over her deepest emotions and fondest memories. It lifted her spirit, reliving those times in her mind, when her heart once beat for another, when even wintry days were filled with sunshine, and love was the magical force that made dreams come true. And just the thought of her father sent those priceless recollections back into hiding.

But that love never died. Like right now, Ellie touched it every day. So strong that the separation felt like a lifetime, that love was safely tucked away long ago, and nothing her father did to others or coerced her to endure could erase it. Marrying Allen Harrison had been easier to do than avoid, and, yes, she loved him. He was sweet, shy, and caring, and as generous as his own father would allow. But she knew she would never be *in love* with him. It simply wasn't in her.

It was security and financial stability in these difficult times, guaranteed by her father, that kept Ellie aligned to him and to her husband—security and financial stability for the baby due in five months.

She closed her eyes briefly, gathering her composure against another rush of futility. She would never regret her choice to bear a child, but wished circumstances could be better. Salaries of both husband and wife were required to raise a family of means in this day and age. This was a fact. While a select upper class reveled in wealth and worry-free success, banking their fortunes and reaping investments, as her husband often recounted, most Americans like herself eked out simple wages and could only dream of such comfortable lives.

For the future Weston grandchild, such an existence would never suffice. Ellie's father had established an impressive trust fund for the baby, all the while pushing both Ellie and Allen to work every available hour and appreciate the struggles of an extremely frugal life and the value of the dollar. He, meanwhile, entertained all sorts of well-connected characters with expensive whiskeys and Cuban cigars.

As if Ellie didn't already resent his interference in her life so many years ago, she resented him even more and trusted him less each day and sank all her energy and love into the child growing within her. She thanked God that her mother somehow remained warm and compassionate despite Ellie's father's years of political gaming. Being closed out by meeting room doors had probably helped her after all. She hoped it still would, because now he sat behind them with the likes of the mayor and the head of the Irish Mob.

"So I think our new messenger girl has a crush."

Alice's none-too-subtle tease yanked Ellie from her thoughts and made her chuckle. Twenty-two-year-old Alice, a bride of one year, grinned over her shoulder as she headed for the filing cabinets across the room. Ellie shook a finger at her, forcing her expression to brighten.

"She's a good worker and polite. That's all that matters, Alice, and you know it."

"I think she just wants all the candy," said Bea from the desk behind Ellie's.

"Uh-uh," Alice corrected Bea, and wagged her finger back at Ellie. "When Ellie's away from her desk, tomboy Vonnie just breezes right by."

"Personally, I don't understand those people," Theresa injected, halting the teasing laughter in the room. She stopped typing and met the eyes watching her. "Well, I mean, *really.* A crush? You'd think that girl's mother would've put a stop to her foolish ways when she was much younger. She needs help. Homosexuals...She's retarded, you know."

"Oh my Lord." Ellie rolled her eyes and turned back to her Underwood. She tried to resume typing, but couldn't resist. "And it's contagious, I suppose?"

She could sense the others stifling their chuckles while Theresa glared at her back.

"That, I don't know," Theresa stated with a huff, "but I for one don't want them near me. The government should do something for the well-being of the normal population."

Ellie sighed. It was pointless to debate with Theresa, Queen of the Office, Knower of All Truth. Besides, the heartfelt memories of her youth now shifted to the forefront of her mind, thanks to Vonnie's familiarity, and Ellie fought back a warm rush of recollection.

Alice noisily cranked a sheet of letterhead into her typewriter. "All I can say is that this country has enough to worry about with the gangsters and their alcohol and gambling. Homosexuals aren't the ones out there machine-gunning people in the streets. Government should go after the Mob."

Theresa issued a subtle "mmm-hmm" as she typed. After several minutes of quiet, she offered, "It won't be long. DA O'Rourke says there's a plan in the works."

All activity stopped abruptly and Theresa, as intended, was the center of attention once again.

"He's going after them?" Bea asked, out of her chair with excitement. "Which ones? Ambrosino?"

Theresa continued to type, her long nose tilted upward slightly. Ellie discerned a smirk on those tightly pressed lips.

"I'm not at liberty to say," Theresa uttered, reading from the paper beside her machine and typing blindly.

"Oh, come on," Alice goaded her, and several others wandered closer to Theresa's desk. "You can't tease us like that. Give us the scoop, girl."

CHAPTER FIFTEEN

"Honest, it's a swingin' joint. Bound to be jumping for the holidays."

Mac studied the street ahead from beneath the tilt of her Fedora. She wasn't nuts about this night-out suggestion of Zim's—and really resented being forced to walk on the inside of the sidewalk—but majority vote had been to get the hell out of the damn house for a change.

She glanced to Zim at her left and nodded. Jersey and Roxie strolled ahead and Hank at the rear. A night of recreation was rare for them as a group like this, and they weren't well practiced.

As much as she longed to sit and enjoy a fabulous meal, drinks, and entertainment at one of Boston's exclusive nightspots, Mac had more than seating reservations about this night. Despite Jersey's reassurances, Mac couldn't shake the creepy feeling that the veil shielding their ghostly operation was slowly being pulled aside. A couple of glitches had turned up on a few of their most recent jobs and finally pushed Mac to cross the line for their own protection: they now carried guns on a regular basis, and they knew how to use them.

Their dress shoes clacked loudly on the sidewalk bricks. It was almost a whole block from where they'd parked the Fordor on this cold, late-December evening, and Mac knew that the longer they walked, the more conscious they became of their vulnerability. Jersey had bitched for ten minutes straight about finding no closer place to park. The occasional white globe lamps that hung from storefronts provided faint light along this isolated back street and Hank's head swiveled as he surveyed dark doorways and pitch-black alleys.

Roxie grabbed the sleeve of Jersey's overcoat when a long-nose Packard curled around the corner up ahead. She teetered in her new pumps, and Jersey made a show of cuddling her "date," wrapping an arm around her waist and snugging Roxie to her hip. She drew her own Fedora down to shadow her face.

The massive car filled the narrow street, *like a chambered shell in a rifle*, Mac thought, and angered quickly for having lost a shaky sense of security to one of helpless exposure.

Heavily chromed drum headlamps, blinding suns the size of dinner plates, flooded the darkness and Mac and associates turned their faces slightly away from the glare. Roxie chose that moment to toss her head back glamorously and laugh flirtatiously at something Jersey said. The clever distraction made Mac smile.

"Keep walking and talking," she said. "Laughter is good." With both hands in her coat pockets, Mac inhaled a calming breath against the overwhelming futility of this moment. She fingered the pack of Luckys she'd taken to smoking lately and her Ronson lighter in her left pocket, and the old-faithful switchblade in her right. She couldn't make a move to the Colt .45 in the shoulder holster inside her suit jacket without being noticed.

Her peripheral vision told her Zim had already reached inside his overcoat for his .38. Jersey, she knew, carried a .38 in her coat pocket, and no doubt had it in hand already. And it was very likely that Hank had clicked off the safety on his .45. Exposing their entire upper echelon, in one place at the same time, was daring at best. Foolish at best, Mac now thought.

Like a locomotive pulling alongside, the powerful Packard glided abreast of them and its guttural rumble muted the patter of tires over cobblestones. Hank issued a boisterous, carefree laugh behind Mac and reached forward to give Zim a raucous slap on the shoulder. Just your average good ol' guys 'n gals out on the town.

Dim light returned to the little street like a refreshing breeze into a stifling tunnel. Zim blew an exhale up to his forehead. Releasing Roxie to adjust her flowing coat, Jersey tossed a guarded look back at Mac and they shared a nod. Jersey's eyes then went to Zim.

"Come up here and get us inside."

They waited uneasily on the dark sidewalk while Zim adjusted his cap and the fit of his wool blazer, and finally stepped beneath the lamp in the entry alcove. Two raps, twice on the black door. A four-inch hole at eye level slid open only long enough for menacing brown eyes to flash at each one of them. The thick door opened halfway and Zim slid in with a side step. Jersey, Roxie, Mac, and Hank followed.

A huge broad-chested man in suit and tie held the door and studied them as they entered the ornate, carpeted foyer, and then closed the door securely behind Hank. Everyone followed Zim's lead, waiting politely for the doorman to open the inner door. They stared at their reflection in the brass-framed mirror ahead of them.

"Quite the place, Zim," Roxie said with a grin. She was on the verge of bouncing in her new patent leather pumps. "How come we've never been here before?"

The doorman swung open the inner door and overwhelmed them with sounds of music, laughter, and clinking glass.

Mac, Jersey, Zim, and Hank removed their hats while Roxie primped with a palm to her glittering beaded hair. Mac's eyes went everywhere at once, and she realized the impossibility of searching every face, assessing every possible threat in such a large, throbbing gathering as this.

"Steffan," the tuxedoed host called as he strutted toward Zim. The others exchanged curious glances.

Roxie leaned against Mac's shoulder. "Steffan?"

"German for Steven?"

The maître d' made a show of coming to a stop and producing a gleaming smile. He offered a slight bow.

Standing as tall as his five-foot-six-inch frame could take him, Zim met him brightly, one hand clapped onto his shoulder, the other extended. "Alfred, looking dapper as always, my man," he said as they shook hands.

Alfred's smile was as broad as his welcoming gesture, an arm reaching toward the busy club room. "So good to see you again." He nodded at them. "Won't you follow me, please? I have the perfect table for you all this evening. Just as I promised."

Zim sent Mac a cocky grin. He led the way behind their host, through a maze of white linen-covered tables, leather club chairs, and parties of varying number. Waiters hoisting trays of steaks and desserts and champagne flutes paused politely as the entourage crossed their paths. Mac took in as much of the scene and its occupants as she could.

She made eye contact with elderly men squinting at them through cigar smoke, smiled pleasantly at gawking couples, and grinned and winked back at an array of seductive, finely dressed women. Thankfully, no one seemed to recognize them.

Alfred finally stopped at their table, situated along the wall at the far end of the long room. Nearby, a seven-piece jazz band was settling in for its next set opposite a massive, highly polished mahogany bar, presently swarmed by thirsty patrons. With another grand gesture, Alfred offered the curved three-person leather booth and its accompanying brass-nail club chairs.

"A waiter will be along directly," he said, and handed them menus. "Please feel free to signal me if I can be of further service. Enjoy your evening."

Their colorful cocktails arrived within minutes, and they settled in, still surveying the crowd, the musicians, and the layout of the club. Roxie's stream of eager dance partners began forming by the band's second song. She'd hardly taken more than three sips of her drink. One blushing young man in gray pinstripes even chose to wait by their table to be first in line when Roxie returned. Thankfully, she had him out on the floor promptly.

Hank shook his head, grinning with the others. "Where does she get that energy?"

"Maybe from this damn drink," Mac said, stealing a sip of the Side Car and wishing she hadn't. "Cognac isn't for me." She coughed. "I'll stick to this Ward Eight rye."

Zim teased Jersey about her "sweet and gentle" pineapple-filled Mary Pickford as Roxie rejoined them, breathless and overheated. They all watched her gulp down her strong drink without blinking.

"Bet I can out-Charleston every girl in this joint," she proclaimed, dabbing at her perspiring forehead with a handkerchief from her purse. "Lord knows the guys don't have it."

"You're just too classy for them," Mac said, smirking.

"Too dangerous is more like it," Hank added.

"Especially in that dress," Jersey said.

Roxie cupped Jersey's chin affectionately. "Why, thank you, darlin'. You brave enough to dance this waltz with me right now?"

Jersey rose to the challenge. She took Roxie's hand and led her onto the crowded dance floor.

Mac felt a twinge of melancholy at the sight, remembering the last time she'd danced with a woman in her arms, the firm softness in her hands, warm breath against her neck, the scent of lavender playing enchanting games with her heart. Funny, she thought, actually chuckling at herself, she hadn't even known how to dance at the time. Olivia made everything easy. Mac blinked when polite applause ended the dance, and her attention returned to the present.

She was content to crowd watch while the others visited the dance floor, but there were never fewer than two at the table with her at all times. Hank rejoined them just as their steaks arrived, and he downed his second beer, then rubbed his palms together briskly in anticipation of the meal.

Roxie returned last, bubbling with energy, and disrupted everyone to claim her seat between Mac and Jersey. "Oooh, that one's name was Robert," she whispered to Mac. "The cat's pajamas, if you know what I mean."

"Down, girl. Eat this scrumptious meal if you want to keep up your energy."

"By the looks he and his buddy are giving you," Jersey said, "I'd say they'll be coming over soon."

Roxie grinned, swirling the ice in her empty glass. "They're both looking over here?"

"Mmm-hmm." Jersey nodded as she chewed.

Hank snickered and pushed away from the table. "Nature call. Be right back. And I'll order more drinks."

Roxie wiped her mouth with her linen napkin and slipped her fingers through Mac's hair. "I've seen a few classy-looking dolls checking you out," she said. She pressed her shoulder to Mac's and lowered her voice. "You're looking very sexy tonight in black pinstripes."

Mac snorted. "Thanks, Rox. You're steak's getting cold."

Roxie ignored the hint. "Listen, Miss Tall and Mysterious. See the blonde in the corner? Sitting with the two older women? She's had her eye on you since we sat down. You need to get off your tight little ass and ask her to dance."

Mac set down her fork and looked Roxie in the eye. Beyond her, she could see Jersey grinning at them.

"What are you smirking about?"

Jersey shook her head and cut another bite of steak. "Nothin'."

"You think I shouldn't?"

Her mouth full, Jersey shared a grin with Roxie and shook her head again at Mac. "I don't think that," she managed to say after swallowing, "I just think you won't."

Zim startled them by slapping a five-dollar bill on the table. Silverware and ice cubes rattled. "A fin says Jersey's right."

Roxie dove into her purse and pulled out a five, too. Mac's eyebrows rose.

"Aw, shit. Now I need a drink. Where the hell's Hank, anyway?"

"See?" Roxie persisted. "The blonde again. She just looked at you over her shoulder. Very seductive."

"It's only a dance, Mac."

Mac scowled at Zim and glared at Jersey. "Bet you think this is funny."

"Yup." Jersey grinned into Mac's glare and sat back with a satisfied sigh. "Damn, that was delicious."

"Fine. Put your money where your mouth is, then."

Jersey chuckled as she reached for her wallet. Roxie leaned toward her and said, "She just looked at Mac again. You see that? The smoky eyes?" She tilted back toward Mac. "She wants you. Go get her, tiger."

Jersey and Zim laughed, and three more fins were added to the pile.

Mac picked up her empty glass and for the third time cursed the solitary ice cube. "What the hell time is it, anyway?" She scanned the large dining room for signs of Hank. He'd been gone almost a half hour.

Zim pulled a pocket watch from his blazer, and Roxie checked the sparkling Bulova on her wrist. "Nine thirty," they said in unison.

Mac looked around the room again. Jersey did, too.

Roxie patted her lips with finality. "Time for me to dance off this meal."

Zim looked to the table where her previous partner sat. "Sorry, sweetie, but the cat's pajamas left. His buddy, too."

Jersey and Mac locked eyes over Roxie's head.

"I'll go," Jersey said, standing and forcing Zim to let her out of the booth.

Mac caught Zim's eye. "Find Hank."

Roxie's dancing jitters became nervous fidgeting. She shot a glance at Mac and then joined her in surveying the room. "That handsome fellow, Robert, talked a lot while we danced. Said he was glad to meet me and hoped to meet my lady friends."

Now she had Mac's attention. "What else did he say?"

Roxie shook her head slowly. "Just that he thought he'd seen Zim here before and that Hank might look familiar, too, but he wasn't sure."

"Hank's never been here, Roxie."

"I know." She toyed with her napkin, then brought it to her lap with both hands. "You think the guy recognized Hank from a job?"

Mac's blood was racing. Something was very wrong. "He's always worn his hair long and had a two-week scruff going before he pulled an inside job. I doubt anyone would recognize him."

But someone did. She could feel it. Hank hadn't worked inside since the previous October, when he posed as an Ambrosino wheelman on a heist they pulled. With all the blood they'd left behind in the truck, nobody should have questioned that he'd ended up in the river.

Mac and Roxie straightened to alert status at the sight of Zim strolling toward them. He cocked his head toward the door as he approached, and Mac went for her wallet. She was counting twenties when he arrived.

"We gotta go. Now."

Mac tossed a handful of bills on the table and they politely bid the doorman a calm good night, complete with ten-dollar tip. On the sidewalk, Zim led them out of the overhead light.

❖

"Jersey's coming with the car. It's a couple of Jimmy's boys. They took off with Hank just as we got out the back door." The Fordor roared up, everyone piled in, and it roared off. Zim half turned in the front seat to continue. "One of the busboys heard mention of the old Mechanics Hall. He said they were sort of dragging Hank along. He wasn't too with it."

"Mechanics Hall is in East Boston." Mac stared out the right rear passenger window. "On the waterfront."

Jersey threw her a knowing look from the driver's seat.

Mac turned to check behind them. This didn't feel good. Hank had to have been made at their last hijacking several weeks ago. At the time, he'd reported a concern that one of Flaherty's four goons had caught a glimpse of him before Hank knocked him out. What swell luck that the guy had picked their nightspot on their night and recognized him. And now they couldn't let the goon get back to Jimmy to rat them out.

Mac checked her Colt and put it away, glancing out the rear window again. She'd been right to buy that hot arms shipment out of Atlantic City last fall. Protection, she'd reasoned. It was time. These days the streets were lousy with trigger-happy hit men. She wanted her people safe. And so here they were, going to collect one of their own, prepared to do whatever was necessary.

Mac took a deep, silent breath as the impact of that fact hit home. Target practice in the deep woods of North Woburn had been fun getaways for all of them, hopping the train and staying with Gleeson's moonshining cousins, and Mac thoroughly enjoyed shooting handguns again. It had been a while since those lessons with Carter and his Colt. This time, they all took to the "sport" and even excelled with shotguns and Tommy guns, hearing but not really listening when cousin Ernest preached, "if you use 'em to play God, that's how you'll die."

She'd been prepared to play God once, or so she'd thought when she jammed a loaded pistol halfway into a thug's brain. But there hadn't been much of a choice at the time. Did they have a choice now? Were they prepared to play God now? *Shit. Happy holidays to us.*

Jersey put the Fordor through the paces, rattling and bouncing over cobblestones, veering hard around Boston's severe, disjointed corners, and rocketing down the alley and slamming to a stop one block from the well-known building.

Mac grabbed Roxie's thigh. "Stay with the car."

"The hell I will—"

"You're not dressed or armed for this. You stay." She watched Roxie leave her Bulova behind. "Rox, please wait here."

"Hurry up." Roxie scooted across the seat and crowded Mac against the door. "Come on. Hank's in there. Get out of the goddamn car."

Jersey tossed her the Fordor's lug wrench as they ran around the block.

The deserted warehouse district backed up to the shipping docks at the edge of Boston Harbor, and dark and desolate on a Saturday night, it reeked of the salty swamp of low tide. The stiff on-shore breeze carried a bone-eating chill this time of year, threatening to render them numb and swallow them whole. Slipping along the side of the building single-file, no one made a sound. An occasional seagull broke the silence, cawing into the monotone of waves against pilings, but they kept their footfalls light.

Mac nudged Zim as they turned the corner and pointed out the Dodge Brothers four-door sedan. At the building's rear door, Jersey took a breath and turned the knob delicately. Miraculously, the door opened without a squeak, and with guns drawn, they stepped silently inside.

As their eyes acclimated to the pitch-black, they reached out to feel for each other. Mac drew Roxie against her side and Jersey tugged Zim to hers. She stepped up to Mac's chest and pressed their cheeks together. They hugged Roxie and Zim closer in the dark.

"A hallway," Jersey whispered, her lips brushing Mac's face, "right ahead. I think there's light down there, probably from under a door."

"I see it," Zim answered. "Come on."

"Mac—behind me. Close." Jersey grabbed her hand and slipped away into the blackness. Mac fumbled for Roxie's hand before letting herself be led away.

The cursing behind the closed door was colorful. Hank apparently wasn't giving the goons anything they wanted—and was paying the price. Just who he was, who he worked for, where his people operated, Flaherty's boys wanted it all and were determined to get it.

They were punching him, most likely had him tied to a chair, and asking questions between blows. Of course, Hank's questioning the goons' heritage didn't help his cause. But when Hank suggested the goons ended up on this earth because their mothers had sold what God gave them, they shot him. In the foot.

But that was all it took for Zim to kick in the door. And when the goons turned guns on them, Zim, Jersey, and Mac shot them dead.

Roxie froze in the doorway, lug wrench dangling at her side. For a moment, they stood stunned by the instantaneous change in the room, the ear-shattering noise cutting to dead silence, and the glaring reality of what they'd done. "Holy fuck."

"Yeah," Mac said. With her free hand, she rubbed at the smoke-induced burn in her eyes. She tore herself away from the hypnotic sight on the floor, the wide-eyed corpses and the expanding pools of blood, and rushed to Hank. She holstered her pistol and cupped his battered face while Jersey untied his hands. "No fucking way we'd let them take you out," she stated firmly.

"I'm gonna…be o-okay, Mac," he said, wincing as she crouched and unwrapped his ankles. Blood dripped, thick and stringy, from his nose and lips onto what had been his finest white silk shirt. "But they may have…shot off my little toe."

She draped his arm over her shoulder, glad she was tall for his sake, and got him to his good foot. Roxie took his other arm. Jersey led them out the way they'd come, and Zim ran ahead for the Fordor.

They sat Hank on a shipping crate near the door, waiting for the car, and Mac focused on Jersey's distant gaze. No doubt she was just as dazed as Roxie. And Zim would feel it too, soon enough. Right now, though, everyone had to buck up. Herself most of all. They had crossed that line—in self-defense—but crossed it nonetheless, knowing full well what rescuing Hank could entail. It wasn't the first trauma they'd had to deal with and probably wouldn't be the last.

She expelled a heavy breath. "Listen, you two." Jersey and Roxie turned to her with vacant eyes. "Roxie and I will take Hank in the Fordor to see Ciro's sister." She glanced at the slumping Hank and set a maternal hand on his head. "Thank God it's only your damn foot." She turned back and found that Jersey's eyes were still on her. "You and Zim take those goons in their Dodge and ditch them, car and all. Dump them at Revere Beach. Let it look like more of their gang warfare with Ambrosino. We'll be right there to get you once we drop Hank off."

against Vonnie's. She patted her stomach. "I'm due in five months. So far, the women at work only suspect."

"No kidding?" She looked down at Ellie's stomach as if she could see the baby. "Wow. You...You must be so excited!" Ellie nodded. "And is your husband gonna make a good father?"

That made Ellie think. "Allen's a very kind man, gentle. Maybe I wish he was a little stronger willed, but I think he'll make a good father, yes. My own father was too strong willed. Still is."

"I'm sorry to hear that. I think...I think I know what you mean."

"Sometimes he's too strong willed when it comes to his family. When I was your age, I desperately needed a more compassionate father."

"Well, at least you have one. And Baby Ellie will have one. I left mine when I was fourteen. In Cleveland."

"Oh, Vonnie, I'm sorry to hear—"

"But it's okay. It was for the best," she insisted, accepting the Coca-Cola bottle from Ellie. "I'm happy here, with lots of friends and a good job."

Ellie suddenly surged off the bench and peered through empty tree branches at the church clock two blocks away. "Speaking of job!" She hurriedly collected her lunch and stuffed the remnants and wrappings into her large purse. "I'm sorry to run away, Vonnie, but I'm going to be late getting back."

Vonnie rose with her. "Don't be sorry, Ellie. I'm glad we got to sit a while and talk. I...I feel like you're a special friend. Thanks a real lot for lunch."

Ellie pulled a bulky napkin from her purse and pushed it into Vonnie's hand. "Dessert. Made them myself. Enjoy." She swung her purse over her shoulder and gripped Vonnie's shoulder. "You take care, okay? See you around the office."

❖

Dressed sharply in spit-polished shoes, pressed black slacks, and matching blazer over a starched white shirt, Mac followed Jersey, Roxie, and Zim into the basement meeting room in Roxbury, the dank, dingy hideout the group had since the very beginning. It had a dirt floor, no windows, three long wooden tables, and a dozen chairs, and it smelled like dust, stale beer, and kerosene. Four oil lamps cast an intimate glow throughout the room, but it still looked more like a cave than anything else. Felt like a cave, too, cold as a meat locker on this mid-January evening. Gleeson turned up the three kerosene heaters, and everyone dared to remove gloves and hats.

Mac took her seat at the center of one table. When the room filled to overflowing, she took off her Fedora and stood.

"Okay, listen, everybody. We're here because the word on the street says the Feds are looking at about a month. I'd guess a couple months. We're working on getting more accurate information, but it's not easy. You know ol' J. Edgar plays close to the vest." A mumble of agreement went round the room. "And we intend to let him be our guest. We're going to just let the ol' boy knock himself out."

Now chuckles circulated among the gang members. "Like to help with that, Mac," Danny quipped, ever eager.

Mac smiled and walked from behind the table, then among those assembled. "You're not alone, but the important thing is that we stay well clear of all the shit that's going to go down. It's doubtful we're in their sights anyway, 'cause we don't have the treasure chests that the big boys have, or the connections everywhere that could 'spring a leak.' And we don't have the firepower, either, or all those wheels they've been tracing. If any of you got a problem, like something you can't get rid of, you know? Stuck in a fix? Go see Zim or Roxie. They can come up with solutions to stuff like that.

"What I'm saying here is that we have enough—for ourselves—to get by comfortably. You all hear me? There's no need to go busting heads for extra cash or cases of booze. Everybody has to stick to the straight and narrow from here on out, until the shit hits the fan. Take no chances. The Feds focus on you, then there's that much less they're focusing on Johnny or Jimmy or Saul or the shitbums at City Hall. And," Mac added with emphasis, pointing into the air, "they focus on you, they focus on all of us. Remember that."

"So you expect to know before it happens, Mac?"

"How much lead time? A week? A day?"

"Probably hours," someone griped.

"Yeah, Mac. What kind of information you gettin'?"

"And how reliable?"

Mac held up her hands and looked at Jersey, who rose and nodded

"Yep."

"Twice."

The gunman angled his head, apparently trying out different firing positions. "You bet. Kept mouthin' off at us. So I took off his right ear. Son of a bitch still wouldn't answer our questions. That's when I put the next shot dead center in his left eye." He lifted the pistol and turned to grin at his accomplices.

They grinned back, obediently, and began wandering around the barn. One of them offered to try his hand at safecracking once they found the Waterses' treasure. Another offered to make Carter "disappear." The third was enthralled by Carter's Runabout pickup and thought it should be part of their payment.

The gunman sighed impatiently. "We find the safe, we rip it out of the fuckin' wall. If we don't find it, we'll take enough stuff from the house to keep the boss happy and get us our cut. And yeah, that truck should be worth some serious dough."

Then Mac nearly fainted when she saw Olivia brazenly walk through the barn's front doors.

She had fire in her eyes and an antique Revolutionary War rifle aimed at the men.

"Just what do you think you're doing?"

How could I forget she was in the house? Mac blinked in hopes the vision would be different. *That thing hangs over the fireplace. She can't think they'll fall for it.*

"Well, sweet Jesus. What have we here?" the gunman said.

"You heard me, mister. You better put that gun down or I'll shoot."

All the men laughed roundly.

"First of all," the gunman said, slowly closing on her. "I'm the one with the real gun here."

"This is a very real—"

"Second of all, that thing doesn't even shoot bullets, Miss Davey Crocket."

"It most certainly—"

"And third of all, even if it did shoot something—assuming you knew how to load it and it didn't blow the fuck up in your pretty face—it would only be once." He glanced over his shoulder at the three men, grinning. He turned back in a flash and yanked the rifle from Olivia's hands by the barrel. "Now. That's much better. Bet you're Jed's daughter?"

Olivia jammed her fists onto her hips, her face nearly as red as her hair. "I certainly am, and I don't know what's going on here, but I can clearly see you've hurt Carter—"

"Eh, so he's not so cute anymore. A good tape job on those ribs and he'll be the same gimp he's always been." He hurled the long rifle into the far corner of the barn.

Olivia steamed. "The police are on their way and they're going to take you all in!"

The man sitting on the Runabout's bumper quickly jumped to his feet. "We can't hang around here, Vito, money or no money."

"Yeah," agreed another. "Boss'd rather lose the load than hand us over to the cops...I think."

Vito fingered the fine silk of Olivia's sleeve and then ran his fingertips through her hair. Olivia slapped him so hard he took a sideways stutter step.

With his men snorting in amusement, he backhanded Olivia across the face. No sooner had she landed hard on her ass, he reached down, grabbed her upper arm, and gruffly hauled her to her feet. "Then we take what we can of value and leave."

"Get your hands off. Let me go, damn it!"

He dragged her along as he stormed toward the back door.

"You're taking her with us, Vito?"

"Why not? Don't you think she's worth a pretty penny?" He pulled her to his side and snickered. "I bet Miss Waters just can't wait to go for a ride with us boys. Ain't that right, sweetheart?"

As Olivia cursed like a sailor and twisted against his grip, they made their way to the doorway where Mac waited.

Where are the damn cops?

Mac unhooked the upright oak crossbar used to keep the barn doors closed and prepared to let it swing down onto selected heads as they emerged. She cocked the hammer back on the heavy Colt and aimed it at the doorway.

At the first sign of their hats, Mac let the twelve-foot plank go. As it crashed directly atop one man's head and across another's shoulders, past Mac to the people lining the wall beyond her. Mac turned and surveyed the ones Jersey indicated.

"With any luck," Jersey said, "we might have the specifics of who, where, and when in a couple weeks. That's if the Feds have even made up their damn minds yet. Could be much longer. We'd love to have it sooner, but it's hard to say right now. We can figure it's going to be last-minute, but all I got for you is that we're working a source."

Mac strolled the perimeter of the room, listening to Jersey's carefully chosen words. She stopped in front of a slim girl seated on a pile of boxes.

The girl dropped what she was eating into her lap, wiped her hand on her pants, and tipped her cap. "Mac."

"Vonnie, right?" she asked quietly.

Wide-eyed with surprise at being known by name, Vonnie could only nod. Mac helped herself to a cookie from her napkin, winked, and moved on.

From the back of the room, Mac took in the sight of her twenty-five-member gang. This could be the end of it all, she mused. Just one slip up and it could all crash down upon them. Their self-imposed family. Her carefully composed, handpicked family, providing its own version of the warmth, companionship, and security she still recalled from her youth.

She was distracted by the cookie and its familiar taste, a vague sensory memory that clashed with the severe realities being verbalized at this meeting. Mac discarded the interruption. Lives had already been lost in the past several years, more could be. If they could just land an inside tip or two and stay underground, lay low through the massive raid that loomed, their small group would make it.

Roxie was standing at the table, reminding everyone of the nitty-gritty items they needed to wrap up. The Feds used fingerprints now, she reminded them, so they all had to watch it. Change all vehicle tires so no tread patterns could be traced. Barrels and empty bottles around the house, manifests, tallies of loads or cash, gasoline cans for the trucks, work shoes, any and all weapons…The list went on, things everyone had to bury someplace distant, or dump in the river or, preferably, burn. Small, discreet barrel fires were always available throughout the city, at the docks, and the North and South Station rail yards, Roxie added.

Mac listened with satisfaction. Her associates were on the ball.

There could be no trace of these last few years. She didn't anticipate a raid on their Victorian, but precautions were under way there as well. Everyone hoped the Feds would systematically round up members of the big three while raiding those headquarters, storehouses, garages, and shops that fronted goods, guns, and alcohol.

Zim took over the meeting to discuss money. Collectively, they had a remarkable stash that could assist each of them for as much as a year, if they were picky about things. All of it was cash on hand, not one cent put into the trust of stuffed shirt bankers. He outlined the plan for payments, and everyone was impressed, grateful to know some decent money would be tossed their way every week to augment the meager jobs they still worked.

Completing her circle of the room, Mac returned to the table as Zim took his seat. Hat in hand, she opened her blazer and sat on the edge of the table.

The squashing of the Mob, she quietly explained, would open a huge void throughout the city of Boston, and if they played their cards right and added only selected associates and choice middlemen, they stood to become the city's biggest, most powerful supplier in short order. But such a position would be short-lived. There was no doubt, she stressed, that remnants of the Mob would fight to regain prominence, but with any luck, their gang already would have the upper hand, and should remain in control for some time. Monopolizing the supply not only stifled demanding politicians and cops, but shut off resources and leverage for any resurgent Mob outfits. Jobs as they knew them, Mac said, would be replaced by a web of connections and deliveries and not be limited to the city proper. As a group—as a *business*—they would cover a larger area and ideally draw even better paydays than they'd seen to date.

"How long do you seriously think we could hold out, Mac?" Buddy asked.

Several questions were voiced at once, and Mac raised a hand.

"Hang on, there." She tossed her hat onto the table behind her and leaned back on both hands. "Only a fool would think we could withstand the Mob without a major overhaul here…like a hundred more guys, an armory, and direct shipments from Henry Ford." Everyone laughed. "But we can make hay while the sun shines, as the saying goes. Look, once the big boys are out of here, you know as well as I do that the

New York and Jersey bosses will be in town, looking to set up their own patsies. Probably take them…what?" She glanced at Jersey for a suggestion and received a shrug and two upraised fingers. "Probably less than two years before their heavy hitters make serious headway."

She stood away from the table and put her hands on her hips. "No one here is naïve. The Mob making headway means they'll dent our operation—financially, and more importantly, personally. I will not stand here and lead or even suggest a war against those guys. No, sir. They use enforcers to make their own fat cats; they kill people so their big man can live in luxury.

"We aren't a gang of assassins. And God knows nobody in our outfit lives like a New York Mob boss. But a .45 stuck in somebody's mouth will get them bastards anything they want pretty damn fast. We know too well how they work. We can go toe-to-toe as long as they stay small-time, but let's face it: Before long—before we lose anybody—we'll have to pack it in.

"By then I want us to have money in our mattresses in homes that are paid for, living quiet little lives, working our quiet little everyday jobs. Hit and run is the name of our business, and there's only so much luck to go around. I want each of us to get every last cent we deserve from this rat race and get the hell out as soon as possible. We're going to be smart enough to know when to get out and stay out."

Hands in her pockets, Mac sat on the edge of the table again. "Remember back when we all were kids, people like cops, firemen, city officials, even mothers and fathers were placed on pedestals. They commanded respect and obedience. Today, and don't ask me how, things pretty much are upside down. All you have to do to see it is leave for a while. You did it," she said, gesturing at Ralph, who'd done four years for embezzlement, set up by one of Flaherty's city councilmen. "You did it, too," she said, and Millie nodded back. Drugged and raped by an Ambrosino hit man who never saw a minute of jail, she'd spent two years in an asylum, committed by her well-reimbursed mother.

"I did it. And so did most of you in some way. But it doesn't mean we have to turn upside down with them. I don't believe life is supposed to be like this." She motioned toward their cavern-like meeting room. "I believe we should be able to earn a living—in the real sense: salaries to live on, not just dream about. Maybe it'll take a miracle, like the banks giving it all up, or another war, but if we completely lose ourselves in this upside-down process, if we stay dug in too long, we'll either end up with nothing or end up dead."

❖

Jersey finished her codfish sandwich and slid the plate aside. The ship's wheel clock above the Union Oyster House door said her contact was a half hour late, and Mac, who'd already finished her chowder, wasn't thrilled about waiting.

The bell on the front door jingled and Vonnie strode in, wired from bicycling the several blocks from the State House. Mac watched the vibrant expression dim when she was spotted.

Jersey gestured to the clock to make a point, but Vonnie sat on the adjacent stool and looked past her to acknowledge Mac with a nod. Mac nodded back, impressed.

"Hi. I didn't know you'd be here. I'm real sorry I'm late. We've run into a snag." She pulled off her gloves and stuffed them in her satchel.

Jersey sipped from her porcelain coffee cup. "*We* have?"

"She's gone."

"What do you mean, she's gone?"

Vonnie inched slightly away. Her eyes flicked to Mac. Jersey leaned across the space and muttered under the breath. "Don't look at her. *I* asked you the question."

Vonnie didn't look away from Jersey when Mac lit a cigarette. "Um…yeah. Well, I-I went in as usual, but I knew something was up when I saw no candy."

Jersey sighed toward the opposite wall. "The point, please?"

"Sure…um…" Vonnie's voice trembled. "No one in the office said much, so I waited outside and caught her friend Alice going to lunch. So Alice said Mrs. H was let go 'cause she's pregnant."

Mac snickered. "That's stupid."

Jersey signaled the waitress and pointed from her coffee to Vonnie.

"Yeah, ain't it though? But…but then Alice said the office girls are taking her to the new Ritz Carlton for lunch next week. I'll speak to her then, don't you worry."

"I'm not worried about you getting to her," Jersey said evenly, raising her cup for another sip. "How she's now supposed to have what we need, though, that *does* worry me."

"She and Alice visit each other all the time," Vonnie said. "That's what Alice told me. So she'd know the score."

The waitress delivered Vonnie's coffee and moved to refill Jersey and Mac's, but a nonchalant wave of Jersey's hand sent the woman away. Vonnie made a project of adding sugar and cream to her black brew, the spoon rattling incessantly against the porcelain, and Mac raised an eyebrow to Jersey.

"Listen, Von," Jersey said, using a softer tone, "You don't need to be nervous, you know. I'm not some thug who's going to hurt you. Is that what you think?"

Mac always enjoyed watching Jersey in action, especially at meetings like this where a good one-on-one first impression went a long way for a long time. Here, Vonnie's self-confidence seemed to wilt in Jersey's presence.

"I knew you wouldn't be happy with me." She started to raise her cup, but her hands shook too much. She set it down carefully.

"I'm unhappy with your news, Vonnie, not you. I think you've done a great job."

"Really? Gee, thanks. I've worked hard, but now this. I didn't know they'd fire her just because she's pregnant."

"Let's hope we can still get what we need."

Vonnie nodded in earnest, then managed to lift her cup and drink. "I hope so. I can't help feeling that I've let everyone down."

Jersey just shook her head.

"You did well," Mac assured her. Extremely well, she thought, but now they had a serious problem. If this Mrs. H no longer had what they needed, they might have to tap someone else. Mac nudged Jersey's saucer and jutted her chin toward Vonnie. Jersey nodded back. She'd give Vonnie another crack at it.

"Will you have something a week from today?"

Vonnie nodded. "Their luncheon is next Wednesday. I could meet you here on Thursday."

"We absolutely have to get something substantial. Who knows what's taking shape right under our noses."

CHAPTER SEVENTEEN

I'm not thrilled about Curley's scheme, Allen, so this won't be easy for me either, but I'll do my best." Ellie squeezed his hand to reassure him as they entered her father's study.

"Ah, the parents-to-be," Jonathan Weston pronounced with a knowing smile. He lowered the evening paper and waved them in. "Now what's this you mentioned at dinner, Allen? Sit right here."

"An after-dinner drink, Dad?" Ellie moved to the Sterling tray on the sideboard, knowing he enjoyed a few fingers of Scotch each evening.

"Of course. Pour one for my son-in-law, too." He narrowed his eyes at Allen. "Looks like the boy could use a healthy jolt."

Allen sat forward in the wingback chair and discreetly took a breath. "Actually, sir, I'll pass, thank you. I've got a rather important issue to discuss. A business matter that comes from the mayor's office."

"I see. But earlier you implied this involved a salary increase, a promotion." Her father accepted the leaded crystal glass from Ellie without a glance or word in her direction. "Was I mistaken to see the flicker of an entrepreneur in you?"

"No, sir. Well, this is a business matter, first, but I'm sure you'll agree the mayor's plan benefits the many parties involved."

Her father chuckled heartily and shook his head before sipping.

"What's amusing, Dad? Allen's quite serious." It never ceased to amaze Ellie how quickly her father could edge his way under her skin.

"Oh, I can tell he is, dear, by the words he chooses when he's around me." He bent toward Allen briefly. "You sound like a politician."

Still standing at her father's chair, Ellie patted his shoulder. "As do you. So you two are bound to see eye to eye about this. It means a lot to Allen—and to us, Dad."

Finally, her father twisted in his chair and looked up. "Are you running for office too, Ellie? I was under the impression your husband was here for some man-to-man discussion."

"Stop," she said, disguising her irritation with feigned disappointment. She playfully slapped his shoulder. "I'm just excited for him to get you on board."

He had turned back to face Allen, and Ellie shuddered at the one-sided dynamics at work between them. He'd once seen Allen Harrison as his daughter's salvation and pushed the educated young man with the upstanding Boston background into Ellie's life to settle her into the role of healthy, wholesome American wife. But after her father's appointment to the city council for South Boston, Ellie watched him tackle life's challenges with a heightened vengeance. As if his black-and-white approach to family hadn't been severe enough, his official stance seemed more tainted, more shadowed than ever.

He addressed Ellie over his shoulder. "You'll excuse us now, Ellie, so we can get on with it."

She didn't expect her husband to rise in her defense, to insist she stay. She didn't expect him to even open his mouth. It wasn't in his makeup, standing his ground, displaying a little courage. And as she closed the polished doors behind her, a multitude of emotions flooded her heart and mind.

She really didn't want to stay and see Curley's plan of graft and Mob activity endorsed by her father and husband. She hated the conspiratorial, pompous gleam that showed too frequently now in her father's eyes. She mourned the state of a kind young man's character, when he willingly succumbed to those who risked the welfare of his family.

She sagged back against the doors, weary, her face in her hands, wishing life could be easier, happier, brighter, but except for the wonder of life growing inside her, she knew better.

She shook her head at how easily she could sense her father's impatience through a heavy door, and could only imagine how her soft-spoken husband was coping.

"You're telling me that Gerald has been 'propositioned' by the mayor's office?"

Ellie cringed at her father's ire. She bit her lip, knowing Allen no doubt was fumbling forward in his father's best interest, when he'd never been able to stand up for her. *How did you ever let this go so far?*

There was coughing in the study now. Ellie balled her fists as she stood eavesdropping. As clearly as if she were standing before them, she could see her father snickering, her non-smoking husband choking on the expensive Cuban cigar that had been pressed into his hand. She was tempted to step in and speak her mind.

"What?" Her father's booming voice vibrated against the doors at her back. "Tell me you're not asking *me* to ensure their protection. What on earth do you expect me to do?"

Ellie half turned and stared at the doors as if expecting Allen to escape. But there was more coughing instead and his muted words she couldn't understand. Lulled into thinking conversation had calmed, Ellie literally jumped when her father yelled.

"Do you think I have any influence with that rat? Flaherty is at the top of law enforcement's list these days, along with Ambrosino and Minsk. What in the name of God do you think I can do? Is there some assumption here that Flaherty and I or the council…are connected? Because, if there is, then you had better—"

"Oh, no, sir! Not at all, sir!"

Allen sounded desperate. Ellie pasted on a broad optimistic smile, knocked with one hand, and stepped into the fray.

"Just checking on you fellas. How's it going in here?"

Both of them turned and stared. Allen was ghostly pale and perspiration glistened across his forehead, while her father sat red-faced in a cloud of cigar smoke.

"Ellie. We're in the middle of business here and don't appreciate the interruption." Her father sat back, his demeanor calm, his face taut, and hurried back into his conversation. Ellie stalled her departure.

"So tell me," he said at last, raising a piercing stare at Allen, "things get a little…testy, who will take care…er…who confers with law enforcement?"

"I—I don't know about such things, sir."

"No, of course you don't." A trace of a smirk appeared at the corner of her father's mouth, and Ellie wanted to slap it off his face. As if sensing her displeasure, he sent her a sideways look. "Ellie. This isn't a woman's business and certainly not yours. Leave the room now."

Ellie felt more inclined to stomp her feet than set them into a retreat motion. She never liked squaring off against her father in this room when she was a little girl, and she still didn't, but she was sorely tempted. *Maybe we'll have our last conversation here, Dad.* He was hot enough now, but if she fanned those flames, they'd engulf her husband.

Biting back her challenge, Ellie looked into her father's vivid blue eyes for an extra second but saw nothing to keep her in the room. She listened keenly to every word they exchanged as she left, and her husband's comment made her press her ear to the door.

"I was fortunate enough to secure a bit of insurance for this plan on the mayor's behalf. You see, he's now watching someone on the city council who's apparently in quite deep with Johnny Ambrosino."

"And you know this how?"

"Well, sir, I...I myself actually overheard a deputy mayor whispering to someone in the men's washroom at City Hall. I'd gone to the finance commission on an errand for my father. I was in the stall, so don't know who they were, but one called the other Archie."

"Archie Tanner?"

The deputy mayor was hardly a City Hall socialite, Ellie mused. He was as tight-lipped as they came, which made his exclusive meetings with her father that much more curious.

"This...This is very disturbing, Allen. Very disturbing. I hope the mayor goes after whoever it is. We have to put our foot down with these Mob characters."

"Yes, sir."

"And in that vein, you go tell your father that I'm no one's errand boy, least of all to someone like Flaherty, and insinuating otherwise could be construed as an insult to my integrity. I'm confident Gerald will see another way clear to secure his investments."

"Oh, well...Yes, sir. I'll explain it all to him. Thank you for your time, sir."

Ellie scurried away from the doorway and into the kitchen. She couldn't leave that conversation or her parents' home fast enough.

"It's probably time I called for our taxi," she said, helping her mother put a stack of saucers on an upper shelf. "Dinner was scrumptious as usual, Mom." She pecked her on the cheek and headed for the living room telephone.

Ellie lifted the receiver and heard the conversation before she began dialing. Her father gushed anxious words at someone who hardly had a chance to respond.

"That could be all he knows. The boy's not that bright, but he's got a big mouth. We've got to keep my association out of this. You hear me? I don't care what you do about Tanner. For all I know, he's a two-timing son of a bitch out to save his own skin, but we can't let the boy make things worse."

Ellie glanced down the hall and spotted Allen chatting with her mother. She was thankful he didn't want to talk with her right away. At the moment, her knees were shaking and she figured her voice would betray her as well.

The man at the other end of the line flicked what sounded like a cigarette lighter and then exhaled hard. Ellie thought his voice came from his shoes. "You forget that the big man's got a fucking temper? Going to be pretty pissed off if all the stuff you two worked out gets flushed down the shithole, so you make sure that don't happen."

"Hey, granted the boy can barely add two and two, but it looks like he's figured out the players and the mechanics. Hell, he somehow fathered me a grandchild. I know he's a bumbler, and that's exactly why I'm worried he could break this wide open on everyone."

"That pussy son-in-law of yours is a problem that needs fixin'. Watch your step or you'll become one, too."

"It's funny you should ask that," Ellie said. She laughed nervously at herself as she and Vonnie strolled through the Public Gardens, Vonnie wheeling her bike alongside. This jaunt in the sunshine was working wonders for her spirit, and probably her physical health, both of which had been suffering of late. She'd been a wreck since hearing her father and some shadow on the phone agree that her husband was "a problem that needed fixing." Having nowhere to turn for help, and forsaking her father for his clandestine ulterior motives, she slept poorly every night, even though she knew it wasn't good for the baby.

"Both Allen and my mother are pushing me to go stay with my parents for these last few months of my pregnancy. I suppose it makes sense, and it will be great having Mom around, but I worry about Allen. And when he and my father are in the same room, you could cut the tension with a knife."

"Your husband's not worried about losing his job, is he?"

"I don't think so. In fact, the Shawmut and the mayor's office could be working out a lucrative deal for the future. But Allen has reservations, I think, because the deal has something to do with Jimmy Flaherty."

Vonnie went wide-eyed. "The Irish Mob boss?"

"Shh."

"But the newspapers said the Feds are planning a move against all the organizations soon."

Ellie stopped walking and glanced around. "Apparently, J. Edgar Hoover himself plans on leading it."

Vonnie uttered a genuine gasp.

Ellie gazed up toward the golden dome of the State House and sighed. "You know, I heard that the raid has been moved to next month, all because Hoover can't get away from some Supreme Court trial about wiretapping. Imagine, just twenty-nine years old. He's certainly out to make a name for himself, so who knows when the Feds will clean up Boston's monsters."

"Maybe they won't wait for J. Edgar."

"Maybe not. Maybe headlines here won't be big enough for the man."

"Well, I just hope the innocent folks get out of the way when the heat does come down," Vonnie said.

"Oh, me too. The Feds are claiming so many people are on the take, but I don't believe all of them are bad. Backed into corners by bad people, is what I think. In fact..." Ellie leaned toward Vonnie and lowered her voice. "Alice heard the Feds believe there's a small gang of hijackers out there driving all the Mob bosses crazy. She said they are all incriminating each other, and that the Feds are sort of amused."

Vonnie stopped walking and stared.

"What's wrong?"

Vonnie resumed their stroll, looking straight ahead. "Hijackers, huh? Wonder why the Feds think that."

Ellie sent her a sideways glance. "Sound like anyone you know?" Vonnie snapped back a response. "Who me? No."

Ellie noted the frown creasing Vonnie's forehead. Her knuckles had gone white with a death grip on the bike's handlebars.

Ellie cringed inside. She'd come to like this girl, hoped she had a happy life ahead. Vonnie reminded her too much of a certain someone whose future had been torn away. She stopped their walking and placed a gloved hand on Vonnie's shoulder, unconsciously rubbing her growing belly with the other.

"Well, if you did know any of these hijackers—and I'm not suggesting you do, of course—but if you did, you probably should suggest they keep their noses clean nowadays. Don't you think?"

"Oh, well, yeah. Of course. Pretty stupid for anyone to get close to those thugs. I mean, with the task force out there and all."

"Vonnie, listen. Do you know a man named Mack?"

"Mack? Eh...no. Why?"

Ellie watched Vonnie grow pale and searched her eyes for the truth. "According to Alice, these hijackers are led by a man named Mack, and it sounds like the Feds are dying to know how he gets details of Mob plans. I guess they want his help."

"But that's crazy. How would the Feds even know about Mac?"

Ellie tossed her chin toward a nearby bench and they sat. She wrapped her long coat around her more tightly while Vonnie hugged her satchel. Neither of them looked at the other.

Ellie drew a small brown paper sack from her purse and handed it to Vonnie. "Hope you liked them the first time," she said softly. "They've always been my favorite."

Vonnie grinned at the cookies inside. "They're wonderful. Thank you."

"I always have some with me these days." She patted the bulge in the front of her coat. "This baby has a wicked appetite." She seized the lighthearted moment to plunge ahead.

"You're a very sweet young woman, Vonnie, considerate, smart, ambitious...Don't be tempted by others to betray your conscience. If you know this Mack or others who do, please keep your distance. And if you can't, please be extremely cautious."

"Well, thank you, Ellie, but really, I don't—"

Ellie squeezed Vonnie's forearm. "Personally, I advise keeping one's distance from the Feds, too. They're out to make arrests, Vonnie. Driving the Mob to distraction is all well and good, but it's really playing with fire. And running around with alcohol is against federal law, regardless of who does it or why. Mack and his hijackers are going to be locked up just as fast as the Mob."

Vonnie nodded solemnly. "Guess we should all plan to stay off the streets, if the Feds will be on the loose," she muttered. "No one has any idea when?"

"Alice heard that they may not wait a month for J. Edgar." She gathered her coat around her again and stood. "I can't let this surprising February weather spoil me, Vonnie. The sun's warm, but I can feel the chill starting."

"Oh, yeah. I agree." She leaped up, swung her satchel to her back, and straightened her bike. "Will you be back to see your friends soon? Like for lunch, maybe? We could sit and chat some more."

Ellie smiled at her shoes as they walked. Her brown ankle-strap pumps were an odd, reminiscent pairing with the scuffed black work boots Vonnie wore. "We didn't make a date, but I'm sure I'll be getting together with the girls before the baby's born."

Seeing Vonnie's shoulders slouch moved Ellie to reconsider. Even if Vonnie did have the crush Ellie's former coworkers suspected, it wouldn't hurt to just visit with her again. She conjured a reason to justify the lengthy trolley ride into the city from her apartment in Hyde Park.

"Well, come to think of it..." She touched a finger to her chin thoughtfully. "I do have an appointment next Thursday right around the corner from here." Vonnie's face brightened. "How about we meet at Brigham's for an ice cream?"

"Oh, I'll be here," she said, nearly gushing. "Maybe I can treat you instead."

❖

Mac stared into the broad gilt-framed mirror behind the Locke-Ober bar, noting every movement made by the pair of finely dressed men at a center table. Her four male associates eyed everything else in the mirror, the doorways, other tables and booths, and the four large bodyguards scattered around the room. Mac didn't get an argument when she took a seat in the men-only establishment, probably because her dark suit, starched white shirt, and Fedora didn't immediately betray her gender, or because her entourage discouraged the bartender from making a fuss.

They studied the two men closely, gathered every spoken word they could. Big Johnny Ambrosino and his attorney, Joe Ginnetti, had no idea who surveyed them, in fact had never had a face to put to her name, and that was the way Mac wanted it. She'd simply stopped in to make dinner reservations and ultimately secured much more.

Ambrosino raised his glass in salute. "Here's to another birthday, Joseph. May you have many more."

Ginnetti nodded back and they drank. "You know I'm getting up there when my high-fashion granddaughter invites *me* to dinner. Next Saturday night. Charlotte's bringing a few girlfriends along to treat them to a bit of Boston history. It'll be Locke-Ober's prettiest table despite my presence," he added with a chuckle.

Ambrosino allowed himself a laugh. "She saying you're historic?"

"They're opening the doors for a 'Ladies' Night.' The dining rooms upstairs will still be by private reservation, but the downstairs restaurant will be much prettier than usual, if I do say."

Ambrosino leaned forward. "I know. When Charlotte called to invite me, a grand idea came to mind, Joe, and I think you'll agree." Ginnetti's eyebrows rose in question. "These are trying times we're in, Joe, and this will address the issues that have been keeping me awake."

"The task force is holding off for another month, waiting until Hoover is available. That's what our boys tell me."

Mac met Zim's eyes in the mirror. Their source anticipated the raid much sooner than that.

"It's good we have that time," Ambrosino said, "because several... situations have arisen these past couple days that call for serious *remedial* action. Saturday night will be perfect. You and your young ladies go celebrate your birthday, old friend, and we'll make it a lovely night out for everyone involved."

"Johnny. Don't be reckless. The timing is not good."

"The timing's perfect."

"You want to share with me these things that have you willing to put everything on the line?"

Ambrosino shook his head at his plight as he spoke. "Let's just say our young friend at the bank and his nosy wife, for starters."

"I suspected we'd eventually have a conversation about him. And she's no longer with the DA. You know she's going to have a baby?"

Ambrosino's eyes flared. "Well, I'm going to have fucking heart failure!" He slammed his fist to his chest.

"Lower your voice!" Ginnetti hissed and looked around the room.

Danny and Zim each ordered another drink and glanced at each other along the bar, past Jackson, Mac, and Gleeson between them.

"Fucking old man finally got him to quiet down," Danny mumbled, and Gleeson shook his head.

"Zim, you and Danny go sit somewhere," Mac said, and the pair took drinks to a nearby table. She glanced at Jackson and Gleeson before upending the rest of her whiskey. "Johnny's hot about something and sounds like he's going to use Ladies' Night."

"He's after that dame at the DA's office," Gleeson said, "the pregnant one, Vonnie's source."

Jackson checked over his shoulder to see how close to Ambrosino's table Zim and Danny were sitting. "Hope they can hear better than we can."

"Give Johnny a minute," Gleeson said, grinning over his beer, "and that Italian temper will crank right back up."

"No, goddamn it," Ambrosino declared. "She's just a kid on a bike, for crissakes." Ginnetti responded so softly Mac couldn't hear, but Ambrosino's reaction reached them easily. "Tipping someone off, obviously. And the husband—" He poked Ginnetti in the chest. "He's talking about us on the *inside*. He's not the pussy I was told about."

Now Ginnetti grabbed Ambrosino's wrist and held it to the table. "Johnny. Enough of this here, okay?" He looked toward the snickering laughter at the bar. "See that?" He rapped Ambrosino's shoulder with the back of his fingers. "They can hear you over there. Even the friggin' bartender's laughing."

Ambrosino scanned the patrons lining the bar and those at the four occupied tables. He snapped his fingers and a mountainous henchman appeared at his chair. "Clear the fuckin' room."

❖

Ralph ushered the young Locke-Ober waiter through the back door of the Victorian and pulled out a chair for him at the kitchen table.

"My sister's friend's son," Ralph announced, pressing the eighteen-year-old onto the seat. He pulled the black-out hood off the waiter's head. "This is Charles. He's been real helpful in the past."

"I really didn't see or hear anything. Honest. I mean…I'm not supposed—"

Ralph gathered the back of Charles's collar in his fist. "You'll tell us what we want to know. No playin' around here. You got that?"

Mac slid him an opened bottle of Coca-Cola and offered a cigarette from her pack. He accepted both eagerly.

"Thanks. Say, that Ambrosino guy sure did tip good."

Mac slapped a twenty-dollar bill on the table.

"Whoa. He didn't tip this good!" He reached for the money, but Mac held it in place. He withdrew his hand. "Who are you?"

"Look," Ralph said, bending close to Charles's ear, "everything they fucking talked about. Let's have it."

"Well, Ambrosino called some guy a puss—" And he blanched when Roxie and Millie entered the room. "Um…"

"It's okay," Mac said. "You can say it."

Charles's eyes roamed Millie's bust line and Roxie's slender figure and Mac sighed loudly. Millie strolled to the young man's chair and whispered against his cheek.

"Say it," she breathed. He shook his head, his face reddening. "You're old enough to look at us like that, you're old enough to say it."

"Mil," Mac growled.

"I want to hear him say it," she persisted in her best Mae West impersonation, and ran her nose along his ear.

"Eh…n-no, I shouldn't say—"

Millie snapped open a switchblade and pressed it to his throat. "Humor me, cutie boy."

"P-pussy. Ambrosino called this g-guy a pussy."

Millie moved the blade away and kissed his cheek. "Good boy."

He sucked a hard drag off his cigarette and flicked ashes into the ashtray. Then he rocked back in his chair when Mac grabbed Millie's knife and stabbed the twenty-dollar bill to the table.

"Talk."

"Yeah, well, um...This...pussy guy and the new Southie councilman I guess are son- and father-in-law and they got some deal going with Jimmy Flaherty, but Ambrosino says he's being double-crossed. Hey, I never smoked a Lucky before. Think I could buy a few off you?"

Mac stared at the baby face that now sported a cocky grin. He stared back, but not for long. Ralph slapped the back of his head so hard, Charles bounced in the chair.

"Ow! Shit! Okay, okay. Ah...Ambrosino says the councilman is *his* guy, gotten him a lot of stuff through the deputy mayor—some Archie guy—but now's telling Flaherty all about it. Says Flaherty's gonna take it to the Feds to save his own sorry ass."

"Shit," Jackson said with a snort. "The Feds should just stand by a while. These idiots will kill each other off in no time."

Charles paused, took another drag, and swigged down most of his Coke. Jersey pried the cap off one for herself and drew a chair up close to his. He worked the cigarette hard and watched her warily.

"So," she began. "The illegal things this councilman and the deputy mayor have been doing for Ambrosino? We're supposed to believe they did them just so the councilman could have something for Flaherty to give the Feds?"

Charles nodded vehemently. "Y'know I really ain't supposed to be talking about—" He stopped when Ralph stepped up to his other side. "I mean, you know what those guys can do to you?"

Jersey reached beneath her bulky red sweater, withdrew her .45, and slowly placed it on the table in front of them. She sat back, leaning against his shoulder, but his eyes never left the gun. "You're quite the sharp fella, now aren't you? Getting all that straight." Finally, he turned wide eyes on her and Jersey grinned. The bottle in his hand shook. "You should continue talking now."

Jersey took what was left of his cigarette from his fingers and ground it out. "I just bet there's more in that smart noggin you should be sharing with us."

"You guys gotta understand," Charles said, his voice rising with his fear. "Please, if they find out I talk—"

Mac grabbed his bow tie and pulled, and his face slammed onto the table. Jersey's .45 rocked at the end of his nose and Charles's eyes bulged as Mac loomed over him, pinning him in place. "Maybe you're not the smart fella we thought you were."

She gave the tie a final twist, hauled him upright with one hand, and flung him back into his seat. "Quit stalling."

Charles coughed deeply, bending forward, his chest heaving. "Can...I...Can I have another Coca-Cola?" He peered up at Mac, Ralph, and finally Jersey.

"Son of a bitch." Jersey yanked him upright by the hair. She shoved her .45 into his groin and leaned on it. "Talk, smart boy!"

"Don't—Give me a ch—" Charles nodded as best he could, squirming in Jersey's grasp. His eyes watered. "Please. I-I'll tell you e-everything I h-heard."

"Careful, Jers," Ralph muttered. "Don't make him piss his pants."

Jersey pulled back and moved her chair away. She waved the .45 at him to proceed.

"Um...Well, A-Ambrosino...He paced and swore a lot. He s-said some good-looking doll who used to work for the DA...She's the councilman's daughter and the pussy guy's wife."

Mac and her associates exchanged surprised looks and Charles appeared to puff with importance.

"It did get kind of confusing. I wasn't with him a hundred percent of the time, you know? Honest. I mean I had to get stuff. But I mostly stood where he told me and waited. And pretended to be deaf like he said."

"The DA woman is related to them?" Mac asked. "The ones working a deal with Flaherty?"

"Yeah. He said she must know about her father, the councilman, doing double duty. He said all three of them know too much to let them near a courtroom."

Mac sat back and considered the fate of Vonnie's contact. Even if Mrs. H was involved with Flaherty, she'd given them time to breathe, time to distance themselves from the heat and slip away. She wished there was a way to spare her Ambrosino's wrath.

"Anything else you can think of?" she asked, watching him gaze at her associates. She slapped the table. "Charles!"

"Oh, n-no. Nothing else, I don't think. Oh, he did say something about a summit, whatever that is. That he needed one real soon and the old man said he'd call it. What's a summit?"

Mac just looked at Jersey and she shrugged back.

"It's a meeting, kid," Jackson finally answered. "A big one."

❖

Once Zim nodded "okay" from beside the front curtains, Mac sent Hank to open the old Victorian's imposing door for Vonnie. It was the seventeen-year-old courier's first visit to the house and Mac wanted her to feel welcome, not intimidated.

The round brown eyes widened noticeably when Vonnie came face-to-face with Hank's hulking frame. Mac chuckled and offered her hand as Vonnie pulled off her gloves.

"C'mon in, Vonnie. Good to see you." The small hand in hers was calloused but warm and Mac wondered how far she'd ridden her bike. "Have a seat," she said, gesturing to a spot on the sofa where she moved to sit.

Jersey offered a smile from across the room and Mac saw Vonnie tense.

Roxie said hello, as did Zim, still by the curtains and fidgeting with the dark blue suspenders that stretched over his undershirt.

Mac reached to the coffee table. "Check this out." She hoisted a carrier of six Coca-Cola bottles. "You can buy them like this now. Six at once. Finally, someone smartened up." She opened one for Vonnie, then for herself. "Technology can bring us Frigidaires and moving pictures that talk, and now what they call 'six-packs,' but it can't bring us peace of mind, can it?"

Vonnie shook her head. "I wish it could."

Mac leaned forward on her knees. "So what happened?"

Vonnie swallowed. "Mrs. H never showed up," she reported, her voice shaky. "We were supposed to meet for ice cream. I-I waited two hours. I even rode around her building, and I rode all through the Common and then the Gardens looking for her, and then I waited another hour. But she never showed."

Mac stared at the floor beyond her folded hands. She nodded slightly. "She's called me by name?"

"Well, her friend Alice overheard the Feds say the name 'Mac.' I don't think any of them know anything about you."

"Enough to know we're hijackers, Vonnie." Mac ran a hand through her hair.

"We *amuse* them," Roxie said facetiously.

The others chortled. Mac shook her head.

"They know we get tips to pull off what we do."

"And they want them," Jersey finished, her arms folded across her chest defiantly.

"Well, they're not getting them." Mac banged her bottle onto the table. She lit a Lucky Strike and offered one to Vonnie, who declined. "Time-wise," Mac said, and she looked to Vonnie to correct her if necessary, "it was a month or less, two weeks ago." Vonnie nodded.

Roxie's head lolled back and she cursed at the ceiling. "And we've still got nothing."

"Not exactly," Mac countered, standing and exhaling smoke. She walked around the coffee table and stopped in front of Roxie. "We have more of an idea when the raid's going down than the others do. It's early March, and we've been prepared for over a month." She met Jersey's eyes evenly. "I'd guess it's any day now."

The statement hung in the air until Zim snapped his suspenders unusually hard. Roxie climbed off the chair and stretched.

"Time to see a man about a dog. Any takers?" She headed to the kitchen. When Zim and Jersey called out drink requests and Hank ordered a 'Gansett, Vonnie obviously caught on.

Mac smiled at the innocent look on Vonnie's face.

"She's picked up too much of that lingo. I give her a year and she'll be back speaking English."

Roxie's head appeared around the door frame. "Hey! Just because you're the cat's ass, McLaughlin, don't think a sassy dame can't handcuff you for life!" She returned to her cocktail chores but had lightened the mood in the room.

Vonnie stood and faced Mac. "I'm sorry I couldn't bring you what we needed, Mac."

"Don't think you let us down. You've done us a tremendous service." Mac steered her toward the foyer. "Of course, we wish we had more definite details, but you certainly did all you could. And I won't forget that."

Vonnie looked toward the floor modestly. "Mrs. H was so kind. Understanding, too. Not that I said much, but I got the feeling she really cared."

"She sounds like a fine lady, Vonnie. Am I mistaken here, or do I detect a little more in your disappointment. Sadness, maybe?"

Vonnie shrugged, but then grinned. "I suppose I liked her a lot."

"Ahuh."

"I mean, she's just so pretty. Gave me advice, cookies...her attention, I guess. She's so easy to talk to. I'll miss her. She's special, Mac."

Stifling a smile at Vonnie's infatuation, Mac put an arm around her shoulders and squeezed. "I'm sure she is. And she'll be a wonderful mother, too, right?"

"Yup." Vonnie nodded, but then her body stilled. She looked up at Mac. "You don't think something could have happened to her, do you? Because she said stuff to me?"

"No. All sorts of things could've come up and caused her to cancel your get-together. Maybe she wasn't feeling well. The weather today, overcast and chilly. Who knows? And remember, she didn't know how to reach you, either."

"Yeah, true."

Mac gave her another squeeze and signaled Hank to open the door. The typically crisp, late-winter evening was still and silent. Except for the lone lamppost on the corner, it was ominously dark. Mac bid Vonnie good night and tamped down a surge of parental concern as she watched her drag her bike from the bushes and pedal away.

Once back inside, Mac found herself lost in thought as Roxie handed out drinks. Hank stood in the parlor entryway, his hands on his hips. "Think something *did* happen to that woman?"

Everyone stopped talking at the thought. Finally, Zim set his drink on the coffee table. "I think Roxie and I'll take the Fordor and follow the girl home."

CHAPTER EIGHTEEN

Sporting a camelhair suit that probably fit him better ten years ago, Gleeson held the chair out for his wife, and their smiling faces joined the others at the linen-draped circular table.

"Jesus. It's like an automobile showroom out there," he said. "Mighty fancy cars all over the damn place. Everyone's showing off tonight."

Mac smiled fondly at him. "Ladies' Night is a big success, huh?"

Frances squeezed his hand and sent everyone a girlish grin. "Not many times in twenty-six years my husband has treated me like a princess. Thank you, Mac."

With a wink, Mac lifted her glass in salute.

Seated to Gleeson's left, Jackson elbowed his arm. "You slacking off, old man?"

Gleeson leaned his bulk into him and spoke in a loud whisper. "At least I knew a good thing when I saw it and I didn't ignore the inevitable." He elbowed Jackson back and flashed a smile at his date. "Good evening, Millie."

She laughed and hooked her arm through Jackson's. "We just enjoy the hunt, don't we, sweet thing?"

Everyone laughed and mimicked "sweet thing" around the table.

Roxie stood up, foxy as ever in a sleeveless knee-length satin sheath and dark silk stockings. She raised her Side Car for a toast. "I just want to say that this is one *fine* looking table, and even though it *took an act of God* for *someone* to come out and play," and she hip-bumped Mac's shoulder, "it's sure worth it." Amused looks fell on Mac, who blushed as she shrugged. "Furthermore..." Roxie urgently whispered down to Zim, "Is that the right word?" He nodded, holding back a grin. "Furthermore, I want to tell each of you how happy I am that you're my family. I missed my real one for quite a few years until you jokers started growing on me. And now... Well, I want you to know that deep in my heart, I'm thankful." She hoisted her glass.

"Hear, hear," Ralph added, and gave his wife Ann a quick kiss on the cheek.

Jackson crushed out a cigarette, shaking his head. "Jesus, cut the mushy stuff, will ya?"

"We love you too, Roxie," Millie said, making Jackson cringe by tickling his ear.

Gleeson raised his beer. "And here's to Locke-Ober for Ladies' Night."

All glasses rose as the table for ten chorused in agreement. The rousing cheer turned the heads of other diners, and Mac caught Jersey's nod toward a striking brunette across the room.

"Flirting from afar?" Mac murmured sipping her Ward Eight. The rye whiskey and fruit juice made her wince. "Damn, why do I drink these?"

"Gee, she's a real doll, Mac. By the windows. Don't look now. There's three of them. With an old man, looks like. Eh, he just left the table." Jersey straightened her navy bow tie and tugged at the fit of her suit jacket, also navy over a pastel blue dress shirt. Mac had deemed her look "smart and sly" as they left the Victorian.

"Maybe you should go ask if they'll be heading next door to dance after dinner." A fun idea but difficult to verbalize, urging Jersey off to connect with someone. And she just knew that Jersey understood, but that didn't make it easier to handle.

Mac tossed back half her drink. There was love between them, but they were destined to be allies in blood from their first meeting, when the scruffy girl dared the skinny girl to fight in that damn boxcar. Time and maturity had not diminished that allegiance one bit. Now, more than ever, their connection was soul-deep and, although the physicality of romance never fully developed, she knew in her heart that they would remain connected forever.

"Maybe *we* should go over there and ask," Jersey said, with a slap to Mac's shoulder. "After a couple more of these." She downed the rest of her highball.

Ralph's wave brought their waiter, Charles, to their table, and standing tall in formal black short jacket and bow tie, he was remarkably professional.

"Good evening, ladies and gentleman. My name is Charles. Another round of cocktails perhaps?"

Mac grinned up at him. "Well, hello, Charles. Yes, we'd love another round, please."

Millie offered a faux whisper toward Jackson's ear. "This is the boy who almost peed his pants?"

They all laughed while Charles bent at the waist to better hear Ralph's words. The pair whispered long enough to make Mac curious, and when Charles wrote on a second page of his notepad and showed it to Ralph, Mac's curiosity turned to anxiety.

Finally, Charles straightened and smiled at everyone. "I'll be right back with those cocktails and menus, sir."

Mac eyed him cautiously, glad to see he spoke to no one as he left the dining room.

She looked back across the table, directly into Ralph's eerie stare. It made the fine hair on the back of her neck stand up. He tilted his head toward the bar at the rear of the long room and stood.

Mac stood. Jersey stood with her.

"We'll be right back, honey," Ralph said to Ann and patted her shoulder. "Just a little business talk."

She rolled her eyes and shared a laugh with Frances.

Jersey positioned herself at Mac's opposite side as the three squeezed together at the elegant but crowded bar. She leaned forward to hear as Ralph spoke softly toward the wood surface.

"All those fancy cars Gleeson mentioned? You got one fucking guess who the hell is here."

Mac stiffened and Jersey took a breath.

"Upstairs, right now," Ralph said in a mumble. "All three in a goddamn summit."

Mac glanced heavenward, sighing at the copper ceiling tiles. "Son of a bitch."

"I don't fucking believe it. Waiter's gotta have it wrong," Jersey said.

Ralph shook his head. "All the help is on alert, their best behavior." He paused as Mac ground out her cigarette in an ashtray and exhaled hard.

Ralph cleared his throat. "Charlie said there's a few city hall hotshots here, too, in the back dining room. Kinda makes sense, considering."

"Yeah," Mac grumbled, "makes for perfect timing for the Feds, too…considering."

"He said we also should know that one of 'em is out here."

Mac gave Ralph a sideways look. "Who is he and where's he sitting?"

"Way behind us, facing a couple at his table, toward us. White hair, gray suit." Mac's eyes instantly went to the mirror, searching. "But get this," Ralph rapped her bicep with his knuckles for emphasis, "Charlie said he's Ambrosino's double-crossing Southie councilman—and he's marked."

Jersey squinted at him. "They wouldn't try anything in here, for sure."

"Jesus, Jersey, think about what you just said." Ralph raised an eyebrow. "He's probably with his daughter and that son-in-law. All three in one spot. Ambrosino couldn't ask for a better opportunity."

"The *Southie* councilman," Mac repeated, still studying the patrons in the mirror. "Wait," and she turned to him quickly. "His daughter is the one Vonnie worked at the DA's office, right?" Ralph nodded. "So do we know him?"

"Don't think so. We know she's married to a guy named Harrison, that's all, but Charlie thinks the councilman's name is Weston."

The name turned Mac's blood cold with shock. *It can't be. And even if it is… Weston on the take?* Bewildered, she turned to Jersey and saw that he recognized the name as well. The thought nearly left her breathless, that if Weston was still around, then Ellie… Jersey set a hand on her shoulder.

Mac squinted harder into the mirror, desperate now to discern the face. The white-haired man in the gray suit was smiling amicably at his two dinner companions, apparently a younger couple, but Mac couldn't detail the face of that man she'd know anywhere. Damn it, she had to be sure.

And probably shouldn't waste any time, now that she could hear arguing coming from the area of the kitchen stairway. If the big three upstairs were at the yelling stage, no doubt gunfire would follow.

She turned them from the bar and headed back to their table, but when she continued past it, Jersey took her arm.

"Don't do it," she ordered in a hard whisper. "You've got to let it go."

Mac stood frozen in place. The racket from upstairs had spread to the kitchen, and patrons appeared puzzled. A stream of state police officers entered from a rear alley door and tried to appear nonchalant as they went to the kitchen.

"Don't," Jersey repeated. "I know what you're thinking, but don't. Not now, at least. We should get the hell out of here."

Mac looked toward the noise and helplessly back to Jersey. She couldn't speak. She couldn't decide. She turned to look over her shoulder, and a woman abruptly halted less than two feet away. Jersey released Mac.

"Hi." The pretty brunette beamed, more at Jersey than Mac. "I was just coming over to invite you to join us." She extended her hand. "I'm Molly Stowe."

Jersey slipped her hand around Molly's and a flustered grin swept across her face. "Eh…Hello. I'm…I'm Jersey."

"Excuse me, won't you?" Mac asked courteously as she backed away.

She took one step and another woman blocked her path. But this one did it from at least twenty feet away.

From nearly the last table, from within spitting distance of Mac's mystery man, Olivia Waters called her name.

"Mac? Mac McLaughlin?"

Stunned, Mac's jaw dropped, and her feet stuck to the floor. Peripherally, she noticed the white-haired man and his dinner companions turn her way, but she couldn't take her eyes off Olivia.

"Oh my God."

Molly appeared at Mac's side, playful eyes darting all over her. "I don't believe this! You know Olivia?"

Jersey practically jumped to Mac's other side. "Did I hear correctly?"

Olivia remained in place, evidently just as surprised, and her sophisticated beauty rendered Mac speechless. Jewelry glittered from her wrists and fingers, a diamond solitaire sparkled at her throat, and matching earrings captured the light of chandeliers. That brilliant smile, those dazzling emerald eyes resurrected a powerful physical yearning Mac had long since learned to quell. Yet, undeniably, here she was stirring things up in a wickedly purple Chanel silk, rebelliously hemmed above her knees, and a lavender feather boa draped casually around her neck and over one naked, edible shoulder.

Molly grinned wildly to Jersey, who in turned surveyed the room in a panic. Heads had turned their way. Indeed, most everyone surely had heard Mac's name, even over the raucous noise in the kitchen. And the noise suddenly rose to a disturbing level, sounds of glasses and dishes shattering, men swearing and fighting. Patrons murmured nervously. Several called for their dinner checks so they could leave.

"Mac," Jersey said into Mac's ear. "This isn't good. I think it's all going down now, Mac. I'm getting everyone out." She signaled the others to leave. "Hey, are you listening?"

Olivia approached Mac with hands extended, and Mac took them reverently.

"My God, you are a heavenly vision as always, Miss Olivia Waters."

"And you are still turning heads, Mac McLaughlin." She leaned back and examined Mac from head to toe. "I just knew it was a woman in a tux," she said, smiling broadly. "Shame on me for not thinking it would be you." She cupped Mac's cheek, leaned up on her toes, and lightly kissed Mac's lips.

"Olivia." Mac turned her head and slowly kissed Olivia's palm. "I am truly thrilled to see you, but your timing is absolutely terrible."

Jersey cleared her throat. "Ahem. Um…Look, I'm really, really sorry to interrupt, but we need to get the hell out of here right now."

Still holding Mac's hands, Olivia looked curiously at Jersey and then Mac. "Just what in God's name *is* going on out there? Our friend Charlotte went upstairs to get her grandfather."

Molly nodded vigorously and looked from Mac to Jersey. "We

were celebrating his birthday, but he had some damn business to attend to upstairs and hasn't come down."

"I think by now all the upstairs business has come downstairs," Jersey injected.

Mac took Olivia by the shoulders, her fingers trailing across the satin skin. She sighed uncontrollably, and Olivia smiled.

"Come," Mac said, struggling to concentrate as she turned Olivia aside. "Let's get your things."

Jersey joined her, guiding Molly back to the table on the far side of the room to collect coats and purses.

From the dining room's front entrance, federal agents charged in with guns waving, yelling for everyone to remain calm and stay right where they were. That sent patrons screaming for the exits. Mac and Jersey rushed their group along.

"Jonathan Michael Weston?" an agent bellowed, catching Mac's attention. Several agents surrounded the small table where the white-haired man now stood with the other couple. Barely able to see through the ring of agents, Mac glimpsed the young man helping a pregnant woman into her coat.

Olivia craned her neck to spot Charlotte in the storm of patrons and agents and police. Molly grabbed her hand as Jersey urged them all toward the rear of the dining room.

"Mac," Jersey barked through clenched teeth. "Mac, goddamn it. Don't just stand there."

Around them, officials were trying to stem the tide of patrons pouring out of the restaurant. Everyone was yelling something. Patrons were being ordered back to their seats, even threatened with arrest when they refused.

Olivia looked back and broke free of Molly's grip to return to Mac. Jersey went after them both.

Then Mac saw his face clearly. After all he'd professed, after breaking his daughter's heart, her will, after destroying Mac's life, his had come to this. *Payback is a bitch.* The Feds cuffed him, and the pregnant woman broke into tears, sagging into the young man's arms. She was devastated by it all. And Mac knew who she was.

Her knees almost gave out. She shook where she stood.

"Mac," Olivia said, wrapping both hands around Mac's arm, tugging. "It's quite scary here."

"It's her."

"What? Who, Mac?"

Jersey grabbed them both by their arms and dragged them away. "Son of a bitch, Mac, I am gonna beat the shit out of you for this."

"Wait! Stop!" Mac worked herself free of Jersey's clutches and they stopped in the middle of the dining room chaos. "Jersey, get Olivia out of here." She stared hard into Olivia's eyes. "Go. Now. Jersey, take her."

"No, Mac." Jersey grabbed Mac by her jacket lapel and practically yanked her off her feet. "You're both coming with me. Fuck this!"

Tumbling after them, Mac watched the Feds head their way with Weston in cuffs, and the young husband, and Ellie, pregnant Ellie, trailing behind. It was a sight Mac could never have imagined.

Another Fed trotted forward, gun extended and eyes boring into Mac's.

"Hey! Your name Mack? Hold it right there!"

Mac's every nerve vibrated. Jersey yanked her onward.

And then, inevitably, came gunfire.

Salvatore Delgado, brother of the late Tito Delgado, once Ambrosino's head of security, blew through the side entrance with five other thugs, Tommy guns spitting fire and hammering lead into everything in sight. The noise alone nearly flattened everyone in the room. The Feds fired back, missing as they sought cover.

People screamed and scrambled beneath anything they could. Mac and Jersey shoved a shrieking Olivia to the floor beneath a table and then dove on top of her. They knocked the table onto its side as the only shield they had and drew their guns while Olivia curled into a ball and stared at them in shock. They huddled tightly together as wood shards flew everywhere. State police crowded the exits, firing at will, adding to the cacophony and the choking gun smoke that clouded the posh dining room.

Bullets shredded tabletops, walls, and oak flooring, smashed glasses, cups, plates, mirrors, and the precious stained glass windows. Sterling silver platters and bowls clanged into the air and bounced off the floor. Shredded furniture exhaled stuffing while amputated chairs scooted around the room in a terrifying dance.

Jersey dared a quick look and fired off two rounds. Mac did the same from her side of the table, dropping one gunman sidling toward them along the wall. Wrapping an arm around Olivia, she slid them back toward a larger heap of furniture, putting a little distance between them and the battered table.

Behind them, the floor was littered with bodies. Four Feds still returned fire, two from behind the bar, and two from interior doorways, but three other Feds, including the one who had called for Mac, lay bloody and unmoving. So did three restaurant patrons—and Jonathan Weston and Allen Harrison.

Mac glanced back. Ellie was gone. She prayed one of the Feds had hauled her out of the room.

Gunfire quieted to sporadic single shots, with either the Tommy guns empty or their handlers shot. Jersey held up a finger and raised her eyebrows. Mac nodded. One left.

The Feds shouted for the last holdout to surrender, but it took running out of ammunition to persuade him.

State police roared into the room.

"Jersey, get Olivia out of here without too much of a scene. I'm heading up front."

"Like hell I will. Don't start that again." She glanced at Olivia, who sat up between them, her makeup smeared and complexion a ghostly white. "Nothing against you, miss. I just won't leave her."

Olivia toyed with the broken diamond necklace in her hand. "You're a smart woman. It's Jersey, right?" She offered her hand.

Jersey chuckled as she shook the delicate hand. "Yeah, it's Jersey. Hell of a way to meet, huh?"

"Are you two finished?" Mac growled.

Olivia frowned hard. "Why are we running away?" Mac and Jersey exchanged glances. "Well? Oh, I see. Shooting gangsters is only legal if you're a cop."

"There's more to it than that," Jersey said. "We sort of have a name too, or at least Mac does. They want her too but don't know what she looks like." That sent Olivia's amazed expression to Mac.

"I don't know what you've gotten yourself into these days, Elizabeth McLaughlin, but it sure as hell is dangerous. Look at me. This Waters woman does not slip into a Chanel and roll around on the floor…well, maybe I *do*, but not to get shot at. Jesus."

But Mac looked past her. "Get out that back door and through Stoddard's. I'm staying 'cause Ellie's here and I'm going to find her."

Olivia set a palm on the satin lapels of Mac's tux jacket.

"Do you bad-girl gangsters have a hideout?"

"What?" Mac's mind was a blur.

"If we get separated, where do you live?"

"One seventy eight Melvern Avenue in Dorchester," Jersey blurted out.

"Olivia," Mac said firmly. "We can talk later. There's—"

"Shh. Another place, another time. Most importantly, we have to get out of here."

Mac was shaking her head, but Olivia was not to be denied.

"I know what you want, Mac McLaughlin. Now, let's see if I can get us out of this ugly situation." She winked as she prepared to stand. "Seems it's what I do best. Trust me."

❖

They crawled out from behind the shattered table just as a Fed and two state cops called to them, searching for someone named Mack.

It took all of ten minutes, a promise to visit the Bureau of Investigation office in the Custom House to give formal statements, and some of the most outlandish lies Mac had ever heard, and then she and Jersey were outside, being hugged by worried friends and stuffed into waiting cars. The "famous stage actress" felt so safe with so many brave agents around, that her "two personal bodyguards" were allowed to step out for some air.

Mac and Jersey simply shuffled out Locke-Ober's rear door, crossed the alley, tidied themselves as best they could, and slipped through Stoddard's hidden back door. They waltzed like restaurant patrons, around the hopping dance floor and right out the front door, keeping themselves and their associates as far away from official recognition as possible.

Olivia insisted to authorities that she be allowed to console her old Radcliffe classmate who'd just lost both husband and father. Escorted to an anteroom, she paused before entering just to gather her wits.

The ornate room was empty, except for the pregnant blonde who sat tucked deeply into the corner of a red leather sofa, sobbing uncontrollably into a handkerchief. Olivia couldn't help the wave of sympathy that overtook her. *Could a woman ever feel so alone?* Ellie had suffered severe loss on this night, but she'd yet to learn she had also won, and Olivia's heart pounded as the opportunity to tell her beckoned.

Standing in the doorway, Olivia allowed Ellie's stare, the inspection of her rather bedraggled coiffure, her Chanel, the diamonds at her ears, and returned the look as compassionately as she could. Ellie was every bit the beauty Mac described, with the most vivid, enchanting blue eyes she had ever seen. Dabbing at them again, Ellie lifted her chin and spoke.

"They...they told me an old friend, a classmate of mine wanted to be with me, but...I'm sorry, I didn't attend Radcliffe. Do I know you?"

Olivia smiled and glanced over her shoulder to make sure they were alone. She came forward, sat close beside her, and rested a gentle hand on her knee.

"Ellie Weston, I presume?"

"Harrison," Ellie corrected her. "But he's...he's gone now." She held the handkerchief to her face until her composure returned. "I'm sorry...It's hard—"

"Good Lord, yes." Olivia gripped her shoulder. "I'm so sorry for your loss. It was horrible out there. Let me get you something? Glass of water?"

Ellie shook her head. "Thank you, though."

"And you are all right? Your baby, too?"

"Yes. The police are taking me to my doctor in a few minutes. My mother is meeting me there." The handkerchief went up to dab a new round of tears. "Thank God she wasn't feeling up to joining us tonight." Ellie squeezed her eyes shut against the image. "Y-you were out there in that massacre?" Olivia nodded. "How? Well...Who are you?"

"I am a friend of a friend. My name is Olivia Lowry, but it doesn't really matter who I am...although one federal agent now believes he has a connection backstage at the Copley for the entire season. But when you've regained your strength and are feeling up to it, I would love to facilitate a reunion of sorts with our friend."

Ellie wiped her eyes again. "I don't even know you," she said sounding as exhausted as she felt. "You want to discuss this now? And why should I agree to some reunion? A mutual friend, you say?"

"Indeed. One who would give…Well, she actually *did* put her life on the line to see you."

Ellie frowned as she gave this some thought. She looked back into Olivia's smiling eyes and thought that, despite the smeared cherry-red lipstick and the streaks of smoky eye shadow, this could possibly be the most glamorous person she'd ever met. It really was preposterous that she and this Olivia woman would have a friend in common.

"She put her life on the line?" Now Ellie looked at her a little sideways. This simply was too farfetched.

"It's not the first time she's sacrificed her well-being for you, either."

Ellie dried her eyes again and studied the handkerchief in her lap. Aside from her mother, only one person had ever sacrificed anything for her. Gradually, from the myriad of tonight's startling, indelible memories, one in particular came to her unbidden: Olivia, this high-fashion socialite, calling a tall, dark-haired woman in a black tuxedo "Mac McLaughlin."

Ellie's heartbeat skipped. Her hands tightened around the handkerchief. *Please, God.* Turning to Olivia, she straightened her posture and took a deep, steadying breath. She knew her cheeks flushed because heat surged through her like a furnace and she started to shake.

"It's her, isn't it? Stick?"

"Who?"

"Oh, no…um…" Ellie shook her head at herself. Closing her eyes, she took another breath and tried again. "Elizabeth." She stood up, too anxious to sit. "Elizabeth McLaughlin."

Olivia stood also. "Yes, Ellie."

Her eyes squeezing shut, Ellie nearly collapsed as she sobbed. Olivia drew her into an embrace and lowered them back to the sofa.

For Olivia, the irony of her present position was not lost. As she shut her eyes and replayed her own memories, Olivia clearly saw that Elizabeth McLaughlin and Ellie Weston needed that stroke of good luck in their lives right now.

She gave Ellie a squeeze and held her out at arm's length. "I know you must want to see her, Ellie, but…well, for the baby's sake, you might—"

"Oh, I can't see her like this."

"Like what? Pregnant? She's already seen you, Ellie. She knows all she needs to know, but agreed you should rest and recover before…"

"Before we see each other and I deliver this baby on the spot?" Olivia laughed lightly. "Something like that."

"How do you know her?" Ellie asked, her tone suddenly sharp. "Are you lovers?"

Olivia cocked an eyebrow at the woman's moxie. She was tempted to ask what it would mean if they were, but Ellie had been through enough. "No," she said softly. "Her heart's always belonged to a certain someone else."

The impact of her statement was obvious and immediate: if Ellie had been standing, she would have staggered. With a hand on her rounded belly and one on the sofa's arm, Ellie inhaled and exhaled with effort. Olivia tried to imagine recalling years of lost love, losing a promising, stable future to the complete unknown. *They're obviously not the same women anymore.*

"Yes, of course I want to see her. I-I just need some time."

"Quite understandable. If you like, I will be back in Boston in two weeks. Would that be satisfactory? I'd enjoy accompanying you. I'll be driving in myself and could pick you up."

Ellie's brain was completely overwhelmed. In one evening, her entire life turned upside down. Her father's secret life with the Mob got him arrested by the federal government and then murdered by gangsters; her husband and father of her baby took two machine gun bullets in the head; their child now would enter the world fatherless; and the love of her life magically reappeared in an entirely different form.

"Whatever you suggest, yes. Thank you, Olivia."

"There's one more thing, however." Olivia held up her index finger. "You should know that Mac…er, Stick…Well, Stick is a wanted criminal."

Ellie stared at her for several seconds as the words penetrated. "Thank God I'm sitting down."

CHAPTER NINETEEN

Roxie unleashed an exaggerated sigh. "Why, pray tell, are you dressed up for a federal hearing? Cripes."

Lighting a Lucky, Mac stalked across the parlor, buttoning the black satin vest over her white dress shirt. She exhaled hard, set the cigarette in the ashtray, and marched to the long mirror in the foyer, where she tugged the vest this way and that, then tucked in her tucked-in shirt again. She readjusted her slim silver belt buckle for the third time and, for the fourth, checked to see that her trousers were buttoned up. Back in the parlor, she shrugged into the form-fitting jacket of her finest custom-tailored black pinstriped suit. She went back to the foyer mirror.

Mac's nervous energy had her pacing all over the house. She would offer everything she had, even her hand in marriage if possible, to have the life she'd always dreamed of with Ellie.

Jersey tried to reach Mac's reasonable side several times during the past two weeks, and Mac appreciated the effort, the concern, but Jersey didn't offer much that Mac didn't already know. Yes, Ellie was her own woman now, not some schoolgirl hanging from her bedroom window. No, she wasn't a sixteen-year-old to woo with stolen candy or hand-made trinkets. Yes, she'd been a wife, had a husband, was now expecting their child. But who was she exactly? Jersey didn't know any more than Mac did.

Mac itched a lot during those evenings Jersey walked on thin ice voicing raw facts. They weren't facts that put Mac's heart and mind at ease. They collided with "facts" her memory provided, how she and Ellie had clicked together, finished each other's sentences, shared the same dreams, kissed with such abandon, loved with such honesty…A woman can't change *that*, Mac reasoned, not feelings that you're born with…

Zim appeared in the kitchen doorway, arms raised in triumph. "Okay, I made the damn oatmeal cookies."

Roxie came out of her slump in the chair and Jersey spun around to roundly applaud Zim's culinary effort. Even Mac became aware enough to chuckle.

"Are they edible?" Roxie grinned, peeking at him over the back of her chair.

Zim stormed over and handed her a sample. "Bitch."

Jersey took one and grunted her approval, then went to work tuning in music on the Borgia.

Mac declined a cookie. She lit another Lucky.

Roxie waved her half-eaten cookie at Mac. "What if she doesn't smoke?"

Mac stopped in mid-step. She looked at the ashtray on the coffee table, then resumed pacing and dragged off the cigarette.

"Everybody smokes nowadays."

Roxie got to her feet. "All right now, pay attention," she commanded, aiming her words at Mac. "In the kitchen we have plenty for cocktails, the coffee is ready, even water for tea. We have ginger ale, Coca-Colas, and maybe some Hires, if Zim hasn't guzzled them all down. We have cookies to nibble on and a ham for supper. You think you can be Miss Hostess by yourself?"

Mac found a smirk on each face. "Thanks for the vote of confidence."

Jersey stepped into Mac's path and put both hands on her shoulders. "We'll take Olivia on a tour of the place and settle into the kitchen for drinks, okay? You two just stay here and relax." She gave Mac a hardy shake. "Please try to relax? She's going to be twice as nervous as you, being in a strange place with us strangers. Put her at ease and you will be, too."

Mac stepped into Jersey and hugged her hard. Jersey patted her back.

"Where would I be without you?" Mac whispered before they separated.

"Or I you, Mac."

On cue, the doorbell rang and Zim did the honors.

Olivia's refined enunciation sang through the foyer as she introduced herself and then Ellie. Mac's brain jammed upon hearing the last names Rowley and Harrison. *So Olivia did marry that milquetoast bastard. Wonder just how "open" her marriage has been so far. And "Harrison." The Mrs. H all this time.*

Zim did an admirable job greeting their guests and ushering them inside, never once stammering or drooling over Olivia or Ellie. In true gentlemanly form, with a light touch to each elbow, he guided them to the parlor. At the threshold, he stopped and bowed slightly.

With a wink to each woman at his side, he mocked British propriety and called, "Announcing Mrs. Reginald Lowry and Mrs. Allen Harrison." They couldn't help but grin, and Zim bowed and stepped back.

Ellie spotted her immediately. She was hard to miss, standing motionless by the fireplace, hands in her pockets, dark and staggeringly handsome. A tentative smile grew across Mac's face and Ellie's skin broke out in goose bumps.

Jersey came forward, rolling her eyes at Zim's antics. She reached for Olivia. "It's great seeing you again, Olivia. Thanks for coming." Jersey kissed her cheek.

Olivia squeezed Jersey's hands. "Wonderful seeing you, Jersey. Thank you for having us."

"Hi, Ellie," Jersey said, stepping into her line of vision.

"Jersey. It's been nine years. I remember the unique name."

Jersey blushed lightly. "Maybe it's just the nature of the business."

"Ah, 'the business.' Yes."

"Yes," Jersey answered defensively, stiffening. "You know, we're all really thrilled you're here. Ah...So...Well, we'll leave you two to get reacquainted." She turned to Olivia. "Let me show you around. A drink first?" she offered, leading her into the kitchen.

"Yes, a drink is definitely in order."

Ellie looked so long into Mac's gaze that her eyes watered. Finally, she blinked and chuckled at herself, smoothing a palm nervously along an invisible wrinkle at her hip. She checked her blue strapless pumps, relieved to see they were on the right feet and still matched the lightweight maternity sweater and skirt outfit she bought for the occasion. She exhaled subtly; no need to advertise how nauseatingly nervous she was.

Across the room, her memory found Stick, tall and slim, with short—very short—wavy auburn hair, and molten brown eyes set so deeply they appeared black. Her nose was straight and formal and her lips thin and firm. Ellie knew all those features better than anyone. Once. Now the eyebrows were a bit more severe, the cheekbones more pronounced, the hollows above her jaws filled with shadow. She was far from being her skinny childhood pal or the emaciated version of her first love. It was with unapologetic purpose that she filled out her expensive suit, from the crisp white collar, to the broad shoulders, to the flattering drape of jacket and trousers, down to the shoes that reflected the room. This beguiling woman she knew but didn't. This woman who once cared for her heart and well being, now…again…was *"a wanted criminal."*

"Ellie." Mac's throat was so dry she almost croaked out her name.

"Stick." Ellie swallowed and fidgeted with her purse in both hands. "Or…It's Mac, now. Isn't it?"

Just hearing her voice nearly felled Mac where she stood. She smiled a little and tilted her head as she shrugged. "For quite a while, now."

Ellie took several awkward steps forward and Mac did the same until they were only a few feet apart.

"Um…Eh, can I get you a drink? Coffee? We have everything."

"Everything?" Ellie smiled.

"Well, I just remember Roxie listing a lot things, so we at least have a lot."

Ellie grinned at Mac's jitters. "Thank you, but nothing for me yet."

Mac gazed at her face, her breasts, her belly. "God, how I dreamed of you…so beautiful, just as I remembered."

"I'm pregnant, St—Mac." Ellie ran a hand over the swell of her belly as if to prove it.

"Oh, that's what that is?"

Ellie shook her head. "Still the wiseguy."

"You're all the more beautiful."

Mac offered her hands and Ellie took them, examined them silently. Mac's skin was darker than hers, and the wide hands filled her palms. Her fingers were long and strong, just as she remembered, but the backs of her hands were lined with experiences she could hardly imagine. She ran her thumb along the raised vein as she often did years ago.

"These hands..." Ellie whispered to herself. She labored to keep precious memories at bay, but then Mac lifted her chin with a fingertip.

"Ellie, how have you been?"

Ellie filled her watery eyes with every frustration, every unrequited desire, every empty day and lonely night, and prayed Stick would somehow just know and not make her speak of them. It had been a working life so far, with minor pleasures and little fulfillment, a life of obedience, duty, and obligation, its only true light due to shine with the arrival of her baby. However, as a widowed mother, she knew that that light now would lead her into a new life entirely and require that she take the independent stand she should have taken many years ago.

Mac's eyes felt familiar and comforting, as if they understood. They warmed her all over with the same sincerity and desire Ellie had cherished as a girl—and sought as a woman. She was more than a bit unnerved by being so swept away. "I've been getting by, Stick—Mac. With Dad, it was never easy, you know that."

"I do."

"What about you? How have you been?" She released Mac's hands to indicate the large, well decorated parlor. "You have a grand house."

Mac stopped her lips with a finger. "Could we get to know each other again?"

"St—Mac, really. Think about how different our lives have become. Think—"

"You're all I've thought about, Ellie. You've been my driving force since I was a kid. And I've done more thinking than you'll ever know. You and I have always been different—and happy—together."

"But St—Mac, so much—"

Mac cupped Ellie's hands. "I'm not sure what you know about me, Ellie, but my heart and soul are still the same. I'll change anything that you don't like about me or my life, God is my witness, just to make you happy." She looked down at their hands and Ellie's belly. "Both of you."

"We already have something special, Mac, but I'm pretty sure you're asking for something far greater, and I simply don't know. Things are different now. We're different." Mac appeared to weaken at every word, and Ellie felt compelled to explain quickly. "I have to make choices now for my child, what's best for him or her. But of course I want us to be friends. I'd love for us to share stories and catch up."

Mac could only nod. She was afraid to open her mouth for fear of fumbling like a fool. She'd played the fool enough already, throwing herself out there like that. Where was her pride?

She'd made a monumental mistake, built up unreasonable expectations, placed all her bets on one outcome, and lost. Ellie's life rightfully revolved around her child, conceived within her marriage to a man. It was just blind foolishness believing through all these years that the love they had for each other as girls was the kind of love a mature woman needed. Such a fool, cornering Ellie. Such a fool for so long. Goddamn it.

Heartsick, she led Ellie by the hand to the sofa and they sat, slightly angled toward each other. "So where do we start, Ellie?" Mac said, angry with herself, with Ellie, with the whole world for letting the most important moment of her life go so badly. "Let's 'catch up.' Do we sit and chat over tea? Reminisce from age sixteen to the present day?" Her voice hardened as anger and frustration crushed her breaking heart. "Or maybe we just hit the highlights for now, hmm? Like prison letters, making babies, or hijacking booze?"

Ellie leaned back, her look of disappointment changing to one of surprised awareness.

"You're Mac the hijacker, aren't you?"

Annoyed, Mac abruptly went to the kitchen, grumbling the name in disbelief, and everyone talking around the table stopped to watch her. She was annoyed at being interrupted, having her pain simply overlooked. And she was annoyed that she'd let her emotions loose once again. She returned to the parlor with two open Coca-Colas, handed one to Ellie, and promptly lit a cigarette. She offered a cigarette from her pack, but Ellie shook her head.

"Mac the hijacker," Mac bitterly repeated, and exhaled a rope of smoke straight across the room. At the moment, she couldn't look at Ellie. She snickered. "How did you come up with that?"

"I used to work in the DA's office, and friends said that's what the federal agents called you."

"Mrs. H."

Ellie's eyes narrowed. "The only person who calls me that is a bicycle courier who works City Hall."

"Vonnie. She's a great kid." Mac poked at ashes in the ashtray with her cigarette. "Ellie, I feel it's only right—and please don't be upset— but I want to tell you that Vonnie was our connection to information about the Feds' raid. Tips she provided helped us take our operation underground and avoid their roundup."

Ellie's eyes turned icy. Mac couldn't tell if she was about to explode with resentment or get up and leave.

"So," Ellie pointed to her chest and stared, "you used me—"

"You can't possibly believe I knew it was you, Ellie."

"Really?" She chortled and shook her head. "We don't even know each other anymore."

"Look, please, I want to be hon—"

"You used me to profit in illegal booze, deal with mobsters, probably kill people, and cheat the federal government. Were you about to say you 'want to be honest'?" Ellie chuckled and leaned closer. "Would that be before or after we 'got to know each other again' and you became an influence on my child?" She sat back, laughing as she shook her head again.

Mac felt the last remnant of her spirit break beneath the heat in Ellie's voice, the vehemence of her gestures. She left her on the sofa and went to the windows.

Children chased a ball down the street in front of the house and Mac shuddered as their carefree happiness clashed with the painful resentment Ellie had thrown in her face. Her breathing went short and tight. She wanted to cry.

This was "how different our lives have become," Mac thought, the difference between aboveboard and behind the back, being hunted and being free. No place for a child. Regardless of how many changes Mac promised to make, Ellie was right, their lives no longer meshed. There probably weren't enough changes in the world to make a difference to Ellie. It all made Mac's heart ache. She turned and spoke softly.

"If you want to leave now, I can have someone drive you home."

❖

Olivia stopped in mid-sip and set her brandy back on the table. Mac wandered to the counter, poured herself several ounces of Canadian Club, and left. Everyone at the table shared a wary look.

Jersey stood. "Cover me. I'm going in."

Olivia pressed Jersey's hand onto the table. "Let me."

She rose and straightened her knee-length shift, then carried her drink into the parlor.

Immediately, she knew Mac was alone. The room was cold in the most meaningful way. Mac stood facing the windows, leaning against the wall, glass hanging from one hand, cigarette from the other. She'd tossed her suit jacket into a pile on the sofa and cuffed her sleeves nearly to her elbows. *Ready for a fight...with herself?* She'd also made rather a mess of her hair. *How much does she want to pull out?*

Mac half turned to see who had entered the room and went back to watching the children play in the street. Olivia approached without a word.

She stopped just off Mac's shoulder, not wanting to crowd or interfere, and for a moment, lost herself in the hint of cedar off Mac's skin. Judging by the butterflies stirring things up inside, her body deemed Mac the sexiest, most arousing person it had ever met. The temptation to stroke her back, to sooth her with a caress across her shoulders was nearly irresistible.

"She didn't want to stay," Mac whispered toward the window. "I offered to have someone take her home, but she left in a taxi. At least I managed to pay the driver." She dragged off her Lucky, and ashes hit the floor. "She's changed, Olivia. We're from two different worlds now, and I should have known. I just never thought she'd be repulsed by me."

Now Olivia did touch her. A hand between her shoulders, warm on the cool satin vest.

"Love doesn't give a damn which world we're from, Mac. Give it time. It took some time to grow apart, didn't it? Give yourselves time to grow back."

Mac emptied the half glass of whiskey in one swallow. "You should have heard her laugh. She knows what we do. I told her I'd do anything for her, that I wanted to be honest with her..." Mac shook her head, staring blindly toward the street. "I groveled and she laughed. She threw it all in my face and fucking laughed."

She squinted, dragging smoke off what was left of her Lucky. Olivia handed her the ashtray.

"Come on," Mac said, leaving the window. "We need more booze."

She sought distraction from the others around the kitchen table for several hours, as everyone ate cashews and oatmeal cookies and smoked and drank away the day's events while the big Borgia's music in the parlor kept the demon silence at bay.

"How is Molly?" Jersey asked, drawing raised eyebrows from her peers. Mac snorted into her fifth drink. "She lives here in the city, right?"

Olivia sent Jersey a coy smile. "She does. And she's well, thank you for asking. Quite busy with her family research and having a grand ol' time these days. She asked when I would be back in the city and wondered if we all might go to dinner."

Jersey's face brightened. "You're serious?"

"Better warn Molly, 'Liv," Mac droned through her stupor. "Give her time to cancel once she learns we're *gangsters*."

"Stop, Mac." She slapped Mac's hand. "Molly's well aware. I filled her in on all the details of our ordeal—well outside Mother's hearing, of course."

Zim shook his head at Mac. "How the hell did you ever survive a year kissing that woman's ass? She sounds like a real b—" Roxie kicked his ankle under the table. "Oh, jeez. Sorry, Olivia."

"Not to worry," she assured him. "I've nearly called her that myself on several occasions...in fact, now that I think of it, I'd say nearly every day."

They all chuckled and Zim repeated his question to Mac, who struggled to pour her sixth drink and no longer sat straight in her chair.

"Mrs. Agnes Waters," she mumbled, leaning forward on the table. She scrubbed at her eyes. "Such a lovely lady."

With a fingertip, Olivia moved a wave of hair from Mac's eye and smiled fondly at her slumping form. "Oh, how she thought you were such a heathen."

"Hey, I corrupted the virginal 'Livia Waters."

Olivia laughed and feigned indignation. "I beg your pardon." Now everyone chuckled. "You did no such thing. We had quite the proper association, *Elizabeth*."

"Yes, Miss Waters."

"I keep trying to picture Mac in one of those cute maid costumes."

Mac closed her eyes on the room and growled at Roxie. "Wretched, fucking, foul things."

"Did you have to curtsy, too?"

"Yes, I fucking did, damn it." Mac sat up and swayed dangerously over the edge of her chair. "Part of playing the fool. I do that so well, you know."

Jersey pushed away from the table and stood, scooping up Mac's left arm. "That's enough. Let's go." She hauled Mac to her feet.

"I'm staying right here. We have comp'ny." Mac tried to sit down, but Jersey threw the limp arm around her neck.

"Let's get you upstairs for a bit." The others wished Jersey luck as she staggered down the hall with Mac.

"Why're you always makin' me go somewhere?" Mac peered at Jersey from close range. "I want to see Oliv-livia, goddamn it." She tripped over the bottom step, but Jersey caught her.

"I'll be here when you wake up," Olivia yelled from the kitchen.

"See?" Jersey said, straining. "She's not going to the moon, for Christ's sake, Mac. You'll see her. But if you don't lie down for a while, you're going to pass out and won't see anything. Now help me here. Jesus, you're too dammed tall."

Olivia soon found herself entertaining the others with tales of Mac's year at the estate.

"She stuck the gun right in his ear and saved the day."

Zim sat back and tossed a hand at her. "Hell, we would've blown them all away."

"Well, Mac was just a maid," Roxie said, grinning, "a poor sweet innocent thing."

Everyone laughed at that until Jersey asked about the delivery those men had stacked in the Waters's barn.

"You know?" Olivia said, her eyes wandering across the floor as she thought, "I don't really know who Dad worked with. I remember as a girl, coming home from school one weekend and having several Irishmen staying at the house. That always stuck with me because I didn't understand a word any of them said. Such a brogue they all had."

Zim looked at Roxie and Jersey. "I didn't think Flaherty reached that far."

"Oh, from what I've heard since the Locke-Ober raid," Olivia said, "all three gangs have been reined in. For now, at least. One of my girlfriends, Charlotte, said her grandfather secured an outside attorney for Ambrosino and he went to the New York Mob for help. Now *that's* far-reaching."

Jersey bolted upright in the wingback chair. "Shit, no?" She looked quickly to Zim and Roxie. "Mac will blow her stack if New York comes to town so soon."

Roxie dragged heavily off her cigarette. "Did she say who he met with?"

Olivia shook her head as she swallowed. "Well, Charlotte did say it was Luciano's people but Charlotte doesn't always get things straight, I'm afraid. She said her grandfather's very careful what he says in jail and often speaks in some confusing code."

"Jesus," Jersey said, and dropped her head into her hands. "Wait till Mac hears."

"We'll wake her when dinner's ready," Roxie stated around an exhale of smoke. "And by the way," she added, turning to Olivia, "we expect you to stay with us."

"We have a guest bedroom," Zim said, eagerly. "Please stay. It's not a posh hotel or a fancy mansion, but it's a comfortable home."

"It's lovely, Zim, and it feels warm and welcoming. Thank you. I accept your invitation."

"And I'll loan you some things to wear," Roxie added. "Don't count on stuff from these guys."

"Speaking of that," Olivia thought aloud, rising from the chair. "I'd like to check on someone, if you'll excuse me."

Zim laughed lightly. "Good luck waking the dead. Last door on the left."

❖

Olivia climbed the stairs, asking herself why. To make sure Mac was still breathing or hadn't choked to death or fallen and hit her head? The list of possibilities grew until she knocked lightly on the door. It floated open, so she stepped inside and closed it firmly behind her.

The room was smaller than she expected for such a large house, and humbly furnished. Mac's double-sized bed, on which she was lightly snoring, took up the right wall along with a nightstand, and the left wall framed an upright bureau next to an old wingback chair and floor lamp. A small writing desk and simple wooden chair sat straight ahead, beneath double windows overlooking the backyard.

Olivia advanced to the desk and peeked down into the yard. Mac's faithful Fordor sat barely visible behind a screen of broad oak trees and shrubs. Part of the life, she told herself, scanning the immaculate, if Spartan desk top. A blank pad of paper, a fountain pen, and a leather cup containing pencils and a ruler were neatly arranged. She wondered what Mac wrote here. She knew the reasons Mac wrote no letters home. She had received just four short notes from Mac since she'd left the estate. And Carter and Mrs. Finnegan only a couple each.

There were no personal touches anywhere in the room, save a smaller version of the framed photograph that hung in the foyer. In it, the four of them posed with two elderly couples, all smiling on the front steps of the Victorian. From the story she heard in the kitchen today, she gathered that the couples were the Germans who previously owned the home and the ones who bought it silently for Mac.

She set the small print back on the desk and searched the walls for any others. Tacked up adjacent to the bureau mirror, a yellowed newsprint picture drew her attention. Up close, Olivia took a quick nostalgic breath to see the advertisement for a Fordor that Mac had saved. It had hung in her room at the estate most of the time she lived there.

From a hook on the narrow closet door, Mac's Fedora called to

Olivia. She smiled as she tried it on, envisioning it on Mac. She angled it back on her head and checked her look in the mirror: on her, sassy; on Mac, suave. She returned to the closet door but was distracted by the gold necklace hanging from the hook. She lifted the gold framed heart, and tears threatened as she remembered the day Mac confessed that she'd never take it off.

"Guess I can put that away now." Mac sighed, watching her from the bed.

Surprised, Olivia turned, forgetting she wore the Fedora. "You don't know that, Mac." She walked to the bed and sat down, reaching for Mac's hand. She jiggled it. "You can't grow maudlin. I told you earlier, you both need time with this. It's not every day that two people turn their lives around and come back together."

"I know. Not too realistic."

"Not too common."

"I should have been smarter and spent the years living now, not for the when-and-if."

"So, you take each day as it comes, Mac. Send her a note in a few days, maybe a week. Just don't push—either of you. Meanwhile remember: if it was meant to happen, it will."

She brushed Mac's cheek, and Mac took hold of her hand and entwined their fingers.

Olivia had to look away, afraid she had overstepped her bounds while a teeny voice in her head hoped she had. "I...ah...Honestly, I just came up to check on you. Supper will be ready soon."

"Ahuh. I like the hat."

"Oh. I'm sorry." She went to remove it, but Mac stopped her.

"Please leave it." Mac reached up and slipped her fingers around the back of her neck.

Olivia's eyes closed at the sensation. "Mac."

An arm like iron cautiously enclosed Olivia's shoulders and drew her down to the bed, knocking off the Fedora, bringing them face-to-face on their sides. Olivia reached around Mac's waist, her hand boldly sliding up beneath the vest, and clutched the hard body closer.

Mac trailed her nose along Olivia's. "I once swore I wouldn't do this," she whispered. "I love the smell of you, that lavender. Makes my head spin."

"That's the CC you guzzled."

Mac shook her head and pressed her cheek to Olivia's, kneading her fingers into the luxurious silk of her dress, the perfectly toned form underneath. It pulled an agonized groan from Mac's depths.

Olivia teased her lips back and forth across Mac's mouth. She writhed hard against Mac's chest, torso, and hips. "Mac, my God, you feel so good. It's more impossible than ever to resist you."

She uttered a soft gasp when Mac's palm covered her breast through her dress, and gently, steadily squeezed, tormenting the nipple with her thumb.

"Lord, Mac, if we had ever done this back then—" Her words were cut off by hungry kisses. Moaning, she seized fistfuls of satin vest and pulled Mac on top of her. "Wow, you're dangerous."

"Gangster," Mac murmured as she left long, firm kisses down her neck, burrowing into the crook of her shoulder. "And you're married."

"With an open relationship," Olivia sighed, her head back.

Mac went after her throat and lingered in the snug heat beneath her chin.

Clinging to Mac's shoulders, Olivia lifted her hips, and Mac ground against her.

"Not real sober," Mac confessed against the tender skin.

"I don't care."

Mac licked Olivia's jaw and slowly dragged her tongue across her lips, while strong fingers grazed Olivia's hip and drew her hemline upward. Mac lifted her head and their eyes met. Mac whispered against her mouth. "How do you do, Miss Olivia Waters?"

CHAPTER TWENTY

Ellie's two-bedroom flat above the bakery in Newton Center was quaintly furnished to save money, mostly with things Ellie had known growing up. Stricken with pneumonia shortly after Ellie's father was killed, her mother passed away nearly three months to the day after him, never having held her new granddaughter for fear of spreading her illness. By late summer, Ellie accepted the challenge of starting her life anew.

Having packed selected belongings from the home she shared with Allen, Ellie sold her family's house in South Boston and nearly all its contents to have sufficient funds to care for baby Katherine without need of a job. Allen's parents insisted that they move in with them, but Ellie proclaimed independence and held firm. There was no way she would live under a father's roof again.

New mother and daughter established a comfortable home, warmed free of charge by the bakery ovens downstairs, and satisfying all Ellie's needs with its water closet and minimal cast iron tub, tiny gas stove, and electric refrigerator. The only expense looming on her horizon was a crib, and she had funds earmarked for when that time came. She even had her father's 1926 Chandler sedan, far more automobile than her beginner's skills could handle, so she housed it in a garage around the corner for a fee of one dozen freshly baked scones per week.

Her new neighborhood was safe and clean and friendly. There was one other tenant in Ellie's building, and even though elderly Mrs. Warren lived on the third floor, she wasn't deterred by flights of stairs. She quickly made Ellie's acquaintance, offering invites for tea, and surprising Ellie with casseroles, desserts, and an endless supply of hand-sewn items for the baby.

These days, baby Katherine was quite content in her bassinet next to Ellie's bed. Each evening after being rocked by the parlor window, catching the priceless August breezes and listening to her mother's lullabies, Katherine slumbered next to Mrs. Warren's homemade pink bunny. Ellie hardly gave the baby's bedroom a second thought. It needed sprucing up, some woodwork repairs and a new coat of paint...maybe gentle yellow...and of course, that crib, but there was no rush.

Thrilled by Katherine's every movement, every sound, Ellie remained in awe of her child, the fair-haired baby with the cornflower blue eyes and turned-up nose. Mrs. Warren constantly echoed the many passersby who predicted that tiny Katherine Harrison was destined for moving-picture stardom, the next Clara Bow. Ellie's neighbor christened her "Little Katie" so there'd be no mistaking her in Hollywood. Ellie beamed and took every compliment to heart. She reveled in the praise of her adorable good-natured child, let it buoy her spirit because there were so many other factors in her life that weighed upon it.

Nearly every quiet night, despite being engrossed in a magazine or crossword book, her thoughts drifted of their own accord back to Allen's panicked face when she told him they were expecting, back to her mother's tear-filled joy, and even to her father's nod of approval and the hour he then spent on the telephone bragging to his associates. She shook her head at the memory of Allen's father and mother hugging him, shaking his hand, and hardly sparing her a glance.

And then there was Stick. *Mac.* Several short notes arrived after their tempestuous meeting at the Victorian back in April, roughly one every couple of weeks, the message always the same but expressed in various ways: *please let part of our past be past, and part be the future.* The handwriting on the envelope always stopped Ellie in her tracks, always had her unfolding the slip of paper with breathless anticipation. But she never responded; she couldn't match words to her feelings. She wasn't sure she had that kind of courage.

Since April, they'd seen each other three times: at the cemetery for the funerals. Distant relatives, associates, neighbors, and friends from school and work attended, surrounding and supporting Ellie, while Mac, Jersey, Roxie, and Zim kept slightly apart, and silent. Often throughout each service, Ellie found Mac's eyes on her, and they would acknowledge each other with a nod. To Ellie, that pushed the pang of loss even deeper, just knowing she was responsible for their separation. But Stick was there for her regardless of Ellie's rejection. Stick's name might have changed, Ellie thought, watching her from afar, but this Mac seemed just as intensely loyal, as smart and coolly handsome, as solidly true to her friends and herself, as Stick ever was. She really hadn't changed. Deep in her heart, Ellie hoped Stick knew their connection was everlasting.

Flowers arrived at the South Boston home on the passing of Ellie's father and husband, and then for the birth of Ellie's baby, and once again, for the passing of her mother. Each time, Ellie knew why certain arrangements came unsigned. Each time, she closed herself in a bedroom and cried. With the passing of her mother, she was completely alone—except for the one soul, somewhere out in the city, who loved her. Ellie cried for nearly a week, and it wasn't until her mother-in-law accused her of being too depressed to properly care for her baby that Ellie tightened her grip on life.

❖

Having put Little Katie to bed, Ellie poured herself a tall glass of lemonade, abandoned her robe, and headed for the rocking chair. With no lights on in the flat, it wouldn't be indecent of her to wear only her chemise by the parlor window on this hot evening. Dusk was settling into night and the glow of streetlamps mellowed the main street below in a comforting way. She closed her eyes in the breeze just as someone knocked softly on her door.

Twice already this evening, Mrs. Warren had delivered a new sundress for the baby. A third one would be a sure sign the woman needed to open her own shop. Chuckling to herself, Ellie draped her robe around her shoulders, switched on the lamp next to the sofa, and swung open the door with a smile. "You amaze m—"

Mac stood perfectly still, smiling tentatively, and with a finger, pushed up the front of her wide-brimmed Panama hat to lift the shadow from her eyes. With her other arm, she offered a bouquet of flowers, a shiny red heart-shaped box of chocolates, and a present wrapped in pink and yellow balloon paper.

Ellie was speechless. She hadn't heard from Mac in almost two months, since before she moved, and hadn't been too forthcoming in giving her new address to anyone. With more than a tinge of reluctance, that included Mac. The Feds had advised her to live a very quiet life and to avoid Boston if possible, until the rumblings from the raid settled down. Cases were just now hitting the newspapers again as trial dates neared, so Ellie kept her profile low. *And she's found me.*

Mac was dapper and bold, daring in far more than just attire. Ellie's heart beat so hard, she just knew that it thumped throughout the building.

"S…Mac. Hello."

Softly, Mac said, "These are for you, Ellie." She still held the gifts out. "I just…Well, I just wanted you to know, I…" She snickered at her own fumbling. "I…um…"

Ellie finally lifted the packages from her arm. *So courageous and undaunted yet reduced to a flustered stutter?* Ellie was deeply moved. "Thank you. I…I don't know what to say."

Mac quickly removed her hat and fidgeted with the buttons of her double-breasted summer suit, a seersucker vanilla over a crisp white shirt. Subtly, she glanced over each shoulder.

"I'm not sure I do either," she said quietly, and her eyes dropped to her shoes, looking disappointed in herself. "I had it all rehearsed. I practiced in the car all the—"

"God, you're handsome."

Mac's head popped up. "Beg your pardon?"

Ellie smiled at Mac's humility. Mac smiled.

Ellie opened the door wider and stepped back. "Come in, please."

Mac turned the Panama around in her hands several times. "You weren't expecting me, and I won't intrude." She stepped back, much to Ellie's surprise. "I…I just—Shit."

"What?"

"Well, I…I just…I know…I mean, the way you're dressed." Ellie drew her robe across her chest. "I know you weren't expecting company, but…See, um…"

"Jesus, St—Mac. Please come figure it out inside." Slipping into her robe, she grinned at Mac's frustrated frown.

"I don't want to intrude," Mac whispered.

"If you were, I'd let you know."

Mac took several steps into the flat and waited while Ellie shut the door and went to the sink.

"I'm putting these carnations in water," Ellie said, "so have a seat. I'll be right there."

Her hands shook as she unwrapped the long stems and searched for scissors to trim them, working by rote as her mind—and her heart— raced. Maybe this was the opportunity to rekindle the friendship, get it back on a healthy footing, she lectured herself, and smiled at the fiery red blossoms that matched the boutonniere in Mac's lapel. *If that's wise. If that's what you really want...and all that comes with it...*

This lecture of conscience wasn't new; the topic cost her months of decent sleep, that familiar face, the uncertainty, the longing, the practicality ever-present. Little Katie's well-being and future were top priorities, and shame on her as a mother to even consider the ridiculous idea of introducing her perfect, innocent child to the shady world of the virtual stranger in her parlor. And then, as always, Ellie felt her heart twinge.

"Thank you for these...Mac. They're so pretty, so full of life. I love carnations." Ellie appeared with Mac's bouquet in an antique vase and placed it on the coffee table.

"I remember your mother's flowerboxes."

Ellie looked up and labored to avoid losing herself in the memories she saw in Mac's eyes. "Would you...ah...How about some lemonade?" She paused to watch Mac move to the sofa, the athletic, refined body so controlled and fluid, a bearing quite distinguished in yet another posh, decidedly masculine suit. "I'm afraid I can't offer anything... stronger. I'm buying some more of that new Kool-Aid tomorrow, but it's probably not something you'd care for." She considered mentioning that she was no fan of alcohol and never kept it in the house.

Mac grinned. "Kool-Aid, you say? Never had it," she said in a subdued tone. She opened her suit jacket as she sat and, again, Ellie was captured by the look of her. She had very little experience socializing with powerful, independent women like Mac, especially those who defied convention in such a remarkable way. And Mac truly was remarkable. "I'm a Coca-Cola girl myself, but lemonade would be great. Thank you."

Even her voice moves me. Ellie practically fled to the kitchen. *I'm in no position to throw caution to the wind like some flapper.* She concentrated on pouring lemonade, trying not to come unhinged by the intoxicating transformation of Stick to Mac. *But what of my own happiness?* She gripped the counter with both hands, closed her eyes, and took a breath. It was all so incredibly difficult to sort out.

Ellie returned with the lemonade and retrieved her own glass before sitting beside Mac on the sofa. "Why are you whispering?"

Mac's eyebrows rose incredulously. "Because I thought I might wake the baby."

Ellie laughed and patted Mac's knee. "Very sweet of you, St... Mac." She blushed at the obvious difficulty she had remembering Mac's name. "Guess it'll take me a while to get used to that."

"Took me a while, too."

"And don't worry. The baby sleeps like a rock. Just like her father."

Mac looked away and sipped her lemonade.

Ellie set down her glass. *Wrong thing to say.* "Would you like to see her?" She was pleased to see Mac's face brighten.

"I'd love to." Mac followed her into Ellie's dark bedroom off the parlor. She tapped Ellie's shoulder and brought her lips close to Ellie's ear. "What's her name?"

Ellie turned so suddenly they collided, her palms landing on Mac's chest. Mac gripped her waist with both hands to steady her, and for a long moment, they stood frozen in time.

Mac's eyes were so dark, Ellie couldn't see them, but there was no denying the surety and warmth that enveloped her, feelings she hadn't experienced in years. The hands near her hips were expansive and sure, confident hands that had done, had held many things—including her, many years ago. *But Lord knows what in recent years...blood? Guns?* Considering where her priorities lay, it hurt to consider the lifestyle.

She stared at her own hands splayed out across the lapels of Mac's suit and could feel the heat of Mac's chest through the layers of fine fabric. It would be so easy to rest her head there, where the top buttons of her shirt opened, for just a moment. Precious memories reached out, daring her to imagine the sanctuary, the tenderness Mac would offer. Challenging her to recall.

"Ellie?" Mac whispered.

Ellie blinked, eager to focus on the flecks of gold in Mac's hidden eyes. "Ah...Her name..." Reality tamped memories back into place and she dropped her hands and stepped away. "Her name's Katherine Rose. Little Katie."

She knew Mac had seen her withdraw. Directly, she occupied her hands by fussing with the thin yellow blanket tucked around Katie and Mrs. Warren's bunny. When Mac set an easy hand on her shoulder and moved closer, Ellie forced herself to relax beneath the touch, exhaling softly as Mac leaned toward the bassinette.

Little Katie pursed her lips in her slumber and appeared to frown. They both grinned.

Mac reached in and straightened one of the bunny's folded ears, then let her fingertips glide over Katie's fine golden hair, over a barely visible eyebrow, along the velvet of her cheek.

"Oh, Ellie, she's so beautiful."

Through misty eyes that surprised her, Ellie burned the image into her brain as if taking a photograph, the formal sleeves of suit and white shirt extending Mac's powerful hand and long fingers in a reverent caress of Katie's delicate features.

Mac turned her own moist eyes on Ellie.

"She looks just like you."

Ellie avoided Mac's eyes. Somehow, she just knew she'd fall apart if that connection was made. Her heart was pounding again and her mind was spinning too fast; she was too torn to risk it. She smiled down at Katie.

"Folks say I should hire one of those press agent people to get her a Hollywood contract." She escaped to the window and spread the drapes apart for air. "Gets a little stuffy in here during these hot nights." She lifted the window beyond halfway. "Eventually, she'll have a crib next door in her own room, once I fix it up. There's more of a breeze in there."

She glanced up at Mac and fell silent. With a haunted gaze, Mac looked past her at the heart-shaped bobble hanging from the window frame, slowly turning on the evening breeze.

A million memories flickered in those eyes and Ellie didn't know what to say or where to begin. Or if she should say anything at all. What Stick had endured, how she had hung on, how she had loved...Ellie knew so little about it all, but could see Stick's past rise up and engulf Mac where she stood.

The heart Stick had carved for her out of discarded glass—her heart—shivering for hours in the Christmastime dark many years ago, hung with the reflections of a mirror, its jeweled emerald hue blackened by the night.

Ellie felt exposed by what Mac could see: that the heart still mattered. But somehow she didn't mind. What ate at her, however, was the hint of desperation in Mac's gaze.

Ellie spoke gently. "I had the glazier down at Trombley's Hardware drill a hole so I could hang it in the sun."

Mac pulled her stare from the dangling memory.

"I...I'm amazed you still have it. You have no idea how happy that makes me."

Ellie reached to Mac's face and lightly wiped away a tear. "Don't you know that no one could ever take your place in my heart?" Ellie gripped Mac's arm and squeezed fondly. "We'll always be special to each other. No matter what, Elizabeth McLaughlin. We grew together right from the start."

Mac blinked slowly. She backed up a step, seeming about to run either with or from Ellie's declaration. She nodded solemnly.

"I think I'm going to go now, Ellie." She returned to the parlor for her hat.

"Now? But you just got here. Why—?"

Mac moved deliberately, not looking back as she picked up the Panama. She rifled a hand through her hair and Ellie was surprised to recognize that nervous, frustrated habit from their youth.

"You didn't expect company tonight, I know, so..." Mac stopped at the door, Panama rotating in her shaking hands. "Thank you for the lemonade. And...for introducing me to Little Katie."

"Wait, Mac. You don't have to go." Ellie approached carefully, seeing a cornered animal's panic in Mac's eyes.

"Yes. Yes, I do." Mac steadied her breathing. "But, well, who knows? Maybe sometime we could...you know, we could...um...Well, we could go grab an ice cream cone or...or go to the park with Katie."

The desperation was back in Mac's eyes, along with a glistening that hurt to see. Ellie lowered her head as her own tears threatened and she wished with all her might that certain decisions in life weren't so damn hard.

Mac turned and opened the door. "I'm really sorry. I didn't mean to be presumptuous."

"You weren't...Mac. Not at all." She didn't bother wiping away the tears that had wet her cheeks.

Mac shook her head as she stepped into the hall and settled the Panama down over her eyes. "Ellie, you're all settled and content and everything. I shouldn't have come."

Ellie rested a palm on Mac's shoulder and found her watery eyes in the shadow of her hat. She lifted Mac's hand and offered a smile. "I pack a mean picnic lunch."

❖

Arm resting on the open window frame, Jersey gazed through the windshield of the faithful Fordor as Mac drove to the dealership in Gloucester. They had been looking forward to this day, each picking up new wheels. Once they handed over the Model T, Jersey would drive them in her new green Pontiac to the dealership down in Brockton, where Mac would take possession of her new white Dodge Victory four-door sedan. It took all morning and part of the afternoon to head north near the Maine border and then backtrack south, well past Boston, but maintaining their anonymity these days was wise. No measure was too extreme.

Federal cases against all three of the big boys would soon begin in succession, and selection of the first jury was already under way. Newspapers were full of innocuous tidbits as desperate reporters scrambled to fill columns until the trials actually began. Every innuendo and rumor made publication, including mention of "Hijack Mack," the mystery man who had stuck his finger into the mix for a few years. Street talk had it that friends of the big boys were just as interested in "talking" to Hijack Mack as were the Feds. None of it surprised Mac or her associates, every one of them grateful they'd prepared for this far in advance.

"Gleeson's taking Zim and me next Friday night to spend the weekend checking out the operation, seeing what we can work out with his cousin and a couple others." Jersey bent forward and cupped her hands around the cigarette she attempted to light. "He says Ernest bumped up production and has good contacts at the North Woburn depot. Runs right into North Station, and we can take the product from there." Cigarette finally lit, she handed it to Mac, who squinted at the harsh Chesterfield before accepting it. "As long as those runners are holding out offshore...They're passing Boston right by these days, Mac, so the demand here's growing by leaps and bounds."

Mac nodded, shooting an exhale of smoke out her window. She waited while Jersey fought the breeze and lit a cigarette for herself.

"I'd still feel better if we just shipped product out. Showing up around here as the new supplier on the block will get our names and faces out there faster'n flicking on a light bulb. Distribution is the bitch, Jers. So, say we get Ernest's product in from North Woburn, and other brewers he knows who are willing to sell. Hell, we could probably even work with the runners ashore at Bulls Point up near friggin' Bath, Maine, but who the hell's going to want to show their face delivering in place of the big boys?"

"But we're on good terms with at least half the joints in the city, Mac. They need the stuff. We don't add the big boys' blood money and our price is golden. And that'll make us"—she thumbed toward her chest—"*us* the ones making them very, very happy. They'll be in the money again, see? So they'll keep quiet. Like being paid off to know nothing."

Mac finished her cigarette in silence. Jersey shifted uneasily at the other end of the seat.

"How about this?" Mac posed. "When we have enough product— and only when we have plenty—we proposition the biggest joints on our list. Cash on delivery. We deliver the next day."

Jersey's eyebrows rose. "The next day?"

"Next day. Couple days later, we make the rounds to the rest of our list and offer them our deal. By then, they'll have heard about the upscale joints. Same deal: next day, cash in hand. Then we disappear for a couple weeks, pick up some more product, wait for the ripples we made to grow into waves."

"Okay, yeah. Easy."

"But." Mac held up a finger. "But before some clowns like us start 'jacking *our* loads, we look elsewhere, like Bangor, Portsmouth, White River Junction...or Worcester, Springfield...There's the whole lower part of New England, there's all of western Mass. Wherever there's a train depot, there are joints in need, and as long as we've got the rail yards on our side, my friend, there's a way. We enlist suppliers and move their product. This is the window we talked about long ago, Jersey, so we can walk away. I don't want any of us around when the likes of Luciano in New York send their goons to take over the Boston action. And you *know* that's going to happen even before these trials are over."

"But Jesus, Mac." Jersey sighed at the ceiling of the car.

"Are you whining?"

Jersey had to chuckle. "Damn it all. Boston's where the money is. From what I hear, there's nothing out in those places but cow shit. And no decent roads. And no women."

Mac grinned. "Now we're down to the nitty-gritty, huh?"

Jersey tossed a hand at Mac and snickered out the window.

❖

"Care to try your magic now, miss?" Ellie challenged Mac with an arched brow.

"Just because she smiled at me once doesn't mean I can stop her crying, you know." Mac sat back against the tree.

"You're afraid to hold her, aren't you?"

"Am not." Mac removed her cap and adjusted the band.

"Yes, you are." Ellie grinned at the reluctance of the *big, bad gangster* while Little Katie complained about the delay in having lunch. "She won't bite you. She doesn't even have teeth yet. And she's well protected from nature's little accidents, so your trousers won't get soiled."

"But really, I'm not af—"

"I'm glad to hear that." Ellie set Little Katie in Mac's arms and sat back to take in the picture. *Never in my wildest imagination...*

Mac cradled the cranky baby in her left arm, snug against her white shirt, and dabbed the tip of Katie's nose with her fingertip. Mac's crooning voice quickly captured the baby's attention.

"Shh there, Little Katie. Thank you for inviting me today. You remember my name? I'm Mac, but you can call me anything you want...except Elizabeth. You'll understand why when your mama calls you Katherine." The reddened face and loud complaints eased immediately, and sky-blue eyes stared up at Mac in wonder. "Thanks for letting me get a word in edgewise. Just look at you, such a little politician. You'd make the most beautiful president these United States have ever seen."

Ellie smiled at the look of fascination on Katie's face, a look Ellie treasured more than most, one of obvious curiosity and rapt attention. Then Katie smiled, her tiny mouth opened, and she giggled. A quick glance caught Mac making faces and laughing along with her, and Ellie's heart beat a little harder.

She slid closer and offered Katie's bottle. "You'll be her knight in shining armor once you produce lunch."

Mac's smiling expression grew apprehensive. "Hmm." She gingerly accepted the bottle and looked back down to Katie. "I'm new at this, so no teasing. I'll just put this thing in the vicinity of where it belongs and you can show off."

Ellie peered over her shoulder. "Wow. You're a natural."

Mac snickered and shook her head, never looking away from the feasting child on her arm. "Last time someone gave me a 'wow,' it wasn't for feeding a baby."

"Care to share?" But the more Ellie thought about it, the less she wanted to know.

"Well…"

"Personal rather than professional, I gather." Mac just nodded. Ellie offered only an "I see."

With Katie snoozing the afternoon away, Ellie and Mac systematically ate their way through a picnic lunch fit for an army. Mac opened the last Coca-Cola in the portable metal icebox and handed it to Ellie, who sipped and handed it back. Closing her eyes, Mac plopped back on the blanket, rubbing her stomach and bemoaning her pathetic self-restraint.

Ellie studied Mac and was taken aback by a surprising desire to curl up against her. *God, this shouldn't be so difficult.* She couldn't remember the last time she lay with someone and surrendered body and soul. There had been a couple eye-opening flings with women while she was a student in Maryland, and then a series of dates her father had arranged before introducing her to Allen, the son of an acquaintance, but none of them won her heart. Only Stick had ever claimed that.

She covered the hand Mac rested on her stomach and wrapped her fingers around it. The dark eyes opened, but Mac didn't rise. Ellie's perceptive gaze traveled the length of Mac's frame and back, a wave of long-lost yearning roiling deep inside when Mac entwined their fingers. There was no returning to their past, but theirs had been the truest, most honest love Ellie had ever known. *No time for lectures now, but you know damn well that love makes you rich, no matter your circumstance. It makes a family whole and hearts full. And life complete.*

Ellie looked at the hope in Mac's eyes until her own moistened. "I don't want you to go away again." Mac sat up and took Ellie's hands in hers. "Mac, please. Never. Promise me?"

Mac took her into her arms and gently stroked her back while Ellie cried.

"I promise, El," she whispered, rocking them slowly, and Ellie locked her arms around Mac's neck. "I promise on my life, honey."

Ellie leaned back until their eyes met. She sniffed.

"I'm sorry I got all dramatic on you," she sniffed again, "but having you here takes a little getting used to." She combed back errant strands of Mac's hair with her fingers, her palm coming to rest on Mac's cheek. "You're just as rousing as ever, Elizabeth McLaughlin, and you get me all flustered inside, but there's more to you than shows on this handsome surface."

Mac's eyes never wavered from hers.

Ellie knew Mac waited on her every word. She set their foreheads together.

"Even so, how can I *not* fall in love with you all over again?"

"Maybe we never fell *out* of love, El," Mac offered gently, a tear slipping down her cheek as she raised her head.

Ellie struggled to keep from crying at the firm press of such tender lips. Nothing compared to these soft, stimulating kisses, and her memory flooded with moments behind her father's rose bushes, in the A&P's old horse barn, on top of homework on her bed...She clung feverishly to Mac's shoulders, and when powerful arms squeezed her tightly, she groaned into Mac's mouth.

Slow, sensuous kisses dotted Ellie's nose and eyes, her jaw, and back to her lips, kisses that lingered and savored, deep kisses that made Ellie weak and filled her with a complete surrender she hadn't felt in many years. She could endure this for a lifetime, but her need was not only to receive such cherished affection. Her fingers trembled across Mac's face, and she returned her kisses with more passion than she ever dreamt possible. She felt Mac's chest constrict against her breasts and knew that this *gangster* fought valiantly to hold back tears.

Gently, Ellie withdrew and traced a fingertip across Mac's lips. "Dear God, it's been so, so long."

Mac could only nod and Ellie lightly kissed her.

"Last spring at Locke-Ober, you reentered my life on a horrific night and you've returned to my thoughts ever since. Through the arrival of the brightest light in my world, and building our new life, I've thought of you." She pressed her nose to Mac's and whispered against her lips. "Night after night, I wondered who Stick became, who you really were. Not knowing—actually being afraid to know—made me scared and unbearably sad. It was like losing you again. Your lifestyle is so threatening…Mac…and…and as much as I don't want you disappearing again, I have to think of Katie's safety."

"I understand. Her safety is what matters most, Ellie. I agree. And you have court appearances coming up, and that doesn't help at all either, I know, but I promise you I will do everything in my power to keep you both safe."

Ellie cradled Mac's face and softly stroked her cheeks with her thumbs. "To make matters even more complicated, I don't think we ever fell out of love, either."

❖

Ralph, Gleeson, Hank, Jackson, and Millie crowded around the battered table with Mac and Jersey. Business talk momentarily took a backseat to the gossip about Roxie and Zim, sleeping off last night's bender—together. It was all pretty amusing, until Millie revealed they'd been doing it for months and that marriage was in the wind.

The tenor of the musty basement meeting room changed markedly as everyone sensed the same thing. Jersey sent Mac a look that asked if she still planned to announce her own change in participation. Mac had called the meeting to let the key players know she would be backing into the shadows of their operation, in advance of withdrawing completely, because there now were two things in her life that mattered more than illegal booze and always packing a gun.

Mac nodded and sat back. She took a long, hard pull off her

'Gansett, setting the bottle down with a decisive knock, and began explaining her position and how she saw the gang's future.

Mac assured everyone that their operation would continue out in the greater Boston area, at least until the Mob started interfering. She explained that a broader business plan for farther outside the area was already in the works and showed great promise. It would be Jersey's show to run, Mac stated, setting a forearm on her shoulder and leaning on it.

"So with Jersey in charge, obviously our great run will continue," she concluded, offering a light to Jersey's Chesterfield, "but with me pulling back and now God-knows-what happening between Romeo and Juliet, she's going to need some people to step up. I'm damn proud of who we are, just regular folks who took back the decent living that was taken from us. So I know she'll have solid support like everyone gave me."

"Was bound to happen sometime." Ralph ran a weary hand through his gray hair. He looked Mac in the eye and lent her a forlorn smile. "You're the best thing that happened to any of us, Mac, and we'll always be grateful. Can't say I know how you pulled off some of the things you did, or how you put up with us, even, but you managed to swing it. You play a mean hand of poker, girl."

"I was dealt a great hand, Ralph. Luciano isn't the only lucky sonovabitch around." Everyone chuckled at that, and Mac reached out and gave Jersey another squeeze. "But, turns out that what I've dreamt about for so long has finally come true, and there's no way I'm going to let her slip through my hands again."

"That baby going to have two mommies?" Jackson asked, rocking back in his chair cockily, and when Mac smiled, he rocked forward and slapped the table. "Well, I'll be dammed." He laughed. "Sorry, Mac, but you don't know nothing about babies."

Hank snorted. "How long she known you?"

Jackson snarled back and returned to Mac. "I just can't see you changing diapers. You even know how?"

Mac couldn't help but laugh with the others. "Shut up, Jackson."

Meanwhile, Hank was the picture of concentration in the group. He leaned on his elbows, his bruiser of a fist covered by his other hand. "Listen, Mac. Me and Ralphie been around this block a few years. We know things are gonna get tight in short order." With Ralph nodding beside him, he looked to Jersey. "So let's lay this new operation on the table and have a look down the road."

Mac could have kissed him. His attention to business and his loyalty to Jersey made Mac not only proud, but deeply grateful as well. To Hank, who'd been widowed at eighteen, work was his life, and he had the utmost respect for anyone who put his or her shoulder to the wheel. He also kicked the asses of those who didn't. Jersey had his respect and, Mac thought, she would be wise to bring Hank in as her second. The smile he put on Jersey's face told Mac that she probably would.

"I want a full meeting to go over everything with everyone," Jersey said. "Jackson, you call it. And get everyone, no excuses. Let's say…night after tomorrow at seven."

Jackson nodded. "You got it, JJ."

Jersey turned quickly. "Don't call me that."

"What's wrong with JJ—Jersey from Jersey?"

"Hmm," Ralph said. "Kinda like it."

"Good way to stay unknown, too," Hank said, nodding.

Millie smirked and slapped a palm to her cheek. "Oh, honey, I just think it's *adorable*."

Jersey looked directly into Mac's eyes. "Shoot me now."

Chapter Twenty-one

For the third time in ten minutes, Millie checked the street below Ellie's flat without moving the drapes. She gave her chewing gum a good loud snap in irritation. "Where the fuck is that fathead dick?"

Ellie and Mac looked up from the map on the coffee table, the colorful language leaving Ellie somewhat aghast and Mac shaking her head.

"How long's it been?" Mac asked casually, returning to the map to draw Ellie's attention from the issue at hand.

"Half hour now. Time enough to grab a sandwich and get his fucking ass back on the job. Goddamn Feds." Millie had Ellie's complete, mesmerized attention as she stalked to the kitchen and came back with a chair. "Mind if I bring this over, honey?" she asked Ellie, making herself comfortable at the drapes.

Ellie shook her head. "Um…I mean, no, Millie. Of course not." She looked to Mac and back. Such complete opposites. "I'll go make us some sandwiches," she said.

Immediately, Mac was at the window, too. "Shouldn't have left his position until relieved," she murmured, peering down the street one way, then the other, searching for the federal agent assigned to protect Mrs. Eleanor Harrison, witness for the prosecution. "Fuck."

They exchanged concerned looks.

"What are you carrying?" Mac asked quietly.

Millie hiked her knee-length skirt. "This little guy," she said of the .25 holstered to her thigh. "And this." She dipped two fingers into her voluminous cleavage and produced a switchblade.

"Thank you."

"Hey, shoe were on the other foot, honey, you'd pulp somebody's face for me. I got no problem being here." She patted Mac's cheek and continued in a hushed voice. "But now, you, sweetie. You're a different story. Playing awful close to the vest, as they say, hanging out right under their noses. And of course you're packin', huh?"

Mac gave a tap to her suit jacket's left lapel, indicating the Colt .45 holstered inside at her armpit.

Millie shook her head at her. "Jesus Christ," she hissed. "What if they question you? Bet you got a pocket gun on your ankle and a blade in your pants, too, right?"

Mac returned to the sofa and the map of New England. "Nobody's getting close to her. There's a .38 wrapped in a towel in the Frigidaire and the sawed-off's taped to the back of the tub."

Millie flew from her chair and leaned over the coffee table into Mac's face. "Have you lost your fucking mind?"

Mac whispered fiercely. "Who would you put your money on— the Feds or the Mob?"

Ellie appeared with a tray of sandwiches and glasses of lemonade. "You can stop whispering now. I'm here. And you're terrible at it, by the way. Both of you."

Millie took half a sandwich and went back to the window. "Sorry, El. This is yummy. Thanks a lot, really."

Ellie took up her seat, close to Mac's side, and leaned into her shoulder. "At first, I was incredibly intimidated by you, not really knowing the 'Elizabeth McLaughlin, wanted criminal.' And then all the federal agents and stuff turned me into a nervous wreck. But now, the Mob is scaring me to death, right in my own home."

Mac turned and kissed Ellie's forehead. "It'll never be me you have to fear, sweetheart."

Ellie kissed Mac on the lips sweetly.

"Hey," Millie teased them. "Take the mushies into the bedroom and let a girl do her job."

Ellie blushed and Millie jumped at the opportunity.

"You know, McLaughlin, your girl and I been doing just fine since I got here yesterday morning, here by ourselves mind you, checking out clothes, hairdos, makeup. Girlie things. And then bad boy Hijack Mac shows up and everything goes to hell."

"If this is 'going to hell,'" Ellie quipped, squeezing Mac's hand, "then it's not so bad after all."

Mac tilted Ellie's chin upward and kissed her wantonly. "Our private time will come," she whispered.

Ellie lost herself in the promise simmering in Mac's eyes. They'd been dating for nearly a month, and Mac's chivalry was slowly eating away at Ellie's sanity.

At least once a week, Mrs. Warren welcomed Little Katie for the evening so Mac could treat Ellie to fine dining and dancing, or to a play or moving picture show. Mac generously reimbursed Mrs. Warren for her time, despite everyone's polite refusals, but Mrs. Warren remained somewhat flummoxed by Ellie's "old childhood friend." There were long strolls with the new baby carriage, the finest one Mac could buy, trips to the Franklin Park Zoo, and even boat excursions to Nantasket Beach with its amusements and carousel at Paragon Park.

But they were rarely alone. And now, with the start of the first of several trials, Ellie wondered how long she'd have Mac's in-house guardians on hand for their most intimate moments. A week ago, Little Katie moved to her grandparents' home, squirreled away for safekeeping until the ordeal ended, but Mac had hinted at stealing them both away to the Victorian for the duration. Ellie just wished the whole damn mess would go away so they could try making a fresh start.

"Do you really have all those guns here?" she asked, watching Mac's finger trace a route out to western Massachusetts on the map.

Mac nodded. "All that matters to me in the whole world, Ellie, is that you stay safe."

"With what I knew about Allen's information and my father's connections, I guess everyone figures I have plenty to tell. But, Lord, Mac, I don't think I do, really, but they must. The government *and* the bad guys."

Millie snorted into the opening of the drapes. "Well, dickhead's finally come back to work. And guess what? Some friends have driven up. Three of them and there's still one behind the wheel." She looked sharply to Mac, who was already at her side.

They watched as the agent was shoved into the strangers' D and driven away.

"Hope he enjoyed his lunch," Millie muttered.

The two men left standing out front looked both wa sidewalk before heading to the first-floor entry.

Mac elbowed Millie in the arm. "Let's go."

Seeing Millie hustle to the kitchen, Ellie rose from the sofa, alarmed and confused. She was about to speak, but Mac stilled her lips with a soft and calming touch of her finger.

"Please get your suitcase."

Ellie spun back to the bedroom. Millie found the .38 in the Frigidaire, and Mac yanked the sawed-off from behind the tub. Ellie rejoined them, staring hard at the abbreviated shotgun Mac wielded like a toy. Mac took her by the hand and they followed Millie into the hallway and down the seldom-used rear staircase to the bakery.

Two hours later, after a circuitous trip back into the city, Millie recounted the episode to others at the Victorian. In the parlor, Mac watched Ellie speak on the telephone to the Bureau of Investigation's special agent in charge. She wasn't positive, Ellie told him, but had glimpsed her agent being driven away in a black Dodge, and when a pair of strangers approached her building, she ran to the home of a friend. And no, she didn't want agents "protecting" her any longer. She reassured the exasperated agent that she would become invisible and still testify as promised.

For the next week, Mac's escort system effectively treated Ellie like royalty. She visited her in-laws on an irregular schedule, tolerating them in order to spend precious days with Little Katie and learning to ignore the presence of Mac's heavily armed associates at the front and back doors.

The Harrisons were outraged by the goings-on, demanding Ellie agree to protection by federal agents and rid the household of nefarious characters. Thankfully, the delicate situation was resolved at week's end, when Ellie was notified that she would testify on Monday. The Harrisons were ignorantly jubilant, clearly picturing their granddaughter returning to a normal, safe routine.

Mac, however, digested the news with a half-glass of Canadian ᵈub.

While Ellie slept in the guest room upstairs, Mac met with Jersey, Roxie, Millie, Hank, and Jackson in the parlor.

ᵋirst thing tomorrow morning," she said softly, "and I mean at ᵋst thing…Wake them the fuck up, I don't care. First thing, ᵉ comes here. I want that baby in this house as fast as we can ᵊen. Anybody gets in your way, fucking shoot them. And I ᵑddamn who it is."

"We'll take three cars," Jackson said, "and can handle anybody who might follow us."

Roxie pointed to Millie on the sofa. "We'll go in and pick her up and get her things, Mac. The Harrisons will probably make less of a scene if two women show up."

"Hank goes in, too," Jersey ordered, and Hank grinned from the chair in the corner. "Those assholes won't stand in his way."

"And Jersey, Zim, and I will watch the outside and the cars," Jackson added.

Mac nodded as the group talked out the details. Ironic, she thought, after all they'd been through and the jobs they'd pulled, that their "business skills" would be put to this use.

"So what do you think, Mac? Mac?" Jersey tapped her knee. "We're thinking tonight. We're going to get her right now."

They were a selfless lot, a special family, and someday she would miss each one of them.

❖

Mac slipped into the guest room soundlessly and swiftly, careful not to disturb Ellie with noise or light from the stairway landing. Of all the moments they had shared these past weeks, why she chose to approach her now, Mac wasn't sure. She just sensed they had to be together tonight. She stopped at the edge of the bed to let her eyes adjust to the dark.

A slim bare arm reached up, beckoning. "If you hadn't come to me tonight, I would have come to you."

Mac leaned down to kiss her. "I need to be with you."

Ellie drew her closer. "And I need to be with you. Finally." She stroked Mac's jaw as they gently kissed. "You know this is our first time, Elizabeth McLaughlin."

"I do."

"Will you...will you lie naked with me?"

Mac promptly abandoned her clothing to a pile on the floor. "I want every inch of you touching me," she whispered, lifting the sheet and carefully sliding in beside her. Nothing mattered more.

Ellie's warm palm came to her shoulder and the possessive grip rippled through Mac's bones. Settled face-to-face, she set a tentative hand onto the gentle curve of Ellie's hip and rested there. Instinctively, her fingers flexed into the softness and made her heart race.

"It seems like we've traveled miles, doesn't it?" Ellie asked, delicate fingertips trailing along Mac's shoulder to her neck and tracing her ear. "We're so far from Henderson's and those days on my front stoop." Mac had no response. No words came to mind, only delirious sensation, a reality that simply couldn't be true. Ellie's touch along Mac's jaw seemed full of a similar wonder. "Someday, will you tell me about it all? You never mention those days, Mac, but even though it'll make me cry, I want to know."

"Anything you ask, Ellie. Everything. The past has made us who we are, you and I, and I want to know about every minute of your life that I've missed, too." She stroked the silkiness of Ellie's hip and back, up to her shoulder, and drew her in tightly, overwhelmed by the creamy softness and Ellie's complete surrender. This was real; the time for fantasy was past. To anchor her mind, she set her forehead on Ellie's.

A tender palm came to her cheek.

"How I ached for you, Mac. It killed me when they took you from me." She slipped her fingers into Mac's hair and spoke onto her lips. "I need you in my life, my Stick. My Mac. All the time, every day and every night."

"It's what I've always wanted, where I've always needed to be," Mac whispered.

She pressed her lips to Ellie's welcoming kiss and moaned gratefully, and as they hugged tightly, bodies fully entwined for the first time, a mystical sort of calm lightened Mac's heart. Long-locked floodgates of emotion opened, and the excited pounding in her chest gave way to a throbbing throughout her entire body, desire overtook propriety, and she allowed pure joy to take control.

"I'll never leave you, Ellie. You're such a part of me, the best part, and I love you." Ellie raised her head enough to kiss Mac firmly, and Mac pressed her back to the pillow, tongues sliding together, tasting eagerly. "Jesus, Ellie," Mac breathed against her lips, "dreams do come true."

"This one has," Ellie answered, sealing her arms around Mac's shoulders and crushing her closer. "You are my dream come true. I love you, Mac. I always have."

Mac kissed her hungrily, a leg slipping into the slick heat between Ellie's upper thighs and locking their hips together. The sensation and texture thrilled her. She lifted up on both arms and hovered over Ellie, searching her face, watching the midnight blue eyes flutter. "You are more amazing than any dream I've ever had."

"You've dreamt of me?"

She kissed Ellie's nose. "Oh, I've had many dreams about you."

Ellie lifted her hips, sliding her sex along Mac's thigh in wordless encouragement. "Ohhh...Is that so?"

"Mmm-hmm." Mac returned the gesture, rocking hard against her.

"God, Mac." Ellie gulped a breath. "Were...were they naughty dreams?"

Mac kissed Ellie's neck, lightly sucking the sweet skin. "Yes, baby. They were very naughty dreams." She licked Ellie's lips and kissed her fully.

Ellie stroked the length and breadth of Mac's back, crisscrossing from one powerful shoulder to the other, reaching along her solid torso to squeeze her ass and pull her pelvis tighter to her own. She needed Mac closer. She'd always needed her closer. And now she couldn't get close enough, to her past or her present, whatever that entailed. She hooked a leg over the back of Mac's thigh to keep her at her center and gasped when Mac drove up against her.

She relished the glide of Mac's movements, feeling her own arousal along Mac's thigh, and she reveled in the significance of it, but what stirred her even further was having Mac's luscious essence wetting her own thigh. Their combined rhythmical motion nearly brought her to tears.

"Show me, Mac," she breathed, as Mac devoured her throat. "Show me what we did in your dreams."

Mac kissed her deeply, caressing her shoulders and upper arms, her mouth trailing along her neck to her chest. Ellie drove her fingers into Mac's hair, drifting in softness remembered from so long ago.

"Aw, Mac...I've...I've wanted this all my life. With you. Do... do you know that?" She clutched Mac to her breast and watched Mac fondle her nipple, slowly suck it into her mouth. Mac pressed inward, burying her face in the plush, full breast, and Ellie's eyes fell closed with pleasure. "Oh, yes."

"I want you, Ellie," Mac murmured, licking one nipple and then the other, cupping each breast to her mouth. "I want all of you."

"You have me, honey, yes. Ohhh…"

Mac pushed up on Ellie's frame and kissed her ravenously. "I want these kisses, these lips," she said, slipping her tongue along Ellie's. "I wanted them then and I'm taking them now." She sealed their mouths with a long, penetrating kiss.

Ellie hugged Mac with all her strength, fingertips pressing so desperately as to bruise. The feel of Mac's solid frame in her hands blurred Ellie's mind, whisked her far from the teenage years when the love of her young life had dwindled to skin and bone. Mac's satin skin harbored muscles of stone, and Ellie couldn't grasp enough of the biceps that swelled, the strapping cords along her back, and the hard, defined abdominals that shaped her feminine body so deliciously. A primal need rose so quickly it stole all Ellie's conscious thought. She broke their kiss to breathe and taste Mac's jaw, her ear, the side of her tantalizing neck, and the thick deltoid of Mac's shoulder.

Mac palmed her breast and squeezed firmly, slipping from Ellie's grasp to claim the hardened nipple between her teeth. "I dreamed of this," she murmured, nipping the sensitive tip, rousing Ellie all way to her toes. Ellie's hips writhed upward, moisture slicking across Mac's flexing abs.

Mac released the nipple and licked her way lower, grazing Ellie's stomach with her open mouth, dropping between Ellie's legs and controlling her hips with deep, massaging strokes.

At the feel of Mac's tongue on her thigh, Ellie's arms drifted weakly onto the bed, and she squirmed against Mac's iron grip and barely stifled a scream when Mac languidly savored the length of her sex.

"Oh dear God, Mac. So…so good."

"I dreamed of this too," Mac whispered, holding Ellie to her mouth. No dream, no previous encounter had prepared her for the wave of emotion that rippled through her body. The love and devotion she'd missed for years was here, earnestly offered with a desire that matched her own. Mac felt a tear escape with her words. "Wanted this…to taste you…give you everything." Grinding her hips into the mattress as her own arousal mounted, she flicked her tongue across Ellie's clitoris until Ellie arched tightly off the bed, quivering. "That's it. Yes. So, so beautiful. Come to me, sweetheart."

"Mac…" Ellie whimpered as she strained beneath Mac's mouth. "I…I…Oh, God. Y-yes, Mac."

Mac was amazed, thrilled beyond reason to climax just as Ellie came and cried out her name.

Ellie smiled into the dark and sighed heavily as she stroked Mac's hair against her thigh. "Bring your magical, handsome self up here right now," she whispered, and Mac promptly obeyed. "Elizabeth McLaughlin, I love you."

Mac kissed her with all her remaining strength. She tucked her face beneath Ellie's chin and draped a possessive arm and leg across her, snuggling close.

Ellie locked her arms around her and squeezed. "I used to fall asleep at night, imagining us just like this, wishing it could be. Then I'd cry because it wasn't and wouldn't be."

Mac leaned up and smoothed back the fine hair in disarray at Ellie's cheek. She brought her mouth to within a kiss. "Shh, my sweetheart. Now it is."

They hadn't been asleep long when Mac became alert to the bedroom door creaking and Roxie's hushed call. She unwound herself from Ellie and slipped into her trousers, cursing herself for not waiting downstairs for her crew to return. Barefoot, she had two buttons done on her shirt when she stepped into the hall.

The only light drifted up from the foyer, but Mac could see the faces around her. They were all smiling. She sent them a curious, sideways look.

"Well? And what time is it?"

Roxie signaled for quiet.

"It's two thirty, Mac," Jersey whispered. "Time for *everyone* to be in bed."

Mac put her hands on her hips, none too pleased by their teasing. She was about to snap when Zim stepped around Millie and right up into Mac's personal space.

"Here," he said softly, gently setting a blanketed bundle into her arms. "We'll set everything else up, but for now, you guys need to be together."

Mac gazed down at Little Katie, sleeping soundly with Pinky, the bunny. Her eyes filled instantly, and she made no attempt to hide her emotions. "Thank you all. So very much." Her voice cracked. She looked directly at each one of them and cleared her throat carefully. "One helluva great family."

❖

U.S. District Court in Boston was a zoo of crazed animals with notepads and cameras, clamoring and pushing and shoving and yelling at each other as well as at the Feds and bailiffs, who fought their own battle keeping spectators in their place. Eventually, trial went into session, the corridor whirlwind subsided, and everyone in anterooms could hear themselves think.

Accompanied by a Fed, Ellie sat in one such room with Millie and Hank, whom she introduced to the court officer as Mr. and Mrs. Walter Maeger, dear friends who had provided her sanctuary. Dutiful and supportive friends that they were, the "Maegers" delivered Ellie as promised—at six o'clock that morning when the janitor arrived—and staunchly remained at her side.

When the door suddenly opened at ten o'clock, the Fed looked up from his newspaper and down at his watch. Hank, by contrast, leaped to his feet in front of Ellie, blocking her from the visitor's view.

Millie didn't hesitate to point that out.

"Isn't it your goddamn job to protect her?" she snapped. "Or are we just here to watch you pretend you know how to read?" She tore the paper out of his hands. "Useless sack of...Get the hell off your ass and do your fu—your damn job."

The bailiff in the doorway fought back a grin and just nodded at the Fed, who, in turn, extended an arm to Ellie. "Time for you now, Mrs. Harrison." He stepped aside politely to let her precede him.

"Wait!" Hank yelled, and everyone stopped moving. He towered over the Fed and outweighed him by a good fifty pounds of muscle. He jabbed at the Fed's tie and rocked the man back on his heels. "Sweet of you to have manners an' all. I'm sure Mrs. Harrison will appreciate that when someone *shoots her in the fuckin' hallway!* Get out there and secure the area. Jesus, do you guys know anything?"

An hour later, duly advised to remain available for the follow-up cases, Ellie emerged from the courthouse via the back door and into the September sunshine, flanked by her stalwart friends, the "Maegers." Three cars idled at the door, and she was quickly ushered into the second. The cars pulled away in unison and changed positions often as they looped through the city.

As expected, two black Chevrolets refused to give up the chase, and when all the vehicles reached the back streets of East Boston, the goons evidently reached the end of their patience. Submachine gun rounds slammed into Mac's three cars with abandon, and Mac heard Ellie's frightened yelp from the back. One of Mac's cars veered off, apparently trying to improve the odds by drawing away one of the pursuing vehicles.

But the Chevys let the car go and pressed on. Drivers Mac and Jersey hunched as low as they could and stomped on the gas. Ricochets pinged like slung gravel and slugs punched holes in the cars' backsides and interiors, narrowly missing the occupants. Both cars' back windows blew out, and glass rained down over Millie and Ellie huddled on the floor of Mac's car. Jersey sped up to close the gap between them as much as she dared. Beside her, Roxie leaned into the backseat and unloaded both barrels of a shotgun through the missing rear window.

Nearly bumper-to-bumper with Jersey and separated from the goons by seconds, Mac led their prearranged race to the docks. She wheeled tightly around a run-down warehouse and Jersey skidded right around after her.

A heartbeat later, the goons screeched around the building and Mac glanced back to see them greeted by Ralph, Gleeson, Danny, Jackson, and Zim with Tommy guns and shotguns. In an ear-shattering instant, buckshot, blood and broken glass were everywhere, and both Chevys careened into the harbor.

CHAPTER TWENTY-TWO

Jersey didn't want to leave the bar, and Mac could understand why. The raven-haired beauty mixing cocktails had a dazzling smile, and when the ebony eyes focused on Jersey, Mac could practically see her sweat.

Zim elbowed Ellie and looked beyond her to Mac. "Jersey's becoming a permanent fixture. Hasn't sat down all night."

"She's very pretty," Ellie whispered.

"I suppose," Zim said, assessing the bartender. "If you like the dark Italian type. Personally"—he drew Roxie closer, chair and all—"I'm sorta taken by a certain Chicago doll."

"And is there going to be a wedding?"

Roxie raised an eyebrow at Zim but responded to Ellie. "If someone can make up his mind. We've been thinking about Chicago. I have some decent family left there, and there's plenty of work."

"In accounting," Zim injected. "We've talked about starting a family of our own, so there'll be no more of this underground junk."

Mac leaned against Ellie's shoulder. "But I hear Chicago's the place to be for that 'underground junk,' Zim. You sure?"

"He's sure," Roxie said, squeezing his arm.

"You know," Mac said, "if all the owners we talked to today come through, it'll be smooth sailing here for a while. Enough to carry the operation through until it's shut down by choice."

Jersey pulled out a chair and dropped into it, not spilling a drop from her Pilsner glass.

"Nice of you to join us," Zim quipped. "Get her name and number? Or doesn't she play for your team?"

"Rosalia," she answered dreamily. "And, yes, I did, and yes, she does." Mac, Zim, and Roxie all clapped. Ellie just laughed and shook her head at their teasing.

"So this place will make number twenty-five?" Mac asked.

Jersey nodded as she swallowed. "It's her ol' man's bar, but he's real sick, she says, so she calls the shots. May even be looking for a partner." Jersey winked at Ellie. "So hurry up and add this joint to the list. We're in."

Zim pulled out the notepad from his suit jacket and jotted something in a code only the four of them could translate.

"Twenty-five is a nice round number," he mused. "Shouldn't be any problem keeping them happy and it'll make a worthwhile run up from Worcester."

"Speaking of that." Mac rose from the table.

"Speaking of what?" Zim asked. "Worcester?"

"What's say we pay a social call on some well-to-do…friends… while we're in the neighborhood?" She bent down and kissed Ellie's ear. "Making a phone call. Be right back."

"Who the hell does she know around here?" Zim asked, and turned to see Mac enter the phone booth in the corner.

Roxie shook her head and Jersey simply grinned.

The next morning, after they left the inn, Mac finally let the cat out of its proverbial bag and issued directions from the backseat to a certain estate in Gardner.

"Haven't been to see them once," Mac said and gave her head a shake. "Boy, you sure can cover a lot of ground in three years."

Ellie brought Mac's hand onto her thigh. "I'm glad of that."

Roxie insisted Mac tell more of her days at the estate so it would be familiar to everyone once they arrived. The idea wasn't all that appealing to Mac, especially considering Roxie really needed to concentrate on driving, but she obliged just to pass the time.

The story, which Jersey lovingly entitled "Mac the Maid," should not have taken the entire half-hour ride, but Roxie's interruptions and giggling prolonged Mac's pain.

"It's easier to tell stories to Little Katie than to you," Jersey chided Roxie from across the seat. Then she chewed up a gum wrapper and spat it at Roxie's face. Roxie shrieked and nearly drove them off the road.

Mac whacked Jersey on the head with her newspaper. "Stop that. She's bad enough. Let her concentrate or we'll all get killed, for Christ's sake."

Jersey looked over her shoulder at Mac and stuck out her tongue. "Why are you defending her? He should be." And she pointed at Zim, safely tucked away in the far corner of the backseat.

"I prefer we stay alive, thank you," Mac answered, displaying Ellie's hand in hers.

Zim crossed his arms indignantly. "And I just can't reach you from over here. Consider yourself lucky."

"So…Mac?" Roxie said, and Jersey groaned. Mac closed her eyes. Ellie covered her grin with her hand. "Mac? You gonna curtsy when we get there?" And Roxie burst into laughter at the image.

Mac passed more gum wrappers up front to Jersey.

Following directions Mac believed to be scars on her psyche, they finally arrived at the imposing front steps of the Waters estate. Everyone poured out of the car and stood around gawking at the manicured grounds and impressive home.

Mac settled her Fedora on her head and took Ellie's hand. The massive door opened, and a young woman of maybe eighteen, formally dressed in the domestic's long black skirt and starched blouse, curtsied in greeting.

Mac heard Roxie snicker somewhere behind her.

The maid studied Mac a bit longer than proper before asking, "McLaughlin party?"

"Yes, we are," Mac answered. "Thank you."

The maid directed them to the parlor as memories pelted Mac from every direction. Ellie squeezed her hand reassuringly. "Stand tall, there, Elizabeth McLaughlin," she whispered.

"Miss Waters will be with you directly," the maid announced. "Please make yourselves comfortable."

The minute she was out of sight, the comments began. Mac just sat in a déjà vu haze. Thank God she had friends with her to keep her mind from compressing into a tiny nugget of some useless substance. Agnes Waters could appear at any moment and bark something that would make her jump. That humbling realization made Mac take a breath. She wanted to splash cold water on her face.

Ellie squeezed her hand again. Reality returned.

Jersey crouched at Mac's knees. "Remember, that woman wanted you in jail, Mac," she growled. "Olivia counts. Her mother doesn't. Put that fire back in your eyes, damn it."

"Shows that much, huh?"

Jersey nodded. "I'd like to kick that woman's fucking brains in." She wandered back to her chair.

"Hey, Mac," Roxie said, strolling around the room. "How'd they get so rich?"

Mac looked up and chuckled. "Take one guess."

Then came an all-too-familiar voice from upstairs. The maid who answered the telephone yesterday had said only Olivia would be home for their visit. She was wrong.

Mac waved at everyone to sit. "She wasn't supposed to be here."

Ellie lifted Mac's hand and kissed her knuckles. "Listen to me, baby." She turned Mac's face to her. "You are the sharp cookie this woman was afraid of. You had the strength and courage to take what the world threw at you and throw it right back. You're a far, far better person. You gave her a whole year of yourself. Don't you dare give her any more. Give the rest to me." She kissed Mac quickly, waited to see the spark return to Mac's eyes, and sat back in her chair.

Agnes Waters took one step into the parlor and stopped. Her eyes locked onto Mac. The connection across the room was electric.

"I was told acquaintances of Olivia's had come calling," she stated, looking nowhere but at Mac. "I daresay this is quite unexpected." She slowly floated over the Oriental rug until she commanded her audience from the center of the room. She glared down into Mac's eyes. "You do realize that you are not welcome in this house, do you not?"

Mac had to chuckle at the irony of it all. *Take your stand.* She slowly rose to her full height, set her Fedora on the chair she had vacated, and walked to within arm's reach of her.

"Hello, Mrs. Waters. How have I been? Oh, I have been well, yes, thank you for asking. And I trust you have as well." She smirked at her spit-polished wingtips and absently smoothed a hand down the front of her suit jacket. "Now that we've finished the formalities, we're here to visit Olivia."

"You and…your kind…will leave the premises at once or I'll be forced to call the police."

"We are here at her invitation."

"Martha!" Mrs. Waters called, and the maid appeared promptly. "Hurry out to the barn and let him know we have trespassers. Now!"

"Yes, Mrs. Waters." The maid curtsied before exiting.

"I'm giving you this opportunity, Miss McLaughlin. Or…or is it actually Mister?"

Ellie seized the arms of her chair in a death grip. Jersey jumped up and stomped forward so suddenly, Mrs. Waters took a startled step back. Mac hurriedly slapped a backhand against Jersey's chest to stop her.

Mrs. Waters smirked. "And are these three women yet more of those you have disgraced with your sick, perverted ways?"

"Hey!" Roxie snapped, slamming her hands to her hips. "Bitch."

Jersey looked to Mac for the okay to destroy this woman. "Mac, you're not taking that from this piece of shit!"

"It's her game, Jersey," Mac said easily. "It's all she knows. Life to her is only about superficial appearances, so you really have to pity the poor woman."

"How dare you!" Mrs. Waters gasped. She turned at the sound of heavy footsteps. "What took you so long?"

The trusty Colt .45 at the end of his extended arm preceded Carter into the parlor, but three pistols were drawn on him by the time he peered into the room. Eyes widening in a combination of shock and fear, Carter dropped the gun and raised his hands.

Also startled by the quick appearance of the firearms, Mrs. Waters retreated and nearly stumbled over the Colt. When she realized what it was, however, she picked it up and pointed it back at the trio holding her and Carter at bay.

Jersey, Roxie, and Zim dove to the floor. Mac pivoted and pushed Ellie behind the brocade sofa. Then she turned and stared at Agnes Waters.

"Goddamn it. Do you know how to use it that thing?"

"Certainly I do."

"Well, then," Mac said, slowly walking in her direction, "prove it."

Mrs. Waters fumbled with the pistol, struggling to position it in both hands, and Mac walked right past her and threw her arms around Carter.

"Hol-y Mother!" he yelled. "Mac! It's you!" He swirled her around the room and kissed her cheek and forehead.

"Put me down, damn it." She laughed, and he did. She straightened her suit jacket. "Jesus, can't say hello when my lungs are being crushed by some feisty ol' bear!" She rose up on her toes and kissed his cheek. "God, it's so good to see you, Carter."

The gasp from behind him silenced the room. Mrs. Finnegan peeked around Carter's shoulder.

"Ohhh, lassie!" Looking a bit uncomfortable in the parlor with a stunned—and armed—Mrs. Waters gaping nearby, Mrs. Finnegan nevertheless shuffled forward and clamped her beefy arms around Mac. Flour from her hands and apron left souvenirs all over Mac's charcoal suit.

"Please forgive me for—Jesus Christ, Mother!"

Olivia blew into the room like a high-fashion hurricane, silks and sheer fabric trailing in her breezy wake as she advanced on her mother. She yanked the pistol from her hand. "What in the name of God were you thinking?"

"They…these people they have guns and they pointed them at us! You have no idea!"

"Mother." Olivia tossed a dismissive hand toward them. "Yes, they have guns. That's okay. That's what they do. But what were you thinking? My God, you could've shot someone!" Olivia gave the old Colt to Carter. "Here. Please take this blessed thing and promise you'll never let it out of your possession around my mother again."

At last, she turned to Mac but her mother pulled her back.

"What do you mean, 'it's what they do'? Elizabeth and these… These are *friends* of yours?"

"Very special ones, in fact. Now, if you don't mind, I'm going to drag them all outside where we can enjoy this beautiful day. But first, at least *one* Waters woman knows her manners."

She approached Mac almost shyly. "Hello, Mac."

Mac took her hands and smiled. "Olivia, ravishing as always."

Olivia placed a telling kiss on her lips that made Mac blush, her mother gasp, and Ellie cock a surprised eyebrow.

Olivia brushed her fingertips along Mac's forearm. "This is a spectacular suit, very dynamic. And it's stunning on you. I'm so sorry about the flour, though. I insist you mail me the cleaning bill."

Mrs. Finnegan took a half step forward, her eyes downcast. "'Tis my fault, lassie. I shall see to the cleanin'."

Mac grinned. "Thank you both, but no."

Olivia patted Mac's chest. "And before you or I get into any hot water here, I want to say hello to someone else."

Ellie already was at Mac's side.

"How've you been, Olivia?" They hugged warmly.

"Well, thank you. And oh my, just look at you," Olivia proclaimed, holding Ellie at arm's length. "Last time we met, you came as a set of two. You look fabulous!" Olivia glanced over her shoulder at Mac. "She's the cat's meow, you know." Ellie grinned. Olivia turned back to her. "And how's the baby?"

"She's just amazing, thank you. Katherine Rose. Almost four months now and growing like a weed."

"The most beautiful girl in the world," Mac injected, an arm around Ellie's waist. "Little Katie is going to be the first female president of these United States."

Olivia laughed. "I see. And she'll get my vote."

Mac nodded eagerly. "It's a fact. She's already decided."

Ellie squeezed Olivia's hand. "Thank you so much for inviting us, such a spur-of-the-moment thing, I know. This has been…well…"

Olivia chuckled. She bumped her shoulder to Ellie's. "Some welcome, I'm sure." She waved for everyone to follow her through the kitchen and outside to tables in the orchard. Her mother could only watch them go.

They all had just settled comfortably at the small tables in the orchard when Mac spotted Martha approaching with an overloaded tray of drinks and went to assist.

"Let me help." She relieved her of a large pitcher of homemade fruit punch.

"Oh, no, miss. It's my function to serve *you*."

Mac walked them toward the tables, knowing Martha eyed her curiously. "I know how it is. I've been in your shoes. Exactly, as a matter of fact."

Martha stopped and stared. "Y-you are Elizabeth McLaughlin? I recognize the name now. I've heard a great deal about you." She curtsied and lowered her eyes. "I'm very pleased to make your acquaintance, miss."

"I can't tell you to stop the damn curtsying, but I wish I could." Martha smiled and looked away. Mac leaned close and whispered, "Agnes Waters is a washed-up mean ol' hag." Martha's eyes widened at the frank words, and she bit back a grin. Mac acknowledged that with a wink. "True. You and I both know it. And Olivia and Mrs. Finnegan and Carter all know it too, but can't show it. So don't feel alone. You're really not."

"Thank you, miss. You're very kind."

By early afternoon, Olivia had everyone, minus her mother, around the dining room table for lunch.

Carter had Mac and Jersey immersed in conversation about life in Massachusetts farm country, and they even dragged secreted details from him about Mr. Waters's bootlegging days. Mac mentally noted the details of the routes he mentioned.

"And you just call or write if you girls need something," Carter said, tapping the table for emphasis. "I can show you around the countryside out here. Plenty of space to get lost in, if that's what you're after, or to set up shop. Beautiful country to raise a family." He looked from Jersey to Mac and grinned.

Mac sat forward in her chair and beckoned Carter closer with a finger. "You know anything about raising bunnies?"

Ellie nudged Olivia's arm, sneaking a moment to admire the expensive French silk sheath and the way the deep green complemented her eyes and the flaming red of her bob. "I've heard someone else lives an exciting life," she hinted gently. "Married life is good for you?"

Olivia deferred to her drink, a slight smile on her painted lips. "Married life is as I expected. It's what I wanted, or...maybe what I thought I wanted. Reggie is away often, so we enjoy our own pastimes, but not having that someone special in your life all the time is harder than I anticipated. Maybe I'm just growing up?" She laughed lightly at herself. "Now, please tell me about you. You certainly must be glad the court business is over. I've followed every word in the *Post*."

Ellie nodded vehemently. "That one day of testimony is one I'll never forget—and never want to experience again. Right after that, I managed to convince the federal attorneys that one time was scary enough and future testimony and future trials would be too much. I'm a widowed first-time mother, after all," she added with dramatic flair. "So we arranged a date at their office and I gave sworn depositions for all the cases. It took all day and exhausted the hell out of me, but I'm done."

"Oh, thank God for that. You were in protective custody, I'm sure."

Ellie and Roxie snickered.

"You could call it that." Roxie said. "We provided the real protection."

"They saved my life, in fact," Ellie added, "but I do worry because they say the Mob never forgets. It makes me wonder if you can ever let your guard down."

Olivia covered her hand on the table. "She'd never let anything happen to you, Ellie. Nor to Katherine Rose. Mac's a very special woman."

"She most certainly is. Sometimes it seems like a dream that we found each other again. And right when we needed each other most."

"I've only read about a love like the two of you share. It's poetic and rare. You're both so lucky, and I wish you all the very best."

Ellie kissed Olivia's cheek. "I don't ever want to lose you in our lives, Olivia. You're too precious to us, too much a part of us to disappear. Swear you'll always stay in touch?"

Olivia's eyes misted and she grinned at their joined hands. "That's what friends are for."

The afternoon closed with a stroll around the grounds, Carter showing off groomed gardens and arbors, and Olivia making introductions to Sunny and Teddy. Mac was particularly touched to see the horses again, and kissed Sunny's velvet nose. Everyone teased her and moved on to the pastures, but Mac lingered and treated the palomino to a small King apple.

"You remember, don't you," she whispered. "You saw it all. We were having such a nice time, and you were eating too many apples. Then the asshole showed up. If only you could've talked, huh, Sunny?"

"Mother wouldn't have listened to her either," Olivia said from the stall opening, leaning against the post. "She'll never change, Mac."

Mac stepped into the doorway, very close to Olivia.

"Reggie's misguided mind caused so much trouble, but there's nothing I would have done differently on that day. And you..." She shook her head, grinning. "Threatening her with your wedding...That's the greatest thing anyone's ever done for me."

Olivia could only smile fondly. That compelling temptation to touch Mac was back again. She straightened off the post and shuffled her feet nervously. It was dangerous to look into those dark eyes but something made her do it.

"The night we shared, Mac...The glorious way you made me feel...I'll never experience anything like it again." She watched Mac's eyes soften. "Will you tell her?"

"Eventually. She hurt me that night, Olivia. I was heartbroken and angry. Also very drunk."

"I know I should never have let it happen. I know better. You were so vulnerable, but I guess a part of me...I apologize, truly, for being so selfish, Mac."

"Don't apologize. I'm not sorry we had that night together. I may not have a clear recollection of details, but I know for a fact that we enjoyed an amazing night." She stroked Olivia's arm with the back of her fingers. "So, there'll be no details, but yes, I'll tell her."

"I don't want her to hate me."

Mac smiled. "She won't. That's not who she is. She's an incredible woman, Olivia, and I love her with all my heart."

"Well, she has a very special light in her life with you, Mac McLaughlin." She clasped Mac's hand as they left the barn. Kicking ponderously at wisps of hay around her feet, she stopped just outside of the barn and looked up at Mac. "Do me one favor?"

"If I can, of course."

Olivia smiled. "Just tell me we fell a little bit in love, once upon a time."

Mac smiled back. "Oh, we surely did, Miss Waters. We surely did."

CHAPTER TWENTY-THREE

Mac took a long swig of Coca-Cola and handed it back to Ellie. Looking back to the road, she pressed both forearms onto the steering wheel to cup her hands around her cigarette lighter.

Ellie grabbed the bouncing wheel and drove from her passenger seat. "Of all the ways to go, Elizabeth McLaughlin, a car accident isn't preferable."

"At least not until we get there," Mac teased her.

"Can't you tell me now? We've been driving since…I don't know, last week, I think, and I've been very patient." She turned in her seat and reached to the back, tucking Little Katie's blanket around her. "Thank God Katie doesn't mind these dirt roads, Mac. Pinky does, though." She grunted, managing to grab the stuffed rabbit off the floor.

Mac made the most of the opportunity to appreciate Ellie's feminine form. *Damn, but that body is something.* She rubbed the back of her hand over Ellie's rear and along the back of her thigh.

Quickly returning to her seat, Ellie seized Mac's wandering hand and kissed her palm.

"Pay attention to the road."

"And once we're there?" Mac wiggled her eyebrows lasciviously.

"We're never going to be 'there,' wherever 'there' is."

Mac laughed. "Yes, we are. In fact, we're almost there."

Ellie rolled her eyes and Mac discreetly watched her study the landscape that zoomed by. It hadn't changed much in the past two hours, except that the terrain was certainly mountainous. But aside from the occasional sprawling farm of corn, hay, or horses, there wasn't much to see.

"We're in no-man's-land," Ellie declared.

Mac chuckled. "Not true. There are plenty of men and women around here. You just don't see the towns or villages from the road."

The Dodge fought its way up another mountain, and Mac pulled off the road so they could take in the view.

"Oh, my goodness, Mac. Look at it!" Ellie scrambled out of the car and stood awestruck. The Berkshire Mountains spread out for miles to the borders of New York and Vermont, decked out in all their autumn glory.

She crossed her arms against the chilly breeze, and Mac stepped up to hold her close from behind. They shared the view, Mac's cheek against Ellie's, and were silent for a long time.

"See the white church steeples here and there?" Mac asked. "Villages. There's what? I see...three...four of them. That's four villages just from this spot. It's not no-man's-land, sweetheart." Neither of them looked away from the multicolored vista.

"But how do people get by, Mac? They must make a whole day of it, just going to market."

"Yeah, probably, but that's an excursion, a little day trip. A treat. They don't often need more than what they already have, and they grow a lot of stuff."

"Like the corn we saw driving up here. The hay."

"Yup. And like gardens—sometimes acres—of vegetables. Tomatoes, beans, squash. Those things, and, I suppose, the livestock for other things, like eggs and milk."

Ellie rubbed her arms briskly, then tugged Mac's farther around her. "I enjoy working with flowers and don't mind getting dirty, but I've never had a garden. You know we didn't even have a Victory Garden growing up."

"Out here, gardens are necessities." Mac poked her nose into Ellie's ear and then kissed behind it. Her heart beat hard in her chest when Ellie giggled.

"And did you say eggs and milk?"

"Yup."

"As in chickens and cows?"

Mac could tell Ellie wrinkled her nose. "No, as in alligators and elephants." Ellie slapped at Mac's arm. "Yes, as in chickens and cows… and maybe horses…ducks…"

Now Ellie laughed. "Oh, can't you just see Katie with ducks? That would be hysterical."

"Ducks can be loud. I do know that."

"And we know Little Katie will never be outdone."

"Definitely. And we shouldn't forget rabbits."

Ellie eyed her excitedly over her shoulder. "Bunnies?" Mac just grinned and nodded as Ellie turned an awestruck expression back toward the view. "So…farmers' crops pay for the livestock feed."

"They do. And don't forget taxes, a mortgage, the cost of whatever heat and light the family has, the upkeep of the place, tools, car or truck. They need to make decent money and barter well."

"God, Mac. They get by on just what they grow?"

Mac nodded. "The ones who know what they're doing. Someone like you or me, a city girl, well…I'd probably need a side job, say, as a mechanic. You, you're a college girl, so maybe you'd work for the local lawyer or doctor." Mac nuzzled her neck. "Of course if you just *happen* to start out with some considerable savings, like a nest egg, it sure would make life easier."

Ellie spun around in Mac's arms.

She delicately traced the angle of Mac's nose and outlined her lips, smiling as she went, then reached to the back of Mac's neck and drew her down. "I love you, Elizabeth McLaughlin."

Mac lifted her into her arms as they kissed. Her mind spun and her heart nearly pounded through her ribs. Her entire life had wound its way to this, to this spot on earth, to this woman. She felt like some fully wound music box whose music was finally set free.

Ellie laced her arms around Mac's neck.

"Ask me, Mac. For Elizabeth, for Stick, for Ellie Weston, for all the days and months and years of us that we lost, ask me now."

Tears slipped from their eyes. Mac's hands shook. She prayed her tremulous knees would keep her upright. *This is what you fought for, why you hung on. She's right here. For you.*

"I've loved you forever, Eleanor Marie Weston. Nothing on this earth has ever meant more to me than you. And if I swear on my life that I will care, protect, and love you to my last breath, will you and

Miss Katherine Rose Harrison please come build a family in my heart and never leave me?"

The words, shaky as they sounded, hung in the air for several poignant seconds until Ellie took Mac's face in both hands and kissed her so hard she actually drew blood. Finally, her crying intensified to the point where they had to stop kissing.

Ellie swiped at her eyes and noticed the spot of blood on Mac's lower lip.

"Oh my God, Mac, I'm sorry."

"Shh. Just kiss me." Mac lowered her head and led the way. She devoured the satin of Ellie's neck and shoulder, squeezing the trim hips in her hands and pulling them into her own. The gnarling want she felt for Ellie was practically beyond restraint, and she groaned hungrily as their bodies fit together. "I want you, Ellie. I want to make love with you forever. I—"

Ellie swallowed Mac's words and cleaved to the full length of Mac's solid frame. "Tonight. At the inn, Mac. I can't wait till we're back in the city," she breathed between kisses. "I want you, too. So very much."

It took Little Katie's faint but distinctive murmurings to bring them back to reality, and they parted slowly, dazed.

"You know," Ellie said softly, grinning as she stroked back Mac's hair, "I can't just run off to some distant farmland with my forever lover without permission."

Entranced, Mac could only watch Ellie back away, that teasing grin never leaving Ellie's lips.

"Someone has to give us her blessing, you know." Ellie opened the car door and lifted Little Katie into her arms. "What do you think, oh wise child of mine?" She returned to Mac and cocked an ear toward the baby. "What's that? Ah. She wants to make sure there'll be no more bad guys or government guys or other scary stuff."

Mac slid an arm around Ellie's waist and smiled down into eyes as pure and loving as her mother's. "I promise you, little one. No more scary stuff." Mac kissed her forehead and then kissed Ellie.

About the Author

A lifelong Massachusetts resident, CF Frizzell ("friz") endures the telecom industry in Boston for a living but dreams of retirement days spent writing at the seashore or in an Adirondack cabin. She grew up in community newspapers and established an award-winning twenty-two-year career that culminated in the role of founder/publisher.

friz discovered her passion for writing in high school, but credits powerhouse authors Lee Lynch, Radclyffe, and the generous family that is Bold Strokes Books for inspiration. She's into history, acoustic guitar, New England pro sports—and most of all, her partner, Kathy, with whom she makes a home in Sandwich on Cape Cod.

Books Available From Bold Strokes Books

Because of You by Julie Cannon. What would you do for the woman you were forced to leave behind? (978-1-62639-199-4)

The Job by Jove Belle. Sera always dreamed that she would one day reunite with Tor. She just didn't think it would involve terrorists, firearms, and hostages. (978-1-62639-200-7)

Making Time by C.J. Harte. Two women going in different directions meet after fifteen years and struggle to reconnect in spite of the past that separated them. (978-1-62639-201-4)

Once The Clouds Have Gone by KE Payne. Overwhelmed by the dark clouds of her past, Tag Grainger is lost until the intriguing and spirited Freddie Metcalfe unexpectedly forces her to reevaluate her life. (978-1-62639-202-1)

The Acquittal by Anne Laughlin. Chicago private investigator Josie Harper searches for the real killer of a woman whose lover has been acquitted of the crime. (978-1-62639-203-8)

An American Queer: The Amazon Trail by Lee Lynch. Lee Lynch's heartening and heart-rending history of gay life from the turbulence of the late 1900s to the triumphs of the early 2000s are recorded in this selection of her columns. (978-1-62639-204-5)

Stick McLaughlin by CF Frizzell. Corruption in 1918 cost Stick her lover, her freedom, and her identity, but a very special flapper and the family bond of her own gang could help win them back—even if it means outwitting the Boston Mob. (978-1-62639-205-2)

Rest Home Runaways by Clifford Henderson. Baby boomer Morgan Ronzio's troubled marriage is the least of her worries when she gets the call that her addled, eighty-six-year-old, half-blind dad has escaped the rest home. (978-1-62639-169-7)

Charm City by Mason Dixon. Raq Overstreet's loyalty to her drug kingpin boss is put to the test when she begins to fall for Bathsheba Morris, the undercover cop assigned to bring him down. (978-1-62639-198-7)

Edge of Awareness by C.A. Popovich. When Maria, a woman in the middle of her third divorce, meets Dana, an out lesbian, awareness of her feelings bring up reservations about the teachings of her church. (978-1-62639-188-8)

Taken by Storm by Kim Baldwin. Lives depend on two women when a train derails high in the remote Alps, but an unforgiving mountain, avalanches, crevasses, and other perils stand between them and safety. (978-1-62639-189-5)

The Common Thread by Jaime Maddox. Dr. Nicole Coussart's life is falling apart, but fortunately, DEA Attorney Rae Rhodes is there to pick up the pieces and help Nic put them back together. (978-1-62639-190-1)

Jolt by Kris Bryant. Mystery writer Bethany Lange wasn't prepared for the twisting emotions that left her breathless the moment she laid eyes on folk singer sensation Ali Hart. (978-1-62639-191-8)

Searching For Forever by Emily Smith. Dr. Natalie Jenner's life has always been about saving others, until young paramedic Charlie Thompson comes along and shows her maybe she's the one who needs saving. (978-1-62639-186-4)

Blindsided by Karis Walsh. Blindsided by love, guide dog trainer Lenae McIntyre and media personality Cara Bradley learn to trust what they see with their hearts. (978-1-62639-078-2)

Blue Water Dreams by Dena Hankins. Lania Marchiol keeps her wary sailor's gaze trained on the horizon until Oly Rassmussen, a wickedly handsome trans man, sends her trusty compass spinning off course. (978-1-62639-192-5)

Let the Lover Be by Sheree Greer. Kiana Lewis, a functional alcoholic on the verge of destruction, finally faces the demons of her past while finding love and earning redemption in New Orleans. (978-1-62639-077-5)

About Face by VK Powell. Forensic artist Macy Sheridan and Detective Leigh Monroe work on a case that has troubled them both for years, but they're hampered by the past and their unlikely yet undeniable attraction. (978-1-62639-079-9)

Blackstone by Shea Godfrey. For Darry and Jessa, the chance at a life of freedom is stolen by the arrival of war and an ancient prophecy that just might destroy their love. (978-1-62639-080-5)

Out of This World by Maggie Morton. Iris decided to cross an ocean to get over her ex. But instead, she ends up traveling much farther, all the way to another world. Once she's there, only a mysterious, sexy, and magical woman can help her return home. (978-1-62639-083-6)

Kiss The Girl by Melissa Brayden. Sleeping with the enemy has never been so complicated. Brooklyn Campbell and Jessica Lennox face off in love and advertising in fast-paced New York City. (978-1-62639-071-3)

Taking Fire: A First Responders Novel by Radclyffe. Hunted by extremists and under siege by nature's most virulent weapons, Navy medic Max de Milles and Red Cross worker Rachel Winslow join forces to survive and discover something far more lasting. (978-1-62639-072-0)

First Tango in Paris by Shelley Thrasher. When French law student Eva Laroche meets American call girl Brigitte Green in 1970s Paris, they have no idea how their pasts and futures will intersect. (978-1-62639-073-7)

CHAPTER SIXTEEN

W hat kind of a sandwich is *that*?"
The incredulous question startled Ellie so badly she almost dropped her Coca-Cola. Vonnie leaned over the back of the park bench, staring hard at Ellie's lunch, steam from her overheated forehead escaping into the frosty January air.

"Hi," Ellie said. "Better not make fun of my sandwich or I won't invite you to sit down."

Vonnie stood and adjusted the satchel that hung diagonally across her chest. She removed her cap and scruffed at her hair nervously. The act was so reminiscent of Stick, Ellie nearly gasped.

"Sorry," Vonnie said, leaning her bike against a tree and pulling at her threadbare gloves. "I's just teasing."

Ellie patted the bench beside her. "Come. Sit. Do you have time for lunch?"

Vonnie looked about her uneasily. "Eh…Well…I got another pickup to make, so…"

She had no lunch. Ellie knew.

"Sit," she commanded, mentally composing the correct offer so as not to insult the girl. "This is a first time for this sandwich," she lied, "fried egg and leftover ham on brown bread. Experiment with me?" She extended a half.

Vonnie nearly drooled at the sandwich. She flicked her eyes up at Ellie. "Um…Well, I could try a bite first, that way you'll know whether to eat yours."

Ellie grinned. "Exactly. You can be my poison tester."

Vonnie laughed and accepted the sandwich with gritty, calloused fingers. Cautiously, she brought it to her mouth and smirked at Ellie. "Catch me if I drop, okay?"

"Just eat it," Ellie said on a laugh.

Vonnie took a delicate bite, no doubt a habit of making her meals last. Her thin frame delivered a powerful sense of déjà vu to Ellie and in just watching her relish the morsel, she saw the shadowy, sunken form of Stick at their last meeting. She wasn't kidding herself about her fondness for Vonnie, even though the vivid memories pained her.

Ellie had no doubt she was famished. "Well?"

Vonnie nodded vigorously. "Delicious! Thank you!" She nearly chomped down the rest but caught herself.

"Want some Coke? Sorry I don't have a straw, but...You don't have any germs, do you?"

Vonnie wiped her mouth with the back of her sleeve and Ellie actually wondered.

"Nope. No germs." She took the bottle and a small sip. "Wow, thanks, Ellie."

"So...How's the job going? You like it?"

"Yeah, I sure do. Really lucky to get it, too. I bike all over town." She nibbled at what remained of her half of the sandwich. "And I meet great people..." She cast her eyes to the sandwich. "Pretty ones, too."

Ellie grinned as she drank. "Are you from around here? Your family?"

Vonnie shrugged. "Not so much family. I have lots of friends, though. All over the city. And we're...We all do lots of odd jobs."

"No family? How old are you, if you don't mind me asking."

"Seventeen." Vonnie's head came up proudly. "On my own a couple years now, and I like it that way."

Ellie could only nod. *Way too many old memories.* "So...nobody special in your life? There's bound to be a boyfriend. A...girlfriend, perhaps?"

Vonnie's eyes met hers with a flash of fear. "N-No. No one. And... you're married, huh?"

Ellie overlooked the obvious subject change and held up her left hand displaying the small gold band.

"Ahh," Vonnie said, nodding, the spark in her eyes dimming slightly.

"I'll let you in on a secret," Ellie added, leaning her shoulder